Healing from Depression
12 WEEKS TO A BETTER MOOD

A Body, Mind, and Spirit
Recovery Program

DOUGLAS BLOCH, M.A.

CELESTIAL ARTS
Berkeley / Toronto

CA

Celestial Arts
P.O. Box 7123
Berkeley, California 94707
www.tenspeed.com

Originally published under the title, When Going Through Hell…Don't Stop!
Distributed in Australia by Simon and Schuster Australia, in Canada by Ten Speed Press Canada, in New Zealand by Southern Publishers Group, in South Africa by Real Books, in Southeast Asia by Berkeley Books, and in the United Kingdom and Europe by Airlift Book Company.

Library of Congress Cataloging-in-Publication Data
Bloch, Douglas, 1949-
    [When going through hell--don't stop]
    Healing from depression: 12 Weeks to a better mood: a body, mind, and spirit recovery program/ Douglas Bloch.
        p.cm.
    Originally published: When going through hell--don't stop! Portland, Or.: Pallas Communications, c2000.
    Includes bibliographical references and index.
    ISBN 1-58761-138-4
1. Depression, Mental--Treatment. 2. Manic-depressive illness--Treatment. 3. Anxiety--Treatment. 4. Depression, Mental--Alternative treatment. 5. Manic-depressive illness--Alternative treatment. 6. Anxiety--Alternative treatment. 7. Self-help groups. 8. Bloch, Douglas, 1949- I. Title.

RC537.B535 2002
616.85'2706--dc21

                      2002019239

Cover design by Catherine Jacobes
Interior design by Betsy Stromberg

First printing, 2002
Printed in the United States of America

1 2 3 4 5 6 7 8 9 10—05 04 03 02 01

SURVIVAL TIPS

If you are in the hell of a major depression or anxiety disorder and feel that you have reached your limit, here are three coping strategies that you can use right now:

1. Set the intention to heal. Make the decision that you want to get well (even if you don't know how).

2. Reach out for support—to other people and to spirit.

3. Ask spirit (or your higher power) for the courage and endurance to stay in the pain until it repatterns.

While I cannot guarantee that you will get better (no one can know the future with certainty), my experience tells me that you will greatly maximize your chances of healing and of making a full recovery if you follow these three suggestions.

If you are on the edge of the abyss, don't jump.
If you are going through hell, don't stop.
As long as you are breathing, there is hope.
As long as day follows night, there is hope.
Nothing stays the same forever.
Set an intention to heal,
reach out for support, and you will find help.

Please feel free to photocopy or remove this page for your personal use.

MORE ADVANCE PRAISE FOR
Healing From Depression
12 Weeks to a Better Mood

"Congratulations on courageously telling your inspiring story. Anyone who has suffered from depression will be uplifted by it."

Harold H. Bloomfield, M.D., best-selling author of *How to Survive the Loss of a Love* and *How to Heal Depression*

"Douglas Bloch writes with the insight and power of message only available to someone who has walked in some of the deepest darkness a human can know. *Healing From Depression* is much more than one man's journey. It is a powerful contribution to anyone seeking help for themselves or someone they love."

Rev. Mary Manin Morrissey,
author of *Building Your Field of Dreams*

"A true survivor's guide that can be used by anyone who is undergoing a dark night of the soul experience. This book is also invaluable for the friend or caregiver of a person suffering from anxiety or depression."

Julie Weiss, Ph.D.

"A superb job. Combines a gripping narrative with a comprehensive self-help manual on healing from depression."

Cynthia Waller, R.N., psychiatric nurse

"Nothing speaks with more authority than the voice of experience. As one who has been there and back, Douglas has created a powerful and useful roadmap for others to follow. His book offers a beacon of hope for those who are still wandering in the darkness of depression."

Michael Moran, Senior Minister, Spiritual Life Center

There is not one of us in whom a devil does not dwell.
At some time, at some point, that devil masters each of us.
It is not having been in the dark house,
but having left it, that counts.

Teddy Roosevelt

*Dedicated to the loving memory of Anne Zimmerman.
Although you could not save yourself, your spirit lives on
in the lives of those whom you loved and served.*

Acknowledgments

It takes a whole village to shepherd a person through a dark night of the soul. At least, that has been my experience. Without the care and concern of a legion of guardian angels who lifted me out of the black hole of a life-threatening depressive illness, this book would not have been written.

My appreciation begins with the staff of the Sellwood Day Treatment Clinic, who provided a safe haven not only for myself, but for twenty to thirty other sufferers of mental illness during the winter of 1996 and 1997. These health care providers include clinic director, Peter Grover; my psychiatrist, Allen Stark; therapists Pat Ritter, Victoria Peacock, Vicki Vanderslice, Mike Terry, Art Kowitich, and Tracey Jones; and office manager, Beth Morphew. Sadly, the day treatment program has now closed.

In addition to receiving expert professional help, I was blessed with courageous friends. Though not everyone had the fortitude to endure my agitated moods, there were those who chose to stand beside me—Stuart Warren, Ann Garrett, Joe Mitchell, Kathleen Herron, Cathy Brenner, Cynthia Waller, and Linda Larsen-Wheatley. During my darkest hours, Raeanne Lewman's loving massage gave me some small pleasure to look forward to once a week.

I also received tremendous support from the patients at day treatment. Evelyn, Kate, Terri, Lynette, Angela, Jacob, Chris, Leon, Robert, Mike, Todd, and Tom—I bless you and pray that you, too, have found some relief from your torment.

My appreciation also goes to Terry Grant and Leslie Newman for their professional home health services.

I will forever be grateful to Marsha Nord for insisting that I would come out on the other side, and to Teresa Keane for teaching me the mindfulness techniques that allowed me to hold on, minute by minute, until help arrived.

This help took the form of the "God group," a group of spiritual friends who gathered together with me at the Living Enrichment Center over a six-month period and held a vision of healing and well-ness for me. They are Mary Manin Morrissey and Eddy Marie Crouch (who initiated the meetings), Pat Ritter, Dennis McClure, Victoria Etchemendy, Judy Swensen, Sally Brunell, Stuart Warren, Joan Bloch, Michael Moran, Ann Garrett, Dianne Pharo, Mark and Tracy Soine, Adele Zimmerman, Sally Rutis, and Jon Merritt.

Thanks to Phoenisis McEachin and Araline Cate, whose body-work helped me to stabilize once the depression lifted.

Last, but not least, my deepest thanks go to Joan Christine Bridg-man—for being such a loyal friend and caregiver (thank you for all those lifesaving walks in Forest Park)—and to Joan Bloch for returning when I most needed her and for giving our marriage a second chance.

Six weeks after my remission began, I was guided to tell the story of my healing in a book called *When Going Through Hell . . . Don't Stop!* At that point, a new crew of helpers appeared to aid and abet the liter-ary process. The first of these were the Reverend Michael Moran and my late therapist, Anne Zimmerman, who first encouraged me to tell my story. Once I became well enough to write, Teresa Keane enthu-siastically stepped in as my primary editor and gave generously of her time as well as of her professional expertise. I am also appreciative of Phineas Warren's suggestion that I create a mini self-help manual to follow the book's personal narrative. Helen Tevlin, Ph.D., became my "technical advisor" and provided helpful feedback about the accuracy and precision of the clinical information that I presented. Helena Wolfe provided her invaluable expertise in designing and formatting the book.

Throughout the two years of writing, my therapist, Pat Ritter, and my Master Mind group (Joan Bloch, Stuart Warren, Ann Garrett, Jon Merritt, Judy Swensen, Beth Hahn, and John Brown) helped me to maintain my emotional stability and serenity.

In addition, the following people agreed to read and comment on early drafts of the manuscript: Miki Barnes, Joan Bridgman, Deanna Byrne, Araline Cate, Al Coffman, Eddy Marie Crouch, Krystyna Czarnecka, Larry Dossey, Chip Douglas, Jim Eddy, Bob Edelstein, John Engelsman, Victoria Etchemendy, Elliot Geller, Penny Gerharter, Joel Goleb, Miriam Green, Beth Hahn, Heather Hannum, Jim Hunzicker, Lee Judy, Ann Kelley, Linda Larsen-Wheatley, Tonia Larson, Brian Litt, Lynne Massie, Dennis McClure, Rhea McDonnell, Michael Moran, Philip Mostow, Marsha Nord, Tracy Pilch, Luella Porter, Pat Ritter, Bruce Robinson, Al Siebert, Vicki Vanderslice, Julie Weiss, and Adele Zimmerman. Thank you all for your invaluable feedback.

A year after *When Going Through Hell . . . Don't Stop!* was published, I decided to teach a series of 12-week classes on healing from depression and anxiety, which incorporated my own experience in recovering from depression with information based on the latest clinical research. These classes provided the inspiration for *Healing From Depression*. I am grateful to the people who came to those initial classes with open hearts and courageous spirits. I also give thanks to my two Portland editors, Michelle Singer and Patricia Koch, who generously gave of their time to read through the material on the better mood program, as well as to Joann Deck and Lorena Jones of Ten Speed Press for their belief in this project.

Finally, I once again dedicate this book to Anne Zimmerman, my late therapist who first encouraged me to write about my recovery, but whose life was lost to suicide during her own depressive episode. I pray that this work, in honor of her memory, may prevent similar tragedies by offering hope and practical coping strategies to those who are still lost in the darkness of depression.

Healing from Depression and Anxiety:
Five Areas of Therapeutic Self-Care*

The goal: To experience a better mood, free from depression and anxiety.

Physical self-care
Exercise
Nutrition
Water intake
Hydrotherapy
Natural light
Sleep
Medication
Supplements
Herbs
Acupuncture
Breathing
Yoga
Touch

Spiritual connection
Prayer
Meditation
Spiritual community
Inspirational texts
Forgiveness
The 12 Steps of AA
Finding purpose
    and meaning

Activities that support my vision of wellness

Lifestyle habits
Structure/routine
Time in nature
Fulfilling work
Setting goals
Relaxation
Pleasurable activities
Humor
Music therapy
Creative self-expression
Time for beauty
Stress reduction
Time management

**Mental and emotional
self-care**
Restructuring cognitive
    processes
Practicing daily affirmations
Releasing negative beliefs
Taming the inner critic
Charting your moods
Feeling your feelings
Thinking like an optimist
Keeping a gratitude journal
Overcoming the stigma
    of depression
Self-forgiveness
Psychotherapy
Healing family of origin issues
Working through grief

Social support
Family
Friends
Psychiatrist/therapist
Minister/rabbi
Support group
Day treatment
Volunteer work
Pets and animals

* This program is meant to support, not replace, any medical treatment you may be receiving.

Contents

PART ONE—
When Going Through Hell...Don't Stop!
A Survivor's Tale of Overcoming
Anxiety and Clinical Depression

PART TWO—
Healing from Depression and Anxiety:
The Better Mood Recovery Program

PART THREE—
Crisis Management and Other Issues

PERSONAL STORIES

Important: Please Read Before You Begin

The subtitle of this book is "12 Weeks to a Better Mood." Please note that this phrase does not promise a cure; it simply offers hope that improvement is possible. As I observe my clients put the better mood program into practice, many report an improvement in their mood and outlook, as well as a decrease in their symptoms during the first three months. In most cases the change has been gradual; in others it had been more dramatic (e.g., finding the right medication).

There are times, however, when external circumstances or internal conditions cause a condition to take longer than twelve weeks to resolve. For example, if someone loses a spouse, it may take years to process the grief. In other instances, a specific depression or anxiety disorder may resist even the best treatments and therapeutic interventions and drag on for many months.

Therefore, if you follow the program outlined in this book and see little or no progress after ninety days, please do not be discouraged. If you set the intention to heal, reach out for support, and persist in your efforts to get well, relief will eventually come.

In addition, if progress is slow try not to compare yourself to others by saying to yourself, "They are getting better, why not me?" or think that you have failed. Depression is a mysterious illness that has its own timing, which is usually beyond our control. What you can control is how you respond to your situation. If you do so with courage and persistence, you will have won a moral victory, even before depression is overcome.

Introduction:
How to Use This Book

Anyone who survives a test is obliged to tell his story.
—ELIE WIESEL, author and survivor of the Nazi concentration camps

If you have picked up this book, it is no doubt because either you or someone you love is in pain. I understand that pain. I know what it is like to feel the despair, the torment, the hopelessness of major depression. I have experienced it and have survived, and my message is that you can get through it, too. There is hope. That is why I have written this book.

Healing from Depression: 12 Weeks to a Better Mood is a resource guide for anyone who is struggling with depression, manic depression (also known as bipolar disorder), anxiety, or a related mood disorder. The book is divided into two main parts. In Part One, I tell the story of how I descended into and emerged from the hell of a major depressive illness. This narrative originally appeared in a book called, *When Going Through Hell . . . Don't Stop! A Survivor's Guide to Overcoming Anxiety and Clinical Depression.* I pray that my story of rebirth will validate your reality, reassure you that you are not alone, and give you the hope that healing is possible.

In Part Two of the book, I present my Better Mood Recovery Program—a body, mind, and spirit approach for living optimally and reducing the symptoms of anxiety and depression. The better mood program was hatched in the crucible of my personal torment. Because my depression did not respond to antidepressant medication, I was forced to put together my "daily survival plan for living in hell"—a series of coping strategies that kept me alive day by day, hour by hour, and minute by minute. These survival strategies were based on five different kinds of self-care activities—physical self-care, mental and emotional self-care, social support, spiritual connection, and lifestyle habits.

After my recovery, my daily survival plan became "my daily wellness plan," which I used to stabilize my moods and to minimize the potential for relapse. Soon, I felt called to share these wellness principles through teaching a 12-week "Healing from Depression" class and support group. In creating the curriculum for the class, I took the self-care strategies I was employing and formulated them into a systematic, step-by-step sequence that could be learned and practiced over a 12-week period. In the year that I have taught the program to my groups, I have been privileged to see many healings and "miracles" in the lives of the group members. I am fortunate to have received permission from a number of my clients to include their recovery stories in sidebars that appear throughout the text. These stories show the power that is inherent in the simple healing tools that you will be learning.

Clinical depression is a serious matter. At any given moment, somewhere between fifteen and twenty million Americans are suffering from depressive disorders, and about one in eight will develop the illness during their lifetimes. Suicide, the eighth leading cause of death in America, is largely caused by untreated depression. Thus, while *Healing from Depression* offers an excellent self-help program for managing the symptoms of depression and anxiety, it is not a substitute for professional treatment. If you (or someone you care about) are severely depressed or anxious and have symptoms that are interfering with your ability to function, please seek out professional help. Information on how to find good mental health resources is located in Appendix C, as well as in Week 2 of the program.

Finally, although my personal narrative and the book's clinical material focus on healing from a depression, I believe that many of the book's principles can be applied to anyone who is undergoing a dark night of the soul experience—which I define as "relentless emotional or physical pain that appears to have no end." It is my deepest wish that the lessons I learned from my suffering and the material contained in this book may give you or a loved one the hope and inspiration to fight on in your darkest hours.

Douglas Bloch
November 9, 2001
Portland, Oregon
dbloch@teleport.com

PART ONE

When Going Through Hell...
Don't Stop!

---

*A Survivor's Tale
of Overcoming Anxiety
and Clinical Depression*

The Descent into Hell

The journey to higher awareness is not a direct flight. Challenges, struggles, and tests confront the traveler along the way. Eventually, no matter who you are or how far you have come along the path, you must experience your 'dark night of the soul.'

—DOUGLAS BLOCH, *Words That Heal*

The notebook by the side of my bed was finally being put to use. Given to me by a friend so I could record my dreams, the lined yellow paper had remained untouched for months, as my sleeping medication made dream recollection all but impossible.

"Oh, well," I mused. "It won't matter much after today."

I looked out the window. There was another of those oppressive Oregon winter skies that moves in like an unwanted houseguest at the beginning of November and doesn't depart until the first of July. The black clouds overhead mirrored those inside my head. I was suffering from a mental disorder known as clinical depression.

Slowly, I reached for the pen and began to write.

November 12, 1996

To my friends and family,
I know that this is wrong, but I can no longer endure the pain
of living with this mental illness. Further hospitalizations will
not help, as my condition is too deep seated and advanced to

uproot. On some deeper level, I know that my work on the planet is finished, and that it is time to move on.

Douglas

I reached over for the bottle of pills that I had secretly saved for this occasion, slowly twisted off the cap, and imagined the sweet slumber that awaited me. My reverie was interrupted by a loud knock at the door.

"Who can that be?" I wondered. "Can't a man commit suicide in peace?"

I turned over in bed and spied my friend Stuart entering the living room.

"Just thought I'd check in and see if you made it off to day treatment," he said cheerfully as he made his way to my bedroom.

I quickly hid the pills, wondering whether I should tell Stuart about my note. Meanwhile, I could feel the stirrings of another anxiety attack. It began with the involuntary twitching of my legs, then violent shaking, building until my whole body went into convulsions. Not able to contain the huge amount of energy that was surging through me, I jumped out of bed and began to pace. Back and forth, back and forth I stumbled across the living room, hitting myself in the head and screaming, "Electric shock for Douglas Bloch! Electric shock for Douglas Bloch!"

I had not always been so disturbed. Just ten weeks earlier, on September 4, 1996, I had taken a new Prozac-related medication in the hopes of alleviating a two-year, chronic, low-grade depression that was brought on by a painful divorce and a bad case of writer's block. Instead of mellowing me out, however, the drug produced an adverse reaction—a state of intense agitation that catapulted me into the psychiatric ward of a local hospital.

Although it took only 24 hours for the adverse drug reaction to totally disable me, the roots of my depression extended far into the past. I have never formally investigated my genealogy, but I know that the illness has run rampant in my family for at least three generations. Five of my family members have suffered from chronic depression; one developed an eating disorder and another a gambling addiction. One uncle died of starvation in the midst of a depressive episode. My mother suffered two major depressive episodes in a three-year period before she was saved at the eleventh hour by electroconvulsive therapy. I strongly suspect that both of my grandmothers lived with untreated depression. The tendency of depression to run in families is probably a combination of both genetic predisposition and family culture. Through observing family dynamics, children learn ways of coping that support or impede mental health. (An example is the phenomenon of "learned helplessness," where a child, through being exposed to painful situations that he cannot control, learns to feel powerless and helpless.)

Though one may be genetically and temperamentally predisposed to depression, it normally takes a stressor (such as personal loss, illness, or financial setback) to activate the illness. A person with a low susceptibility to depression can endure a fair amount of mental or emotional stress and not become ill. A person with a high degree of vulnerability, however, has only a thin cushion of protection. The slightest insult to the system can initiate a depressive episode.

Two such incidents had occurred in my life at the ages of twenty-six and thirty-three when the loss of love relationships plummeted me into deep depressions. The first breakdown resulted in a four-month stay in Berkeley Place in Berkeley, California; the second led to a one-month residence in a New York psychiatric hospital. Fortunately, I was able to emerge from these ordeals fully intact (I later described the journey from trauma to recovery as breakup, breakdown, breakthrough). In 1984, I moved to Portland, Oregon, bought a house, married, found a great therapist, and began my present career as a writer. I was sure that I had left the dark house forever.

In 1993, however, a marital separation initiated a slow crumbling of my psyche that culminated in February of 1996 when the divorce became final. I found myself too depressed to write and two months later learned that two of my most beloved books had gone out of print.

By summer's end, I was, in the words of a friend, "barely limping along." Although previous trials of antidepressants had been unsuccessful, on the advice of a psychiatrist, I decided to try a new Prozac-related medication that had recently been approved by the FDA. Instead of calming me down, however, the drug catapulted me into an agitated depression—a state of acute anxiety alternating with dark moods of hopelessness and despair.

Diagnostic Criteria for a Major Depressive Episode

A depressive illness is a whole body illness, involving one's body, mood, thoughts, and behavior. It affects the way you eat and sleep, the way you feel about yourself, and think about things. It is not a passing blue mood or a sign of personal weakness.

Depressive illnesses come in different forms, the most serious of which is major depression. The following criteria for major depression are taken from the *Diagnostic and Statistical Manual of Mental Disorders (DSM-IV)*. If you or someone you know fits these criteria, seek professional help.

A. Five or more of these symptoms should be present during the same two-week period and represent a change from previous functioning.

1. Depressed mood most of the day
2. Markedly diminished interest in pleasure
3. Significant change in appetite, leading to weight loss or weight gain
4. Insomnia or hypersomnia (too much sleep) nearly every day
5. Psychomotor agitation or retardation nearly every day
6. Fatigue or loss of energy nearly every day
7. Feelings of worthlessness or excessive or inappropriate guilt
8. Diminished ability to think or concentrate, or indecisiveness
9. Recurrent thoughts of death, recurrent suicidal thoughts without a specific plan, suicide attempts, or specific plans for committing suicide

B. In addition, these symptoms cause clinically significant distress or impairment in social, occupational, or other important areas of functioning.

It soon became clear that taking this antidepressant had created a permanent shift in my body and mind. Before ingesting the drug, I felt crummy, but not crazy; emotionally down, but still able to function. My suffering was intense—but not enough to disable me, not enough to make me suicidal. Now, I had entered a whole new realm of torment. The drug's assault on my brain caused something inside of me to snap, sending me into an emotional freefall and creating a life-threatening biochemical disorder. The closest analogy I can use to describe my state is that I was on a bad LSD trip—except that I didn't come down after the customary eight hours. In fact, the nightmare was just beginning.

There were two things about my predicament that made it different from anything I had ever experienced—the sheer intensity of the pain and its seemingly nonstop assault on my nervous system. During my hospitalization, I discovered that my official diagnosis was "major depression" combined with a "generalized anxiety disorder." Here is what I learned when I asked my doctor about these terms.

Major Depression

If there is hell on earth, it is to be found in the heart of a melancholy man.
—ROBERT BURTON, seventeenth-century English scholar

Before I describe my own experience of major depression (also known as clinical depression), I would like to delineate the difference between the medical term "clinical depression" and the word "depression" as it is used by most people. Folks say they are depressed when they experience some disappointment or personal setback— e.g., the stock market drops, they fail to get a raise, or there's trouble at home with the kids. While I would never want to minimize anyone's pain, clinical depression takes this kind of suffering to a whole new level, making these hurts look like a mild sunburn.

Major depression can be distinguished from the blues of everyday life in that a depressive illness is a whole body disorder, involving one's physiology, biochemistry, mood, thoughts, and behavior. It affects the way you eat and sleep and the way you think and feel about yourself, others, and the world. Clinical depression is not a

Gustave Dore's illustration of purgatory in Dante's *Divine Comedy*

passing blue mood or a sign of personal weakness. Subtle changes inside the brain's chemistry create a terrible malaise in the body, mind, and spirit that can affect every dimension of one's being.

On page 4, I have listed the official symptoms of major depression, taken from the *Diagnostic and Statistical Manual of Mental Disorders (DSM-IV),* the official diagnostic resource of the mental health profession. Describing how depression actually feels, however—especially to someone who has never been there—is not so straightforward. If I told you that I had been held hostage, put in solitary confinement, and beaten, you might receive a graphic image of my suffering. But how does one describe a black hole of the soul where the tormentors are invisible?

I remember a diagram from my high school biology class depicting what happens when you put your hand on a hot stove. The nerve receptors in the skin send a message up the arm and spinal column to the brain, which interprets the situation as "Ouch, that's hot!" The brain then sends a message back down the spine telling the hand to remove itself from the burner. All of this takes place in a fraction of a second.

The pain of depression is not so easy to track. It cannot be described as stabbing, shooting, or burning; neither can its sensations be localized to any one part of the body. It is an all-encompassing malignancy—a crucifying pain that slowly permeates every fiber of one's being. Being consumed by depression is not like being gored by a bull; it is more akin to being stung to death by an army of swarming wasps.

When one is clinically depressed, the capacity for (and the memory of) pleasure vanishes. The best that one can hope for is a kind of negative happiness that results from the temporary absence of distress. Life fluctuates between the horrible and the miserable. A sense of humor, that wonderful analgesic that existed even among some concentration camp prisoners, is completely absent. (Many friends marked the beginning of my depression as when I lost the ability to laugh.)

Even though depression is called a mood disorder, mood is only one of the many bodily functions that are disrupted by a disorganized, misfiring brain. Eating and sleeping are disrupted (along with one's sex drive), and energy levels dwindle so low that even the simplest task can seem impossible. In the words of one depressive, "Pouring milk over my cereal feels like climbing Mount Everest."

For me, this lethargy manifested as a heaviness in my body, as if I were trying to walk through a vat of molasses. In other instances, I experienced a massive, suffocating pressure in my chest, like being pinned to the ground by a 350-pound wrestler. During such times, I was so exhausted that I would curl into a fetal position and lie there for hours. "A slug," I thought to myself, "has more energy than I do."

"If you want to get an idea of what depression feels like," says UCLA neuropsychiatrist Peter Whybrow, "combine the anguish of profound grief with bodily sensations of severe jet lag." That's how it felt to me—like breaking up with my first true love and then being run over by a truck.

William Styron, whose memoir *Darkness Visible* chronicles his descent into a major depressive episode, describes the agony of depression this way:

"Melancholy," by Edvard Munch

It is not an immediately identifiable pain, like that of a broken limb. It may be more accurate to say that despair, owing to some evil trick played on the sick brain by the inhabiting psyche, comes to resemble the diabolical discomfort of being imprisoned in a fiercely overheated room. And because no breeze stirs this cauldron, because there is no escape from this smothering confinement, it is entirely natural that the victim begins to ceaselessly think of oblivion.

Time on the Cross

I am now the most miserable man living. If what I feel were equally distributed to the whole human family, there would not be one cheerful face on earth.
—ABRAHAM LINCOLN

The pain of depression is not only agonizing, it is chronic, persistent, and seemingly unremitting—like having an emotional toothache. Although psychological factors may trigger a major depressive episode, at some point the disorder manifests as a biological illness. Hence, I could not will or affirm myself out of my malaise. Positive thinking was useless. Nor could I apply any metaphysical, psychological, or self-help techniques to stop the pain. There was no inner child to nurture or heal. I was ill at my biochemical core.

In the past, if I were in a funk, enjoying the simple beauty of nature would help to improve my condition. Thus I was taken aback when on a beautiful summer's day, I hiked in a pristine old-growth forest, and my mind, in its continued downward spiral, persisted in contemplating suicide. Though the environment was heavenly, it could not assuage my inner suffering. The pain was just too intense, as if some invisible phantom were clanging a pair of cymbals inside my brain. I now understood the meaning of "endogenous" depression (i.e., a depression that arises from within). I was at the mercy of a deranged biochemistry that I could neither understand nor control.

When asked by Art Buchwald whether his depression was improved by being in the country, William Styron replied:

> It's all the same. You're carrying the thing around with you. It's like a crucifixion. It doesn't matter where you are; nothing in the outer world can alter it. You could be in the sublimest place you could possibly imagine. For example, [Mike] Wallace went down to St. Martin, which is a wonderfully attractive place. But he had his darkest moments there.

As Styron knew only too well, there is little respite from the hell of a major depression. You cannot curl up in bed with a few good videos, drink chicken soup, and expect to feel better in seven to ten days. Unlike most physical ailments, depression does not improve with rest. Being alone in bed actually makes matters worse, as the mind turns further inward and tortures itself with imaginary demons.

I felt like some sadist was twisting my arm behind my back and would not relent even after I yelled "Uncle!" With each unfolding day, the pain seemed to increase. I complained to my friends, "This is the worst I've ever felt!"

"But that's what you say every day," they countered.

It didn't matter. There was something freshly horrible about the pain, as if I were being kicked in the stomach once every minute.

I was sure someone had created a cruel parody of Psalm 139 in which David says to God, "Where can I go from your spirit? Or where can I flee from your presence? If I ascend into heaven you are there. . . If I take the wings of the morning and dwell in the uttermost parts of the sea, even there your left hand shall lead me and your right hand shall hold me . . ." except that in depression it is not God, but the devil who follows you everywhere. And there is no escape.

Generalized Anxiety Disorder

There may be no rest for the wicked, but compared to the rest that anxious people get, the wicked undoubtedly have a pastoral life.
—RUSSELL HAMPTON, *The Far Side of Despair*

Although no one knows exactly why, a great number of depressions are also accompanied by anxiety. In one study, 85 percent of those with major depression were also diagnosed with generalized anxiety disorder (see the symptoms listed in the sidebar), while 35 percent had symptoms of a panic disorder. Because they so often go hand in hand, anxiety and depression are considered the fraternal twins of mood disorders.

Believed to be caused in part by a malfunction of brain chemistry, generalized anxiety is not the normal apprehension that one feels before taking a test or awaiting the outcome of a biopsy. A person with an anxiety disorder suffers from what President Franklin Roosevelt called "fear itself." For a reason that is only partially known, the brain's fight-or-flight mechanism becomes activated, even when no real threat exists. Being chronically anxious is like being stalked by an imaginary tiger. The feeling of being in danger never goes away.

Even more than the depression, it was my anxiety and agitation that became the defining symptoms of my illness. Like epileptic seizures, a series of frenzied anxiety attacks would descend upon me without warning. My body was possessed by a chaotic, demonic force that led to my shaking, pacing, and violently hitting myself across the chest or in the head. This self-flagellation seemed to provide a

Diagnostic Criteria for Generalized Anxiety Disorder

How do you know if you are suffering from clinical anxiety? The following criteria are taken from the *Diagnostic and Statistical Manual of Mental Disorders (DSM-IV)*. If you or someone you know is experiencing these symptoms, seek professional help.

A. Excessive anxiety and worry occurring more days than not for at least six months.

B. Difficulty in controlling the worry and anxiety.

C. The anxiety and worry are associated with three (or more) of the following six symptoms:

1. Restlessness or feeling keyed up or on edge
2. Being easily fatigued
3. Difficulty concentrating or mind going blank
4. Irritability
5. Muscle tension
6. Sleep disturbances (difficulty falling or staying asleep, or restless, unsatisfying sleep)

D. The anxiety, worry, or physical symptoms cause clinically significant distress or impairment in social, occupational, or other important areas of functioning.

E. The disturbance is not due to the direct physiological effects of a substance (e.g., a drug abuse or a medication) or a general medical condition (e.g., hyperthyroidism).

physical outlet for my invisible torment, as if I were letting steam out of a pressure cooker.

The force of my symptoms was so great that I considered the possibility that I might be possessed by some malevolent demon. I remembered the film *The Exorcist* and set up an appointment with a priest who specialized in satanic possession. After taking a thorough case history and questioning me about my religious beliefs, the priest concluded that I was not possessed by the devil.

"It certainly feels that way," I replied.

I then consulted a psychiatrist who told me that my symptoms were not those of a panic disorder. I did not experience palpitations, pounding heart, sweating, trembling, shortness of breath, chest pain, fear of dying, and so on. The word "agitation" was the closest I could come to describing the feeling of wanting to jump out of my skin. Hence my disorder was eventually diagnosed as "agitated depression."

Agitated depression is not a good diagnosis to have. Clinicians have observed that when anxiety occurs comorbidly with depression, the symptoms of *both* the depression and the anxiety are more severe compared to when those disorders occur independently. Moreover, the symptoms of the depression take longer to resolve, making the illness more chronic and more resistant to treatment. Finally, depression exacerbated by anxiety has a much higher suicide rate than depression alone. (In one study, 92 percent of depressed patients who had attempted suicide were also plagued by severe anxiety.*) Like alcohol and barbiturates, depression and anxiety are a deadly combination when taken together.

In addition to physical agitation, my anxiety was accompanied by obsessively rhyming voices. In my book *Words That Heal,* I suggested that people rhyme their affirmations because "words that rhyme make a more powerful impression on the subconscious than blank verse." Now my own subconscious had decided, in a malicious way, to take my advice to heart. Rhymes such as "electric shock for Douglas Bloch," "the River Styx in '96," and "suicidal ideation is a

---

* *Clinical Psychiatry News,* 27, no. 6 (1999): 25.

More than any other image, Edvard Munch's
"The Scream" depicts the out-of-control anxiety
that was threatening to destroy me.

hit across the nation" flooded my mind. (The rhyme "electric shock
for Douglas Bloch" was an allusion to ECT, electroconvulsive therapy.) When my anxiety became extreme, I shouted these rhymes out
loud, further upsetting myself and those around me. Although I did
not actually hear these verses—they were more like obsessive
thoughts—their presence led my doctors to give me a final diagnosis
of *agitated depression with psychotic features.*

Because my anxiety emerged from a disordered brain, it, like
the depression, was outside of my conscious control. Yet virtually
everyone—my friends, family, men's group members, and even
health professionals—interpreted the anxiety as some sort of acting
out that I could modify at will; they did not understand that I was
sick. Some people even became angry and abusive in response to my

distress. The most dramatic illustration of this occurred on the night of my first hospitalization.

The day had begun with a major anxiety attack, an aftershock from the overly anxious reaction to an antidepressant I had taken two days earlier. At my request, my ex-wife, Joan, telephoned the on-call psychiatrist who advised that I hospitalize myself, given the extremity of my symptoms. It took most of the day for my managed care insurance to precertify my admission, so by the time we left for the hospital it was already late in the evening.

As Joan and I made our way out Sunset Highway, my terror escalated as I recalled the trauma of my psychiatric hospitalizations during my previous episodes. Five blocks from the unit, realizing that history was about to repeat itself, I attempted to jump out of the car and was prevented only by the automatic door locks that Joan activated from the driver's side.

We arrived on the psychiatric ward at midnight, and after being searched and having my belongings confiscated, I was led to a stark, barren room with a hospital cot and a glaring overhead light.

"What did you expect?" the night nurse commented, when she saw the distress on my face.

From her tone of voice, I could sense that order, not compassion, was this woman's priority. She spoke in carefully measured phrases, as if competing with a metronome to see who could keep the most exact beat.

"Isn't there a reading lamp here?" I asked timidly. "It helps me to relax if I can curl up in bed with a book."

"Lamps are not allowed in the rooms," she replied. "We can't risk having our patients strangle themselves with the cord."

Pondering that morbid remark, I asked the nurse for a tranquilizer to help me get to sleep.

"You don't need medication," she replied in a clinical voice. "Take some deep breaths and try to control yourself."

"I'd like to, but I can't," I responded. "That is why I was admitted to the hospital—because I'm out of control. Please call the psychiatrist and ask him to order me a sleeping pill."

Big Nurse was unmoved. My anxiety escalated, and I began to pace the floor. Whack! Whack! I hit myself in the head, then across the chest.

"If you can't restrain yourself," she warned in a high-pitched voice, "I'm going to call security and tell them to strap you down."

Upon hearing these words my mind raced forward to a scene of being forcibly put in a straightjacket. I felt myself suffocating and was filled with terror. My worst fear was about to come true— I was going to die in a mental hospital. I spotted a bottle of tranquilizers that was sitting unattended at the nurse's station and moved toward it. "I'd rather get it over with now than die of fright," I decided.

Fortunately, Joan was still on the unit. Sensing my distress, she grabbed me by the arm and escorted me for a long walk around the ward. When we returned, the on-call psychiatrist had ordered a 50-milligram tablet of Mellaril (an antipsychotic tranquilizer in the same family as Thorazine). With a prayer of thanksgiving, I gulped down the medicine.

Even with the Mellaril, I still felt a bit agitated, and I asked Joan to rock me to sleep. When the nurse made her rounds a few hours later, she spotted Joan and became livid. "What are you doing here?" she howled. "I thought I told you to leave!" At that moment, I realized that the notorious Nurse Ratched (from the book and movie *One Flew Over the Cuckoo's Nest*) was not just a fictional character.

Unfortunately, this experience was repeated two months later in a different hospital. My anxiety in the new environment was exacerbated by the fact that I was residing in a locked unit. The only outdoor space available for exercise was a small courtyard surrounded by barbed wire. Here, restless patients took their smoke breaks. The air was so full of secondhand smoke that I could hardly breathe, let alone jog or run in place. My exercise options all but eliminated, I paced back and forth in the halls for hours at a time.

One day, upon witnessing my agitation, a mental health therapist took me aside.

"Why don't you practice the cognitive therapy techniques you learned in your behavior modification group?" he asked.

"I think a Klonopin would be more effective." (Klonopin is an anti-seizure medication that is also used to treat anxiety.)

"You can control your thoughts and your behaviors without medication," he insisted.

"Don't you understand?" I replied emphatically. "I AM NOT IN CONTROL OF MY NERVOUS SYSTEM. I AM NOT IN CONTROL OF MY NERVOUS SYSTEM."

Instead of a straightjacket, the nurses and therapist decided to put me in the "quiet room"—a euphemism for a padded cell with no windows. "Just what a claustrophobic needs to calm his anxiety," I mused.

Such lack of compassion on the part of trained professionals shows their ignorance of a basic medical fact—that in *extreme* cases of anxiety, the agitation *chemically interferes* with the brain's ability to hold positive thoughts over a sustained period.

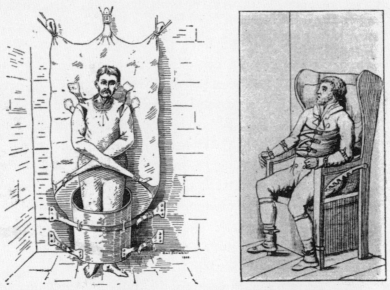

This illustration depicts two types of restraints commonly used in 19th-century hospitals. Modern day methods are more humane and are used only when a person is a danger to himself or others.

It was not until six months later that the legitimacy of my symptoms was validated by a savvy nurse-practitioner who taught stress reduction to patients with chronic pain. "When your brain gets whacked out to this extreme," Teresa advised, "you literally need to burn off those agitating chemicals; I recommend intense exercise." Following her counsel, whenever my anxiety began to escalate, I ran down to my neighborhood pool and swam a mile or more until I dropped. (I called this ritual swimming for my life.)

Meanwhile, I was living in the inferno, a concentration camp of the mind. I felt as if my brain were being batted back and forth by two drunken Ping-Pong players—one named anxiety and the other called depression. I had never believed that hell was a place you went to after death, but rather a state of consciousness that one could experience here on earth. Now I had the living proof. About four months after my first hospitalization, my psychiatrist asked, "Douglas, are you afraid that if these symptoms persist, you will become chronically mentally ill?"

"What do you mean?" I replied incredulously. *"I already am chronically mentally ill."*

CHAPTER TWO

There Is No Room at the Inn: Because Managed Care Has Not Preauthorized Any Stays

---

*If there were a physical disease that manifested itself in some particularly
ugly way, such as pustulating sores or a sloughing off of the flesh accompanied by pain of an intense and chronic nature, readily visible to everyone,
and if that disease affected fifteen million people in our country, and further,
if there were virtually no help or succor for most of these persons, and they
were forced to walk among us in their obvious agony, we would rise up as
one social body in sympathy and anger. We would give of our resources,
both human and economic, and we would plead and demand that this
suffering be eased. There is not such a physical disease, but there is such a
disease of the mind, and about fifteen million people around us are suffering
from it. But we have not risen in anger and sympathy, although they are
walking among us and crying in their pain and anguish.*

—RUSSELL HAMPTON, *The Far Side of Despair*

The extreme symptoms of depression and anxiety I have just
described did not come upon me overnight. The dissolution of
my psyche was more akin to the gradual washing away of a sandcastle
by the encroaching ocean tides. I had hoped that my hospitalization in
September 1996 would halt the downward spiral that had begun with

the adverse drug reaction the previous week. However, I was released
within forty-eight hours of my arrival, long before I had an opportunity
to emotionally heal—a consequence of managed care. I was sent home
with no recovery plan other than my psychiatrist's advice to "be your
own physician" and to take low doses of Mellaril "as you see fit."

For the first few days after my release, I maintained a shaky stability. I returned to work, hoping that the focus of a job would alleviate my anxiety. Instead, my moods turned inexorably downward.
With each passing day, I felt more and more fragile. Early morning
awakenings (a classic symptom of depression) intensified. My depressive moods blackened. The anxiety attacks, which had begun sporad-
ically, increased in frequency to two to three times a week. I was less
and less able to concentrate on my sales job, crying at the slightest
upset. Like the Bizarro Superman I used to read about in the comic
books, I felt as if the old Douglas had been replaced by some mal-
functioning impersonator.

My predicament brings up a pertinent question that has enormous social implications—what happens to a person who is incapacitated by clinical depression? Where does he or she go when he reaches
the point that he can no longer cope? There are no halfway houses for
depressives, although with fifteen to twenty million Americans suffering from depression, you would think there would be. Neither are
there any 12-step groups called Depressives Anonymous. Many people
in the throes of depression tough it out and continue their daily
routine in spite of the incredible pain, becoming what William Styron
calls "the walking wounded." I did not have that luxury. The symptoms of my anxiety were simply too extreme for me to be on my own.

Although I had many wonderful friends, they were busy with
their jobs and family obligations and could not monitor me throughout the day. (It is also easy for friends to get burned out caring for
someone who is clinically depressed. To find out what friends and
family can do, please refer to Part Two, chapter 14, "When Someone
You Love is Depressed.") My ex-wife, Joan, had moved in with me
that September to become my caretaker, but was actively looking for a
full-time job. This crisis was too big to be handled by friends and
family alone; I needed the support of a therapeutic community.

"The Sleep of Reason Produces Monsters," by Francisco de Goya

During my previous depressive episodes, I had stumbled across two such environments. In 1976, I spent four months residing at Berkeley Place, Inc., a halfway house that transitioned hospitalized patients back into the community. (Although I had no history of hospitalization, I was allowed to stay because I was homeless.) Then in 1983, my parents admitted me to New York Hospital for a one-month stay (at that time, a month was considered a short-term stint). During these respites my symptoms significantly improved, and by the time of my discharge I was on the mend. I believe that each of these institutions saved my life.

Now, however, it was 1996. With managed care insurance companies in charge of mental health treatment, the landscape was anything but patient-friendly. I consulted a number of psychiatrists and psychotherapists in the hopes of getting healed through outpatient therapy, but none of them would work with me. "You're too agitated and out of control to benefit from therapy," they said. "You should spend at least four to six weeks in a residential setting in order to get stabilized." The prescription was sound, but it overlooked a critical point—psychiatric hospitals no longer provided long-term care. Beginning with the 1960s, each decade has seen a gradual reduction of inpatient time allotted to the mentally ill.

For example, in the mid '60s I knew a woman who suffered from schizophrenia and who spent two years getting well at McLean, Harvard's famous psychiatric teaching hospital. (Many celebrities have resided at McLean—including Sylvia Plath, Robert Lowell, Ray Charles, and singer James Taylor, who wrote about the experience in his first album. Novelist Susanna Kaysen also recounts her stay at McLean in the book *Girl, Interrupted.*)

Not only patients, but psychiatrists are becoming increasingly frustrated with a managed health care system that puts profits above the welfare of the individual. One psychiatrist told me that he is forced to treat many of his severely ill patients—who at one time would have been hospitalized—on an outpatient basis.

In *The Far Side of Despair*, author Russell Hampton recounts his six-month hospitalization for anxiety and depression during the early 1970s. In 1985, author William Styron spent six weeks in a hospital recovering from a major depressive episode. By the time my crisis hit, the average stay had been reduced to seventy-two hours. Even McLean, champion of milieu therapy, had switched over to short-term treatment.

"Slit your wrists and a hospital will have to take you in," a friend advised when I told him of my predicament.

"If it were only that easy," I replied, as I thought of my ex-roommate Dan, whom I had met during my first hospitalization. A high school physics teacher in his mid-thirties, Dan had been admitted after his wife found him wandering in the woods with a gun, threatening to blow his brains out.

"What is your treatment plan?" I asked over breakfast.

"I don't know," he replied with an apathetic look on his face. "I get discharged later today."

"But you're not ready to leave!" I said incredulously. "You were only admitted last night!"

"I can't help it. My insurance company said my time is up."

As he predicted, Dan was discharged later that afternoon, less than twenty-four hours after he was admitted. I frequently think of him, wondering whether he is still alive, in spite of the system that failed him. Looking back, I am convinced that if long-term residential care had been available to me (as it was in 1976 and 1983), my recent illness would have resolved far sooner. The absence of adequate facilities for people suffering from extreme depression and anxiety is a major failing of our mental health care system.

As I struggled to find someone (or someplace) to be my caregiver, I imagined the ideal healing environment for someone in Dan's or my state—a restful, peaceful asylum in the country modeled after the old health sanatoriums of Europe. Here is the vision that came to me:

> This center is designed to treat the whole person, combining the best of medical with alternative care—diet, exercise, light therapy, acupuncture, vitamin and mineral supplementation, prayer, psychotherapy, group therapy, vocational counseling, and so on. Unlike traditional hospitals, the entire facility is a place of beauty. The buildings are open and spacious with plenty of natural light. Soothing classical music fills the air, and gorgeous works of art decorate the hallways and the walls of the patients' rooms. Nutritious meals are served using fresh foods from the ground's organic gardens. Various forms of physical therapy such as massage and whirlpools provide relaxation for patients and staff. Puppies and kittens are available for everyone to love. In short, the center provides a holistic therapeutic milieu, the goal of which is to return the individual to society as soon as possible, but not before he or she is ready.

Aside from its role in reducing the human suffering caused by mental illness, such a facility might well pay for itself by reducing the $43.7 billion annual cost that depression places on the U.S. economy.

Unfortunately, the only institution that remotely resembled my fantasy was the world-famous Menninger Clinic in Topeka, Kansas. While Menninger had an excellent reputation, the price tag was daunting—$30,000 for a month's stay—an amount that no insurance would cover. Moreover, I was scared of being transplanted to the Midwest without friends or family support. For the next five months I agonized about whether to take the radical step of going to Menninger.

Just as I was about to give up hope, I learned of a residential clinic that seemed to fit my needs. Springbrook, a drug and alcohol rehabilitation center located forty-five miles southwest of Portland, had everything I had hoped for: a minimum twenty-eight-day residency (with a possible sixty-day extension); group and individual therapy; recreational therapy that included a gym, a weight room, and access to a city pool; a beautifully manicured twenty-five-acre campus with walking paths; a balanced diet consisting of excellent food provided by Marriott Food Service (the only complaints about the food are that the servings are too big); and 12-step spiritual orientation. Finally (this is the most amazing fact), in most cases insurance companies would pay for 50 to 80 percent of the treatment cost.

There was, however, a small catch—one had to be an alcoholic or a drug addict to be admitted.

"I'm not an addict," I explained to the admissions officer over the phone, "but I am in as much pain as one."

"I'm afraid that you don't meet our criteria," she replied.

"But I read in your brochure that you treat people for depression."

"Only if you have chemical dependency as your primary diagnosis."

"Let me understand this," I said, pondering the absurdity of the situation. "If I were to self-medicate with drugs or alcohol to nullify the pain of my depression, and consequently developed an addiction, I would be able to pursue long-term recovery in an elaborate treatment center. But if I choose a healthier outcome and resist the temptation to abuse myself, I am limited to a three-day stay in the local psych ward."

"I see your point," she said sympathetically, "but I have to abide by our policy."

I had heard of people slipping through the cracks of society's institutions, but this felt more like falling into the crater of an active

volcano. "It's no wonder that depression is the leading cause of suicide," I thought, "when people can't get the help they need."

Many people with mental disorders, especially the poor, end up
behind bars. According to the U.S. Bureau of Justice and Statistics,
prisons now house more than 280,000 mentally ill inmates (16 percent of the inmate population). People who are ill need treatment,
not incarceration.

The issue, it seemed to me, is that depression is not a tangible
problem like substance abuse. And since depressives as a rule do not
make the headlines with their self-destructive acts—like driving a
BMW into a tree while loaded on cocaine—their illness is not taken
as seriously.

For a while, I contemplated getting hooked on drugs so I might
receive some decent care and attention. A few months later I read
Elizabeth Wurtzel's *Prozac Nation* and discovered another depressive who faced the same dilemma. Wurtzel writes:

> I found myself wishing for a real ailment, found myself longing
> to be a junkie or a cokehead or something. . . . It seemed to
> me that if I could get hooked on some drug, anything was
> possible. I'd make friends. I'd have a real problem. I'd be able
> to walk into a church basement full of fellow sufferers and have
> them all say, "Welcome to our nightmare! We understand!
> Here are our phone numbers, call any time you feel you're
> slipping because we're here for you."

Meanwhile, there was no one—i.e., no institutional structure—that
was there for me. As I paced back and forth, hitting myself furiously
while I waited for Joan to arrive home from work, I was left pondering,
"Where can I find a therapeutic environment that will nurture me
back to health?" Discovering the answer to this question was becoming
a matter of life and death.

"Melancholia I," by Albrecht Dürer

CHAPTER THREE

Treading Fire

When a man finds that it is his destiny to suffer, he will have to accept his suffering as his single and unique task. No one can relieve him of his suffering or suffer in his place. His unique opportunity lies in the way in which he bears his burden.

—VICTOR FRANKL

War is hell. So is mental illness.

—BINFORD W. GILBERT

The towering door closed behind me with a grave finality. "Are you sure you have to keep it locked?" I asked the orderly. "I voluntarily checked myself in here, so I don't think I'm going to try to escape."

"It's not you that we are worried about," he replied. "With all of the addicts on this ward, we can't risk having any more drugs smuggled into the unit. That's why no one is allowed to go outside."

This was not the private facility at Springbrook with its manicured walking paths. With all of my other options exhausted, I had entered Pacific Gateway Hospital, a dual diagnosis psychiatric facility in the Portland area. Unlike Springbrook (and other drug and alcohol treatment centers), Gateway accepted patients who suffered solely from mental disorders. While Springbrook's clientele consisted of

Words of Hope

Only two hours remained before I was to be admitted to the psychiatric ward of Pacific Gateway Hospital. As my partner, Joan, packed my suitcase, I became increasingly anxious about being taken to an unknown and threatening environment. My friend Kathleen shared with me the following words of hope and encouragement:

1. You are falling apart in order to be put together in a new way. You will come through this because you are loved.
2. As a result of this breakdown, you will emerge a better person.
3. You are strong; you made a decision not to give up in the past, and you will not give up now.
4. All of the good you have done will help you to a better future.

doctors, lawyers and other professionals, Gateway ministered to the common folk. Like pilgrims converging on Mecca, they streamed in from all parts of the Pacific Northwest, seeking salvation from the "three Ds"—drinking, drugging, and depression.

At Gateway, instead of having seventy-two hours to get better, my managed care provider had granted me seven to ten days (an inadequate time to heal from depression, let alone get clean and sober). It was the best I could muster.

My days at Gateway were spent attending group therapy, playing backgammon, and being beaten at speed chess by a mercurial manic-depressive who supported his drug habit by hustling chess games on the street. During my stay, my condition declined, not because of the environment (Gateway had an excellent reputation), but because the depressive illness had taken on a life of its own and was metastasizing through me like a psychic cancer. The downward trajectory of my disease was evidenced by the increasing frequency and duration of my anxiety attacks. Without the option of outdoor exercise, I was reduced to pacing the hallways, wearing out both the carpet and my welcome.

Admission Summary: Pacific Gateway Hospital

Patient: Bloch, Douglas. This is the first Pacific Gateway hospitalization for this 47-year-old white male.

Reason for Admission: The patient is depressed, anxious, and increasingly out of control.

Mental Status Examination: Patient is a well-developed, well-nourished adult male appearing stated age. Patient's speech was variable in flow from slow to pressured. Thought content was that he was overwhelmed, hopeless, helpless, and out of control, and that he needed help. His mood was markedly anxious with an undercurrent of depression. His affect was mildly labile. Recent memory based on object recall is good. Remote memory based on historical reconstruction is good. Intelligence, based on vocabulary, fund of knowledge, and educational achievement is above average to superior. His insight is fair. His judgment is poor. He presents as extremely dependent and hopeless. He denies suicidal or homicidal ideation at this time.

Strengths and Assets: (1) The patient is very intelligent.
(2) The patient tends to form a good therapeutic alliance.

Attending Diagnosis: (1) Major depression. (2) Recurrent, severe panic attacks with agoraphobia (patient reports episodes in which he is so anxious he cannot leave the house). (3) Generalized anxiety disorder.

INITIAL TREATMENT PLAN:
Problem List: (1) Depression. (2) Anxiety.
Medication: I will probably increase the Zoloft. He took 50 mgs. the first time today. May increase the Elavil and may increase the Klonopin.
Plan of Treatment: Admit the patient to the adult unit. Work with the patient on the issues of stress management and anxiety reduction. Get the patient stabilized on medication. Work with him on issues of self-esteem. Get him transitioned to day program.
Estimated Length of Stay: 5 days.
Goals, Discharge Criteria: (1) The patient will be stable on medications. (2) The patient will be able to manage his affairs outside the hospital.

Signed Dr. ██████████████ 10-23-1996

My sorry plight earned me the sympathy of the hard-core heroin users who housed the ward. ("We thought we had problems," I heard them say among themselves, "but this dude is really messed up.")

As the day of my release grew closer, I began to panic. Joan was now working full time, and if I could not create an alternative support system, I would be shipped off to the state hospital in Salem.

One day, shortly before my release, I noticed a new person in the lunchroom who wasn't from our unit.

"Hi." I reached out my hand. "My name is Douglas."

"My name is Tom Peters," came the reply.

"Are you a patient on the ward?"

"I attend day treatment next door."

"What's that?"

"It's where people go after they leave the hospital. It's pretty good, actually. We attend groups most of the day and come here for a free lunch."

The lunch I couldn't have cared less about. The full-time structure was another matter.

"What are the hours?"

"Nine-thirty till three-thirty, kind of like going to school."

Later that day I approached my psychiatrist, who confirmed that the program was for real.

"How soon can I get in?" I inquired.

"The program is crowded right now, but they may have space for you. I'll introduce you to the director, Mike Terry, tomorrow at lunch."

Two days later, on November 1, 1996, after just nine days, I was discharged from Gateway. I left the hospital's main entrance, made a right turn, walked one block, and found myself at the doorstep of the Sellwood Day Treatment Clinic.

Day treatment was a highly structured outpatient program consisting of group and individual therapy that was available to recently hospitalized patients. The center was housed within a historic landmark—the home of Dr. Sellwood, after whom the Sellwood district of Portland is named. The two-story dwelling was constructed in 1906 and expressed the Victorian charm and elegance of the homes built during that era. The cheerful, well-lit rooms and tasteful furnishings conveyed a sense of home and family. Day treatment was more than a psychiatric clinic; it was a true therapeutic community. Its healing milieu supplied three ingredients that were crucial for my stabilization:

1. **Containment:** Being in a structured environment with defined limits and daily tasks decreased my anxiety.

2. **Contact:** Nurturing connection and support from staff and patients helped me to focus outward and to escape my inner nightmare.

3. **Routine:** A regular, daily rhythm with predictable activities calmed and soothed my nervous system.

The heart of the program was group therapy, which ran from 9:30 A.M. to 3:30 A.M. and was facilitated by members of the treatment team— a psychiatrist, three psychologists, two social workers, a nurse, an art therapist, a movement therapist, and two drug and alcohol counselors.

Day Treatment Schedule

9:30–10:30	Living Skills	Managing Emotions	Living Skills	Managing Emotions	Social Skills
10:30–11:30	Coping Skills	Problem Solving	Problem Emotions	Relationship Trauma Survivors	Coping Skills
11:30–12:30	Medical Group Evaluation	Women's Group / Men's Group	Relationship Group Psychotherapy	Mind & Body Group Psychotherapy	Communication Skills
12:30–1:30	LUNCH	LUNCH	LUNCH	LUNCH	LUNCH
1:30–2:30	Movement Therapy	Self-Esteem	Stress Management	Crafts	Self-Esteem
2:30–3:30	Relapse Prevention	Art Therapy	Anger Management	Relapse Prevention	

Day treatment provided me with a complete, *uninterrupted* support system that far surpassed the assistance any single therapist could offer. For the next nine months, this program would play a pivotal role in my survival. (Not all cities have such a comprehensive program. If a day treatment center does not exist in your area, you can seek out 12-step groups, depression support groups, or any combination of structures that work. Mental health support groups can be located by calling your local hospital or by contacting the organizations listed in Appendix C.)

It was not the content but the context of day treatment that I found so healing. The psychological information presented in the groups was fairly elementary; I had learned most of it in my first year of undergraduate studies. It didn't matter. I was not attending the program to add to my intellectual knowledge; I was there because I needed the structure and support. I decided to humble myself and to accept the help that was so generously offered.

Asking the Right Question

Shortly after my arrival at day treatment, I was assigned my individual therapist, Pat Ritter. Pat was a registered nurse and a recovering alcoholic who, having been clinically depressed herself, understood mental illness from both sides of the hospital door.

"This is your life," Pat stated matter-of-factly at our first meeting. "For reasons we may not understand, the universe has given you the challenge of major depression right now. You do not get to choose whether you have this mental illness. Your choice lies in how you are going to deal with it."

"But what about those self-help books that say you can create anything you want if you just apply the right technique?" I asked. I was thinking about all the "can do" motivational self-help tracts I had read (and written) in my quest for self-improvement.

"They may work in other contexts," she replied, "but not in this one. This time you are dealing with a force that is more powerful than your ego."

As Pat spoke, I imagined myself as a sailor who had survived a terrible shipwreck and was lost at sea. I shared my image with Pat.

"What is that sailor's task?" she asked.

"To try to stay afloat until help comes."

"Precisely! Your job is to create an 'emotional life raft' that will keep you afloat until the pattern of your illness shifts."

"And how do I do this?"

"In AA we have something called the '24-hour plan.' Instead of promising never to drink again, we focus on keeping sober for the current twenty-four hours. I suggest you adopt a similar strategy."

Pat was right. Whenever I contemplated the prospect of dealing with my pain over the long term, I became overwhelmed. But if I could reduce my life to a single twenty-four-hour segment of time— that was something I could handle. If I could tread water (or, being in hell, tread fire) each day, then perhaps I could survive my ordeal.

A Survival Plan for Living in Hell

My definition of a man is this: a being who can get used to anything.
—DOSTOYEVSKY

Working together, Pat and I created what I called "my daily survival plan." The central idea was simple—to develop coping strategies that would get me through the day, hour by hour, minute by minute. Because I was fighting a war on two fronts, I had to devise and employ techniques that would deal with the depression and the anxiety. I used my coping strategies to create four categories of support, which I have summarized on the following pages. These categories are: *physical support, mental and emotional support, spiritual support,* and most importantly, *people support.*

Putting together a survival plan did more than help me cope. In designing and carrying out this program, I became the captain of my ship, an empowering move for someone who felt powerless. As Pat later reflected, "When you made the decision to do more, I saw a glimmer of hope in your eyes."

Here, then, is the plan we created.

A Daily Survival Plan for Responding to Depression and Anxiety

What follows is a brief outline of my daily survival plan. I have rewritten it in the second person so you can adapt it to your individual needs. Remember, the goal is to identify coping strategies that will keep you safe and get you through each day until the pattern of the depression shifts.

A. People Support

Find a way to structure your daily routine so you will be around people much of the time. If there is a day treatment program in your area, some form of group therapy, or depression support groups at your local hospital, attend them. Don't be embarrassed about asking for help from family members or friends. You are suffering from an illness, not a personal weakness or a defect in character.

B. Physical Support

1. Exercise is one of the best ways to elevate and stabilize your mood, as well as to improve your overall physical health. Pick an activity that you might enjoy, even if it is as simple as walking around the block, and engage in it as often as you can (three to four times a week is ideal).
2. Eat a diet that is high in complex carbohydrates and protein, avoiding foods such as simple sugars that can cause emotional ups and downs.
3. Adopt a regular sleep schedule to get your body into a routine.
4. Take your medication as prescribed. Check with your health care professional before making any changes in dosage. Be patient and give the medicine enough time to work.

C. Mental and Emotional Support

Monitoring self-talk is an important strategy in helping to stabilize one's mood. Although you may not be able to control your depression and anxiety, you may be able to modify the way you think about your symptoms. You may wish to work with a therapist who specializes in cognitive therapy.* He or she can help you to replace thoughts of catastrophe and doom with affirmations that encourage you to apply present-moment coping strategies. Perhaps the most powerful thought you can hold is "This, too, will pass."

D. Spiritual Support

If you believe in God, a higher power, or any benevolent spiritual presence, now is the time to make use of your faith. Attending a form of worship with other people can bring both spiritual and social support. If you have a spiritual advisor (such as a rabbi, priest, or minister), talk with that person as often as possible. Put your name on any prayer support list(s) you know of; don't be bashful about asking others to pray for you. The universe longs to help you in your time of need.

Because of the disabling nature of depression, you may not be able to implement all of these strategies. That is okay. Just do the best you can. Do not underestimate the power of intention. Your earnest desire to get well is a powerful force that can draw unexpected help and support to you—even when you are severely limited by a depressive illness.

---

* Please see Week 5 of the Better Mood Recovery Program in Part Two for information on cognitive and other forms of therapy used to treat depression.

People Support

The centerpiece of my survival strategy involved being around people. Interacting with other human beings drew me out of my tormented inner world and gave me something external to focus on. Talking with others was often the only intervention that would calm me down in the midst of a major anxiety attack. Like a screaming infant who is held by his mother, I found human contact tranquilizing and soothing.

My sense of connection with people also gave me a reason not to harm myself. I did not want to afflict my friends and family with the anguish that would result from my self-imposed departure. Kim, a lifeguard at the pool where I swam, agreed with my thinking. "Other people are a good reason to stay alive," she affirmed.

Knowing the curative effect of human caring and connection, I committed myself to attending day treatment. Unfortunately, getting to the clinic was not so simple. Like many people who suffer from depression, my symptoms were most severe in the morning. Oftentimes I would wake at 6:00 A.M., paralyzed by fear and overwhelmed by anxiety. To deal with my immobility, I asked five of my friends to each pick a day of the week to call me and roust me out of bed (hearing a caring person's voice on the other end of the telephone line served as a natural tranquilizer). The plan worked beautifully, and on those days when I was totally incapacitated, my friend Christine would drive me to day treatment. Instead of being home pacing the floors and hitting myself, I had a place to go where being around others ensured that I was safe.

In addition to group therapy, the other cornerstone of day treatment was my individual therapy, which took place on Tuesdays and Thursdays. These sessions did not consist of the usual insight-oriented psychotherapy. Being in *survival mode*, my goal was to focus on present-moment coping strategies. For example, I often entered Pat's office in the middle of a full-blown anxiety attack and spent the session pacing the floor while Pat gently coaxed me into taking a Klonopin. In this way, Pat functioned as a cheerleader, encouraging me from the sidelines, even though she could not directly influence the outcome of the game.

Attending day treatment was like going to a regular job—except here the task was to get well. My "coworkers" suffered from a wide range of mental disorders—depression, anxiety, manic-depression, schizophrenia, multiple-personality disorder, and PTSD (post-traumatic stress disorder). The patients at day treatment did not fit the stereotype of crazy people that I had learned as a child. These were brave souls who struggled against powerful and deadly brain disorders. They were my comrades in healing, and together, we formed a brotherhood of pain.

Many of my fellow group members lived on SSI (supplemental security income) or SSD (Social Security disability) while Medicare paid for their therapy. (More information about financially surviving a mental illness can be found in chapter 12.) My friends commuted to the clinic on the bus, often traveling many hours over long distances. Some were homeless and were forced to live in whatever transition shelters would accept them. (I, who owned my own home, felt like Bill Gates in comparison.) Suddenly I realized that our celebrity-obsessed culture had it all backward—that these nameless souls, stigmatized by their poverty and mental illness, were our true heroes, for they possessed what Woody Allen, in the opening lines of the film *Manhattan* rightly called the most important human attribute—courage.

Day treatment was a true life raft that kept me afloat during the most critical period of my illness. The program's only limitation was that it did not provide twenty-four-hour care. Groups ended at 3:30 P.M. on Monday through Thursday, and 2:30 P.M. on Friday. Since Joan and my friends were all working, I needed to find additional support for the rest of the afternoon. The solution came in the form of Terry, a home health aide whom I located through an agency in the Yellow Pages. (The cost of hiring a home health aide can be reasonable, about $10 to $12 an hour.) Terry was a guardian angel who stayed with me on weekday afternoons and guided me through various mundane tasks that kept me focused—cleaning the house, balancing my checkbook, mailing books to my readers, buying vegetable starters for the garden, taking a leisurely hike in Forest Park, and so on.

Weekends were also a challenge because they lacked the structure that day treatment provided. I organized my time as best as I could, asking Joan and my friends to take shifts as my caretaker (the task was too big for any one person). Walks in nature alternated with car drives along the Columbia River Highway, games of Scrabble, piecing together jigsaw puzzles, and watching movies (when I could focus). Since it is extremely demanding to be around someone who is emotionally and physically agitated, I will always be grateful to those people who displayed saint-like patience and understanding in the midst of my ordeal.

Support is critical in helping someone to cope with all kinds of extreme circumstances. Survivor researcher Julius Siegal emphasizes that communication among prisoners of war provides a lifeline for their survival. And for those who are prisoners of their inner wars, support is equally crucial. In chronicling his own depressive episode, novelist Andrew Solomon wrote:

> Recovery depends enormously on support. The depressives
> I've met who have done the best were cushioned with love.
> Nothing taught me more about the love of my father and my
> friends than my own depression.*

Physical Support

The second aspect of my daily survival plan consisted of finding ways to nurture my physical body.

Exercise. Research has shown that regular exercise can improve one's mood in cases of mild to moderate depression. In the midst of my clinical depression, exercise provided a decided, if only temporary, reprieve from my emotional torment. For years my favorite physical activity had been swimming; now it became a cornerstone of my survival strategy. My 9:00 A.M. swim helped calm my morning anxiety and prepared me for day treatment. My evening swim elevated my mood and alleviated whatever residual anxiety was still present. When the attacks were particularly bad, I would swim thirty to forty laps until I collapsed in exhaustion.

---

* Andrew Solomon, "Anatomy of Melancholy," *New Yorker*, 12 January, 1998; 73, no. 42: 51.

On weekends I exercised by hiking in the Columbia Gorge, around Mount Hood, or in Portland's beautiful Forest Park. Although walking in the woods did not eliminate the depression or anxiety, it provided a safe structure in which I could physically burn off a portion of my distress.

Eating and sleeping. To stabilize my emotions, I ate a diet high in complex carbohydrates and protein (fish, chicken, vegetables, whole grains, pasta, whole wheat breads, potatoes, yogurt, and so on) and avoided foods, such as simple sugars, that produce mood swings (see Week 3 of the Better Mood Recovery Program for more information). Fortunately, loss of appetite was not one of my symptoms, I ate regularly.

Although my prior depressive episodes had been marked by severe insomnia (few things are as debilitating as waking up at 3:00 A.M. and not being able to get back to sleep), this time I was able to rest, thanks to small doses of the antidepressant Elavil as well as the antianxiety drugs Klonopin and Ativan. This allowed me to keep a regular sleep schedule, which helped my body get into a rhythm.

On those nights when I experienced early morning awakenings (a classic symptom of depression), I reminded myself that no one ever died of insomnia. If I couldn't fall asleep within twenty minutes, I would get up and read (if I could focus), walk around the block, watch some television, or do some simple housework. Within an hour, I was usually back to sleep.

Medication. While antidepressants did little to alleviate my depression, I learned to use Klonopin to manage my anxiety. Klonopin is an antianxiety medication that is a member of the benzodiazepine family, which includes Xanax, Ativan, Valium, and Librium. Despite my fears of getting hooked on the drug, I soon realized that the benefits of taking Klonopin (i.e., containing my anxiety) outweighed the risks—depression combined with anxiety is more likely to result in suicide. Thus when my anxiety began to escalate, I ingested a half milligram of Klonopin and was guaranteed two to three hours of temporary relief. Although I sometimes felt a bit groggy, being sedated was preferable to jumping off a bridge.

Mental and Emotional Support

Although I could not always control the painful symptoms of depression and anxiety, I could influence the way I thought and felt about those symptoms.

Monitoring self-talk. Monitoring one's self-talk is an integral strategy of cognitive-behavioral therapy, a talk therapy widely used in treating depression. The catch-22, of course, was that the part of me that was supposed to do the monitoring—my thinking self—was itself diseased. I felt like a legless man who is told that the only way to save his life is to get up and walk.

Fortunately, before the onset of my illness I had spent eight years writing books and articles on the subject of positive self-talk. With Pat's help, I used a process from my book *Words That Heal* to create specific affirmations that would counter the all-too-frequent thoughts of gloom and doom that dominated my brain. For example, the sentiment "My depression will never get better" was replaced by the affirmation "Nothing stays the same forever" or "This, too, will pass." (I'll say more about this process in chapter 5.)

I had to switch from negative to positive self-talk once, twice, sometimes ten times a day. Since the depressed brain tends to see life through dark-colored glasses, monitoring my inner dialogue proved to be a constant and unending challenge.

Keeping a mood diary. One of the survival techniques I used to stay alive in my hell was to keep track of my anxiety and depression on a day-to-day basis. To this end, I created a daily mood rating scale (see the sidebar on opposite page).

Somehow, the simple act of observing and recording my moods gave me a sense of control over them. I also used my mood diary to track my reactions to pharmaceutical drugs and to record daily thoughts and feelings. This ongoing log served as an important progress report, both for myself and for my health care providers. It also provided an operational definition of recovery—my psychiatrist defined my getting well as seeing both the depression and the anxiety ratings decrease to a score of 2 or below for six consecutive weeks. As my mood scale for the month of January 1997 indicates,

Daily Mood Rating Scale for Anxiety and Depression

1–10 Depression Scale	1–10 Anxiety Scale
8–10 despair, suicidal feelings	8–10 out of control behavior, hitting, rhyming voices
6–7 feeling really bad, at the edge	6–7 strong agitation, pacing
5 definite malaise, insomnia	5 moderate worry, physical agitation
3–4 depression slightly stronger	3–4 mild fear and worry
1–2 minorly depressed mood	1–2 slight fear and worry
0 absence of symptoms	0 absence of symptoms

however, I was light years from that goal (see January Mood Diary, page 42).

Venting when I need to. Part of surviving meant being able to express my feelings—especially anger and grief about my plight. With Pat's encouragement, I vented my rage and fury through yelling, pounding a pillow, or painting my feelings in art therapy.

Later, I learned that the body's immune system is actually strengthened by expressing feelings and that both positive (joyful) and so-called negative (sad or angry) feelings are equally therapeutic. There is something about catharsis—giving full expression to one's deepest feelings of anguish—that is good for us. Perhaps that is why the Book of Psalms contains as many lamentations as songs of praise.

Being compassionate with myself. As part of my emotional self-care, it was important that I release the toxic feelings of blame, guilt, and shame that are so often felt by a person who is depressed. As Pat reassured me, "Depression is an illness, like diabetes or heart disease. It is not caused by a personal weakness or a defect in character. It is not your fault that you have this disorder."

Once again I turned to the affirmation process. Whenever I started to judge myself for being depressed, I would repeat, "It's not my fault that I am unwell. I am actually a powerful person residing

January Mood Diary

Date	Depression	Anxiety	Personal Notes
Jan 1	6	2	
Jan 2	6	4	Interview at OHSU hospital to see whether I should go in.
Jan 3	4	4	
Jan 4	9	6	
Jan 5	9	3	Take Lithium; go on hike and feel worse.
Jan 6	2	4	
Jan 7	9	10	Call Menninger Institute in Kansas to see about long-term stay.
Jan 8	4	2	
Jan 9	4	10	
Jan 10	4	8	Get acupuncture in the morning; it does not last.
Jan 11	10	8	
Jan 12	4	9	
Jan 13	3	10	Major anxiety attack at the pool; take Klonopin.
Jan 14	8	10	
Jan 15	10	8	
Jan 16	10	9	Suicidal feelings. On the verge of hospitalization.
Jan 17	6	8	
Jan 18	5	2	Best day in a month because of support; spend day with Kathleen, Judy, and Joan.
Jan 19	8	4	
Jan 20	5	6	
Jan 21	6	10	How long can I take this?
Jan 22	8	8	
Jan 23	8	10	
Jan 24	8	2	Start out anxious. Take Klonopin and go into depression, which is just as bad.
Jan 25	2	7	

Jan 26	5	9	Superbowl Sunday. Spend day at LEC for support.
Jan 27	2	5	
Jan 28	5	2	
Jan 29	5	1	
Jan 30	3	1	Best day in three months. Spend time with friends.
Jan 31	1	1	Stayed home from day treatment; opened mail and did finances. Went to look for a kitten to adopt.

inside a very sick body. I am taking good care of myself and will continue to do so until I get well."

Focusing on the little things. One day I asked Pat, "If all I am doing is trying to survive from day to day, how do I find any quality in my life?"

"The quality is in the little things," she replied.

How true! Shortly after Pat's comment, Portland was unexpectedly blessed with a sunny day. As I beheld with awe and wonder the magnificent pinks and red hues of the sunset, I recalled the words of poet Robert Browning: "God's in his heaven—all's right with the world." My experience was made all the more poignant by its transitory nature; I knew that in a matter of hours my depression would return, and I would be cast back into outer darkness.

In another instance, a friend and I spent an evening listening to the celestial chants of some Taize monks, founders of an intentional spiritual community located in the south of France. I was particularly moved by one refrain: *Within our darkest night, you kindle the fire that never dies away, that never dies away.* . . . As my voice merged with the voices of the audience, I was momentarily catapulted into ecstasy. Like a trapeze artist balanced on the high wire, I stood suspended above the abyss of my suicidal thoughts, safe from harm.

Having moments like this was akin to making deposits into an emotional bank account. When I sank back into my depression, I would draw upon my stored memories and affirm that life could still be beautiful, if only for an instant. Although I have described the pain of depression as seemingly unrelenting, there were moments of respite. Every now and then a day or two of relief from the intense pain would offer me a time to relax, recoup, and feel a tiny bit of hope. If the pain were 100 percent continuous, no one would survive a clinical depression.

Adapting to the cyclical nature of the illness. Another adjustment I had to make was understanding the up and down nature of my depressive illness. This occurred at two levels. First, I observed that days of intense anxiety would alternate with those of immobilizing depression.

Second, like the person with a chronic physical disease such as cancer, I came to learn that periods of progress and recovery were often followed by unwanted setbacks. Such relapses were particularly dangerous, for my accompanying disillusionment led to despair and suicidal thinking. To counteract these thoughts, I trained myself to say: "One day, the respites will last. One day, they will turn into a genuine recovery." I also reminded myself of Dougal Robertson's famous counsel from his manual describing how he and his family survived thirty-eight days lost at sea. Robertson wrote, "Rescue will come as a welcome interruption of the survival voyage."

Spiritual Support

The spiritual aspect of my struggle centered around a single word—*faith*. I wanted desperately to believe that my suffering had meaning and purpose, and that one day it would end. The irony was that I had authored a number of spiritual self-help books that provided readers with healing affirmations and spiritual encouragement in the face of fear, doubt, and despair. Over the past decade, I had received hundreds of letters and phone calls from people who testified that my words had helped them to overcome a variety of physical and emotional challenges. "Read your own books!" my friends would tell me. I did so from time to time, but whatever comfort I derived from the passages was drowned out by my pain, which gave evidence to the conviction that God had truly abandoned me.

Despite my absence of faith, I began to attend church again. My place of worship was the Living Enrichment Center (LEC), a large, nondenominational church located in Wilsonville, Oregon. It taught many principles of the Unity School of Practical Christianity, whose philosophy I had studied for twenty-five years. (The Unity School of Practical Christianity was founded by Charles and Myrtle Fillmore in 1889. It was formed to teach how the principles of the Old and New Testaments can be practically applied to helping people live fuller, more abundant, and joyful lives.) Like day treatment, attending LEC gave structure to my day and provided me with a community of like-minded people with whom I could hear messages of hope and inspiration that I had once believed.

To help bolster my waning faith, one of the ministers at LEC suggested that I take up an old hobby—gardening. On the day I planted my garden, I was so agitated that three people had to steady me while I sowed the seeds in the fertile soil. Nonetheless, the message I gave the universe was clear: "I expect to be alive in the fall to reap the harvest."

These, then, were the main components of my daily survival plan. Like a soldier on the battlefield, my primary job was to keep myself alive until the end of the day. Following is an example of how this strategy worked during a typically hellish twenty-four hours.

A Day in the Inferno

I have developed a new philosophy . . . I only dread one day at a time.
—CHARLIE BROWN

The phone rings once, twice, three times. I reach to pick it up. "Rise and shine!" sings the cheery voice. "It's your friend Christine with your daily wake-up call."

As I emerge from my oblivion, I quickly scan my body for signs of agitation. I feel my left leg starting to twitch, the first sign of an oncoming anxiety attack. I take a few deep breaths and attempt to relax, but it's like trying to maintain my ground in the face of a charging bull.

Depression Life-Raft Card

At Pat's suggestion, I wrote down some of my main survival strategies on a three-by-five card and carried it around in my pocket. Reading the card helped me to stay on task and keep me focused in the present, instead of catastrophizing about the future. Today, I still refer to the crumpled card when I feel myself losing my center.

I am surviving one day at a time.
I do this by practicing these self-care and self-nurturing strategies:

- I follow a routine.
- I go to day treatment.
- I do deep breathing.
- I say my affirmations.
- I eat three meals a day.
- I take my daily swim.
- I see my therapist and psychiatrist.
- I take walks around the block.
- I talk on the phone with my friends.
- I socialize as much as I can.
- I go for my weekly massage.
- I take my Klonopin.
- I pray for healing.
- I tell myself, "This, too, shall pass."

"I think I'm going to need some help. Could you drive me to day treatment?" I ask feebly.

"Sure," my friend replies. "I'll be right over."

As Christine hangs up, the agitation becomes so strong that I can no longer lie in bed. I hurriedly get up and begin to pace the floor. It is the start of another day in hell.

Knowing that Christine is on her way helps to calm me a little. Still, my body is shaking as I struggle to dress, so I take half a milligram of Klonopin with some orange juice. Soon, Christine arrives and drives me to the community pool, where she waits in the lobby while I take my morning swim. Because my anxiety is high, I thrash about in the lap lane, barely avoiding a collision with oncoming swimmers. After ten minutes of frenetic activity, I jump into the hot tub. The warm, relaxing waters add to the sedating effects of the Klonopin. I'm glad that Christine is driving.

I arrive at day treatment in time for the 10:30 A.M. goals group. I sit through the meeting in a daze. Sedation is better than agitation. Then in the 11:30 A.M. medication group, the Klonopin wears off, and I start to feel the initial sensations of an anxiety attack. In a few minutes my body becomes so agitated that I start rocking to and fro like an autistic child.

"Christ!" I think to myself. "I was starting to calm down, and now this has to happen. It's futile. I'll never get better." With each new catastrophic thought, I feel myself being dragged into the mire of hopelessness and despair.

Suddenly a voice in my head cries out, "CANCEL! CANCEL!" I realize what my mind is doing and switch gears to repeat my affirmations.

This attack will not last forever.
I've been here before and have survived.
I can get through this.
I have options. I can take a Klonopin, talk to a staff person, or
 walk around the block.

Fortunately, we are about to go to lunch, which is served at the hospital next door. Our group marches rank-and-file to the hospital lounge, where I engage in my daily ritual of doing the newspaper crossword puzzle to distract myself from my pain. At 12:30 P.M., the receptionist asks me to stop, and our group files into the lunchroom. Along the way, we pass the barbed-wire courtyard of the psychiatric ward where I once resided. I wave at the patients, some of whom I recognize, knowing that I could rejoin them at any time.

At lunch, the hospital food is atrocious, but the fellowship is healing. I enjoy the one-on-one interactions with a counselor and a fellow patient. At a quarter past the hour, we are asked to leave the lunchroom. The next group starts at 1:30 P.M., but with a new anxiety attack coming on, fifteen minutes seems like an eternity. How will I contain myself without losing control? I grab a patient, saying, "I can't be alone right now. Please walk with me." And he agrees.

After I ingest a second Klonopin, the afternoon sessions go a bit smoother, and at 3:30 P.M. Christine picks me up and drives me to my weekly massage. My massage therapist lives and works in a houseboat on the shores of the Willamette River. During the session, I am soothed by the gently lapping waves and the singing of the birds. For the next forty-five minutes, I experience a respite from the pain.

All too soon I am awakened from my reverie by the sound of Raeanne's voice telling me it is time to leave. "No!" I protest. "I want to lie here forever." Moments later, a gentle nudge tells me that I must make room for the next client. I quickly dress and walk along the moorage back to the shore. The colors of the sky are a thousand shades of indigo blue, and the clouds look like elephants; I feel as if I am on a drug—which I am. I don't like the side effects of these antidepressants.

Christine drives me home. After thanking her, I go inside to check my schedule. At 6:00 P.M., I will take my evening lap swim and then have dinner with my friend Ann. What will I do for the next hour? Unstructured time is the enemy; I can't be alone with the anxiety right now. I call the Metro Crisis Line and explain my predicament. Talking to someone gives me a focus and decreases my agitation. Human contact is my salvation.

By 6:00 P.M., I am calm enough to drive myself to the community center's swimming pool. As I begin my second lap swim of the day, I feel the Klonopin wearing off. To cope with the anxiety, I synchronize the rhythm of my strokes and my breathing to a 4-4 beat, using my affirmation to fend off despairing thoughts:

"I am peace-ful, I am peace-ful, I am calm."
1 2 3 4,   1 2 3 4,   1 2 3 4.
"I am peace-ful, I am peace-ful, I am calm."
1 2 3 4,   1 2 3 4,   1 2 3 4.

It takes two repetitions of my affirmation to swim one length of the pool; four repetitions equals one lap. As the laps unfold, my nervous system unwinds. My brain releases a few endorphins. I am swimming not for my health, but for my life.

After my swim, I eat dinner with my friend Ann and watch an intriguing episode of *Mystery!* on PBS. Like many people who suffer from depression, I am most anxious and depressed in the morning and feel calmer as the day progresses. On this particular evening, the black cloud lifts and I actually feel normal again. Later, as I drift off to sleep, I pray that my newfound peace will carry over into the morning. "Maybe this is the turning point," I think. "Maybe tomorrow will bring my salvation."

But like Bill Murray's character in the movie *Groundhog Day,* I awake at dawn to find myself in the all-too-familiar anxious and depressed state. It's time to tread fire all over again.

As I have shared in this account, my battle to survive was waged not just day by day, but hour to hour and minute to minute. Like a volatile stock market, my psyche was subject to unpredictable episodes of anxiety and depression that rained down upon me like showers blowing in from the Oregon coast. As each downpour subsided, I was granted momentary relief—until the next front came in. Because I never knew when an anxiety attack would strike, I had to be ready at a moment's notice to readjust my plans (quite a lesson in learning to be flexible!).

Living this way was quite draining. I felt as if I were at the mercy of a strong undertow dragging me out to sea. I would struggle with all my might to swim a few strokes toward shore, only to be pulled back toward the ocean by the overpowering current. By the end of the day, I was run down and exhausted, which at least helped me fall asleep. But as the constant battle against the unrelenting black tide began to wear me down, I wondered whether the struggle was really worth it. Soon, my rhyming voices had composed a new verse: "Madness or suicide, it's yours to decide."

CHAPTER FOUR

Madness or Suicide, It's Yours to Decide

The pain of depression is quite unimaginable to those who have not suffered it, and it kills in many instances because its anguish can no longer be borne. The prevention of many suicides will continue to be hindered until there is a general awareness of the nature of this pain.

—WILLIAM STYRON

I am the wound and the knife! The victim and the executioner.

—CHARLES-PIERRE BAUDELAIRE

Philosopher Albert Camus once wrote that the only real philosophical question to ask is whether or not to kill yourself. To a person suffering from depression, however, the question of suicide is not academic. The pain of depression is intense, seemingly ever present, and it feels like it will never end. Being clinically depressed can be compared to having an ongoing nightmare where the only way to end the dream is to annihilate the dreamer. According to the National Institute of Mental Health, 15 percent of those diagnosed with a major depressive disorder who are not treated (or who fail to respond to treatment) will end their lives by suicide (this is thirty-five times the normal rate). Suicide in America kills more people (about

32,000 a year) than homicide. Comparing this figure to 43,000 breast cancer deaths per year and 42,000 driving fatalities, it's clear that suicide is a major undiagnosed health problem in this country. Moreover, for every one person who commits suicide, sixteen attempt it, which translates to five hundred thousand attempts per year, or one every minute. People with serious illnesses such as cancer and heart disease do not kill themselves in large numbers; depressed people do.

Many theories attempt to explain the motivation for suicide. Freud postulated a death instinct. Others have suggested that man is endowed with "a drive to destruction." But to anyone who has experienced suicidal pain, the explanation is so simple, that it requires neither psychiatric nor psychological jargon. Death is chosen because suffering is so agonizing, that there comes a time—depending on the individual's tolerance for pain and the available support—that *ceasing to suffer* becomes the most important thing. The DSM-IV supports this "aggregate pain model" of suicide in its section on major depression:

> The most serious consequence of a major depressive disorder is attempted or completed suicide. Motivations for suicide may include a desire to give up in the face of *perceived insurmountable obstacles* or an intense wish to end an *excruciatingly painful emotional state* that is perceived by the person *to be without end*. [Emphasis added.]

During my dark night, I met a woman who was battling cancer. She wrote a poem about her struggle and her hope for recovery called "The Crawl through Hell."

> So I crawl. Slowly I crawl. I inch my way through hell.
> Count the days. Each one is one less to endure.
> Each day I am closer to the end.
> Back to the world. Back to life.
> Life is the light at the end. The tunnel will end.
> It is long but it has an end.*

---

* Used with permission. Excerpted from "The Crawl through Hell," in the *The Buttercup Has My Smile*, by Lynne Massie.

The wailing woman in Pablo Picasso's "Guernica"

To the depressed person, however, there is no light at the end of the tunnel. One does not crawl, because there is no *place* to crawl to. Both ends of the tunnel are sealed off, and a sign on the door reads No Exit. (Other images of hopelessness include: being trapped in a *dense black fog;* falling into a *bottomless abyss;* being locked in a *cold, dark dungeon;* sitting helplessly on a *melting ice floe.*)

People in life-or-death survival conditions, such as being lost in the wilderness or being held prisoner of war, will dream and plan for the future in order to make their present conditions tolerable. The critically ill heart patient expresses his faith in his upcoming surgery by making a date to play golf six weeks after the operation. The imprisoned soldier dreams of being reunited with his wife and family. But the depressed person sees no viable future. There is nothing to look forward to, no dreams to fulfill, only the never-ending agony of the eternal present. In this context, I saw suicide not as an act of self-destruction, but as an act of self-love.

To Be or Not To Be

To remain as I am is impossible.
I must either die or be better, it appears to me.
—ABRAHAM LINCOLN

I first began to experience suicidal feelings (the clinical term is "suicidal ideation") in November 1996, shortly after I began the day treatment program. As my pain intensified and I became overwhelmed with the thought of eternal suffering, I remembered Nietzsche's words: "The thought of suicide is a great consolation: by means of it one gets successfully through many a bad night." Realizing that I could always end my life when the agony became intolerable granted me a sense of peace and relief.

This was by no means the first time I had contemplated suicide. During my two previous depressive episodes, I had made two half-serious attempts—the first time swallowing some tranquilizers with a bottle of beer, and the other, taking a handful of Valium before driving on the Long Island Expressway. (It remains one of the unexplained miracles in my life that I returned home safely.) Moreover, I had been close to at least a half dozen people who had committed suicide, the most recent of whom was the psychotherapist I had seen before Pat. In a sense, the suicidal demon had pursued me my whole life. Like the legendary St. George, I was locked in mortal combat with a deadly dragon—and he was winning.

I knew I was serious about killing myself when I drew up a will, named my brother the executor, and sent copies to him and a good friend. I wanted to put my financial house in order before I died.

Putting one's house in order is one of the classic signs of someone who is serious about committing suicide. There are other signs as well; for example, people who talk about suicide are more likely to act on it. If someone you know is exhibiting these danger signals do not ignore them! Get the person to a hospital or someplace safe.

Having taken care of my remaining fiscal responsibilities, I spent countless hours deliberating on the most efficient way to terminate my existence. My first choice was to use a gun because it seemed so quick and final. Then I remembered a crisis counselor telling me about a man who suffered irreparable brain damage when he shot himself in the head. "I wouldn't try it," the counselor warned. "You might end up a vegetable."

My next plan was to jump off a building, but after picturing myself walking to the ledge and looking down, I remembered that I was afraid of heights. Also, a friend at day treatment had asked me an unsettling question—"What if, halfway to the ground, you change your mind?"

I later learned that taking pills is not always lethal and, like a gunshot wound, can cause permanent brain damage. Even jumping off a bridge doesn't guarantee death, as I learned from a man who broke his back trying. "Remember Murphy's Law," the suicide counselor had emphasized. "It's not so easy to kill yourself."

Finally, I resolved to take an overdose of the antidepressants and tranquilizers that I had saved up over the past few months. This also frightened me, since I didn't really want to die, and was concerned about the people I would leave behind. I knew that if I killed myself, my friends and family would not only be grief stricken, but would feel angry and guilty as well. "Why should I drag all of these people into my nightmare?" I thought.

My concerns about the impact of my death on others were shared by a fellow patient at day treatment.

"Don't do it!" Dennis cried emphatically, when I told him of my plans.

"Why not?"

"My brother offed himself twenty-five years ago, and I still haven't forgiven the bastard. Don't make your friends and relatives go through what I did."

"All right," I replied. "I'll try to be more considerate."

Later that day, I reported this conversation to Pat.

"It seems like your friend has developed an ethical injunction against suicide. Do you have any similar moral beliefs?"

"No," I replied. "I don't believe it is a sin to commit suicide. I can't see why a loving and merciful God would punish someone for wanting to end his suffering."

"I'm sorry to hear you say that," Pat responded solemnly.
"Why?"

"Studies have shown that people who lack a moral or religious belief that suicide is wrong are more likely to act on the impulse."

Pat's analysis was true. Without a clear moral reason not to kill myself, my resolve to avoid suicide was only as good as the kind of day I was having. When graced with five or six hours without symptoms, I would think, "Maybe I'm in remission," and hope for the best. Too often, however, the respite would give way to a downturn in mood that brought with it the voices of doom, i.e., "Suicidal ideation is a hit across the nation" and "Madness or suicide, it's yours to decide." My choices seemed clear—either spend the rest of my life in hell (I believed I would live out my days in a state mental hospital) or put an end to the pain. Both outcomes were unacceptable, but I could not imagine a third alternative. In my anguish I cried out, "God! Show me another way, or at least give me some hope that another way is possible."

Meetings with Angels

For we are saved by hope: but a hope that is seen is not hope
for why would a man hope for that which he sees? But if we hope
for what we see not, then *do we with patience wait for* it.
—ROM. 8:24–25

When the Apostle Paul wrote "We are saved by hope," he was not speaking in platitudes. Research has shown that the risk of depression is correlated more with hopelessness than with the intensity of the depression. It seems that we can endure all sorts of pain and suffering if we are even remotely optimistic that things will get better or that there is a meaning to our suffering. Conversely, people with lesser degrees of depressive pain can become suicidal if they lose hope for a better future. Hopelessness, not sadness, is the antecedent to suicide.

If a way out of hopelessness did exist, I knew that I could not find it alone. Since my mind was trapped inside an "either-or" thought loop (as depicted by the rhyme "Madness or suicide, it's yours to decide"), it would take another person to lead me out of my mental prison.

The first person I turned to for help was the Reverend Mary Manin Morrissey, the spiritual director at the Living Enrichment Center. Having known me from the early days of LEC, Mary took a special interest in my case.

"When you start to think that all is hopeless and that there is no solution except suicide," she said, "remind yourself that you are under the influence of a 'drug' called depression. This chemical imbalance is distorting your view of reality. Thus, you should not consider your feelings of hopelessness as a reflection of the truth of your situation."

"How do I prevent myself from giving in to the despair?" I asked.

"Try to think of your depression as a bridge instead of as an abyss, a transition period instead of an end point. There is a universal law of polarity that says all states of consciousness eventually *turn into their opposites*—i.e., pleasure becomes pain and pain becomes pleasure. Likewise, your suffering will one day turn into joy."

"That's impossible," I replied. "To me, depression is a bottomless black hole from which there is no escape."

"Then you will need to have the soul strength or spiritual endurance to stay in the pain until it repatterns and transmutes," Mary replied. "There is a higher power that is more powerful than any condition, including this depression. Maybe you had this breakdown so you would be forced to turn to God above anything else."

"Do you have any ideas on how to do that?"

"I know that you are a student of the Old and New Testaments," Mary replied. "Throughout the Bible, especially in the Book of Psalms, we hear about God's promises of deliverance. I suggest you read through the psalms and write down the verses that give you comfort or hope. You might even want to post them in your home where you will be sure to see them on a regular basis."

I was glad that Mary had faith in my recovery. In the days that followed, I took her suggestion to heart. I located a number of psalms, as well as inspirational quotations from my book *I Am With You Always,* and placed them in strategic locations in my office, bedroom, and bathroom. (The quotations I used can be found on pages 272 to 273.) Looking for additional words of spiritual encouragement, I visited my local bookstore and spoke to the store owner, Lisa, about my ordeal. After listening intently, she walked over to the new arrivals' table and pointed to a beautifully decorated book called the *Celtic Tree Oracle.* Lisa explained that the text describes the symbolism of the twenty-five letters of the Celtic alphabet. Each letter was associated with a tree or bush and was linked to a specific aspect of Celtic philosophy and cosmology. (The Celts were an ancient tribal culture that inhabited the British Isles before the time of Christ. The Druids, the wise elders of the Celts, had a very special relationship with the natural world and considered trees to be particularly sacred.)

I have always felt an affinity to the tree kingdom, which I have nurtured through a quarter century of hiking in the forests of the Pacific Northwest. "Perhaps," I thought, "these trees could speak to me now." During the Middle Ages, it was customary for monks to open up the Bible at random, point to a passage, and receive guidance from it. "Why not do the same with this book?" I thought.

With a prayer on my lips, I opened the volume and found myself staring at a page with the Celtic letter "Eadha," which translates as "white poplar." The interpretation reads as follows:

> This tree is concerned with finding the *spiritual strength* and *endurance* to face the harsh realities that life presents to us, often over a *long, debilitating period* of time. It conveys a sense of the ability to *endure* and *conquer.* In this way it *prevents death* and the urge to give way under the *impossible odds you must overcome.* It is, therefore, of great assistance on the journey towards *rebirth.* [Emphasis added.]

I was deeply moved by how clearly the reading depicted my predicament, as well by as the hope that it offered.

"This is an auspicious event," Lisa remarked after I showed her the passage. "It indicates that you want to live, and that spirit will help you to survive your ordeal." Lisa then photocopied the image

The White Poplar

of the poplar (as well as its interpretation) so I could carry it around as a symbol of protection. In future weeks and months, I looked at the picture and read the words of encouragement whenever I felt myself slipping.

Next, I visited a spiritual counseling service sponsored by a New Thought church in the Portland area. As I approached the space where the lay ministers were seated, I wondered how they would respond to my situation. If I have one criticism of New Thought spirituality or its psychological counterpart—the power of positive thinking—it is that it focuses exclusively on the good and neglects the dark side of life. And so it came as no surprise when the volunteer approached me with a cheery smile and said, "What shall we affirm today? Prosperity? Health? Happiness? Creative self-expression?"

"Actually, I was thinking of committing suicide," I replied.

With a combination of concern and amusement, I watched the volunteer's face turn white. "I think I should get my supervisor," she said as she hurried out the door.

When the supervisor arrived, I assured her that this was no joke, that I really was depressed and needed help. Understanding the seriousness of my predicament, she sat down with the volunteer and recited two positive prayers that affirmed my capacity for healing and wholeness.

I find no fault with the church practitioner for being overwhelmed. Many friends, and even some psychotherapists, could not handle the intensity of my suicidal pain. Whenever I tried to share my suicidal thoughts, they would either get angry or abruptly change the subject. Only those people who were specifically trained to treat major depression, or who had "been there and back," could deal with my extreme condition.

One such person was a social worker named Judy. Having attempted suicide herself, she knew firsthand what goes on in the mind of a suicidal individual. Judy saw her clients, many of whom were in severe crisis, out of her small Victorian home, nestled in the Columbia River Gorge, twenty-five miles east of Portland. At our first meeting, she got right to the heart of the matter.

"Suicide is not chosen," Judy said emphatically. *"It comes when emotional pain exceeds the resources for coping with the pain."*

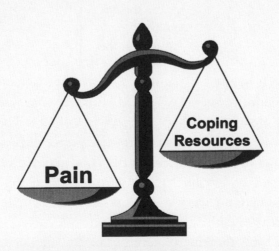

While speaking, Judy showed me a picture of scales to illustrate her point.

"You are not a bad or weak person," she continued. "Neither do you want to die; you just want to end your suffering."

I nodded in agreement.

"Your problem is that the scales are weighed down on the side of your pain. To get the scales back in balance, you can do one of two things: discover a way to reduce your pain, or find a way to increase your coping resources."

I explained that the former option seemed impossible.

"Then let me give you a coping resource that I'm sure you will find lifesaving," Judy said, as she handed me a pamphlet titled "How to Cope with Suicidal Thoughts and Feelings." I read it briefly and felt a mild sense of hope. (The information from this sheet, as well as other strategies for preventing suicide, can be found in chapter 11.)

"One more thing," Judy added. "I know you think that killing yourself will end your pain. But according to what I've read, consciousness continues even after death. Some people even believe that we reincarnate and return to earth in order to work out issues that we didn't resolve in this life. Perhaps there is no easy escape."

"What other option are you suggesting?"

"Stick around until you get better."

"Beating Michael Jordan in a one-on-one basketball game would be more likely."

"Crises, including suicidal ones, are time-limited," Judy countered. "Eventually, something's got to give. Provided you don't kill yourself, you will be around to experience the next chapter of your life."

"That's easy for you to say, but you're not in this hell. My intuition is telling me that I'm stuck here forever."

"Cognitively, you cannot help but think 'I am permanently frozen in horrible pain.' This is what depression is—a failure of the imagination. The chemical imbalance in your brain is preventing you from envisioning a positive future. Nevertheless, I want you to at least make room for the *possibility* that some unexpected good might grace your life."

Sensing that I was stuck in unbelief, Judy leaned back in her chair and recounted the following parable.

According to an ancient tale, a Sufi village was attacked and captured by a group of warriors. The king of the victorious tribe told the vanquished that unless they fulfilled his wish, the entire village would be put to death the following morning. The king's wish was to know the secret of what would make him happy when he was sad, and sad when he was happy.

The village people constructed a large bonfire, and all night long their wise men and women strove to answer the riddle: What could make a person happy when he is sad, and sad when he is happy? Finally, sunrise dawned and the king entered the village. Approaching the wise ones, he asked, "Have you ful-filled my request?" "Yes!" they replied. The king was delighted. "Well, show me your gift." One of the men reached into a pouch and presented the king with a gold ring. The king was perplexed. "I have no need of more gold," he exclaimed. "How can this ring make me happy when I am sad, and sad when I am happy?" The king looked again, and this time he noticed that the ring bore an inscription. It read, *This, Too, Shall Pass.*

"It is an immutable law of the cosmos," Judy continued, "that the only constant in the universe is change. Haven't things happened to you that you never would have predicted?"

I nodded my head as I recalled the many experiences, both good and bad, that life had unexpectedly brought me.

"Since you cannot know your future with absolute certainty, then, allow for the possibility that a healing may be waiting for you around the corner. Pat tells me that you have already created a sur-vival plan for yourself."

"I use it to get through each day."

"Good. Then stick with your strategy. Instead of fretting about the future, simply create the support that you need to stay alive, one day at a time. Please repeat this statement: "I am creating the sup-port that I need to stay alive, one day at a time.""

"*I am creating the support that I need to stay alive, one day at a time,*" I said meekly.

"Good! Now I want you to repeat this affirmation every day. It doesn't matter whether you believe it; keep saying it anyway. I know that you are going to live."

Judy's heartfelt sincerity and intensity left a deep impression on me. Although I felt hopeless, she seemed so confident. "Maybe she's right," I mused.

In addition to her counsel, Judy gave me her phone number as well as the number of the American Suicide Survival Line (888-SUICIDE) and said that I must call *anytime* I was in danger of harming myself. She also gave me a number of Internet sites on suicide prevention that proved to be amazingly helpful (see Appendix C).

Lisa, Mary, and Judy were three guardian angels who came to me in my darkest hour. They presented a vision of healing to me that I could not see for myself. Although their faith in my restoration did not remove my physical and psychological pain, it did give me a reason to hang on. And as long as I stayed alive, a miracle was possible.

Prayer for Going through a Dark Night of the Soul

This is a combination prayer and affirmation that I composed and read during my depressive episode. I hope that it may be a support to you as well.

- I accept the fact that I am going through a dark night of the soul. I am dying to the me that I have known.
- I embrace my pain fully and accept my present condition. I understand that on some level my soul needs this experience.
- Although I feel all alone, I know that God is with me.
- I realize that this experience has a purpose and teaching, and I ask spirit to reveal it to me.
- Although I am in pain, I know that my travail will end, and that love, inspiration, and direction will reenter my life.
- I ask the universe to give me the strength, courage, and guidance to see my way to my rebirth.
- I give thanks for my situation just the way it is.

CHAPTER FIVE

Bearing the Unbearable Pain

The mind is its own place, and in itself
Can make a heav'n of hell, a hell of heav'n

—JOHN MILTON

In the weeks following my conversation with Judy, the image of scales as a metaphor for suicide haunted and obsessed me. To put the scales (and my life) back in balance, I realized that I must increase my coping resources or find a way to reduce the pain.

"Reduce the pain?" I thought incredulously. "How can I find relief from agony this extreme?" I recalled what William Styron had told his daughter on the eve of his hospitalization: "I would rather have a limb amputated without anesthesia than to be suffering the kind of pain I am feeling at the moment."

It was at this point that an old college friend of mine serendipitously reentered my life. Teresa Keane was a registered nurse who worked at the Oregon Health Sciences University Medical School, where she taught stress reduction to patients with chronic pain. Her classes were based on the groundbreaking work of Jon Kabat Zinn, a meditation teacher featured in Bill Moyers's 1996 PBS documentary, "Healing and the Mind." Kabat Zinn teaches the Buddhist practice of "mindfulness meditation" to patients suffering from intractable physical pain. Through employing his techniques, they learn to alleviate not only their physical discomfort, but their accompanying emotional distress as well.

I met with Teresa in her office at OHSU, where I described the nature of my torment.

"Facing pain is a learned skill," Teresa responded. "When you are in a lot of pain, whether it is a migraine headache or suicidal torment, the pain dominates all of your awareness and becomes all encompassing. It's hard to remember a time when the distress was absent, and it's hard to believe that it will ever go away. It's as if both past and future are blotted out, and you are left stranded in your present misery."

"At least you understand," I remarked.

"However," Teresa continued, "if you can release your judgment of your pain and just observe it, you will notice a very important fact about the nature of pain—pain comes *in waves!"*

Upon hearing these words, I remembered the grief I felt after my divorce. There were times when I was so overwhelmed by sorrow and loss that I could barely function. After a period, however, the pain and the longing let up, perhaps for a day or two—until the heartache returned and began the cycle all over again—pain turning into relief, which turned into more pain, followed by more relief, and so on.

"This is the body and mind's built-in protective mechanism," Teresa explained. "If the pain were truly nonstop, you wouldn't survive. And so you are granted a few gaps in between the intense sensations to stop and catch your breath."

"But it feels like the pain is unrelenting," I protested. "If you were clinically depressed, you would understand."

"The key to reducing your perception of pain," Teresa continued dispassionately, "is to uncouple the sensations in your body *from the thoughts about them."*

"What does that mean?"

"You are feeling two levels of pain," she explained. "The first level is physiological—the raw pain in your body. The second level (and this is where you have some control) consists of how you interpret your experience. Perhaps you are thinking, 'This torment is killing me,' or 'This will last forever,' or 'There is nothing I can do about it.' Each of these despairing thoughts creates a *neurochemical reaction* in the brain that creates even more distress. If you can learn to detach yourself from these judgments, much of the pain that arises from them will diminish."

Detail from Michelangelo's "The Last
Judgment" in the Sistine Chapel

"How do I do this?"

"Think of your anxiety or depression as a large wave that is
approaching you. As the wave makes contact, see if you can ride the
wave by focusing on *your breath*. Breathe *through* the sensations,
breathing in and out while attending to the sound of your breathing.
Don't try to analyze what is happening, just breathe. It's not even
about getting through the day; it's about getting through each breath."

When I had worked as a salesperson in the corporate world, I
learned the skill of breaking large goals into manageable parts. Now
I discovered that one could divide pain into manageable parts. If I
couldn't handle getting through the day, I would try to make it
through the next hour; if an hour seemed too long, I set my sights
on the next minute or second.

Teresa showed me another powerful technique to use with my
self-talk when my pain became intense. Whenever I cried, "My pain
is unbearable!" Teresa would reply, "Tell yourself the pain is *barely*
bearable."

"The pain is barely bearable," I repeated aloud. There was a
shift and I felt it.

In another session I screamed, "I can't take it anymore!"

"You can *barely* take it," Teresa responded.

"I can barely take it," I replied.

Mental Illness As a Spiritual Practice

Emotions are like waves;
Watch them come and go in the vast ocean of existence.
—NEEM KAROLI BABA

Teresa was teaching me the practice of mindfulness, a spiritual practice of living in the present moment. In traditional meditation, when the mind wanders, one gently brings it back to a central focus (the breath, a candle, and so on). I was challenged to do the same, especially when, in response to intense emotional pain, I projected my present condition into the future using catastrophic self-talk that led to suicidal thinking; "If I have to put up with this suffering for the next thirty years, I might as well end my life now."

"Just return to the here and now," Teresa would say. "Over a period of time you can learn to relate differently to your pain. You can work with the pain and live around the corners of pain and develop your life around it. Eventually the turbulent emotional waters will become calm again. In the meantime, you can find inner stillness and peace right within the most difficult life situations."

"You've got to be kidding," I responded somewhat angrily. "How do you expect me to stay centered when the emotional equivalent of a migraine headache is pounding my skull?"

"Stop fighting the pain and see it as your life," Teresa calmly replied. "It doesn't mean you should *like* your discomfort. But there is something transformative that happens when we simply *allow* ourselves to experience our pain without trying to judge, change, or resist it in any way. Let me show you."

At that moment, Teresa reached over and pressed a tender point between my right thumb and index finger (I later learned that it was a particularly sensitive acupuncture point).

"Ouch! That hurts," I protested.

"Breathe into the place in your body where you feel the pain," Teresa responded compassionately. "See if you can ride the waves of sensation as you would ride the ocean's waves. As you do this, notice how the experience of your pain begins to change."

Back to the Present

One of the most challenging aspects of practicing mindfulness was having to deal with my catastrophic thoughts and feelings about the future. These would inevitably arise when I suffered an unexpected anxiety attack or was engulfed by particularly bad depression. Self-statements such as "I can't go on like this" or "I won't live the rest of my life in this pain" further escalated my despair and hopelessness and drew me closer to the prospect of suicide.

As a way to keep me safe, Teresa and I devised a simple but powerful three-step technique for responding to catastrophic and despairing self-talk. I have rewritten these steps in a prescriptive fashion so others can use them.

1. Notice what is happening. Become aware that your mind is dwelling on thoughts of catastrophe and doom. Identify the catastrophic thought, e.g., "I'll never get better."
2. Realize that these thoughts are not about the present but about the future. Since the future has yet to occur, it cannot harm you.
3. Refocus onto the present moment through positive self-talk and constructive action. For example, you might replace the statement "I'll never get better" with "What self-care strategy (such as calling a friend, going for a swim, or taking an antianxiety medication) can I choose *right now* to get me through this period?" Then put the strategy into action.

I cannot recall how many times this simple process allowed me to endure a day, an hour, or a minute of intense pain. In giving me a way to manage my catastrophic (and potentially dangerous) thinking, this technique literally saved my life.

I breathed into the soreness and observed that the pain in my hand softened and decreased until I could hardly feel it.

"Good work," Teresa replied. "Now see if you can do the same with your emotional pain."

On days when my depression and anxiety fell below a 5 on my mood scale, Teresa's technique worked well. As I breathed into the pain of depression and stopped resisting it, the pain diminished. But during those all-too-frequent instances when the agony registered close to 10, I simply could not surrender. "Get the hell out of here!" I screamed at the hurt, and then felt guilty because I was not able to detach and let go.

"This is not about right and wrong," Teresa responded. "It's about *struggle* and *practice*. It's about learning to cope—discovering which options work for you and which ones don't."

(Teresa also told me that those who have experienced childhood violence or sexual abuse may find that relaxation techniques such as deep breathing elicit feelings of anxiety. If this occurs, consider practicing meditation or relaxation under the supervision of a trained therapist who can help you process these feelings.)

Mindfulness meditation did not work all of the time, but it worked enough. The moments of peace it provided, when combined with intense exercise and small doses of the antianxiety drug Klonopin, interrupted the pain cycle sufficiently so as to make my suffering barely bearable.

CHAPTER SIX

Overcoming the Stigma of Depression

The last great stigma of the twentieth century is the stigma of mental illness.

—TIPPER GORE

In the school of life, the best students get the hardest problems.

—ANONYMOUS

Up until this point, I have been describing the pain of depression as I experienced it on a physiological and emotional level. There existed a second level of distress that, though less primal, was nonetheless debilitating in its own way. This was the *guilt* and *shame* I felt about being depressed.

Despite the fact that such celebrities as Mike Wallace, William Styron, Patty Duke, Tipper Gore, and Ted Turner have publicly shared their battles with depression or manic depression, the stigma of mental illness remains. After my first hospitalization, I remember the dilemma I faced in trying to explain my three-day absence to my employer. If I told the truth—that I was being treated for anxiety and depression—I stood a good chance of losing my job. Instead, I reported that I had been treated for insomnia at a sleep clinic. *Sixty Minutes* reporter Mike Wallace faced a similar predicament during his first episode of clinical

71

depression. "Because I wanted to keep working," he explained, "I chose to keep my illness a secret."

"Clinical depression is a medical condition, similar to diabetes or heart disease," my psychiatrist responded when I confessed how I had concealed my hospitalization. "We need to stop making depression a moral issue. Is the person with a disorder of the pancreas or the circulatory system weak-willed, lazy, or defective? Of course not. And neither is the individual who suffers from depression."

Unfortunately, a recent survey taken by the National Mental Health Association revealed that 43 percent of Americans still believe that depression is the result of a weak will or a deficit in one's character. Many doctors also subscribe to the "defect in character" theory. Consider the observations of physician A. John Rush:

> Doctors are still reluctant to make the diagnosis [of depression] because they, too, feel like, "Oh you must have done something wrong. How did you get yourself into this pickle?" which sort of means the patient is to blame. It's okay if you have a neurological disease—Parkinson's, Huntington's, urinary incontinence, a busted spine because you got into an auto accident—but once you move up to the higher cortical areas, now you don't have a disease anymore; now you have "trouble coping"; now you have a "bad attitude."*

I have often wondered why it is so scary to be open about our frailties. With the revelation that depression and other forms of mental illness have a biological component, people should no longer feel that their symptoms are caused by personal inadequacies or a lack of willpower. On the contrary, only a *strong* and *courageous* person could bear and ultimately transform so much pain.

I believe that the stigma surrounding mental illness arises from living in a culture where feelings of vulnerability are considered weak and unacceptable. This is especially true for men who are raised with

---

* As quoted in the chapter "Overcoming the Stigma and the Shame," from the book *On the Edge of Darkness: Conversations About Conquering Depression,* by Kathy Cronkite (New York: Doubleday, 1994), 79.

the injunction that "big boys don't cry," that it is not okay for men to be vulnerable and show their feelings.

The price that men pay for being stoic, stuffing their feelings, and holding the pain in, is depression. Family therapist Terrence Real says that when men are not in touch with their painful emotions, they may act them out through alcoholism, domestic violence, and other antisocial behavior. An example of this is the recent spate of mass shootings—all done by depressed men or boys.

This fear of being seen (by themselves and others) as vulnerable and weak, leads many men to lose touch with their own feelings and to avoid being in situations where strong emotion may be present. For example, the observant reader will note that thus far my entire support system has consisted of women. A good male friend who avoided me during my illness later confided, "When you were depressed, I was afraid to be around you for fear that I might 'catch' your depression." What he meant was that being in my presence might cause him to tap into his own *latent* depression, a proposition that was so uncomfortable, he had to split.

Women also suffer from this bias against feeling. If a woman works in a male-dominated field such as construction, policing, or law, she is forced into the same mold as men. Women attorneys or construction workers who cry are criticized or passed over for promotions, just as men in these professions would be. A woman working in a nontraditional field who feels and expresses her emotions is labeled as unstable, unreliable, and weak. One woman police sergeant tells a story of being sent by the men on the force into a domestic violence situation on her first day at work to see whether she was "tough enough to be one of the guys." It was made absolutely clear that she should show no fear or sadness about the attack the batterer had made upon his wife and children.

Politics is another field, traditionally the province of men (now being entered by women), where vulnerability is unacceptable. In 1972, presidential candidate Edmund Muskie was considered unfit to hold office after he allegedly cried in public. Similarly, Thomas Eagleton, the Democratic vice presidential candidate in the 1972 election, was forced to exit the race when it became known that he had received ECT to

Abraham Lincoln is one of many
famous people who have suffered
from depression.

treat his depression. I find it incredible that this bias still exists, given
the fact that many great political leaders—Abraham Lincoln, Teddy
Roosevelt, Eleanor Roosevelt, Joan of Arc, and Winston Churchill (who
called his malady "the black dog")—suffered from depression.

Abraham Lincoln is a particularly intriguing example of someone who achieved greatness in spite of the fact that he experienced
bleak, despairing periods of depression throughout his life—no doubt
brought on by the early death of his mother and cold treatment at the
hands of his father. A typical depressive episode is described by Karl
Menninger in his book *The Vital Balance:*

> On his wedding day, all preparations were in order and the
> guests assembled, but Lincoln didn't appear. He was found in
> his room in deep dejection, obsessed with ideas of unworthi-
> ness, hopelessness, and guilt. Prior to his illness Lincoln was an
> honest but undistinguished lawyer whose failures were more
> conspicuous than his successes. This was when he was consid-
> ered well—before his mental illness made its appearance. What
> he became and achieved after his illness is part of our great
> national heritage.*

---

* K. Menninger, M. Mayman, and P. Pruyser, *The Vital Balance: The Life Process in
Mental Health and Illness* (New York: Viking Press, 1967).

In today's political climate, where image, style, and sound bites are more important than substance, one wonders whether someone like Lincoln, or other introverted American presidents such as Thomas Jefferson, could be elected. (Even spiritual people get depressed. The Biblical figures of Moses, Saul, David, Elijah, Jeremiah, Jonah, Paul, and Jesus [in his human form] experienced depression. David's laments are evidenced throughout the Book of Psalms.) Clearly, it is time to reassess our evaluation of what makes a leader.

The Challenge of Being a Nobody

For many people, the stigma of being depressed is compounded by shame and guilt about not being a "productive member of society." The depressed person may become a "nobody" when his disability makes him unable to work or to earn a living. How, then, does an individual measure his self-worth when he or she is not working or producing?

This is the question I asked myself as I struggled to come to terms with not living up to the expectations of my cultural programming. I was the firstborn son, raised in an upwardly mobile, middle-class Jewish community, where competition for entrance into Ivy League schools began in the third grade. Unlike my Catholic friends, who attended a nearby parochial school and were taught to avoid the seven deadly sins, I learned that there was only one deadly sin—not living up to one's potential. This potential was very specifically defined—unless you became a doctor, a lawyer, or ran your father's business, you were considered a failure. There were, of course, exceptions. One could always teach at Harvard, make a fortune on Wall Street, or win the Nobel Prize. As long as the gods of Status and Recognition were served, our parents and teachers would be happy.

Such pressure to produce necessarily takes its toll. I distinctly recall my sadness when, in the middle of my junior year in high school, a good friend of mine suddenly stopped coming to class. Rumor had it that he had suffered a nervous breakdown and was whisked away to a special school in Connecticut. Understanding that other promising minds had likewise succumbed to mental illness was my only consolation as I filed for Social Security disability benefits at the age of forty-eight, while many of my classmates lived in half-million-dollar homes and earned six-figure incomes.

Lacking money, power, and prestige (the standards by which I was raised to judge myself), my sense of failure and inadequacy continued to plague me. One day, I was invited to a potluck dinner, where I met an attractive woman who had just been hired as a professor at the prestigious Reed College, after having obtained her Ph.D. from Harvard. After describing her exploits in great detail, she asked the dreaded question—"And what do you do for a living?"

I paused for a moment to contemplate my response. Recalling my father's injunction to always tell the truth, I responded, "I attend day treatment and collect disability income."

The woman looked at me with a mixture of bemusement and pity before making a discrete exit. I felt as if someone had placed a nametag on my shirt—the kind you get when you attend a singles group or a self-help seminar—that read "Worthless."

This interaction (or lack of it) hammered home the question, "What happens to a person's self-esteem when a lifelong emotional disability such as clinical depression interferes with his ability to be productive in societal terms?" Like the former athlete who is confined to a wheelchair after a paralyzing accident, I had to accept my limitations and find a new way to define my existence. I knew from my spiritual studies that a human being's essential worth and goodness come from who he is, not what he does. I understood that friends and family were working overtime to keep me alive, not because of my degrees or my bank account, but because they loved me. Moreover, being down in the dumps had its advantages. Like the fallen hero in Bob Dylan's "Like a Rolling Stone," being stripped of my privilege dissolved my arrogance and made me a more humble and compassionate human being.

Still, given my programming, it was an ongoing struggle to validate myself in the absence of external markers. Then one day, one of the members of my group at day treatment who knew of my struggle said:

"Douglas, *who you are* is not a function of how much money you make."

"Douglas, *who you are* is not a function of how many credentials you have."

"Douglas, *who you are* is not a function of your vocational identity or occupational title."

My therapist Pat commented, "Sam has done a good job of defining who you are not. Can you find a positive way to describe who you are?

At that moment, I blurted out, *"Who I am is a spiritual being who is on this earth to grow in love and wisdom."*

From then on, I strove to redefine my identity in nonachievement terms. For example, one day I noticed that I said a few kind words to a fellow patient at day treatment. Instead of taking that act for granted, as I usually might, I focused on it and valued it. Rather than dismissing it as a minor event (compared to doing something "really great"), I saw it as important.

Pat supported this attitudinal shift.

"Your brother may work on the sixty-sixth floor of an office building in Manhattan, but your 'work' right now is to heal from this illness, a much harder job than being a vice president of Citibank."

"How do you figure that?" I asked.

"Just managing to stay functional, given your level of pain, is a major achievement. I'm sorry that no one is giving you stock options for your display of courage. But the absence of financial reward does not invalidate the important work you are doing."

Over the next few months, I struggled to release the toxic feelings of blame, guilt, or shame that so often accompany the stigma of mental illness. Rather than judging myself as "weak" or "defective," I strove to love myself and to affirm my strength and goodness.

It is my hope that one day our attitudes toward depression will evolve similarly to those about cancer. Years ago, people were ashamed to admit they had cancer. Now that cancer is out of the closet, we have fund-raising events such as "Race for the Cure," which publicizes and raises money for victims of breast cancer. One day, I would like to see a similar fund-raising event for the treatment of depression.

Such change does not occur overnight. The roots of shame-based conditioning and society's prejudice against the mentally ill run strong and deep. My progress, while slow and sometimes painful, is steady. Ultimately, I am learning to let go of what Pat called "the weapon of comparison" and to see that my essential goodness is dependent not on what I do, but on who I am—a spiritual being who is on this earth to grow in love and wisdom.

CHAPTER SEVEN

God Is My Antidepressant

*Scientific prayer or spiritual treatment is really the lifting of your conscious-
ness above the level where you have met your problem. If only you can rise
high enough in thought, the problem will then solve itself.*

—EMMET FOX, "What Is Scientific Prayer?"

*Ask and you shall receive. Seek and ye shall find. Knock and the door shall
be opened. For everyone who asks receives, and he who seeks finds, and to
him who knocks, it shall be opened.*

—MATT. 7:7–8

By this point you have probably asked the question, "Why doesn't
that poor fellow just take some Prozac and put an end to his
misery? After all, ever since their discovery after World War II, antidepressants have become the first line of treatment for clinical depression, and for good reason—they work. All of my fellow patients at
the day treatment center were on some combination of drugs—
usually an average of three to five medications—which were constantly being readjusted and fine-tuned. Sometimes an entire regimen
would be stopped, and a host of new antidepressants would be tried.
Many patients were periodically readmitted to the hospital so the
new medications could be carefully monitored. In the long run, all
of this tinkering offered a tentative peace, and in some instances a
marked improvement of mood.

79

My own experience with antidepressants, however, had a far different outcome. I began with the well-known SSRIs (selective serotonin reuptake inhibitors), Prozac, Zoloft, and Paxil. Unfortunately, each of them made me feel as if I had received intravenous shots of double espresso. I later discovered that I had experienced a phenomenon called SSRI overstimulation. It seems that certain anxiety-prone individuals may experience a transient excitation, often described as a speeding sensation, when they first take an SSRI drug such as Prozac or Zoloft. In some instances, this reaction can result in a full-blown panic attack.* Later I learned that starting out on minute doses of a medication can decrease the intensity of this stimulation. But the standard quantities I was taking at the time made me far too agitated and anxious.

I then turned to the older tricyclic antidepressants, which for many people are just as effective as the SSRIs, at one-tenth the cost.** Yet aside from Elavil, which sedated me so I could sleep, they too failed to diminish my symptoms.

Finally, it was on to Nardil and Parnate antidepressants, which are hardly used these days because of their dietary restrictions. Once again, I experienced nothing except a racing heart and some bizarre hallucinations. In total, I experimented with about fifteen antidepressants, including some of the newer drugs such as Wellbutrin, Luvox, Serzone, and Remeron—all of which failed to produce the expected results.

I specifically remember being jealous of the manic depressives at day treatment because they had a magic bullet—lithium—that miraculously evened out their moods. I found no such biochemical panacea that would heal my symptoms.

Finally, I asked my psychiatrist, Dr. Stark, for an explanation.

"You have a case of treatment-resistant depression," he said. (This is also known as refractory depression.)

"What does that mean?"

---

* Valerie Raskin, *When Words Are Not Enough* (New York: Broadway Books, 1997), 99.

** Erica Goode, "New and Old Antidepressants Are Found Equal," *New York Times,* 19 March 1999, A1.

"It means that your type of depression is not helped by our available medications. Although 80 to 90 percent of patients benefit from antidepressants, a small minority do not—either because they can't handle the side effects or because they simply don't respond to the drugs."

"If antidepressants don't work for me, is there another way for me to heal?"

"I would try ECT."

ECT (electroconvulsive therapy), commonly known as electric shock therapy, is the treatment of last resort for clinical depression. In ECT, the brain is stimulated with a strong electrical current that induces a kind of epileptic seizure. In a manner that is not clearly understood, this seizure rearranges the brain's chemistry, resulting in an elevation of mood.

Like many people, I was put off by the gruesome reputation of ECT (as popularized in the movie *One Flew Over the Cuckoo's Nest*)—until I saw it heal my mother of a life-threatening depression. ECT also stabilized my partner Joan's aunt, who suffers from manic depression, as it did a number of patients at day treatment. I thought to myself, "If electricity can jump-start a stalled heart, why can't the same current be used to heal a sick brain?"

Intrigued, I consulted a number of medical journals and learned that ECT is very effective in certain types of major depression and mania. (A more detailed description of ECT and how it works can be found in chapter 11, "Therapeutic Interventions for When Things Are Falling Apart.") Nonetheless, I was terrified at the prospect of having my brain zapped with a lightning bolt and then waking up with a blistering headache and not remembering what I had eaten for breakfast. (One of the significant side effects of ECT is short-term memory loss, especially for events that occur around the time of the treatments.) Thus, I was in no way disappointed when the doctor who evaluated me for ECT said that because of my nervous system's hypersensitivity, he was reluctant to try the procedure. (There are two "milder forms" of brain stimulation called RTMS [Rapid Transcranial Magnetic Stimulation] and Vagnus Nerve Stimulation. They are being explored as alternatives to ECT and are discussed in chapter 11.)

"Praying Hands" by Albrecht Dürer

I returned to Dr. Stark with my findings.

"Medication doesn't seem to work, and I'm not considered a good candidate for ECT," I moaned.

"That leaves prayer," he replied.

Actually, I already was following Dr. Stark's advice. For the past four months, I had been placing weekly prayer requests in the prayer boxes at the Living Enrichment Center. Adele, one of the prayer volunteers, had taken a personal interest in my case and was writing back to me once a week. Concerned about the gravity of my condition, Adele contacted the Reverend Eddy Brame, head of pastoral counseling at the LEC, and told her of my predicament. Shortly afterward, I received a call from Eddy.

"When one of our congregants was dying of cancer," Eddy explained, "we decided to bring all of her supporters—her family, friends, minister, physicians, and social worker—together in one room. Their combined prayers created a powerful healing energy that allowed Carol to live far longer than anyone expected. I think that the same principle might work for you."

Answered Prayers

Here is one of the many letters I received from the LEC prayer ministry in response to my weekly prayer requests.

April 20, 1997

Dear Douglas,

Thank you for trusting your prayer request to the Living Enrichment Center Prayer Ministry. We are praying with you and for you, knowing and accepting that God's grace is guiding you toward a complete healing from depression and anxiety. We see you making the best choices, and with God's loving guidance, moving into health, joy, and vitality.

On a separate page we have enclosed an affirmation that can support you in knowing the truth. As we put our focus on God and the divine qualities of wholeness, balance, creativity, peace, and oneness, we know that transformation occurs. As you repeat your affirmation, know that there are many others supporting you in prayer.

Blessings,
Adele

Affirmation
My body is a holy temple, infused with divine intelligence.
Every organ, cell, and tissue is bathed in the revitalizing power of spirit.
The power to experience miracles is in me now.
I open my mind to the healing love of God.

"Mary, myself, and members of the prayer ministry would like to schedule a meeting with you on Monday, July 14, at 4:00 P.M. in Mary's office. Can you attend and bring members of your personal support team?"

The invitation could not have come at a better time. By the early summer of 1997, I was truly desperate. My depressive episode was now in its tenth month, and during the prior ninety days my anxiety and depression had reached all-time highs—eclipsing the dark days of the previous November and December. In pursuit of relief, I had tried every conventional and alternative treatment I could find, including:

- Sitting at the feet of, and being blessed by, two Tibetan monks who were disciples of the Dalai Lama
- Receiving a soul retrieval, a shamanic healing, and a series of acupuncture treatments
- Ingesting Chinese herbs, homeopathic remedies, megadoses of vitamins, and a panoply of antidepressants

Despite my concerted efforts at finding a traditional and/or alternative cure, I still remained trapped in the black hole of depression. "What have I got to lose?" I thought. I told Eddy that I would accept her invitation. I now had three weeks to prepare for what I believed was my last hope for survival.

The God Meetings

We do not come to grace; grace comes to us.
—M. SCOTT PECK, *The Road Less Traveled*

As the time of the meeting with the LEC ministers drew nearer, I suggested to my partner, Joan, that we spend a day in retreat at a Trappist monastery located in the small town of Lafayette, Oregon, twenty miles southwest of Portland. Thomas Merton had been one of my spiritual mentors, and I hoped that spending time in his order might be a source of inspiration to me. It was one of those glorious Oregon summer days that almost compensates for the other nine months of interminable rain. We arrived at the monastery at midday and spent the afternoon hiking the lovely grounds. Afterward, I wandered into the library, where I stumbled upon an audiotape by ayurvedic physician Deepak Chopra, whose books on holistic health and spirituality were all the rage in the United States. In his talk, Chopra asserted that the brain had its own "internal pharmacy," as evidenced by its ability to manufacture painkilling endorphins.

"There really is such a thing as healing from within," I thought. "If only I could find a way to access my body's natural healing system." I walked to the chapel next door, got down on my knees, and prayed for such a healing.

The following day, Monday, July 14, did not begin auspiciously. I woke up in my normal agitated state and barely made it to day treatment for the morning groups. After lunch I returned home, where I met Joan and my friend Stuart. At 3:00 P.M., we drove out to LEC, just avoiding Portland's daily rush hour traffic madness.

The Reverend Mary Morrissey's spacious office was located on LEC's ninety-five-acre campus on the second floor of the main building. Pictures of Jesus, Buddha, and other spiritual teachers adorned the walls, complemented by a large magnolia tree that bloomed outside a picture window. Mary had arranged the chairs and couches in a circular pattern around a glass coffee table, at the center of which sat an angelic figurine. Ten other individuals were present besides Stuart, Joan, and myself—six staff people from LEC (including three ministers), a minister friend from a local Unity church, the leader of my men's group, my therapist, Pat, and Judy, my social worker. I was deeply moved that twelve people had taken time out of their busy schedules to support me.

Mary facilitated the meeting in a straightforward fashion. She began by leading us in an affirmative prayer, taken from the writings of New Thought writer Jack Addington:

> *There is no power in conditions;*
> *There is no power in situations;*
> *There is only power in God;*
> *Almighty God within me right now.*
> *There is no person, place, thing, condition, or circumstance*
> *that can interfere with the perfect right action*
> *of God Almighty within me right now.*

I am pure spirit, living in a spiritual world.
All things are possible to God through me. *

Mary then asked the participants to introduce themselves, recount how they had met me, and describe their thoughts on the ultimate outcome of my ordeal. As people shared their perceptions, a common theme emerged—everyone affirmed that I could be healed of my affliction. Although I disagreed with their prognosis, I was moved by the unanimity of their faith.

When my turn arrived, I briefly recounted the history of my depressive episode as well as my present feelings of hopelessness and despair. Normally, I would have stopped there, but the previous day Mary had given an inspired sermon on "the mental equivalent." This is an ancient metaphysical principle that states that before something can manifest in the outer world, there must first exist an idea or "mental equivalent" of it in the world of thought. I complimented Mary on her talk and said that I wished to create a mental equivalent of *what wellness would look and feel like for me.*

The group embraced my idea, and so I asked each participant to join with me in affirming my picture of wholeness over the next thirty days. I promised to write out my vision and send it to the members by the end of the week. The plan was that every day (preferably at 9:00 A.M.) each person would read my vision statement while picturing me as whole and well. The meeting ended with a prayer of thanksgiving.

The Rebirth Statement

I left the group feeling nurtured by the loving attention I had received, but without any sense that a healing had taken place. If anything, things seemed to get worse as my anxiety increased over

---

* Throughout this and subsequent chapters, I will be using the term "God" to describe a higher power or creative intelligence that infuses the universe. If the traditional concept of God seems alien to you, you may wish to think of such ideas as the vastness of the human spirit, an intelligent order in nature, the life force, creative inspiration, or qualities such as goodness, truth, love, beauty, peace, justice, and so on. The words we use are less important than the universal reality they describe.

the next two days. Then, on Thursday morning, July 17 (ironically, what would have been my thirteenth wedding anniversary), I awoke with a clarity and a peace that I had not experienced in five months. The normal symptoms of intense agitation and feelings of hopelessness were totally absent. I felt as if a dark cloud had lifted.

I could scarcely believe it. "Is this a miracle or a mirage?" I asked myself. I had experienced other remissions, but they had usually lasted only two or three days (the longest I had gone without symptoms was ten days in February). Grateful for what little peace I did have, I spent the afternoon walking with a friend through the holy grounds of the Grotto, a local Catholic shrine dedicated to the Virgin Mary.

The next day I faxed my rebirth statement to the ministers at LEC and to the rest of my support team. The opening lines read:

> With help from God, I am reborn to a new life. I have learned the lessons that the anxiety and depression came to teach and thus have fully and freely released these symptoms from my body and mind. They are replaced by inner peace, emotional stability, vitality, wholeness, wellness, and joy. My brain chemistry is stabilized and in perfect balance. I am healed and made whole.

The remainder of Friday passed without symptoms. That evening, I recorded in my mood diary that my anxiety and depression had dropped below a 2 on my symptom rating scale. (This was my psychiatrist's definition of remission.) In my journal I wrote, "I actually feel good. There is no pain to bear, no suffering to endure." A person who has not lived with chronic, debilitating anxiety and depression cannot fully appreciate what it feels like to be liberated from one's anguish. For me it was as if a ten-month migraine headache had suddenly ceased.

On Saturday, July 19, I hiked to Multnomah Falls with a friend and watched the full moon rise over Mount Hood. "I haven't seen you this well since your illness began," Kathleen joyfully observed. Sunday morning I attended church and spoke with Mary Morrissey about my remission. Referring to the support group, Mary exclaimed, "That was a God meeting!"

"What do you mean?" I asked.

"I could feel the presence of spirit fill the room with love and peace."

(The other people I spoke to at LEC said that they too had sensed a light and a lightness of being in the room that day.)

"So what do you think is happening?"

"I sense that you are having a spiritual healing."

For the next twenty-one days, I continued to experience a life without anxiety and depression. Then, exactly four weeks after the God meeting, I experienced a relapse, brought on by a recurrence of cellulitis a severe infection of the soft tissue in my lower leg—and an unexpected separation from a close friend (once again, loss triggered a depressive episode). For a brief time, the old symptoms returned and I was back in the inferno as my depression and anxiety levels skyrocketed to 8 and above. Fortunately, a second support meeting had been scheduled for August 26, just two weeks away. Because I believed that the injection of light from the first meeting had catalyzed my remission, I had faith that my symptoms would end as soon as I met with my support team. Although I was in great pain, I was no longer hopeless about my recovery.

At the second God meeting, people commented that I had clearly improved (there were now fourteen people beside myself who attended). Members of the group remarked that even with the relapse, I seemed more vital, less agitated, and more lighthearted. I read my rebirth statement aloud and received helpful feedback on how to make it stronger and more definite. By the next day, my mood had once again improved. My rebirth statement was taking form.

Subsequently, Mary scheduled our God meetings once a month so that I might receive regular injections of spiritual energy. (This is similar to what occurs in conventional treatment for major depression, where patients who have been treated with electroconvulsive therapy receive monthly maintenance doses of ECT to prevent relapse.) With each new dose of light, I became stronger and more stable. By the conclusion of the third God meeting in September, my

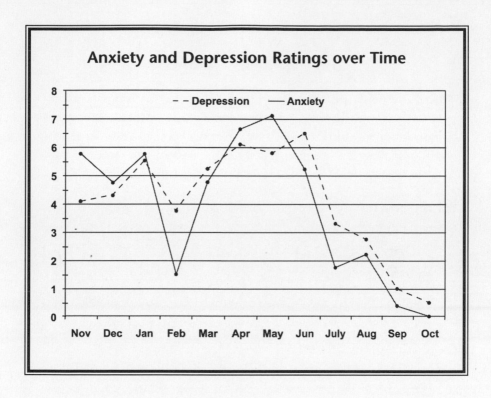

Anxiety and Depression Ratings over Time

mood swings had ceased. I no longer contemplated suicide. My sense of humor returned. I was able to concentrate and to spend long periods of time by myself. I no longer needed shifts of people to monitor and keep track of me. In short, my depression and anxiety had healed without drugs or other conventional medical treatment (see the Anxiety and Depression Ratings over Time graph).

Three additional God meetings were held at LEC in October, November, and December. At the October meeting, the group supported me in disposing of the tranquilizers I had saved for a future suicide attempt. The male members accompanied me to the men's room, where we emptied several hundred tablets into a large ceramic container. Then, each of us blessed the pills and dropped them, one handful at a time, into the toilet bowl. After a prayer of thanksgiving, we flushed them into oblivion.

At the November gathering, the group and I created another potent ritual. I burned the suicide note I had written the previous

From Despair to Gratitude

No matter how hopeless things seem or feel, each new day brings the opportunity for a new beginning. To reinforce this attitude, I made a photocopy of the suicide note I had written in 1996, and then inscribed a new set of affirmative statements at the bottom of the sheet. Below, I have replicated both the note and a letter I wrote to myself that contains the new beliefs.

> To my friends and family,   Nov. 12, 1996
>   I know that this is wrong, but I can no longer endure the pain of living with this mental illness. Further hospitalizations will not help, as my condition is too deep seated and advanced to uproot.
>   On some deeper level, I know that my work on the planet is finished and that it is time to move on.
>   Douglas

11-20-97

A reminder to myself,

The words on this sheet were written at the depth of my depression. I am keeping a record of them so, if I ever experience this state again, I can remind myself that no matter how bad things look or feel, there is always a reason for hope.

I now let go of the despair expressed in this note and replace it with thoughts of hope and optimism. I turn the page on the past and begin a new chapter of my life.

year, but not before photocopying it. On the back of the duplicate copy I wrote the following:

> The words on this sheet were written at the depth of my depression. I am keeping a record of them so if I ever experience this state again, I can remind myself that no matter how bad things look or feel, there is always a reason for hope. I now let go of the despair expressed in this note and replace it with thoughts of hope and optimism. I turn the page on the past and begin a new chapter of my life.

Each group member added his or her words of affirmation and encouragement to make the blessing complete.

During this three-month period, I continued to submit my weekly requests for healing, which were prayed over by the LEC prayer team and the entire ministerial staff. By the year's end, my support team felt that I was stable enough to continue the God meetings without the church's help. My first reaction to the prospect of losing the church's support was that of fear. Fortunately, my therapist, Pat, assured me that I was well enough to make it on my own. The God meetings have since continued in my home as "Master Mind groups" in which group members both *give* and *receive* spiritual support (see page 271 for more about this).

Because my healing was not caused by a physical substance, it is difficult to substantiate what occurred. No one photographed or recorded the doses of spiritual light I received. I possess no X-rays depicting that a cancerous tumor had shrunk. Neither did I throw away my crutches or "take up my bed and walk." And yet it was clear that something miraculous had taken place.

There is a story in the Gospel of John in which the disciples, after seeing a man who was blind from birth, asked Jesus, "Rabbi, who sinned, this man or his parents that he was born blind?" Jesus answered, "Neither this man nor his parents sinned, but that the works of God should be revealed in him." Likewise, on some level, I believe I was stricken with depression so spirit could work a miracle in and through me—and that others could witness it.

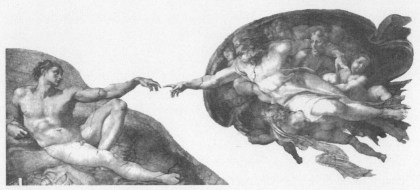

Michelangelo's "The Creation of Adam"

The Power of Prayer

At the height of my illness, Mary Morrissey had said, "There is a power within you that is greater than any condition you may face. If you ask that higher power for its assistance, help is available."

The healing power of prayer was not a new idea to me. The spiritual tradition of Unity and other New Thought metaphysical schools teach what is called "affirmative prayer"—a process of building and affirming an inward consciousness of what one desires. When this inner picture manifests in the external world, it is called a "demonstration." I had demonstrated many things in my life—a new car, a lovely home, a book contract (even a pair of tickets to a sold-out Grateful Dead concert)—but never a healing of this magnitude. Fortunately, I was graced with a group of dedicated people who collectively held a vision of my wellness.

It is my belief that the key ingredient in my healing was the presence of *group energy*. I had met and prayed with Mary Morrissey many times; I had prayed with other ministers and members of the prayer team, as well as with my therapist—and still I continued to decline. It wasn't until someone said, *"Let's put all of your support people together in one room"* that the healing power of prayer became fully activated. The *combined* prayers and positive thoughts of the group members set up a spiritual energy field through which divine love moved and healed my body and soul. (This energy is described in many spiritual traditions. In the gospel of Matthew, Jesus tells his disciples, "Where two or three are gathered together in my name [i.e., my nature], there am I [Divine consciousness] in the midst of them." In the Jewish religion, the power of group consciousness is the rationale for a minyan—the requirement of a minimum of ten Jews for a communal religious service.)

Given the fact that many cases of depression have been known to resolve on their own, some doctors have suggested that I might have recovered without any spiritual intervention. Nonetheless, I choose to believe that my healing was a divine blessing. During my illness, a good friend had given me a book about the apparition of the Virgin Mary at Lourdes and the subsequent healings that had followed. I knew that a similar miracle was occurring in my life when, on the drive home from the second God meeting, Joan, Stuart, and I witnessed four magnificent rainbows illuminating the Oregon afternoon sky. Referring to Noah's encounter with the rainbow after the Flood, and God's promise of reconciliation, Stuart exclaimed, "This is just like living in the Bible!" And so it was.

The Power of Support

It was not only God who healed me; it was people. One cannot overcome an illness like major depression (or any dark night of the soul experience) by oneself. The weight of the agony is too immense, even for the strongest-willed individual, to bear alone.

During my illness, two people close to me, a previous therapist and a fellow student of metaphysics, committed suicide in the midst of similar bouts of depression. The cause of their tragedies, I believe, lies in the words of Spanish philosopher Miguel de Unamuno, who said, "Isolation is the worst possible counsel." My friends had retreated into environments in which they were cut off from family, friends, and therapeutic assistance. Fortunately, many people in the Portland area extended themselves to me—the staff and patients at day treatment, my partner, Joan, countless friends, and the prayer ministry of LEC. Without them, I would not have survived.

In a recent special aired on National Public Radio, Mike Wallace, William Styron, and Art Buchwald spoke candidly about their depressions and about the lifeline of support that developed among them during their episodes. (All three were living on Martha's Vineyard at the time of their ordeals.) In his acknowledgment of Art Buchwald's support, Styron said:

> I have to give Art credit. He was the Virgil to our Dante. Because he'd been there [in hell] before, like Virgil. And he really charted the depths, and so it was very, very useful to have Art on the phone, because we needed it. Because this is a new experience for everyone, and it's totally—it's totally terrifying. And you need someone who has been there to give you parameters and an understanding of where you're going.

(For a cassette copy of the radio program *A Conversation with Mike Wallace, Art Buchwald, and William Styron,* call the Dana Alliance for Brain Initiatives at 800-65-BRAIN.) In my depressive state, I did not have a Buchwald—a brother or sister survivor who had been to hell and back—who could assure me of my future deliverance. What I did have, however, was a committed group of individuals who "kept the high watch" by holding a vision of my healing until it came to pass. And so I learned the lesson that is granted to survivors of emotional and physical trauma: when divine love heals us, it most often comes through the healing love of other people.

As I read over the description of my recovery, I feel moved to add an important postscript. Just because spiritual intervention was a catalyst for my recovery, it doesn't mean that this is the path for everyone. For some people, healing may come from finding the right medication or nutritional supplement; for others, it may be through falling in love or pursuing a passion. Since the majority of people who are treated for depression eventually get better (i.e., most depressions are episodic), if you can endure the pain and set a strong intention to get well, you will likely be graced by some healing modality that works for you. (The key is to hang on until the pattern of the illness shifts.)

In addition, many people have observed that I attracted a particularly large support network of committed people. While this is true, I believe that support is available to anyone who earnestly seeks it. Potential resources include family; friends; coworkers; mental health professionals; one's church, synagogue, or other place of worship; 12-step meetings; 24-hour crisis lines; and telephone prayer lines (listed in Appendix C).

Even with the many resources that are available, some people feel too ashamed, shy, or anxious to reach out for help. If asking for assistance seems hard, please reconsider calling *someone*, even if it is a crisis line. Reaching out *will* make a real difference in your recovery. I promise.

Dante and Beatrice experience the beatific vision in the conclusion of "Paradisio," from Dante's *Divine Comedy.* The poet wrote, "A light there is in the beyond which makes the creator visible to the creature, who only in beholding him finds peace." The artist is Gustave Doré.

CHAPTER EIGHT

After the Pain, the Joy

No one is as capable of gratitude as one who has emerged from the kingdom of night.

—ELIE WIESEL

Enlightenment begins on the other side of despair.

—JEAN-PAUL SARTRE

There is an ancient spiritual truth that states that "Every adversity contains within it the seed of an equivalent or greater good." Like the lotus flower that blooms in the depths of the mud, something redeeming can emerge from even the most horrendous situation. This was certainly true of my experience of major depression. When I awoke from the nightmare, I found that the illness had left unexpected gifts in its wake. The black cloud of depression had a silver lining.

The first of these blessings was compassion. As a result of my ordeal, my empathy has deepened—for all who suffer, and especially for those who are afflicted with mental illness. Having gained a greater understanding of the frailties of human existence, I am less likely to judge others. Before my episode, I might have said about a person with a neurosis, "How could he stay in that dysfunctional marriage?" or "Hasn't he cured his addiction yet?" Now, when I meet a person who is in pain, I release my judgment and say silently,

"Friend, I know what it is like to be at the mercy of your demons. I bless you and pray that you, too, will find your way home."

On the eve of my second hospitalization, Joan had remarked, "Think of your stay in the hospital as a training ground for learning how to cope." In many respects, my *entire illness* was a lesson in learning how to manage intense pain. Thus, a second gift of the depression has been the development of emotional coping skills that I now use to create stability and serenity in my daily life.

In addition, I have gained a new perspective about the meaning of distress. Whenever I start to get irritated because something is not working out as planned, I say to myself, "What's the big deal? I almost died. I almost committed suicide." What was once a crisis, I now regard as an inconvenience. I am reminded of the saying "Don't sweat the small stuff." After you have stood at the brink of the abyss and faced death, everything is small stuff. As author, Martha Manning, wrote after her own hellish experience with clinical depression, "My baseline for awful will never be the same."

Yet another blessing I have received has been the reconciliation of my marriage. My divorce in 1996 initiated an overwhelming reaction of grief and loneliness, which created the depression that ultimately led to my breakdown. During my illness, my ex-wife, Joan, became a major support in my healing—accompanying me to LEC's Sunday services and driving me to the monthly God meetings. Our commitment to my recovery and to our spirituality rekindled the love that drew us back together.

Finally, my reconciliation with Joan was part of a bigger picture. Having my own "near death" experience made me realize what I truly valued in life—the love of my wife, friends, and family.

Breaking Down to Breakthrough

The depth of darkness to which you can descend and still live
is an exact measure of the height to which you can aspire to reach.
—LAURENS VAN DER POST

In 1977, Czech physical chemist Ilya Prigogine won the Nobel Prize for his theory of dissipative structures. Prigogine showed that "open systems" (those systems having a continuous interchange with the environment) occasionally experience periods of instability. When this imbalance exceeds a certain limit, the system breaks down and enters a state of "creative chaos." Yet out of chaos and disorganization, a new and higher order spontaneously emerges. This phenomenon—known as spontaneous transformation—has been recognized as the basis of physical evolution.

"Job and His Family Restored to Prosperity," by William Blake

I believe that what holds true on the physical plane is valid on the psychological plane as well. Hence, so-called nervous breakdowns can be seen as rites of passage into a more mature spiritual consciousness. As survivor researcher Julius Siegal describes it:

> In a remarkable number of cases, those who have suffered and prevail find that after their ordeal they begin to operate at a higher level than ever before. . . . The terrible experiences of our lives, despite the pain they bring, may become our redemption.

Although I would never want to trivialize the suffering that depression brings, I do feel changed for the better by my healing experience in ways that would not have occurred had I undergone a lesser ordeal.

What Goes Down Must Come Up

Ten years ago, I wrote the following in my book of affirmations, *Words That Heal:*

> *What goes down must come up.*
> *There can be no death without rebirth.*
> *Every ending is followed by a beginning.*
> *The experience of hell is a precursor to the glory of heaven.*

These words are no longer an intellectual supposition. Having learned their truth firsthand, I have a personal message for anyone who is going through a dark night of the soul experience:

> *If you are on the edge of the abyss, don't jump.*
> *If you are going through hell, don't stop.*
> *As long as you are breathing, there is hope.*
> *As long as day follows night, there is hope.*
> *Nothing stays the same forever.*
> *Set an intention to heal,*
> *reach out for support, and you will find help.*

I realize that not everyone can develop the spiritual endurance to hold on, and there is no shame in that. But for those whose will to live is greater than their suffering, there exists the eternal promise of resurrection and rebirth. Like the mythical phoenix, we who are consumed by fire will rise again from the ashes.

I began this part of the book with a quotation from Teddy Roosevelt, a courageous soul who experienced numerous episodes of depression during his life. His words, "It is not having been in the dark house, but having left it, that counts," form a credo for all souls who have been to hell and back.

Because depression tends to recur, there is a possibility that I might one day revisit Roosevelt's "dark house." If that happens, I hope to put this book's body, mind, and spirit recovery program to good use. But for now, I would rather join with the psalmist in singing the 126th Psalm, in which David praises God for the deliverance of his people:

> The Lord has done great things for us, whereof we are glad.
> Those who sow in tears shall reap in joy.
> He who continually goes forth weeping,
> Shall doubtless come again with rejoicing,
> Bringing his sheaves with him.

(The phoenix was the Greek name for the mythological bird that was sacred to the sun god in ancient Egypt. An eagle-like bird with red and gold plumage, the phoenix lived for five hundred years, then built its own funeral pyre on which it was burned to ashes. Yet, out of the ashes a new phoenix arose. Symbolic of the rising and setting of the sun, the phoenix later appeared in medieval Christian writings as a symbol of death and resurrection.)

"The Invisible Helper," by Mary Hanscom

Amazing Grace

You have survived the winter because you are, and were, and always will be, very much loved. And long, long before you felt my warmth surrounding you, you were being freed and formed from within in ways so deep and profound, that you could not possibly know what was happening

—MARY FAHY, *The Tree That Survived the Winter*

It is a fact that even on the most overcast of days, though its rays are hidden from view, the sun is still shining. In a similar manner, I believe that God's light continues to bless us even in our darkest moments. As I reflect back over the period of my illness, I see that a benevolent, unseen force was protecting me. This amazing grace guided me to the day treatment clinic, to my therapist Pat, to those people who steered me away from suicide, and ultimately to the healing at the Living Enrichment Center.

Nowhere is the principle of divine protection more beautifully illustrated than in the anonymous essay "Footprints in the Sand." I first encountered this inspirational passage in an Ann Landers newspaper column a year before my illness. Soon I began to see the text inscribed on parchment and plaques that were sold in various souvenir shops. One day, in the depths of my depression, I bought a copy for myself. Afterwards, I read the words and found them to be a source of solace and hope. I present them here for those readers who have yet to encounter their inspiring message.

Footprints in the Sand

One night a man had a dream. He dreamed he was walking along the beach with the Lord. Across the sky flashed scenes from his life. For each scene he noticed two sets of footprints in the sand, one belonging to him and the other to the Lord.

When the last scene of his life flashed before him, he looked back at the footprints in the sand. He noticed that many times along the path of his life there was only one set of footprints. He also noticed that it happened at the very lowest and saddest times in his life.

This really bothered him, and he questioned the Lord about it. "Lord, you said that once I decided to follow you, you'd walk with me all the way. But I have noticed that during the most troublesome times in my life, there is only one set of footprints. I don't understand why when I needed you most you would leave me."

The Lord replied, "My precious, precious child, I love you and I would never leave you. During your times of trial and suffering, when you saw only one set of footprints, it was then that I carried you."

"God Answers Job Out of the Whirlwind," by William Blake

Chronology of Events

Although the world is full of suffering. It is also full of the overcoming of suffering.

—HELEN KELLER

The following is a brief summary of the events that led up to and took place during my episode of major depression.

December 1990. Serious cracks in my six-year marriage begin to appear.

April 1991. I enter group therapy to deal with my marital crisis and to work on family of origin issues.

September 1993. After much deliberation, Joan and I decide to separate.

April 1994. The book that I am writing under contract for a New York publisher is unexpectedly turned down after I submit it. I am now without a creative focus or a love focus. I begin to develop insomnia.

December 1994. I am stricken with the first of a series of chronic bacterial infections in my lower right leg. Intravenous antibiotic therapy is required to vanquish the cellulitis.

September 1995. I file for divorce.

November 1995 and February 1996. Two additional attacks of cellulitis occur.

February 28, 1996. My divorce from Joan is finalized.

March 1. I am laid up with another bout of cellulitis. My mood
blackens.

April 1–7. A trip to the Grand Canyon temporarily lifts my spirits.

June through August. I try a number of antidepressants in an
attempt to heal my melancholy, none of which help.

August 10. I take the antidepressant Zoloft before bedtime and
spend the next two days feeling extremely agitated.

September 4. I take the antidepressant Effexor before bedtime and
wake up at three in the morning in a state of major agitation and
panic. It takes two hours to get back to sleep. I finally wake up
at noon, and experience a black depression for the rest of the day.

September 7. I awaken with out-of-control agitation and panic.
Joan drives me to a psychiatric ward in a local hospital. My
major depressive episode officially begins.

September 10. I am discharged from the hospital with a diagnosis
of "agitated depression."

September 11. Joan moves in with me and becomes my part-time
caretaker.

September 12–October 22. My general mood takes a slow,
downward direction. I begin to experience daily anxiety attacks
that can only be contained through long walks in the woods.

October 21. Joan begins work at a full-time job.

October 23. I admit myself to Pacific Gateway Hospital.

November 1. I am discharged from Pacific Gateway. I begin
attending the day treatment program at the Sellwood Day
Treatment Clinic.

November 12. I prepare to commit suicide by taking an overdose
of tranquilizers, but I am serendipitously interrupted.

November 15. Sedated on the antianxiety drug Klonopin,
I rear-end a pickup truck during rush-hour traffic.

December 4–13. A temporary lifting of symptoms is followed by
a return to the inferno.

January 2, 1997. I consider admitting myself to the hospital as
suicidal feelings return.

February 13. I begin to submit prayer requests to the prayer
ministry at the Living Enrichment Center.

February 21–28. I experience a week of unexplained calm
and peace.

March 1. The old symptoms return with a vengeance.

April 20. I hire a home health aide to be my companion on weekday afternoons.

May 13. I plant a small vegetable garden.

May 25. After months of agonizing, I decide not to go to the Menninger Psychiatric Clinic in Topeka, Kansas.

June 19. The Reverend Eddy Brame of the Living Enrichment Center asks me to attend a support meeting to be held on my behalf with the LEC ministerial staff. This proves to be the turning point in my illness.

July 14. A two-hour meeting to support my healing is held in the Reverend Mary Morrissey's office and is facilitated by Mary. Twelve people attend. I decide to create a vision statement depicting what wellness would look like for me. The group agrees to affirm this vision with me on a daily basis.

July 17. I wake up free of symptoms. This remission will continue for three and a half weeks.

July 20. Mary confirms that the spirit was present at our meeting. I spend the day relaxing at the Oregon Coast.

August 11. I experience a relapse and spend two weeks back in the dark house.

August 26. The second God meeting takes place. Fourteen people are present. I share my rebirth statement with the group and receive helpful feedback.

August 27. My symptoms once again go into remission. I stop attending day treatment.

September 21. I begin to feel the return of some anxiety, but it is less severe than it had been.

September 25. The third God meeting takes place. Eddy Brame is now the main facilitator.

September 26. My symptoms disappear again, this time apparently for good.

October 19. I am able to focus again. I begin to tutor mathematics to high school and college students.

October 23. The fourth God meeting occurs, at which I dispose of the medication I had saved up for a possible suicide attempt. This is the one-year anniversary of my being admitted to Pacific Gateway Hospital.

October 26. As a symbol of my rebirth, I begin to remodel my home.

November 9. I begin writing an article about my recovery from depression for a local newspaper.

November 20. The fifth God meeting takes place.

November 25. The symptoms of anxiety and depression have been absent for eight weeks. This means that my major depressive episode is now officially in remission.

December 10. My inner guidance tells me that I am supposed to write an article about my experience.

December 18. The final God meeting is held at the LEC.

January 15, 1998. The first Master Mind group meeting is held at my house. Six members of the God group and I participate. Subsequent meetings will be held biweekly.

February 22. On my forty-ninth birthday, a party is held at my house to celebrate my emergence from my dark night of the soul. Many of my friends and the LEC support people attend. My article has turned into the beginning of a book.

December 10. The first draft of the book is complete. It's working title is *When Going Through Hell . . . Don't Stop!*

November 30, 1999. The book is published.

December 4. A book blessing is held at my home.

December 12. I make my first public appearance at the Living Enrichment Center during which I share my story.

December 13. The U.S. Surgeon General releases a groundbreaking report on the nation's mental health.

January 2000. I begin giving workshops on my five-part "better mood" program.

July 2000. I create a Web site in order to share my work (www.healingfromdepression.com).

July 14. I celebrate the three-year anniversary of the first God meeting.

March 2001. I begin to lead "Healing from Depression" classes and support groups to offer to others the same group support that healed me.

PART TWO

Healing from Depression and Anxiety

The Better Mood Recovery Program

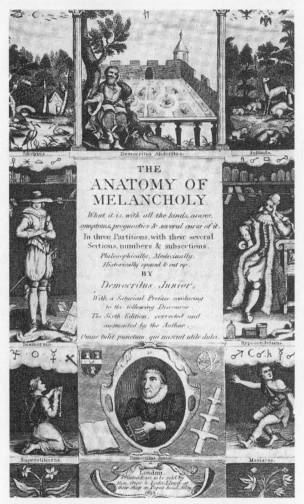

The title page to *The Anatomy of Melancholy*
by Robert Burton, first published in 1621

CHAPTER NINE

What Is Clinical Depression and How Do I Know Whether I Have It?

Depression is an illness. I am sick. I need to be here not because I'm defective, not because I am a moral leper, not because I've fallen from grace or turned my back on God, but for one simple reason: I am sick.

—TRACY THOMPSON, *The Beast*

Before we can begin the better mood recovery program, we need to take a look at what we will be treating—the syndrome of depression. This chapter will provide you with an overview of the causes and symptoms of clinical depression.

The voice on the phone did not sound like the Jesse I knew. The tone was flat and tentative, the usual confidence visibly absent. "I'm not doing so good," he mumbled.

"What's going on?"

"I'm having a hard time keeping up in my first term at college. I just can't seem to concentrate on my studies."

"That seems odd. You were so motivated to do well in high school."

"I know. But I just don't have the energy I used to. My sleep is messed up. I wake up in the middle of the night with my mind racing and spinning, and I can't get back to sleep. In the morning, I can't seem to get out of bed to get to class. Sometimes I wonder if it's all worth it."

Such talk was uncharacteristic of my nephew who had been an honor roll student throughout high school. Two weeks later I received the following E-mail: "Blackness, darkness, the walls are closing in. It won't be long, now." I called Jesse's dad. The next day we withdrew Jesse from the university, and escorted him to the crisis triage center at Providence Hospital in Portland, Oregon.

"It's major depression, isn't it?" I said to the resident psychiatrist.

"How did you know?"

"I just experienced my own episode last year," I replied. "Once you go through a hell like this, you never forget it."

As we enter the twenty-first century, Jesse and I are far from being alone. Depression has now become the second most disabling condition in America (surpassed only by heart disease) and the fourth most disabling worldwide. The disorder does not discriminate among its victims; it affects all age groups, all economic groups, and all gender and ethnic categories. While the average age of onset was once a person's mid-thirties, it is now moving toward adolescence and even early childhood. At any given moment, somewhere between fifteen and twenty million Americans are suffering from depressive disorders, and about one in five will develop the illness at some point during their lifetimes.

The first step in becoming liberated from the mental straightjacket of depression is to recognize and understand the nature of the condition. Getting proper help for depression begins with proper diagnosis. The purpose of the pages that follow is to provide a clear understanding of the signs and symptoms of major depression so you can determine whether you or a loved one may need to seek treatment.

What Is Clinical Depression?

A depressive illness is a "whole body" disorder, involving one's physiology, biochemistry, mood, thoughts, and behavior. It affects the way you eat and sleep, the way you think and feel about yourself, others, and the world. Clinical depression is not a passing blue mood or a sign of personal weakness. Subtle changes in the brain's chemistry can create a terrible malaise in the body, mind, and spirit, which can affect every dimension of your being.

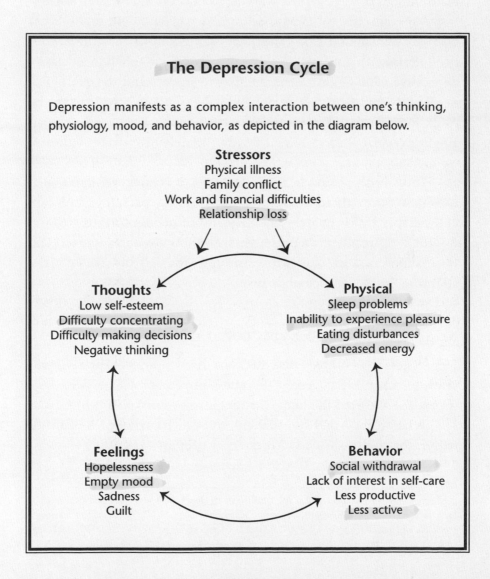

The Depression Cycle

Depression manifests as a complex interaction between one's thinking, physiology, mood, and behavior, as depicted in the diagram below.

Stressors
Physical illness
Family conflict
Work and financial difficulties
Relationship loss

Thoughts
Low self-esteem
Difficulty concentrating
Difficulty making decisions
Negative thinking

Physical
Sleep problems
Inability to experience pleasure
Eating disturbances
Decreased energy

Feelings
Hopelessness
Empty mood
Sadness
Guilt

Behavior
Social withdrawal
Lack of interest in self-care
Less productive
Less active

Depression is called the common cold of mental illness, not because its symptoms are mild but because the disease is so widespread across cultures. It is the most diagnosed mental health disorder in the United States, among the most debilitating, and the most lethal (15 percent of all untreated clinical depressions result in suicide). According to an estimate in the *Journal of Clinical Psychiatry,* each year depression accounts for a $43.7 billion burden on the American economy, as measured in medical costs, lost productivity in the workplace and at home, and lost contributions of wage earners who die from depression-related suicide.

Although depression has become the malaise of our times, it has plagued humankind since antiquity. King Saul of the Bible (who needed David's music to soothe his despondency) was a classic depressive. The Greeks were the first to understand the biological nature of depression and gave it the name "melancholia" (from the roots "melaina chole," meaning black bile). In the seventeenth century, English scholar Robert Burton wrote the definitive work of the era on the subject—*The Anatomy of Melancholy.*

Though depression is a serious illness, it is *highly treatable,* as it normally responds to a combination of antidepressants and psychotherapy. Unfortunately, the majority of people with depression do not seek treatment because the symptoms are unrecognized and misdiagnosed, and/or because the individual is deterred by the stigma surrounding mental illness.

What Are the Symptoms of Depression?*

Depression is a complex disorder, and its symptoms express themselves on many levels. Depression creates physical problems, behavioral problems, distorted thinking, changes in emotional well being, troubled relationships, and spiritual emptiness. The symptoms of major depression can be divided into three categories:

---

* Much of the information about the symptoms of depression was provided by the Depression Awareness, Recognition, and Treatment Program (D/ART) of the National Institute of Mental Health. Call 800-421-4211 for free literature, or visit their Web site (www.nimh.nih.gov).

1. Disturbances of emotion and mood

2. Changes in the housekeeping functions of the brain—those that regulate sleep, appetite, energy, and sexual function.

3. Disturbances of thinking and concentration

The most common symptoms of clinical depression include:

- a chronically sad or empty mood
- loss of interest in ordinary pleasurable activities, including sex
- decreased energy, fatigue, feeling slowed down, slowed movement, and slurred speech
- sleep disturbances (insomnia, early morning waking, or oversleeping)
- eating disturbances (loss of appetite and significant weight loss or weight gain)
- difficulty concentrating, impaired memory, and difficulty in making decisions
- agitated actions (such as pacing or hand-wringing)
- feelings of guilt, worthlessness, or helplessness
- feelings of hopelessness and despair
- thoughts and/or talk of death and suicide
- irritability or excessive crying
- social withdrawal or isolation
- chronic aches and pains that don't respond to treatment
- suicide attempts
- an increase in addictive behavior

In the workplace, depression can be recognized by the following symptoms:

- morale problems or a lack of cooperation
- difficulty concentrating
- safety problems, accidents, and listlessness
- absenteeism
- frequent complaints of being tired all the time
- complaints of unexplained aches and pains
- alcohol or drug abuse
- blaming others
- increased complaints about a spouse or significant others

For those who are at home, these symptoms may appear as:

- a lack of interest in daily self-care routines
- less attention paid to children (dependents)
- not wanting to go out of the house
- not finding any meaning in one's day
- increased addictive behavior kept secret
- feeling overwhelmed by ordinary tasks
- feelings of guilt and worthlessness

In order to best apply this cluster of symptoms to your own situation, think of your symptoms in terms of three words: *number, duration,* and *intensity.*

1. **Number.** The symptoms of depression are additive—that is, the greater the number of symptoms you have, the more likely you are to be clinically depressed. According to the *Diagnostic and Statistical Manual of Mental Disorders (DSM-V)*, five or more of these symptoms should be present for a person to be considered clinically depressed.

2. **Duration.** The longer you have been down in the dumps, the more likely it is that you are clinically depressed. According to the DSM IV, the five or more symptoms must exist for at least *two weeks* for a diagnosis of major depression to be made. (In the case of dysthymia, or chronic low-grade depression, symptoms must be present for *two years* or more.)

3. **Intensity.** Many of us can feel emotional pain and still cope with our daily existence. Some experiences of depression are within the normal course of living. The pain of major depression can be so great, however, that its intensity (along with the number and duration of symptoms) can significantly impair one's ability to cope.

Getting proper help for depression begins with a proper diagnosis. Of the seventeen million people in America who suffer from depressive illnesses, over two-thirds (about twelve million) receive no treatment whatsoever. The minority who do seek help typically consult a number of doctors over many years before being properly diagnosed. The questionnaire on page 118 may help you to determine whether you (or a loved one) suffer from depression.

Diagnostic Criteria for a Major Depressive Episode

A depressive illness is a whole body illness, involving one's body, mood, thoughts, and behavior. It affects the way you eat and sleep, the way you feel about yourself, and think about things. It is not a passing blue mood or a sign of personal weakness.

Depressive illnesses come in different forms, the most serious of which is major depression. The following criteria for major depression are taken from the *Diagnostic and Statistical Manual of Mental Disorders (DSM-IV)*. If you or someone you know fits these criteria, seek professional help.

A. Five or more of these symptoms should be present during the same two-week period and represent a change from previous functioning.

1. Depressed mood most of the day
2. Markedly diminished interest in pleasure
3. Significant change in appetite, leading to weight loss or weight gain
4. Insomnia or hypersomnia (too much sleep) nearly every day
5. Psychomotor agitation or retardation nearly every day
6. Fatigue or loss of energy nearly every day
7. Feelings of worthlessness or excessive or inappropriate guilt
8. Diminished ability to think or concentrate, or indecisiveness
9. Recurrent thoughts of death, recurrent suicidal thoughts without a specific plan, suicide attempts, or specific plans for committing suicide

B. In addition, these symptoms cause clinically significant distress or impairment in social, occupational, or other important areas of functioning.

Self-Rating Scale for Depression

Have either of the following symptoms been present nearly every day *for at least two weeks?*

  A. Have you been sad, blue, or down in the dumps?

  B. Have you lost interest or pleasure in all or almost all the things you usually do (work, hobbies, interpersonal relationships)?

If either A or B is true, continue. If not, you probably do not have a depressive illness. Now continue by answering the following statements:

Have any of the following symptoms been present nearly every day *for at least two weeks?*

  1. Do you have a poor appetite or are you overeating?   No   Yes

  2. Do you have insomnia—trouble falling asleep or nighttime awakenings?   No   Yes

  3. Are you oversleeping (going to bed a lot earlier than usual, staying in bed later than usual, taking long naps)?   No   Yes

  4. Do you have low energy, chronic fatigue, or do you feel slowed down?   No   Yes

  5. Are you less active or talkative than usual?   No   Yes

  6. Do you feel restless or agitated?   No   Yes

  7. Do you avoid the company of other people more than you used to?   No   Yes

  8. Have you lost interest or enjoyment in pleasurable activities, including sex?   No   Yes

  9. Do you fail to experience pleasure when positive things occur, such as being praised or being given presents?   No   Yes

  10. Do you have feelings of inadequacy or decreased feelings of self-esteem, or are you overly or increasingly self-critical?   No   Yes

11. Are you less efficient or do you
accomplish less at school, work, or home?   No   Yes

12. Do you feel less able to cope with the
routine responsibilities of daily life?   No   Yes

13. Do you find that your concentration
is poor and that you have difficulty
making decisions (even trivial ones)?   No   Yes

14. Do you think and/or talk of death and suicide?   No   Yes

15. Have you at any time in the past been
acting unusually happy for more than two weeks?   No   Yes

If A or B is true and if you answered yes to five or more of the above questions, you may have a major depressive illness. If you answered yes to number 15, you may consider whether major depression is but one phase of a bipolar disorder.*

For the diagnosis to be complete, however, you should have a complete physical exam and blood workup to rule out other medical problems such as anemia, reactive hypoglycemia, and low thyroid, all of which cause symptoms that may mimic those of major depression. Specifically, you will want a test of the thyroid function called the TSH (thyroid stimulating hormone) stimulation test as well as the TRH (thyrotropin releasing hormone) stimulation test. (The TRH test is complicated to perform and is thus rarely ordered by doctors; however, it can pick up on thyroid disorders that the TSH test cannot.)

What Are the Different Types of Depression?

We began this chapter by stating that getting proper help for depression begins with a proper diagnosis. This is easier said than done, since depression, like the mythological Hydra, is a many-headed beast. There are many types of depressive disorders, each of which contains a multitude of symptom patterns and representations. Here

---

* Adapted from Donald Klein and Paul Wender, *Understanding Depression* (New York: Oxford University Press, 1993), 13–15.

is a list of the most common depressive disorders as listed in the
Diagnostic and Statistical Manual of Mental Disorders (DSM-IV):

- major depression (also called clinical depression)
- manic depression (bipolar disorder)
- dysthymia (low-grade chronic depression)
- cyclothymia (mild manic-depressive cycles)
- postpartum depression
- seasonal affective disorder (SAD)
- existential depression
- mood disorders due to a medical condition
- medication-induced depression
- substance-induced mood disorder

This chapter discusses the most common depressive disorder, clinical
depression. The remaining depressive disorders are described in detail
in Appendix A.

What Occurs in the Brain of a Depressed or Anxious Person?

Just as coronary heart disease is a disorder of the circulatory system and
diabetes is a disorder of the pancreas, depression and anxiety are disorders of the brain. When people become severely depressed or anxious,
the brain literally becomes sick, although no one knows precisely how.
This is because the brain is both *inaccessible* (it is surrounded and protected by our thick skulls) and incredibly *complex*—possibly the most
complex structure in the known universe. At birth, an infant's brain
contains one hundred billion nerve cells, called neurons—a quantity
that rivals the number of stars in the Milky Way. But when we marvel at
this complexity, we are not just talking about the sheer numbers of cells.
Rather, it is what these cells do. Unlike other cells in the body—a muscle cell, fat cell, or liver cell, for example—the neurons of the brain and
nervous system carry on complex conversations with one another. Each
one of these billion neurons carries on thousands of conversations with
its neighbors. Consider the challenge of being on the phone and talking
with one thousand or ten thousand people simultaneously and trying to

Images of Depression

Depression is a unique malady that is extremely difficult to put into words. Perhaps the best way to convey the *actual experience* of depression is through image and metaphor. Here is a sample of apt descriptions taken from those who have been there:

- the black dog (Winston Churchill)
- the hypo (Abraham Lincoln)
- The Beast (reporter Tracy Thompson)
- a mental straight jacket (writer Philip Roth)
- suffocating to death in a fiercely overheated room (author William Styron)
- darkness visible (poet John Milton)
- a funeral in my brain (Emily Dickinson)
- a season in hell
- the underworld
- a black hole
- sinking in quicksand
- being submerged underwater—everything seems distorted and far away
- being trapped at the bottom of a well without any rungs that one can use to climb out
- being trapped in a tunnel with both entryways sealed off and a sign reading No Exit
- sitting helplessly on a melting ice flow
- being immersed in a dense, black fog that settles in for an eternity
- falling into a bottomless abyss
- being locked in a cold, dark dungeon
- being forced to wear a five hundred-pound jacket, twenty-four hours a day
- having your finger caught in a slammed car door
- an emotional toothache

Anatomy of a Neuron

The diagram below depicts the four parts of a nerve cell: the cell body, the axon, the dendrites, and the synapse—the space between one nerve cell and the next.

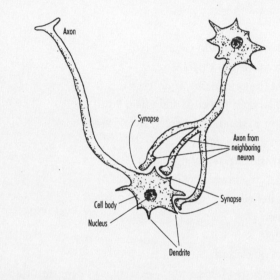

keep all the conversations straight. In depression, these conversations get disrupted, with catastrophic consequences.

Two areas of the brain are believed to be affected in clinical depression. The first area is the space between the cells, known as the *synapse*. In these spaces we find chemical messengers known as *neurotransmitters*, which allow the nerve impulses to be fired from one cell to another. There are two neurotransmitters that have been specifically linked to mood disorders—*serotonin* and *norepinephrine*. Originally, it was thought that too few of these messengers existed in the synapses between the nerve cells, and that antidepressants restored the right amount by preventing them from being reabsorbed into the brain cells. Recently, this theory has been discarded as being too simplistic, and attention has been turned to other theories of what is going awry.

The Limbic Brain*

The hypothalamus and amygdala are two parts of the emotional brain that have been implicated in depressive and anxiety disorders.

The cortex of the new mammalian brain

The Cingulate Gyrus of the Limbic Lobe

The Frontal Lobe (where emotional memories are stored)

The Hypothalamus (the housekeeping functions)

Olfactory Bulb (involved in smell)

The Limbic Lobe

The Thalamus (the brain's telephone exchange

The Hippocampus (the memory transducer)

Amygdala (the emotional sentinel)

The Spinal Cord

The Temporal Lobe (in which the amygdala is found)

* From *A Mood Apart* by Peter Whybrow copyright © 1997 by Peter Whybrow. Reprinted by permission of Basic Books, a member of Perseus Books, L.L.C.

The second aspect of the brain that is affected by mood disorders is the *limbic system,* also known as the emotional brain. The limbic system is the mediator of human feelings. It receives and regulates emotion, governs sexual desire, and, through a walnut-sized gland called the *hypothalamus,* oversees the smooth running of the physical body's housekeeping functions: thirst, appetite, sleep, pleasure, sexual desire, and aggression. These, of course, are the precise activities that get thrown out of whack in depression.

Finally, the *amygdala,* an almond-like structure in the limbic system, has been implicated in anxiety disorders. The amygdala controls the brain's fear reaction. For example, if I were walking down the street and spotted a bear, the amygdala would send signals to my brain to begin the fight or flight response that would increase breathing, heart rate, blood pressure, and so on. Panic attacks and phobias are disorders of this fear system that occur when the amygdala gets activated, even when there is no apparent threat.

Healthy Sadness versus Depression

Many people confuse depression with sadness. While intense sadness may be a component of depression, depression is a whole body disorder that contains many other dimensions of imbalance and dysfunction. The chart below contrasts these two states.

Characteristics of Healthy Sadness

- You are sad, but don't feel a loss of self-esteem.
- Your negative feelings are an appropriate reaction to upsetting events.
- Your feelings go away after a period of time.
- Although you feel sad, you do not feel discouraged about the future.
- You continue to be productively involved with life.
- Your negative thoughts are realistic.

Characteristics of Depression

- You feel a loss of self-esteem.
- Your negative feelings are out of proportion to the event that triggered the bad mood.
- Your feelings continue and do not let up.
- You feel demoralized and are convinced that things will never get better.
- You give up on life and lose interest in your friends and your career.
- Your negative thoughts are exaggerated and distorted, even though they seem valid.

What Are the Causes of Depression?

For many decades, a bitter argument has been raging in the psychiatric community between those who believe that the causes of depression are genetic and biological illness and those who believe that they are psychological and social. Fortunately, an increasing number of clinicians are subscribing to the "fertile ground" theory, which says that depression is a genetic disorder of the mind, body, and spirit that occurs when *predisposing factors* combine with *environmental stressors*.

In other words, for clinical depression to occur, two factors are usually present:

1. A biochemical or physical predisposition (which provides the fertile ground).

2. A triggering stressor, which brings on the actual episode. (There are times, however, when an episode can mysteriously begin out of the blue.)

Predisposing Factors

A predisposition to clinical depression can be caused by a variety of genetic, biochemical, and environmental factors:

- **Family history.** Depression, like heart disease, runs in families. If one parent has suffered from depression, there is a 25 percent chance that a child will develop the illness; if both parents are depressed, the risk rises to 75 percent.
- **Biological imbalances.** These include imbalances in the brain's neurotransmitters as well as hormonal imbalances (such as low thyroid function).
- **Early childhood trauma.** These include abandonment, abuse, neglect, birth trauma, death of a parent, and divorce. Such trauma permanently alters the nervous system as seen by the fact that the best predictor of depression in adulthood is the death of a child's parent before the age of eleven.
- **Our basic temperament.** Harvard psychologist Jerome Kagan's work with infants clearly demonstrates that we are born with a "temperamental bias." In his research with infants, Kagan has identified two types of children:

1. The **inhibited, high-reactive child:** This child is shy, reserved, anxious, cries easily, and tends to withdraw in novel social situations. He or she may become quiet, hold a parent's hand, or retreat altogether.

2. The **uninhibited, low-reactive child:** This child is outgoing, open with strangers, and at ease in new social situations. Rather than cling to the mother or hide, he or she will openly explore the novel environment. This child is described as spontaneous, playful, and quick to laugh or smile.

Kagan believes that these babies were simply born with different brain chemistry. When I first encountered Kagan's work, I was astounded to see how the high-reactive temperament so accurately portrayed my personality as an infant and young child. It also removed some of my guilt and shame by making me realize that I did not create my basic temperament; it was not my fault that I was born with a predisposition to depression.

Neuroscientist Richard Davidson has confirmed Kagan's research by demonstrating in his laboratory that the low-reactive children have pronounced activation in a region of the brain called the left prefrontal cortex and less activity in the amygdala (the brain's fear mechanism). Conversely, Davidson has found that depressed, unhappy people have more activity in the right prefrontal cortex of their brains (not the left), and have especially overactive amygdalas.

Environmental Triggers

In addition to the genetic and biochemical causes, depression may have environmental causes. Environmental factors include:

- **Loss and separation.** Death of a loved one, divorce, marital separation, or any interpersonal conflict are major triggers for depression.
- **Financial stresses.** Loss of a job or being in debt can cause depression.
- **Physical illnesses.** Any chronic illness, such as heart disease, cancer, AIDS, multiple sclerosis, or Parkinson's, can trigger symptoms of depression.
- **Infections.** For example, streptococcal bacteria—those that cause strep throat—also attack the basal ganglia in the brain, and have

been implicated in obsessive-compulsive disorder, anorexia nervosa, and Tourette's syndrome. Other pathogens, such as T Pallidum (the syphilis-causing bacteria) and the human immunodeficiency virus, have been known to cause anxiety, delirium, psychoses, and suicidal impulses.

- **Adverse reactions to prescription drugs.** There are a number of common prescription drugs whose side effects can cause depression. See Appendix A for details.
- **Social isolation.** Many studies identify isolation as a contributing risk factor for depression. For example, a British study showed that single parents were more likely to become depressed than married ones.
- **Environmental toxins.** For example, certain noxious chemicals in new carpets or furniture trigger feelings of depression and anxiety in sensitive individuals.
- **Moving or changing employment.** Moving can be very disruptive to the psyche and trigger feelings of loss from the past.
- **Substance abuse.** Drug and alcohol use can clearly elicit the symptoms of depression.

Biology Is Not Destiny

The fertile ground theory tells us that, although environmental factors play an important role in mood disorders, people do not suffer from serious episodes of depression and anxiety without a biochemical predisposition. Does this mean that we are doomed by our genes and temperament? Not necessarily, says Jerome Kagan:

> For example, if a high-reactive infant is raised in a good environment by great parents, is good in school, and has lots of friends, then this child will not end up unhappy, but relatively happy. It's just that he's got to fight the bias. Remember, if you're born with a gene that says you're going to be 6 foot 9, then you're biased to be a great basketball player. But there are some short men who are great basketball players. They overcame their bias. And that's true for everything in life.*

---

* From the cassette, *Gray Matters: Emotions and the Brain* by The Dana Alliance for Brain Initiatives, 800-65-BRAIN.

Other neuroscientists concur with Kagan. Joseph Ledoux, the scientist at New York University who has done pioneering work on anxiety and the brain, says, "The brain has plasticity, the ability to *rewire itself* in response to environmental stimuli and any kind of learning." Scientists now know that neurons in many parts of the brain continue to undergo structural change not just through childhood and adolescence *but all through life*. These scientific discoveries are life changing, for they tell us that we are no longer helpless victims of our genes and/or biochemical makeup. No matter how many episodes of depression and anxiety you have suffered (or are suffering), your brain and nervous system can be rewired and reprogrammed. This is what we will be seeking to accomplish with my better mood recovery program.

Anxiety and Depression Symptoms Inventory

The following questions are designed to help you understand your history and symptoms of depression so you can better treat them. You can answer in the spaces provided or on a separate piece of paper. You may also wish to purchase a journal in which to record your answers to this and the other questionnaires that will appear in this book.

1. Is there a history of either depression or anxiety in your family? Name any relatives who suffered from these disorders.

2. Researchers at Harvard have identified the "inhibited, high-reactive child" who is more likely to be shy, reserved, fearful, and pessimistic. How closely did your childhood temperament match this description?

3. Can you identify any early childhood stress or trauma (e.g., loss, abandonment, abuse, or neglect) that increased your likelihood of becoming depressed or anxious as an adult?

4. Write down what you consider the most prominent symptoms that you experience during times of depression or anxiety (refer to the symptoms list in chapter 9).

1.

2.

3.

4.

(continued on next page)

5. Once a person is vulnerable to depression, it usually takes an external trigger or stressor to elicit symptoms. What events, thoughts, or feelings in the past (or in the present) have triggered your feelings of anxiety or depression?

6. Depression is episodic and cyclic. If you have had a previous episode of depression, what were the events and circumstances that helped bring you out of it?

7. If you are currently in the middle of an episode of depression, how does knowing that you have emerged from a previous episode help to reassure you that "This, too shall pass?"

CHAPTER TEN

Introducing the 12-Week Better Mood Recovery Program

To optimize the function of the healing system, you must do everything in your power to improve physical health, mental and emotional health, and spiritual health. . . . One must see the whole picture of health, and under-stand the importance of working on all fronts.

—ANDREW WEIL, *Eight Weeks to Optimal Health*

A wise physician once told me the following proverb: "If you lose your possessions, you've lost a lot. If you lose your health, you've lost a great deal more. But if you lose your peace of mind, you've lost everything!"

Depression and anxiety rob us of this most precious gift—our emotional serenity. Over the next twelve weeks, we are going to recover this lost gem, a treasure more valuable than all the riches of the world.

The way back to mental health lies through what I call the "better mood recovery program." Drawing upon my professional expertise as a counselor as well as my personal experience in recovering from depression, I designed the better mood recovery program as a com-bination of self-care activities and coping strategies whose purpose is to rewire the brain and to balance its biochemistry. This structure has been thoroughly tested—by myself during my four years of recovery, as well as by hundreds of people in my workshops and depression support groups.

Please consider using the better mood recovery program if you find yourself in any of the following situations:

- You are currently experiencing an episode of *clinical depression* or *manic depression* (bipolar disorder).
- You are currently experiencing episodes of *anxiety* or *panic* that often accompany clinical depression.
- You are suffering from *dysthymia* (low-grade chronic depression) or *cyclothymia* (a less severe form of manic depression) and desire to elevate or to stabilize your mood. (See Appendix A to learn how to identify these conditions.) While dysthymia and cyclothymia do not disable, they take the zest out of life and keep you from functioning at an optimal level.
- You have already experienced one or more episodes of depression or anxiety and wish to *live optimally* and *prevent a relapse*.
- You wish to *cope better* with everyday stress, remain calm in times of turmoil, or create a better mood more often in your life.

How to Use the Program

As the name implies, the better mood recovery program is designed to improve your overall mood and bring you closer to emotional serenity. I define "mood" as a consistent extension of emotion in time. While emotions can change in seconds or minutes, our mood is our emotional set point that remains fairly neutral and stable unless it is disrupted by a mood disorder such as depression or anxiety.

This program will not remove all of your symptoms or effect a total "cure." Recovery from depression and anxiety is an ongoing process, not a one-time event. What you will gain from the program is a set of tools that you can use to significantly improve your state of mind and help you to stay well so you don't have to experience future depressive episodes.

Before you begin the program, I would first like you to ask your-self the question, "How am I doing right now? How distressing are my symptoms?" With regard to the hellish realms of depression and anxiety, you probably fall into one of two categories:

1. You are "in hell" trying to get out.
2. You are "out of hell" trying to stay out.

If you fall into category number 2 and you are in between depressive episodes or you suffer from a mild form of depression or anxiety, you should be able to read through each weekly lesson, complete the assignments, and meet with your recovery partner to report your progress and get support. This also applies if you are using this program to cope with stress or improve your overall mood.

If, however, you fall into category number 1 and are in extreme psychological and/or physical pain, completing the program will be more difficult. You may have difficulty concentrating or reading, or you may lack the energy or motivation to pursue even the simplest of tasks. If this is the case, my advice is simple—DO THE BEST YOU CAN. (Meanwhile, make sure you are getting good medical or psychiatric treatment.) Even if you can only read a paragraph or a page at a sitting, I encourage you to do so. I know that you will find something of value in these pages. Another idea is to have a friend or family member read the weekly chapters to you or at least summarize them.

In addition, let me suggest the following coping strategies to you:

- **Set the intention to heal.** Make the decision that you want to get well, even if you don't know how or don't believe that it is possible.
- **Reach out for support**—to other people and to spirit. Seek the help and support of friends, family, and others. Make sure that you are receiving proper *medical treatment,* both from a psychiatrist or prescriber (for medication) and from a therapist. Place your name on one of the twenty-four hour telephone prayer lines (see Appendix C). The thirty-day *prayer support* you receive will make a big difference
- **Locate a day treatment program** in your area (also known as day hospital or partial hospitalization) and attend it. Call your local hospital or mental health clinic for a referral. The daily structure and support can be lifesaving.

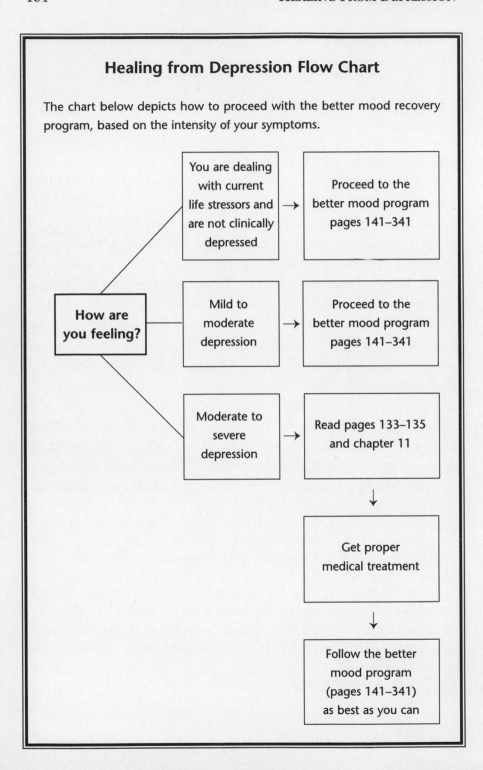

Healing from Depression Flow Chart

The chart below depicts how to proceed with the better mood recovery program, based on the intensity of your symptoms.

How are you feeling?

You are dealing with current life stressors and are not clinically depressed → Proceed to the better mood program pages 141–341

Mild to moderate depression → Proceed to the better mood program pages 141–341

Moderate to severe depression → Read pages 133–135 and chapter 11

↓

Get proper medical treatment

↓

Follow the better mood program (pages 141–341) as best as you can

- Consider **hospitalization** if you feel totally overwhelmed or are not feeling safe (see chapter 11).
- If your pain feels unbearable, break it down into **manageable bits** by asking, "What can I do to get through each day?" Live one day at a time, one hour at a time, one breath at a time.
- **Ask spirit** (or your higher power) to help you manage the pain until it repatterns. Read (or reread) chapters 4 and 5 of my personal story to see how I coped with extreme emotional pain.
- Locate the phone number of your local **mental health crisis line,** and call it as often as you need to. You may also call the National Hope Line toll free at 800-784-2433.
- Have someone repeat to you again and again, *This, too, shall pass.* Know that the vast majority of people who have experienced this kind of pain have come out the other side.
- Take heart in the fact that you are reading these lines **written by a survivor.** Use my story in the first half of this book to provide the hope that survival is possible.
- **If you are feeling suicidal, reach out for support.** Talk to others. Call 800-784-2433 for immediate counseling.
- **Turn to chapter 11,** where you will learn about five interventions for dealing with acute symptoms of depression and anxiety.

If you follow the above suggestions while hanging on and reaching out for support, you will be delivered from your dark night of the soul. As your pain diminishes and you begin to feel more stable, you will gain the motivation and focus to work through this program and reap its benefits.

Program Structure

I have tried to make the better mood recovery program as user friendly as possible, having broken the information into small, bite-sized steps so you can easily digest and integrate it over time. Although I am presenting my plan as a twelve-week program, it also can be viewed as a series of steps that you can implement over *any time frame.* You don't need to rush yourself and feel that you *must* complete the program in exactly twelve weeks. Recovery is not a race. While some folks do best with a highly structured time-limited approach, others heal better when they follow their own pace.

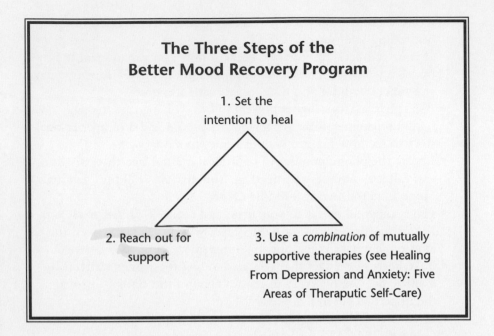

**The Three Steps of the
Better Mood Recovery Program**

1. Set the
intention to heal

2. Reach out for
support

3. Use a *combination* of mutually
supportive therapies (see Healing
From Depression and Anxiety: Five
Areas of Theraputic Self-Care)

So, if it takes you four to six months to integrate these self-care principles into your life, that is fine. Please don't pressure yourself or make yourself feel guilty if you haven't completed the chapters in the specified amount of time. What is most important is that you make these wellness habits a part of your daily life.

In addition, you can pursue the twelve-part program in *any order* that feels right to you. For the ease of using this book, it makes most sense to work through the material in the sequence that I have presented it. (This is especially crucial for Weeks 1 and 2.) If, however, a certain topic calls out to you, skip ahead and preview that week.

Program Overview

The better mood recovery program consists of these three life-changing steps.

Step 1: Set the intention to heal. Make the decision that you want to get well, even if you don't know how. Setting the intention to heal is the starting point of all recovery. You will learn about this principle in Week 1 of the program.

Healing from Depression and Anxiety:
Five Areas of Therapeutic Self-Care*

The goal: To experience a better mood, free from depression and anxiety.

Physical self-care
Exercise
Nutrition
Water intake
Hydrotherapy
Natural light
Sleep
Medication
Supplements
Herbs
Acupuncture
Breathing
Yoga
Touch

Spiritual connection
Prayer
Meditation
Spiritual community
Inspirational texts
Forgiveness
The 12 Steps of AA
Finding purpose
     and meaning

Activities that support my vision of wellness

Lifestyle habits
Structure/routine
Time in nature
Fulfilling work
Setting goals
Relaxation
Pleasurable activities
Humor
Music therapy
Creative self-expression
Time for beauty
Stress reduction
Time management

Mental and emotional self-care
Restructuring cognitive
     processes
Practicing daily affirmations
Releasing negative beliefs
Taming the inner critic
Charting your moods
Feeling your feelings
Thinking like an optimist
Keeping a gratitude journal
Overcoming the stigma
     of depression
Self-forgiveness
Psychotherapy
Healing family of origin issues
Working through grief

Social support
Family
Friends
Psychiatrist/therapist
Minister/rabbi
Support group
Day treatment
Volunteer work
Pets and animals

---

* This program is meant to support, not replace, any medical treatment you may be receiving.

Step 2: Reach out for support. Love and connection are an essential part of the healing process. In Week 2 of the program, you will take your first steps toward building a personal support team that will guide you to recovery.

Step 3: Treat your symptoms using a combination of mutually supportive therapies. An example of this integrative approach can be seen in the way we treat heart disease. If you went to a cardiologist and wanted to know how to prevent a heart attack (or to recover from one), he or she might prescribe a cholesterol-lowering medication and tell you to eat a low-fat diet, exercise three to four times a week, and cut down on the stress in your life.

In a similar manner, depression can also be treated holistically, i.e., on a variety of levels. In working to achieve my own emotional balance, I have identified five such levels: physical self-care, mental and emotional self-care, social support, spiritual connection, and lifestyle habits. (A visual overview of these areas is depicted by the diagram, Healing from Depression and Anxiety: Five Areas of Therapeutic Self-Care, page 137.) These holistic therapies will be covered in Weeks 3 to 12 of the better mood recovery program.

Healing from depression can be likened to assembling a jigsaw puzzle. For the puzzle (and ourselves) to be whole and complete, all of the pieces must be in their proper place, as shown in the diagram below.

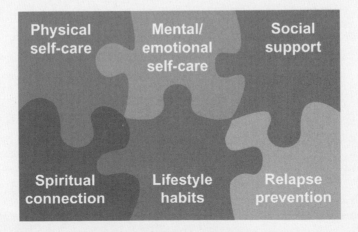

Physical self-care   Mental/emotional self-care   Social support

Spiritual connection   Lifestyle habits   Relapse prevention

Taking the First Step: Self-Assessment

Before you proceed to Week 1 of the twelve-week better mood recovery program, I would like you take the initial step of assessing where you are now in your treatment. Take a moment and look over the diagram of holistic self-care strategies on the page 137. As you read through the activities listed under each of the five headings—physical self-care, mental and emotional self-care, social support, spiritual connection, and lifestyle habits—I would like you to think about which strategies you are already practicing in your life. Perhaps you have a satisfactory exercise routine or a good therapist. Maybe you are already meditating once a day, getting out in nature, or are engaged in volunteer work. List those strategies that you are already using under the appropriate category in the diagram on page 140; e.g., meditation under spiritual connection, time in nature under lifestyle habits, volunteer work under social support. Whatever you are doing that is working for you now—whatever is helping you to feel stable and well—write it down under the appropriate heading. When you are finished, you will have a portrait of the *current state* of your recovery program.

Next, I would like you to look over the therapeutic self-care diagram (Healing from Depression and Anxiety: Five Areas of Therapeutic Self-Care, page 137) and determine which of those activities *you would like to add* to what you are already doing. Then, list them *in a different colored pen or pencil*. As you work with the better mood recovery program, you will be adding these tools and strategies to your daily routine. At the end of the program, you will have the opportunity to reevaluate where you are and note the progress you have made.

A significant advantage of this kind of active participation is that it puts you in charge of your healing. You are about to become your own personal trainer, your own coach, your own guide and healer. My experience has shown this level of involvement to be a powerful antidote to the feelings of powerless that so often accompany the experience of depression. Or, as one group member put it, "Good things happen when you take the throttle."

Now, let's begin the better mood recovery program.

Healing from Depression and Anxiety:
My Five Areas of Therapeutic Self-Care

The goal: To experience a better mood, free from depression and anxiety.

In the space below, write down those self-care activities that are now a part of your daily life. As you learn the better mood recovery program, you will be adding new tools and activities to the list.

Physical self-care

Spiritual connection

Activities that
support
my vision
of wellness

Lifestyle habits

Social support

**Mental and emotional
self-care**

Setting the Intention to Heal

It's not who you are, or what your parents decided for you, or what you were fated to be that counts. What counts is knowing who you want to be and asking for it.

—BRUCE WILKINSON, *The Prayer of Jabez*

FIRST WEEK OVERVIEW

In this week, you will set the intention to heal by creating a vision of wellness.

The Taoist philosopher Lao-tzu once said, "The journey of a thousand miles must begin with a single step." Today, you are setting out on a journey of healing from anxiety and depression. What is your first step as you begin this quest? It is simply to state your intention to get well.

This may seem like a simple act, but it has profound ramifications for your future health and well being. It doesn't matter how long you have suffered from anxiety or depression. Perhaps, like myself, you have been struggling since childhood, or maybe your first episode began six months or six weeks ago. Regardless of the time involved, the first step is the same—making the decision to heal.

For some readers, this may be asking a lot, since depression robs us of energy, motivation, and hope. Fortunately, at this point, I am

141

not asking you to *do* anything, only to make a *decision*. You don't
have to know *how* your healing will take place. You don't have to
believe that it is possible. If you are feeling particularly hopeless or
discouraged right now, ask yourself this question: "Is there a part of
me, even if it is ten percent or one percent, that wants to feel better?"
If you can find just a molecule within you that says, "I WANT TO
LIVE," your healing journey will have begun.

By setting the intention to heal, you will stimulate and support
your body's healing system—its innate capacity to control disease
and bring itself back into balance. Physician Andrew Weil describes
this phenomenon in the book *Spontaneous Healing*. Weil writes:

> The body can heal itself. It can do so because it has a healing
> system. At every level of biological organization, from DNA up,
> mechanisms of self-diagnosis, self-repair, and regeneration exist
> in us. Medicine that takes advantage of this innate healing is
> more effective than medicine that simply suppresses symptoms.

Although we call depression a mental illness, the disorder manifests
with debilitating physical symptoms. And as anyone who has survived an episode of depression knows, the brain and body can heal
themselves if they are given the right support. Saying, "I want to feel
better," is the first step in changing your brain chemistry.

Intention is not like wishful thinking, which is abstract, vague,
and passive. Like an arrow flying toward a target, intention is clear,
specific, and has the power of commitment behind it. It is this one-
pointed commitment that activates a benevolent aspect of the universe that will support you in realizing your desire to be well. Perhaps
this is why W. H. Murray, in *The Scottish Expedition*, writes:

> Until one is committed, there is hesitancy, the chance to draw
> back, always ineffectiveness. Concerning all acts of initiative
> (and creation), there is one elementary truth, the ignorance of
> which kills countless ideas and splendid plans: that the moment
> one definitely commits oneself, then Providence moves too.
> All sorts of things occur to help one that would never other-
> wise have occurred. A whole stream of events issues from the

decision, raising in one's favor all manner of unforeseen events and meetings and material assistance, which no one could have dreamt would come their way.

I have learned a deep respect for one of Goethe's couplets: "Whatever you can do, or dream you can, begin it. Boldness has genius, power, and magic in it." Begin it now.

Clearly, not all of our wishes are granted. Many people diagnosed with terminal cancer die though they possess a strong will to live. Depression, however, does not have to be terminal. If you set the intention to heal and receive the right type of support, recovery is possible.

Once again, I wish to emphasize that I am not asking you to do anything, only to get in touch with your desire to be well. If you don't believe that healing is attainable, be open to the possibility. Be willing to be healed.

For example, during my most recent episode of major depression, I thought that my chances of surviving were close to zero. But just as Dorothy in *The Wizard of Oz* never lost sight of her desire to return to Kansas, I continued to say to the universe, "Heal me from my affliction. Please release me from this pain." Eventually, the higher powers responded to my request and delivered me from the abyss.

Healing Tool #1: Your Vision of Wellness

Lord, we know what we are, but know not
What we may be.
—WILLIAM SHAKESPEARE, *Hamlet*

There are two basic tools that you will be using to translate your intention to heal into a reality. The first and most important is a vision statement. Essentially, your vision statement will answer the question, *"What would my life look and feel like if I were free from the symptoms of anxiety and depression?"*

A vision statement is based on the second habit from Steven Covey's *The Seven Habits of Highly Effective People:* Begin with the end in mind. According to Covey, this habit arises from the principle that "all things are created twice," first in our mind and then in the world of form. In writing a vision statement, you create an exact mental blueprint or picture of health that you are seeking to bring into your life.

Vision statements have been used for years in the business community. Most organizations have some form of mission statement that defines their purpose and influences the way they carry our their daily activities. Olympic athletes also engage in creative visioning through the practice of visual rehearsal. For example, a gymnast will play over his entire routine in his imagination before he sets foot on a mat. In so doing, he is programming his nervous system to direct his body to perform optimally.

In a similar fashion, you can communicate a vision of health and healing to your brain and nervous system. The following exercise will show you how.

Composing a Vision Statement

Imagine for a moment that you are in a state of health and wholeness. Imagine that your mental and emotional health are functioning at optimal levels. What would it be like for you to be in a better mood?

How would your body look and feel? How much energy would you have available to you?

How would you be feeling most of the time? What types of thoughts would you be thinking?

What types of relationships would you have? What kind of work would you be involved in? What would your spiritual life be like?

Drawing on the answers to the above questions, on a separate page, write a paragraph (or more) describing your vision of mental and emotional health.

See if you can use all five senses—sight, hearing, touch, smell, and taste—to depict your experience. Set it down in the present tense, as if the experience were happening now.

Barbara's Vision of Health and Wellness

This vision statement was written by Barbara, a professional author and a member of my depression support group.

I am a woman of strength and resilience. I accept the ebb and flow of life with humor and openness, knowing I am always safe. I take love with me wherever I go. I gratefully receive the love and support of my friends and make my strength, love, and support available to them in appropriate ways.

I can say "no" when I feel overextended and continue to love and accept myself and to be loved and accepted by others. If someone is unused to my saying "no" and becomes upset, I can simply bless them, remembering that they, too, are only human. I continue to love and respect myself.

My body is strong and capable. Every cell hums with vibrant good health. I love to exercise and to feel my body work. I let all body sensations, nervous or otherwise, flow through me as I relax and rest in the comfort and care of a higher power. The true me is always at peace.

I enjoy the world and spend time each day in nature and with people. I am eager to start work each day. The work is challenging and fun! I trust my talent and relax into my work schedule, looking forward just as eagerly to the end of the workday—time to venture out into the world!

I love getting out and about, as comfortable when I'm by myself as I am with others. I love to explore new places and new activities. The world seems like a friendly place, and I am secure and strong within it.

I easily stay in touch with friends and family. Whether or not I have accomplished all I expected to, I remember the lilies of the field and the sparrows—they don't work for God's love and care; it is a free gift.

When I get into bed at night, I fall asleep with a peaceful mind, a grateful heart, and a body that feels comfortable and alive. I sleep well and awaken refreshed and with new confidence and energy to begin another adventure!

As you proceed with this exercise, do your best to write something, even if recovery from depression seems like a distant reality. If you can't imagine yourself being completely well, choose to see yourself feeling a little bit better. One woman simply stated, "I just want to feel my life force again." Remember, I am not asking you to believe in your healing, only to desire it.

If this still seems like too much, ask someone to help you write your vision statement—a friend, family member, your counselor, or your doctor. *You don't have to do this work alone.*

There are many ways to write a vision statement. I have printed three sample vision statements of different length on adjacent pages. Barbara is a professional author, and her statement is the longest. Laura's is short and simple. Michael's is medium length.

As these examples illustrate, there is no specific way to compose a vision statement. Your statement doesn't have to be beautifully written, it just needs to speak to you. Trust your own voice. Let the words come from your heart. There is no need to compare yourself to others.

Also, don't worry about creating a perfect vision statement the first time. Over the next few weeks, you will have numerous opportunities to modify your statement. My own vision statement went through five drafts until it arrived at its current form.

In addition, you might want to include visual imagery, such as a tree, that gives you the feeling of strength and wholeness. Meditating on this image every day will help your subconscious mind to make your vision of wellness a reality.

Another option is to create a collage where you depict images of wellness using cut-out pictures from old magazines. When I attended art therapy at day treatment, creating these collages allowed me to give expression to my feelings and dreams that I could not verbalize. A sample of such a collage appears on page 149.

The important thing is to start someplace, even if it is to wish for a tiny improvement. Remember, the journey of a thousand miles begins with a single step.

Laura's Vision of Health and Wellness

The following vision statement is only two lines, but it perfectly captures the essence of joy and wellness.

I am healed, whole, and complete.
I am fully alive, filled with love, joy, and gratitude.

Michael's Vision of Health and Wellness

Michael, a group member who suffered from anxiety as well as depression, wrote this vision statement to describe his desire to return to his old life.

I am calm and peaceful. My energy is strong and good; I am engaged in life with my family, friends, and coworkers. I am happy and easygoing. I sleep well and peacefully at night. I wake up in the morning looking forward to my day, whether it is new design challenges at work or weekends where nothing is planned.

I look forward to being with and doing things with my friends and family. I travel extensively and I love it. I am a body builder enjoying my great body and my workouts.

I am a good influence on my kids, and they look to me for advice and support that I easily and positively give. I love my life.

Healing Tool #2: Setting Goals

*When attention is not focused on a goal, the mind typically begins to be
filled by disjointed and depressing thoughts. The normal condition of
the mind is chaos. When the mind is involved in a goal-directed activity,
it acquires order and positive moods.*
—MIHALYI CSIKSZENTMIHALYI, *Flow*

Once you create your vision of wellness, the next task is to break that
vision down into smaller bite-sized steps, or goals. In setting goals,
you define what you want, and then formulate a concrete plan by
which you can manifest them. Goal setting will give you the means
to take your vision of wellness and make it a present reality.

Virtually every self-improvement book on the market recommends formulating and setting short and long-term goals. Here is
what Richard Williams, father and coach of tennis prodigies Venus
and Serena Williams, told the *New York Times* after Venus won the
Wimbledon and the U.S. Open:

> It doesn't take money to be successful in tennis or golf. It takes
> determination to do what you're going to do. With that deter-
> mination and a great player and a great deal of hard work, you
> will succeed. I really believe that in order to be successful, you
> must have a plan. It can't be one in your head either, it's got
> to be one that's *written out so your optical nerve can take it to
> your brain.* [Emphasis added.]

Just as the Williams sisters had a game plan for excelling at tennis,
you will be creating a game plan for getting your life back on track.
The constructive and focused aspect of setting goals will calm your
mind as you experience yourself as proactive rather than reactive.
Here are some important characteristics of goals:

- Goals are specific. This usually involves making a change in
  a specific behavior or in the way you feel about things.
- Goals are doable, seeable, and reachable.
- Goals are usually time limited (they must be accomplished by
  a certain date).

A Picture of Wellness

"A picture is worth a thousand words," says a Chinese proverb. The collage below was created by cutting and pasting images from magazines.* It gives a pictorial representation of someone's vision of wellness.

If you are having a difficult time putting your thoughts and feelings into words, you might consider gathering some old magazines and creating your own wellness collage. Or, if you are artistically inclined, you may want to draw or paint your picture of wellness. The book, *Life, Paint, and Passion* by Michelle Cachou, can help you to access important healing images through painting, especially if you have no drawing experience.

- Goals are big enough to matter, but small enough to reach.
- Goals should be committed to in writing. When written down on paper, they become much more tangible and real.

There are two kinds of goals that I would like you to work with for this program. The first is a set of *long-term goals* for this program. To formulate these goals, ask yourself, "Over the next twelve weeks what types of changes would I like to see in my thoughts, feelings, and behaviors?" One simple way to answer this question is to take some of your current symptoms (e.g., poor sleep) and turn them

*From the *2002 Master Mind Goal Achiever's Journal* © 2002. Reprinted with permission from Master Mind Publishers.

into their opposite (sound and restful sleep). A good place to start is to look at the symptoms that you listed for question 4 of the Anxiety and Depression Symptoms Inventory in chapter 9 (page 129). Which ones would you like to see healed? I have provided a better mood recovery program goal sheet where you can write down these goals.

Another way to formulate long-term goals for this program is to read over your vision statement and observe what thoughts, feelings, and behaviors were contained in your picture of optimal health. You may write these goals down in the sheet on the opposite page or in your personal journal.

The second type of goals that you will be working with are your *weekly goals*. Each week you will decide on one or more simple steps that you can take that will bring you closer to your vision of wellness. You can write your weekly goals on your weekly goal sheet located at the end of each week's lesson. Filling out your weekly goal sheet will become an integral aspect of your recovery program over the next twelve weeks.

Putting It All Together

The tools that I have provided—the vision statement, the better mood goal sheet, and the weekly goal sheets—are designed to take your heartfelt desire for healing and translate it into daily self-care activities that will positively change your brain chemistry and elevate your mood.

An example of how this process works can be seen in the life of Barbara, whose vision statement appeared earlier in this chapter. In the third paragraph of her vision statement, Barbara states, "My body is strong and capable. . . . I love to exercise and to feel my body work." Barbara took this statement and made it her first goal on her better mood goal sheet:

Goal #1: To incorporate exercise into my daily routine.
Barbara then wrote down the series of steps that it would take to make her goal a reality.

My Goals for the Better Mood Recovery Program

In the space below, list at least three goals that reflect the changes you would like to see over the next twelve weeks.

One simple way to create a goal is to take a current symptom (e.g., poor sleep) and turn it into its opposite (sound and restful sleep). Thus the problem of low self-esteem would become the goal of healthy self-esteem, the problem of difficulty making decisions would become the goal of improvement in decision-making and so on.

To locate symptoms you wish to heal, you can refer to the symptoms you listed on question 4 of the Anxiety and Depression Symptoms Inventory in chapter 9. Now proceed to write your goals.

Goals

Write down things you would like to change about:

1. Your thinking

2. Your feelings

3. Your physical well-being

4. Your behaviors

List any further goals below.

Initial steps:

1. Call the local gym to research their rates.

2. Call the local pool and find out lap swim hours.

3. Talk to fitness instructors about the merits of treadmills versus swimming.

Later steps:

4. Work out at the gym at 9 A.M. on Monday, Wednesday, and Friday.

5. Swim at the pool on Tuesday and Thursday after work.

Barbara made these steps her weekly goals. With encouragement from me and the members of the support group, she followed through until she was regularly exercising at the gym and pool.

Clearly, this type of process takes motivation and effort, two qualities that can be sorely lacking in someone who is depressed. That is why next week we will turn to the next crucial step in healing from depression and anxiety—attracting the right support.

Goals and Assignments for Week 1

Congratulations on having begun the journey of healing from depression and anxiety. I know that you may not have a lot of energy right now, so I am going to keep the first week's assignments pretty simple. If you need more time to take these initial steps, that's okay. Recovery is not a contest or a timed test. The important thing is that you get started.

1. Taking all the time that you need, begin to work on your vision statement. Don't worry about how it looks or sounds. Come from your heart, and honestly set down how you would feel if you were whole and well. Follow the guidelines and recommendations listed in the vision statement exercise. If you need help in completing the task, ask someone close to you to lend some support.

2. In the better mood recovery goal sheet on page 151, write down your goals for this twelve-week course. If this seems hard, just try writing one simple change you would like to see.

3. Fill out your weekly goal sheet below. Your goals should describe one or more steps that will move you closer to a long-term goal.

4. Congratulate yourself for having made a commitment to your healing! If there is any way you can give yourself a treat or find a small way to nurture yourself, please do so. You deserve a pat on the back for having taken this courageous step.

My Goal Sheet for Week 1

This week's starting date _____

Goal or goals _____

_____

Benefits of attaining this goal _____

_____

Action plan _____

_____

Assessing the Week

What did I learn from this week that will help me plan for the next week?

_____

_____

_____

_____

Where Do We Place Our Attention: On the Problem Or the Solution?

We began this week by learning about the principle of *intention.* Now I would like to speak to an equally powerful principle—that of *attention.* This principle states that whatever we put our attention on is what we will create—i.e., attention directs energy. Or, as my therapist puts it, "where the attention goes the energy flows."

In approaching a challenge such as depression, we can either put our attention on the problem or place it on the solution. These two perspectives are contrasted below:

Problem Framework
- What's wrong?
- How long have I had this problem?
- Why do I have this problem?
- How many ways does this problem limit me?
- Whose fault is it that I have this problem?
- When was my worst experience with this problem?

Outcome Framework
- What do I want?
- When do I want it?
- What can I start doing to get what I want?
- What resources do I have available to help me get what I want?
- How can I best utilize the resources that I have?
- How will I know when I have what I want?
- When I get what I want, what else in my life will improve?

Healing from depression usually begins with diagnosing our condition and focusing on the problem. At some point, however, we must turn our attention to the healing that we seek. This does not mean denying the pain of depression or pretending that it doesn't exist. Yet, we can be with our suffering and *simultaneously* focus our *intention* and *attention* on creating what we want.

Over the next eleven weeks, I will be asking you to follow the outcome framework and keep your eyes on the prize by reading your vision statement and setting weekly goals. This *ongoing focus on health* will eventually attract the manifestation of health to you.

Reaching Out for Support

Anything that promotes a sense of isolation often leads to illness and suffering. Anything that promotes a sense of love and intimacy, connection and community, is healing.

—DEAN ORNISH, *Love and Survival*

SECOND WEEK OVERVIEW

In this week, you will begin to build a support team by locating two healing allies: a recovery partner and a mental health professional.

We have learned that setting the intention to heal represents the first step on the road to recovery. Now I would like to share an equally important principle: *the power of intention is magnified when it is shared with another person.* When we state our vision of wellness in the presence of one or more supportive people, that vision becomes strengthened and exponentially magnified.

This principle of mutual support is demonstrated by the success of Alcoholics Anonymous. No cure existed for alcoholism until two drunks came together and said, "Let's do together what neither of us can do alone." Each day, tens of millions of people gather together in AA and other 12-step communities to join in love and caring to mutually support each other's healing.

Having support in your life is not just helpful in promoting recovery; it is essential. One cannot overcome an illness like major depression (or any dark night of the soul experience) by oneself. The weight of the illness is too immense, even for the strongest-willed individual, to bear alone. Symptoms invariably worsen for people who withdraw, isolate, or try to beat the illness on their own. Conversely, when people take the risk and reach out for help, they open themselves to a healing force more potent than any known drug. As Dean Ornish writes, referring to the healing power of human connection:

> I am not aware of any other factor in medicine—not diet, not smoking, not exercise, not stress, not genetics, not drugs, not surgery—that has a greater impact on our quality of life or incidence of illness.*

Finding Allies in Healing

Over the next twelve weeks, you will learn how to build a support team—a group of professionals, family, and friends who can walk you through your episode of depression and anxiety. In this week, you will locate two important people—a recovery partner and a mental health professional—who will become major supports as you work through this program.

Your Recovery Partner

When I first learned how to swim at camp, my instructor had us participate in the buddy system. Each novice swimmer was paired with another swimmer who served as his or her buddy. Whenever one of us went to the deep end of the lake, we were instructed to take our buddy with us—for companionship, for moral support, and for safety.

I have found that the buddy system is a wonderful tool to promote healing from depression. I would like you to start this week by

---

* Dean Ornish, *Love and Survival: The Scientific Basis for the Healing Power of Intimacy* (New York: HarperCollins, 1998), 2–3.

An Ally in Healing

A person in the black hole of depression cannot see his way out of the darkness. In the following letter, my partner, Joan, expressed her faith in my recovery and held a vision of my healing when I could not do it for myself.

It my belief that anyone who suffers from serious depression needs at least one other person (a family member, friend, doctor, spiritual advisor, and so on) to focus on the goal of wholeness and healing. This will be the function of your recovery partner during this course.

Dear Douglas,   Christmas day, 1996

Love is the greatest healing power. May the power of love work through you to do the work it needs to do to move you toward your healing.

May you be led to the right medicine to bring you into balance. I have great compassion for what you are going through. There is a mystery to this illness that your mind can't understand. There is a *higher* force at work here.

I send you so much love and healing and light on this Christmas day! Douglas, please don't give up. May you receive the inspiration you need to keep going from day to day and moment to moment—especially when you feel the deepest despair and loss of faith. There is a way out. Somehow, some way, you will be led to the light!

I am here in love and support for you during this healing crisis.

May your soul hear this.

Love,

Joan

thinking of a particular person (or persons) who might serve as your recovery partner for the remainder of this program. Each week you will check in with this individual, share your vision statement, and work on your goal of the week. Forming this type of alliance will help you in at least three ways:

1. When you state your weekly goals in the presence of your recovery partner, you have someone to be accountable to. Most people find that it is far easier to keep a promise they have made to someone else than one they have made to themselves.

   For example, let's say I tell my recovery partner, Marilyn, to call me on Friday at 4 P.M. to see whether I have written the introduction to my newest book proposal. Friday afternoon arrives, and I still have not begun the proposal. Being a good procrastinator, I might think, "This would be a good time to mow the lawn." But then I remember that Marilyn will be calling in an hour. Rather than break my word to her, I sit down at the computer to start writing.

2. By sharing your vision, you will benefit from the Master Mind principle, which says that whenever two or more people come together for a positive purpose, a benevolent spiritual energy (known as the Master Mind) is activated. This invisible force helps to bring our goal(s) into manifestation. (We will learn more about the Master Mind in Week 9.)

3. Your recovery partner can hold your vision of healing for you, even when you cannot! He or she can look at your vision of wellness with full belief, without being burdened by the baggage of fear and doubt. This was precisely what occurred in my life when a group of twelve loving individuals came together at the Living Enrichment Center, a New Thought church outside of Portland, and held a collective vision of my healing. (They did this by reading my vision statement every day for thirty days while visualizing me as whole and well.) Although I was totally convinced that I could not recover, my support team *knew* in their hearts that I would get well. Eventually the power of their conviction became translated into my reality. (For a more detailed description of this healing and additional explanations as to how my healing took place, please refer to chapter 7, "God Is My Antidepressant.")

My experience is not an isolated case. Since my recovery, I have worked as a midwife to help others emerge from episodes of anxiety and depression. In each case, the individual's recovery would not have been possible without the loving support of one or more people. Thus, while I cannot *guarantee* that you will get better (no one can know the future with certainty), my experience tells me that if you set the intention to heal, reach out for support and follow the remaining guidelines in this book, you will greatly maximize the chances of reducing your symptoms and making a full recovery.

Locating Your Recovery Partner

Take a moment and see whether you can think of one to three people who might serve as your recovery partner(s) for the remainder of this program. These individuals could include a friend, therapist, family member, clergy member, or someone like yourself who wants to heal from anxiety or depression. (The advantage of working with a fellow sufferer is that you can become *each other's coach and healer*, thereby forming a true mutual partnership.) Write the names of one to three people below or on a separate piece of paper.

1.

2.

3.

Over the next week, I would like you to call or E-mail these people and ask them whether they could be a support person for you during this program. If you are like many people suffering from depression, this may be easier said than done. Perhaps you feel ashamed, shy, or undeserving of help. Or maybe you fear rejection or don't want to feel like a burden to others. If asking for assistance seems hard, please consider the following:

- You are worthy of receiving support. The universe longs to help you in your time of need.
- If you are afraid of being a burden, realize that most people *enjoy* being supportive. The act of giving is its own reward.
- Also remind yourself that you will only be communicating with this person one or twice a week, so it won't be an imposition.

If asking someone to be your recovery partner still seems like too much, you can start out with a small step, such as talking with another person for fifteen minutes, even if it means calling a crisis line. Remember, not only is it okay to reach out for support, it is a vital step in the recovery process. Asking for help *will* make a real difference.

In his or her role as a recovery partner, this person should act in the following way:

- be available in person, by phone, or by E-mail at least once a week
- be a good listener
- be totally committed to the goal of your recovery
- validate your feelings (not talk you out of them)
- provide feedback and engage in problem solving when you request it
- share what has worked for them
- be both compassionate and firm, as he/she holds you accountable to your goals and commitments

Meeting With Your Recovery Partner

Once you enlist a support person, set a weekly time to meet with him or her for approximately thirty minutes to an hour. Your meetings should be structured as follows:

1. For the first block of time, share with your recovery partner what you have learned from the topic of the week. (For example, during Week 3, you might talk about what physical self-care activities have had a positive effect on your mood.) Also, share any homework assignment that you have been working on as well as *your goal of the week*. Conclude this part of the meeting by *reading your vision statement of wellness*.

2. Next, give an update on your mood (using the Daily Mood Scale shown later in this chapter) and share how you are faring in your recovery, reporting any successes, challenges, insights, and so on.

   During this sharing, your recovery partner's role is to listen attentively and to refrain from interrupting or giving advice. After you have finished with your update, you may ask your partner for feedback and suggestions about what you have shared. (It is also okay not to ask for feedback.)

3) Finally (and most importantly), *request support* for the coming week. This request should focus on:
   - your current goal (e.g., "I would like support for exercising three times this week" or "I would like support for saying my affirmations")
   - an aspect of your vision statement
   - a specific life challenge you are facing

Feel free to make more than one request if you like. After you have finished speaking, ask your recovery partner to affirm you silently or by using an affirmation such as, "I see you attaining your goal and hold for you a vision of your success." If your partner is also participating in his or her own twelve-week recovery program, you can switch roles and let her or him share while you become the supporter.

Between meetings, your partner will continue to hold a vision of healing for you on a daily basis (and you for him or her if that is requested). You may also stay in touch by phone or E-mail. Having this kind of regular contact and reinforcement will become a central piece of your recovery program.

Locating a Mental Health Professional

A second ally that you will want to have during this program is a mental health professional, as well as a prescriber if you need to take psychiatric medication. There are a great many qualified and compassionate health care professionals who offer care and treatment for depression. They include:

- psychiatrists
- clinical psychologists
- clinical social workers
- psychiatric nurse practitioners
- family practice physicians and internists
- marriage and family counselors
- pastoral counselors
- clergy
- drug and alcohol counselors

Although only psychiatrists, physicians, and nurse practitioners can prescribe medication, members of the other groups offer psychotherapy and often refer out for the medication component. Thus, you may end up seeing two mental health professionals—medical doctor for your medication and counselor for therapy. (Your therapist or counselor may also serve as your recovery partner.)

The relationship between doctor and patient, or therapist and client, plays a critical role in the healing process. Your relationship with your mental health care provider will be as important as any treatment you choose. Consequently, it is important that you feel comfortable with him or her. In this respect, it is a good idea to interview several counselors or therapists before you make a final decision about the person who will be your guide and advocate.

Obtaining the proper referral is an important first step in your healing. There are several ways to do this.

1. **Word of mouth.** Ask people you know (family, coworkers, friends, a family physician, or internist) for the name of anyone who has been helpful to them or others they know.

2. **State licensing boards.** You can call and ask for referrals. Feel free to ask about a practitioner's credentials, how long he or she has been in practice, and his or her experience in treating major depression.

3. **Associations of helping professionals.** You can contact these organizations for referrals to mental health professionals in your area. Here are some phone numbers to start with (additional information is provided in Appendix C):
   • American Psychiatric Association, 202-682-6220
   • American Psychological Association, 202-336-5800
   • National Association of Social Workers, 800-638-8799
   • American Association for Marriage and Family Therapy, 202-452-0109
   • American Association of Pastoral Counselors, 703-385-6967
   • American Society of Clinical Hypnosis, 312-645-9810

When you find the right therapist, you will most likely be treated with one or more of the following forms of psychotherapy:

- **The psychodynamic approach,** pioneered by early psychiatrists such as Freud, Jung, and Adler, relates the development and maintenance of depressive symptoms to unresolved conflicts and losses rooted in childhood. This approach focuses on helping the individual to gain insight into the nature of his or her problems, work through conflicts, and find new ways to look at relations with others.

  The therapist-patient relationship is a key part of the treatment because of the client's tendency to transfer unresolved feelings about a parent or authority figure onto the therapist (a process called "transference"). Since many depressions are caused by unexpressed mourning, the patient may also be encouraged to grieve his or her early losses, including deaths and the emotional unavailability of primary caregivers. Such grieving can help a person to gain closure with the past and allow a gradual healing to take place.

- **The cognitive-behavioral approach** teaches the client with depression new ways of thinking to replace faulty beliefs about himself, the world, and the future. Specific focus is placed on identifying erroneous assumptions, expectations, and conclusions ("This will never end"), and on letting go of self-destructive thoughts (e.g., "I'm worthless" or "No one can love me when I am depressed").

  In addition you will learn strategies such as meditation, visualization, progressive muscle relaxation, and biofeedback, which can produce physiological changes in the brain and nervous system.

- **Interpersonal therapy** looks at the role of interpersonal relationships (or lack of them) in contributing to depression. In this therapy, the client learns new skills for interacting with people and developing healthy, functional relationships.

- A fourth therapeutic approach, more popular in Europe than in the United States, consists of the existential psychotherapies, the most noted of which is **logotherapy**—created by psychiatrist Victor Frankl—author of *Man's Search for Meaning,* which helps patients discover the meaning and purpose of life and find worthwhile ideals to live for.

Each of these approaches has proven valuable in treating various levels of depression. The technique (or techniques) you choose should depend on your temperament, your level of functioning, the severity of your depression, and the therapist's training and background. Research has shown that any of these therapies can be beneficial if used by a competent professional. Moreover, in today's therapy office, it is not unusual for therapists to be familiar with several psychological theories and to combine several approaches to meet each individual's needs.

The important thing is to try some type of therapy with a professional trained in assessing and treating depression. Studies show that the combination of psychotherapy and medication is *more effective* in treating depression than medication alone, especially in maintaining long-term mental health. (If you are between episodes and are *doing really well,* you might be able to forego seeing a counselor. On the other hand, this would be an ideal time to practice preventative medicine and use therapy to maintain your current stability.)

Counseling and Finances

One of the issues that anyone seeking a mental health professional may encounter is financing—i.e., "How do I pay for my therapy?" A sizable number of my clients have no health insurance (like thirty-seven million other Americans who are without health insurance). Even those who are covered under a plan (usually managed care) discover that their mental health coverage gives them a limited number of visits (for example, twenty sessions with a therapist over a two-year period). Furthermore, actually getting in to see someone can be extremely problematic.

For example, in the opening session of one of my healing from depression support groups, a man announced to the group that his symptoms were so extreme that he was thinking of "ending it all." When I asked him to make an appointment with his psychiatrist, he said his HMO told him that the earliest he could be seen was in three weeks. (Fortunately, we were able to get this person appropriate help.)

Under conditions such as these, it makes the most sense to pay out of pocket to a private counselor, if you can afford it. Otherwise, it is best to work within the limitations of whatever health insurance plan you have. If you don't have insurance, you can turn to a number of low-cost mental health agencies where you can meet with a counselor and pay fees on a sliding scale. Check the community health listings in the white pages of your phone book, or call your local mental health crisis line.

We will return to the issue of social support in Week 8. For right now, locating your recovery partner and your mental health professional is a good first step in building your support team.

Goals and Assignments for Week 2

Here are your assignments for the upcoming week:

1. Invite someone to be your recovery partner for the remainder of this program. Write this goal down on the weekly goal sheet at the end of this chapter. If you are able to find a partner this week, meet with him or her. Share what you have logged in your Daily Mood Diary. Also talk about any insights you had about your condition or syndrome after reading about the characteristics of depression in chapter 9.

2. If you are not currently working with a mental health professional, set the intention to find one. Write this intention down on your goal sheet. Use the suggestions from this chapter to find at least two possible candidates. Then make appointments to see them.

3. Read over your vision statement each day. If you feel like making small changes, feel free to do so. Share it with your recovery partner and anyone else who unconditionally supports your healing and recovery.

4. Start tracking your moods using the Daily Mood Scale, which appears on the next page. Use this scale to assign a numerical value to your mood, ranging from −5 to +5. Record your score each day in the Daily Mood Diary, which appears on page 168.

    To get started with this process, think about how you are feeling today and ask yourself, "How have I been doing? Have I experienced any symptoms of depression or anxiety? How has my general mood been?" (Given that my mood can fluctuate during the day, I always take inventory before bedtime and then evaluate what my mood has been over the course of the day.) After noting how you have been feeling, assign your mood a number between −5 and +5 and write it beside today's date in the second column of the Daily Mood Diary. Record your energy level during the day in the third column. Ten means high energy; 5 is average energy; and 1 means, "I feel like a slug. I can hardly get out of bed." I like tracking energy because it is a measure of vitality and health, and it closely correlates to levels of depression.

Finally, record the day's events or go into more detail about your state of mind in the comments column. If you need more space, you may create your own version of this diary on a larger piece of paper. You may also record your moods at the bottom of the following weekly goal sheet. In addition to tracking your symptoms, you can use the Daily Mood Diary to track your recovery. I tell my clients who are severely depressed to define recovery as having the numbers on their mood scale be *in the positive range* for at least six weeks. If you are doing well right now, keeping your rating at zero or above is a good goal to shoot for. Having your scores drop into the negative numbers will alert you to the early warning signs of a depressive downturn so you can take appropriate action to prevent an episode.

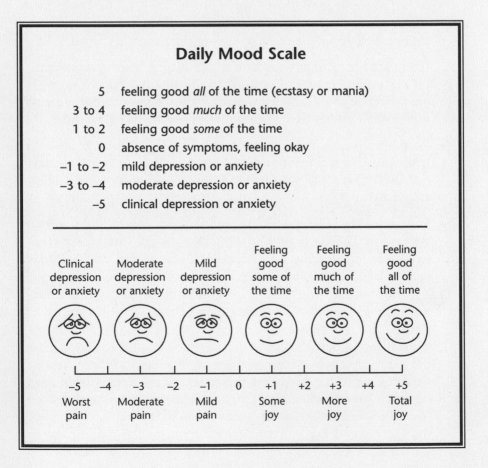

Daily Mood Scale

5	feeling good *all* of the time (ecstasy or mania)
3 to 4	feeling good *much* of the time
1 to 2	feeling good *some* of the time
0	absence of symptoms, feeling okay
−1 to −2	mild depression or anxiety
−3 to −4	moderate depression or anxiety
−5	clinical depression or anxiety

Clinical depression or anxiety	Moderate depression or anxiety	Mild depression or anxiety	Feeling good some of the time	Feeling good much of the time	Feeling good all of the time

−5	−4	−3	−2	−1	0	+1	+2	+3	+4	+5
Worst pain		Moderate pain		Mild pain		Some joy		More joy		Total joy

My Goal Sheet for Week 2

This week's starting date: _____ My recovery partner: _____

Date and time we will connect: _____

Goal or goals: _____

_____

Benefits of attaining this goal: _____

_____

Action plan: _____

_____

Ongoing goals (check off the ones as you accomplish them)
_____ Read my vision statement daily (upon awakening or before bed)
_____ Chart my moods in the Daily Mood Diary
_____ This was my average mood on the daily mood scale (–5 to +5)

How was my mood this week?
Record your moods below for each day of the week. (–5 to +5)

Day	Mood	Comments
Mon		
Tue		
Wed		
Thu		
Fri		
Sat		
Sun		

Daily Mood Diary

Record your moods below for each day of the month of _____

DATE	MOOD	ENERGY	COMMENTS
1			
2			
3			
4			
5			
6			
7			
8			
9			
10			
11			
12			
13			
14			

15			
16			
17			
18			
19			
20			
21			
22			
23			
24			
25			
26			
27			
28			
29			
30			
31			

Physical Self-Care: Focusing on the Basics

No less than two hours a day should be devoted to exercise, and the weather little regarded. If the body is feeble, the mind will not be strong.

—THOMAS JEFFERSON

THIRD WEEK OVERVIEW

In this week, you will learn ways to take care of and nurture your physical body that will have a profound impact on your mood.

It is the third week of our recovery program, and you have reached an important juncture in your journey to heal from depression. Having set the intention to heal and having reached out for support, it is time to take action to alleviate your symptoms and to create a better mood. But how?

The first person most people turn to when they are feeling blue is their family physician. If your doctor is familiar enough with the symptoms of depression to make a proper diagnosis, he or she will most likely write you a prescription for Prozac (or some other anti-depressant) and have you return in three weeks. While there is nothing wrong with medication, there is *so much more* that you can do. Because depression is a complex, multifaceted disorder with a variety of causes, you can approach its treatment from a multitude of directions and modalities.

Take a moment and review the Healing from Depression and Anxiety: Five Areas of Therapeutic Self-Care diagram in chapter 10. Over the next ten weeks, you will learn how you can use each of these areas and their corresponding self-care activities to change your brain chemistry and your mood. I encourage you try a combination of these mutually supportive therapies; you will greatly maximize your chances of attaining the healing that you seek.

Now, let's begin with the first step in attaining a better mood—taking care of and nurturing your physical body.

The Body-Mood Connection

Although depression is characterized as a mood disorder, it primarily affects the physical body. Those of you who have suffered from clinical depression know the agonizing physical symptoms—loss of appetite, disruption of sleep, the inability to experience pleasure, fatigue, lethargy, heaviness, agitation, and so on. In many ways, being depressed is like having the emotional flu. Conversely, when we feel great physically—full of vitality, energetic, awake, and alert—it is almost impossible to be in a bad mood. As my friend Beth who suffers from anxiety is fond of saying, "It is so much easier to think positively and be calm and serene after a good night's sleep!"

Another reason to focus on physical health is that it deals with our most *basic* human needs—food, water, air, sleep, touch, and movement. Because these needs are so elemental, many people take them for granted. But when we ignore our basic needs, the entire body—as well as our mood—gets thrown out of balance. (Researchers like Candace Pert have shown that "molecules of emotion" are located not just in the brain, but throughout the body.)

Because of this body-mood connection, I believe that the starting point of healing from depression and anxiety is physical self-care. In the pages that follow, you will learn many ways you can create a better mood by nurturing your physical body.

Ten Basics of Physical Self-Care

Here are ten basic physical self-care habits that can form the foundation of your physical self-care recovery program.

1. Avoid putting junk in your body. Start with the obvious toxins like tobacco, alcohol, and hard drugs. In addition, eliminate or reduce processed foods such as soft drinks, diet sodas, candy, cookies, cakes, and prepared entrees made with artificial ingredients.

2. Exercise your body sufficiently at least twenty minutes a day, five days a week, in a way that breaks a sweat. The practice of yoga is particularly helpful in conditioning the body, calming the nervous system, and balancing emotions.

3. Drink plenty of water, at least sixty-four ounces a day (one ounce for every two pounds of body weight) and more if you are active. Make sure the water is pure, not city water. To ensure this, use a good water filter.

4. Meet your body's need for sufficient *sleep* with a regular and consistent sleep schedule.

5. Eat a diet that contains a wide *variety of fresh* unprocessed *foods,* buying organic whenever possible. Make sure you eat at regular intervals to keep your blood sugar stable.

6. Learn how to properly oxygenate your body through deep, diaphragmatic *breathing.*

7. Get enough exposure to *natural light* (morning hours are best), especially if you have SAD (Seasonal Affective Disorder). Light boxes are therapeutic for some people.

8. If you wish to explore *medicine* that directly impacts your brain chemistry—whether it be conventional antidepressants such as Prozac or

(continued on next page)

Zoloft, herbal remedies such as St. John's Wort and Kava, or amino acids such as 5-HTP or SAMe—find an appropriate prescriber or nutritionally oriented physician to work with.

9. Find a way to fulfill your body's need for *touch* through hugs, therapeutic massage, physical intimacy, and so on.

10. Take care of your *daily hygiene* by showering, shaving, combing your hair, brushing your teeth, and so on. Feeling clean will help you to feel better.

Exercise

Exercise—any physical activity that promotes endurance, flexibility, or strengthening—is a natural antidepressant. The latest scientific research at the Cooper Research Institute in Dallas, Texas, demonstrates that as little as three hours a week of regular exercise reduces the symptoms of mild to moderate depression as effectively as Prozac and other medications. Aerobic exercise in particular improves circulation, brings increased blood flow and oxygen to the brain, and releases endorphins, the body's painkilling chemicals. The only side effects of aerobic exercise are a stronger cardiovascular system and better overall health. Even if you have no history of mood disorders, regular exercise can profoundly improve the quality of your physical, mental, and emotional well-being.

Regular exercise has become the central pillar of my recovery program. On weekdays, I ride my stationary bike and lift weights in the morning and swim in the evening. On weekends, I take long walks in the forest. When I miss my routines for even one or two days, I am more likely to become depressed or anxious. When I return to my schedule, the self-doubts, fears, and anxieties melt away.

One of the reasons that many people resist exercise is that they see it as something arduous and unpleasant. To heal this resistance, see if you can turn the "e" in exercise to the "e" in enjoy. In other words, strive to make exercise fun by connecting it to activities that give you pleasure. Such activities might include:

- gardening
- hiking
- jazzercise
- folk dancing
- listening to or playing music while exercising
- planned active activities with friends (note that the word activities has "active" in it. Instead of going out with a friend to your favorite French restaurant, enjoy a hike on one of your favorite nature trails.)

Mark's Story:
Exercise Makes the Difference

At the age of thirty-seven, I fell into a major depression. I lost my ability to concentrate, my ability to sleep, and my ability to feel any type of joy or pleasure. Everything that had color became gray. Eventually, I got stabilized on medication. Yet I never felt that I had regained the joy of living that I had before the depression struck.

Then I enrolled in Douglas's depression support group and learned about the value of exercise in relieving the symptoms of depression. I decided to try something different. One thing that Douglas emphasized during class was to set and monitor goals. So I chose to make engaging in a regular exercise routine my primary goal and mission.

My first step was to start a regular workout program at my health club consisting of a one-hour aerobic class, three days a week. Each week at the support group, I told my fellow members of my exercise goals. Knowing that I would have to report my results the following week made me want to follow up on my commitment. Being held accountable to others was a huge support in keeping me motivated.

After three months of sticking with my plan, I have noticed amazing results. My mood has improved, I feel less on edge, and I am more confident. Under my psychiatrist's guidance, I plan to discontinue my medication. There are times when I don't feel like working out, but I remind myself that exercise has become my "mental health therapy." The improvements in my cardiovascular fitness are just a bonus to being free from depression and anxiety. Nothing else I have done so far has given me such a return on the time invested.

Another way to approach exercise is to incorporate it into your daily activities. (Our agrarian ancestors didn't need to set aside special times in their busy schedules to work out at the gym.) Some mundane activities that will give you a natural workout include:

- doing the laundry
- walking up the stairs in your office building
- walking to the grocery store
- pruning roses
- edging the lawn
- pulling out weeds
- planting and harvesting veggics

Our bodies were made to move. Whether it is a daily walk in the park, a water aerobics or yoga class, or dancing to your favorite music, get into motion. Start with small steps and remind yourself that you don't have to be perfect. At the pool where I swim, I see many disabled, elderly, and overweight people taking part in water exercise classes. Even if you have a physical disability or carry extra pounds, it is usually possible to engage in some form of movement.

A Healthy Diet

A major key to keeping depression at bay is to get your nutritional needs met through eating a balanced diet of healthy foods. Good nutrition supports the optimal functioning of your brain and body. Eat organic produce as much as possible to minimize the intake of chemicals and preservatives that can cause problems, especially in sensitive individuals.

Another part of nutritional self-care means cutting back on the sweets. Studies have shown that too much sugar can foster anxiety as well as depression. Excessive intake of sugar may also weaken your immune system, foster allergies, and increase the risk of diabetes and reactive hypoglycemia.

In her book *Potatoes Not Prozac*, Kathleen DesMaisons, Ph.D., an addiction and nutrition expert, claims that many people who are prone to addictive disorders, as well as to depression, are also sugar sensitive—their body chemistry reacts in extreme ways to sugar and refined carbohydrates. The reaction throws off not only the blood sugar levels, but also the levels of serotonin and beta-endorphins (nature's pain killers) in the brain. This in turn causes an inability to concentrate; creates feelings of exhaustion, hopelessness, and despair; and contributes to confusion, irritability, and low self esteem— symptoms of clinical depression! Such symptoms lead the person to seek out a sugar fix to relieve his or her distress. This, of course, sets up the classic vicious cycle, leading to emotional ups and downs as his or her blood sugar levels fluctuate wildly.

Fortunately, DesMaisons has discovered that eating the *right foods* at the *right times* can often bring the body and emotions back into balance. Her dietary recommendations include:

- eating three regular meals a day, spaced no more than five to six hours apart
- eating the recommended amount of protein (a portion the size of your fist) at every meal
- replacing simple carbohydrates with complex carbohydrates
- reducing or eliminating sugars (including alcohol)

DesMaisons's plan has achieved a high success rate with recovering alcoholics as well as with people with mood disorders who are striving for emotional stability.

Another book that I have found helpful is the *Metabolic Body Type Diet* by William Wolcott. This book is based on the simple but often overlooked premise that different individuals process the same foods and nutrients differently. For example, a high-carbohydrate diet can help one person lose weight, while causing a second person eating the same food to gain weight. One person's meat becomes another's poison.

Wolcott introduces a technology called *metabolic typing* that analyzes individual nutritional differences. Metabolic typing contends that a number of factors—including the oxidative system (how slowly or quickly you burn foods) and the autonomic nervous system (whether you are sympathetic or parasympathetic dominant)—work together to determine your dietary needs. This analysis identifies three general metabolic type categories: *the protein type* (high protein, high fats and oils, low carbohydrates); *the carbo type* (low protein, low fats and oils, high carbohydrates); and *the mixed type* (requires a relatively equal ratio of proteins, fats, and carbohydrates).

Wolcott's metabolic-type self-test revealed that I was a protein type who had been living on a carbo diet. When I switched to the protein regimen and added meat back into my diet, my need for sleep declined, my energy increased, and my weight dropped. (My partner, on the other hand, gets much better results from eating more carbohydrates and less protein, demonstrating that one size does not fit all.)

In addition, other researchers have discovered a connection between depression and food sensitivities and allergies. Although no one has proven that sesitivities and allergies can cause depression, it seems reasonable to assume that they can aggravate both depression and anxiety. For example, in her book *Depression-Free Naturally,* Joan Matthews Larson describes the phenomenon of alcoholics who were supersensitive to alcoholic grains they drank. After they chose to replace their alcoholic intake with lots of pastas, breads, cereals, and other wheat products, they continued to complain of depression and fatigue. Common food allergens include dairy products, wheat, and corn. If you think you might have food sensitivities or allergies, consult a doctor who specializes in allergies or environmental medicine.

Adequate Water Intake

To maintain healthy body functioning, it is important to drink adequate amounts of fluids, at least two quarts a day. Your body is composed of 70 percent water, while the brain is about 90 percent water. Water is essential to proper metabolism, circulation, and elimination. It flushes out toxins and restores chemical balance to cells, tissues, and organs. Many of my clients have reported a direct improvement in mood, as well a cessation of physical symptoms such as headaches, once they increased their water intake.

Research indicates that you should drink at least sixty-four ounces of water a day (ideally, one ounce for every two pounds of body weight) and more if you are active. Adults lose nearly two to three quarts of water a day (twelve cups) through breathing, perspiration, and urination.

Your thirst reflex is not a good indicator of dehydration; by the time you feel thirsty, you should have been drinking water hours ago. This is why many people are chronically dehydrated and don't even know it. A mere 2 percent drop in water in your body can trigger fuzzy short-term memory, trouble with basic math, or difficulty reading. For many people, the thirst mechanism is often mistaken for hunger. A University of Washington study showed that one glass of water shut down midnight hunger pangs for almost 100 percent of dieters.

When I presented this information at one of my seminars, a man who leads river raft trips through the Grand Canyon informed me that whenever his passengers become irritable, anxious, or angry, he gives them water and watches their mood even out. The moral of the story is clear—don't wait until you are thirsty to drink. Carry water with you and sip it throughout the day. Your body and your mind will thank you.

Exposure to Natural Light

Another physical need of the human body is getting enough exposure to natural light. For those people who are light sensitive, inadequate exposure to light can create depressive syndromes such as seasonal affective disorder (SAD). (See Appendix A to learn more about SAD.) If you live in a dark climate and suffer from SAD, use full-spectrum lights to enhance your exposure to light. (I use halogen lamps because I prefer the warmer, yellow color.) An hour of exposure to outdoor light in the early morning can also make a difference. Some people find that lighting candles on a dark winter's day brings warmth and coziness to an otherwise dreary environment.

Sleep Schedule

Part of staying physically balanced means developing regular sleep patterns that give you adequate amounts of rest. According to Dr. Peter Hauri, author of *No More Sleepless Nights,* more than one hundred million Americans have sleep disorders. Try to develop a sleep schedule—a regular time of going to sleep and arising—and stick to it. Sleep irregularities are among the early warning signs of *both* mania and depression. These symptoms include:

- trouble falling asleep
- trouble staying asleep
- early morning awakenings (followed by ruminations)
- sleeping too much

Depressed individuals who sleep too much will inevitably tell you that they wake unrefreshed, indicating that their sleep is not restorative sleep. (Sleep may also be a way of escaping emotions that are too painful.) It also seems that people with depression experience an excessive amount of dreaming sleep. They primarily rest in this lighter stage of sleep, during which rapid eye movements and dreams occur. There seems to be something about an excess of rapid eye movement sleep that is depressigenic—it makes people feel depressed.

Also, researcher Eve Van Couter discovered that when volunteer students were deprived of sleep, their brains did not effectively process glucose, the major fuel for brain function. As we saw earlier, impaired sugar metabolism is linked to depression.

Sleep medication and tranquilizers can be useful in trying to break a pattern of sleeplessness, but they are only designed for short-term use. Low doses of the antidepressant Elavil can induce sleep over longer periods without risking addiction or dependence. Behavioral changes, such as those listed in the book *No More Sleepless Nights* by Peter Hauri, can be extremely effective. These include:

- developing a sleep schedule—a regular time of going to sleep and arising—and sticking to it
- reducing caffeine and alcohol and eliminating cigarettes
- using your bed only for sleep and sex, not for other activities such as reading
- practicing bedtime relaxation techniques
- getting regular exercise during the day

In addition, you may wish to be evaluated at a sleep clinic to rule out the possibility of physical problems such as sleep apnea. (Sleep apnea is a temporary suspension of breathing that occurs repeatedly during sleep. It often affects overweight people or those who have an obstruction in their breathing tract.)

For those who have experienced crippling insomnia, establishing regular and restorative sleep patterns makes all the difference in the world. Here is a an affirmation or mantra that I received from a client who repeated it to himself as he drifted off to sleep in order to stop his obsessive thoughts. It was written by a thirteenth-century English monk and reads as follows:

> *All shall be well,*
> *and all shall be well,*
> *and all manner of things shall be well.*

Abdominal Breathing

One of the most powerful ways to impact the emotions and the involuntary nervous system is through the breath. In Sanskrit, the word for breath is *prana,* which also means "life" or "spirit." Most people in our society breathe rapidly and shallowly, using only the upper part of their chests. This is especially true for depressed individuals, whose life force is at a low point, as well as for people who are chronically anxious.

Abdominal breathing (also called diaphragmatic breathing) involves using your entire chest and abdominal cavity to breathe. Through abdominal breathing, you can slow down racing thoughts and increase your body's life force and vitality. Here is a brief description of the process.

Sit in a comfortable position with your spine straight (you can also do this lying on your back). Place both hands on your abdomen, right beneath your rib cage, with the fingers of each hand spread out and just touching each other. Now, inhale slowly and deeply, sending the incoming air as low down your chest as you can toward your tummy. As your belly fills up with air, the fingers of your two hands will slowly *move apart.*

When you have taken a full breath, pause momentarily and exhale slowly through your nose or mouth. As you do so, you will see your abdomen deflating, much like a balloon as its air lets out. Let your body go limp as you watch your hands on your abdomen slowly return to their original position. Your fingers should be touching again.

Try repeating this eight to ten times, breathing deeply and slowly without gulping in air or letting it all out at once. You may wish to count to four on the inhale and to eight on the exhale, or whatever rhythm works best for you.

I first learned about abdominal breathing in a yoga class many years ago. You can also learn diaphragmatic breathing techniques in any stress reduction clinic, biofeedback center, pain clinic, or from any individual who has practiced yoga.

Physical Touch

Human touch is profoundly healing for body, mind, and spirit. Phrases such as "You touched me" or "Keep in touch" reflect the importance of human touch to emotional and physical health. There are many ways of experiencing touch—by extending a hug, holding a hand, or giving a back rub.

One way to receive healing touch is through therapeutic massage. Massage relaxes the muscles, promotes lymph drainage, and stimulates the immune system. While many people are touch hungry, those folks who have experienced physical violence or sexual abuse may need to be desensitized to their negative conditioning around touch before they feel safe and open to its healing benefits. If you think this may be true for you, consult with your therapist or someone who specializes in treating survivors of physical or sexual trauma.

For myself, my weekly massages provided one of the few moments of relief I had during the ongoing torment of my clinical depression. Now that I am in recovery, I still nurture myself with massage as well as with regular soaks in a hot tub.

This Week's Goals and Assignments

Here are your assignments for the upcoming week:

1. Fill out the Physical Self-Care Wellness Inventory below. This will help you to see how well you are caring for your physical body. I suggest that you buy a *simple journal* or *spiral bound notebook* that you can use to record your answers to this questionnaire and others that will follow. This will be your Better Mood Journal. You can also use your Better Mood Journal to record any thoughts, feelings, or important events that occur during the remainder of the program.

2. Complete the worksheet on Creating Goals for Physical Self-Care that follows. Then choose a self-care activity as this week's goal.

3. Start to track how many ounces of water you drink each day. On a blank sheet of paper, note each time you take a drink and how much fluid you ingest.

Ongoing Self-Care Activities

- Read your vision statement daily.
- Chart your moods in the Daily Mood Diary.
- Meet with your recovery partner.

Physical Self-Care Wellness Inventory

The following questions are designed to help you assess how you are doing in the area of physical self-care. You can answer in the spaces provided or in your Better Mood Journal.

1. Overall, how would I rate my physical health? (1 low, 10 high). How is my energy level? Do I think of myself as primarily ill or well?

(continued on next page)

2. What types of physical activities make my body feel good? What types of exercise do I participate in? How many times a week do I exercise?

3. How would I describe my relationship with food? What kinds of food comprise the majority of my diet? Are there any comfort foods that I turn to when I am stressed?

4. Do I eat the right amount of food given my activity level? Do I drink sufficient water (eight glasses a day)?

5. How is my sleep? Do I sleep too much, too little, or about the right amount? How is the quality of my sleep? Am I able to sleep through the night without interference, or do I get up periodically? How do I feel when I awaken in the morning—refreshed or still tired?

6. Many people use a shower, bath, whirlpool, hot tub, or pool to soothe them physically and emotionally. Do I use water therapy in this way? If not, how might I do so?

7. Are there aspects of my health that prevent me from feeling vital and alive? If so, what are they?

8. Are there any exercise or health habits that I would like to develop? Are there any that I would like to eliminate?

Creating Goals for Physical Self-Care

Using the list of physical self-care activities below as a guide; write down those that you are already practicing and those that you would like to incorporate into your life.

- Regular exercise
- Good nutrition
- Adequate water intake (sixty-four ounces or more per day)
- Hydrotherapy (swimming, saunas, or jacuzzis)
- Exposure to natural light
- Regular sleep
- Antidepressant medication
- Complementary medications (vitamins, herbs, or amino acids)
- Deep breathing
- Yoga
- Hugs and/or therapeutic massage

Physical self-care strategies that I am already using:
1.

2.

3.

Physical self-care strategies that I would like to make part of my life. Examples include, "I would like to exercise three times a week," or "I would like to eat a better balance of fruits and vegetables," or "I would like to sleep more regular hours."
1.

2.

3.

Now, take one of these activities and make it a goal for the coming week or a future week.

My Goal Sheet for Week 3

This week's starting date:_____ My recovery partner:_____

Date and time we will connect:_____

Goal or goals: _____

_____

Benefits of attaining this goal:_____

_____

Action plan:_____

_____

Ongoing goals (check off the ones as you accomplish them)
_____ Read my vision statement daily (upon awakening or before bed)
_____ Chart my moods in the Daily Mood Diary
_____ Participate in some form of exercise or movement
_____ This was my average mood on the daily mood scale (–5 to +5)

How was my mood this week?

Record your moods below for each day of the week. (–5 to +5)

Day	Mood	Comments
Mon		
Tue		
Wed		
Thu		
Fri		
Sat		
Sun		

Antidepressants and Their Alternatives

The fastest way to change your state of mind is to change your physiology.
—TONY ROBBINS

FOURTH WEEK OVERVIEW

In this week, you will learn about the benefits of antidepressants (such as Prozac) as well as their natural alternatives (such as St. John's Wort).

In the first and second weeks of the better mood recovery program, you set the intention to heal and reached out for support. In the third week, you learned about the body-mood connection—how nurturing your physical body and meeting its basic needs for food, water, air, sleep, touch, and movement can make you feel better emotionally, as well as physically. In this week, we will be taking the body-mood connection a step further by exploring the impact of antidepressants on brain chemistry—and hence, mood.

In modern psychiatric medicine, antidepressants have become the treatment of choice for people with major depression. Before World War II, these drugs did not exist. In the 1950s, two drugs, one an antipsychotic and the other a tuberculosis medication, were accidentally found to elevate the moods of depressed individuals. Since then, a host of new substances has been synthesized, specifically for the treatment of depression. Most recently, medications have been developed that specifically target the particular neural pathways of depression with less generalized neural impact and, therefore, far fewer side effects. For many, these medications can be likened to a "penicillin for the mind," a miracle drug that puts them on the road to emotional stability.

Current theory links the biochemical causes of mood disorders to a deficiency of three of the brain's neurotransmitters—serotonin, norepinephrine, and dopamine. Antidepressants don't actually create more serotonin, norepinephrine, and dopamine. Instead, they are believed to limit the reabsorption of these chemicals into the brain's nerve cells, thereby increasing the amounts of neurotransmitters available in the space (synapse) between the sending and receiving cells. This in turn causes a better neural transmission from cell to cell, resulting in an elevation of mood.

What Are the Major Antidepressants?

There are three groups of antidepressants. All three groups of antidepressants take two to four weeks to begin working, and six to eight weeks to achieve full effectiveness. The first and oldest group is the *tricyclics* (so named because of their three-ring chemical structures). Examples include Imipramine (Tofranil) and Amitriptyline (Elavil). The tricyclic side effects may include dry mouth, blurred vision, sexual dysfunction, fatigue, weight gain, constipation, and abnormalities in the cardiovascular system. Such discomforts can often deter a person from staying on the medication long enough for the beneficial effects to be felt.

The second group of antidepressants is called *monoamine oxidase (MAO) inhibitors,* or MAOIs for short (examples are Nardil and Parnate). Monoamine oxidase is an enzyme that breaks down neurotransmitters. Hence, by inhibiting the production of MAO, these drugs increase the amount of neurotransmitters retained in the synapses. Unfortunately, the MAOIs have cumbersome dietary restrictions. They cannot be taken with foods that contain the amino acid tyrosine—such as aged cheese, beer, wine, chocolate, and liver.

The third and most recently developed class of antidepressants is known as the SSRI—*selective serotonin reuptake inhibitors*. This group, which includes Prozac, Zoloft, Celexa, and Paxil, is as effective as the tricyclics in treating depression, but generally has fewer and milder side effects. Nonetheless, the SSRIs may be highly agitating for some patients (producing anxiety and insomnia), who thus may require additional sleeping medications.

There is also a class of *atypical* antidepressants that includes Serzone, Effexor, and Wellbutrin. They are called atypical because their chemical structure and method of action are pharmacologically distinct from the tricyclics, MAOIs, and SSRIs.

No one class of antidepressant is better than any other, as medications work differently for different people, depending on the complex interaction between an individual's biochemistry and the drug's pharmacology. This is why finding the right medication is often a matter of trial and error and good medical follow-through.

Antidepressants do not get you "high"; neither are they addictive. They work by reestablishing the right proportion of neurotransmitters in your brain so nerve impulses can be effectively communicated from cell to cell.

What Should I Expect When I First Take an Antidepressant?

Unlike most other drugs, antidepressants do not take effect immediately. Usually there is a four- to six-week period before their beneficial effects are fully felt, although some people have reported improvement within the first week. Hence, while waiting for the medication to take effect, you may have to endure side effects, which may (or may not) be temporary, before you know whether the antidepressant will work for you. Moreover, since the art of prescribing psychiatric medicine is an inexact science (because each person's body and brain chemistry is unique), it may take several trials on different drugs before you find the right one. You will need to increase your self-care and seek moral support during this time.

Once you find a medication that provides relief from the hell of depression, enduring the side effects may seem a small price to pay. Moreover, in many instances the side effects are temporary and fade with continued usage.

It is also important to note that in a small minority of cases, some people experience a recurrence of depression while still on medication, a phenomenon known as "Prozac poopout." When this occurs, you usually can obtain relief by changing medications or dosages under careful medical supervision.

How Long Should I Take My Medication?

The short answer is *as long as you need it*. This will depend on how well your body can rebalance its biochemistry on its own. Some people have only one major episode and never need treatment again (just as some individuals suffer just one heart attack or one bout with cancer).

Others heal from depression, go off their medication, and continue to feel well until a later date when the depression returns. This usually requires going back on medication and/or engaging in other forms of treatment until the episode passes.

However, some folks discover that as soon as they stop medication, their symptoms return. These people usually need to take antidepressant medication on a long-term basis in order to correct underlying biochemical imbalances.

What about Adverse Side Effects?

People vary greatly in their sensitivity to drugs.
One person's remedy may be another person's overdose.
—DR. JAY S. COHEN

If you have read my personal narrative, you know that my depressive episode was triggered by an adverse reaction to an antidepressant drug. While such instances are rare, they have been documented in the literature. In addition, many antidepressants have the potential to induce a manic episode in individuals who have a bipolar disorder.

Roger's Story: Finding the Right Medication

From time to time in my life I've gone through periods of anxiety, fear, and despair—from moderate to severe. The most recent lasted for eight months and culminated during a two-week period when I became so immobilized that my wife took me to the emergency room. There, the doctor prescribed for me the antidepressant Wellbutrin.

I started the medication that night, and within a few days began to feel my energy and motivation return. I took on a project that I had been putting off for months—and finished it with confidence and ease. It was as if someone had pushed the "on" switch inside my brain. As the days progressed and the anxiety decreased, I was no longer distressed by my old fears. I felt like myself.

I've now been taking the medication for a month, and it continues to work well. Because I am job hunting and am under financial pressure, I still have mild bouts of anxiety. The difference is that before, I would have been overwhelmed. Now I am able to do temp work while looking for a full-time job. I am also using cognitive therapy to respond rationally when I worry excessively about the future.

If after taking an antidepressant you experience extreme symptoms, such as intense emotional or physical agitation, anxiety, violent thoughts, mania, or suicidal thinking, tell your prescriber immediately! Most likely lowering the dose will result in a diminishing of your symptoms.

There are a number of ways to reduce the risk of having an adverse or "paradoxical reaction" to an antidepressant.

- If you are thinking of going on medication, find a well-trained pharmacologist who is up to date on the latest research and can carefully monitor a drug's known and unknown side effects.
- As an informed consumer, you should always read the package insert that comes with an antidepressant to learn about potential contraindications. Ask your pharmacist for a free insert. If you see a particular side effect listed that you have experienced before in a negative way, tell your prescriber.

• Another way to diminish the risk of a negative reaction is to start with a very low initial dose, especially if you are sensitive to medication. Ask your prescriber if you can begin with half the minimum dose. (You can cut the pill in half to do this.) Then you can slowly adjust the dose upward. The following table provides more helpful information on selecting the right dose.

Personally, I have found that it is preferable to begin a new medication during the day. At night my defenses are down and my

How Big a Dose? Ask the Patient

Before writing a prescription, doctors should give every patient a questionnaire to determine whether he or she needs the standard dose. Here are some sample questions your doctor should ask you.

• Are you sensitive to any prescription or nonprescription drugs?
• How does alcohol affect you?
• Do some drugs make you tired or sleepy; such as cold or allergy remedies or antihistamines? Tranquilizers or anticonvulsants? Motion-sickness remedies or antinausea agents?
• Do some drugs give you energy or cause anxiety or insomnia; such as coffee, tea, chocolate, or other caffeine-like substances? Appetite suppressants (prescription or nonprescription)? Cold or allergy remedies or decongestants?
• Have you ever had a reaction to epinephrine (adrenaline chloride, which dentists often inject along with pain-numbing medication)?
• Have you ever had any side effects from any other prescription or nonprescription drugs (such as impaired memory or coordination, blurred vision, headaches, indigestion, diarrhea, constipation, dizziness, palpitations, rashes, swelling, or ringing in the ears)?
• Overall, how would you describe yourself with regard to medication: Very sensitive? Not particularly sensitive? Very tolerant—i.e., you usually require high doses?

* Excerpted from Denise Grady, "Too Much of a Good Thing? Doctor Challenges Drug Manual," *New York Times,* 12 October, 1999, D1.

unconscious is open, making me more vulnerable to adverse reactions. I suspect that this may be true of a percentage of other people who suffer from depression and are prone to anxiety.

If I Have Resistance to Taking Medication? How Should I Deal with It?

If you need to stay on medication to remain well, try not to think of this as a personal weakness. When your body requires assistance to remain in balance, it is no different than having any other illness that requires medication (e.g., insulin for diabetes, antihypertensive drugs for high blood pressure, or cholesterol-lowering drugs for heart disease).

Unfortunately, most people have mixed feelings about taking psychiatric medication. Many of my clients tell me, "I should be able to lick this on my own. Why do I have to be dependent on a pill?" (Meanwhile, they see no problem in taking insulin or antihypertensive medication.) Some folks never do get used to the side effects, while others complain of feeling "flat" or "emotionally removed."

My reply to these concerns is that taking medication is a trade-off. While some of the side effects may be bothersome, their discomfort is negligible compared to the agony of experiencing a clinical depression. Nonetheless, even people who are helped by medication display ambivalence about being "dependent" on these drugs.

Not surprisingly, studies show that 70 percent of patients prematurely discontinue their medication or discontinue their medication abruptly rather than gradually. Such premature or abrupt cessation is associated with a 77 percent increase in the rate of relapse or recurrence of the depressive episode. The moral of the story is clear: Do not make any changes in your medication regimen without first consulting your physician or prescriber.

What Should I Know about My Medication?

To increase the likelihood that a medication will work well, patients and families must actively interact with the doctor who is prescribing it. Questions you should ask include:

Alphabetical Listing of Medications by Trade Name

Antidepressant Medications

Trade name	Chemical or generic name
Adapin	doxepin
Anafranil	clomipramine
Asendin	amoxapine
Aventyl	nortriptyline
Celexa	citalopram
Desyrel	trazodone
Effexor	venlafaxine
Elavil	amitriptyline
Ludiomil	maprotiline
Luvox	fluvoxamine
Marplan	isocarboxazid
Nardil	phenelzine
Norpramin	desipramine
Pamelor	nortriptyline
Parnate	tranylcypromine
Paxil	paroxetine
Pertofrane	desipramine
Prozac	fluoxetine
Serzone	nefazodone
Sinequan	doxepin
Surmontil	trimipramine
Tofranil	imipramine
Vivactil	protriptyline
Wellbutrin	bupropion
Zoloft	sertraline

Antimanic Medications

Trade name	Chemical or generic name
Cibalith-S	lithium citrate
Depakote	divalproex sodium
Eskalith	lithium carbonate
Lithane	lithium carbonate
Lithobid	lithium carbonate
Tegretol	carbamazepine

Antianxiety Medications

Trade name	Chemical or generic name
Ativan	lorazepam
Azene	clorazepate
BuSpar	buspirone
Centrax	prazepam
Dalmane	flurazepam
Klonopin	clonazepam
Librium	chlordiazepoxide
Paxipam	halazepam
Serax	oxazepam
Seroquel	quetiapine
Tranxene	clorazepate
Valium	diazepam
Xanax	alprazolam

- What is the name of the medication and what is it supposed to do?
- When and how often should I take it, and when should I stop taking it, if at all?
- What, if any, food, drinks, other medications, or activities should I avoid while taking the prescribed medication?
- What are the potential side effects, and what should I do if they occur?
- What written information is available about the medication?

The table on the adjacent page lists the most commonly prescribed drugs for depression, bipolar disorder, and anxiety by their generic (chemical) names and trade (brand) names. If your medication's trade name does not appear, look it up by its generic name or ask your doctor or pharmacist for more information.

What If the Medication Doesn't Work?

There is no single panacea for depression. As helpful as antidepressants can be, they do not work for everyone. In 1999, Steven Hyman, director of the National Institute of Mental Health, was quoted as saying, "Given how common depression is, it is a major public health threat that 20 percent of people don't get more than a modest benefit from any of our therapies."[*] Psychiatrists say that the number of people who don't respond to drugs is closer to 10 percent. Nonetheless, if you are one of those one in ten, please do not give up. We will be exploring natural antidepressants whose side-effect profile is lower and which you may tolerate better. (This is the case with my partner, Joan, who finds that she can tolerate St. John's Wort much better than the synthesized drugs.) In addition, if you are extremely depressed, electroconvulsive therapy (ECT) can be a major lifesaver. There are also less intrusive methods of stimulating the brain (such as RTMS and vagus nerve stimulation) that show favorable outcomes in the initial studies. Moreover, depressive episodes are usually time-limited so they often resolve on their own. Sometimes a period of rest is all that is needed.

---

[*] As quoted in Joannie M. Schrof and Stacey Schultz, "Melancholy Nation: Depression Is on the Rise, Despite Prozac. But New Drugs Could Offer Help," *U.S. News and World Report,* March 8, 1999, Volume 126, Number 9: 57.

I experienced healing of my major depressive by means other than medication. In my most recent episode, I was healed through the power of prayer. Many people whose memoirs are listed in the bibliography improved without drugs (authors William Styron and Jeffrey Smith are examples). Thus, while antidepressants should be your first line of treatment in major depression, please know that you still can get better even if they do not work for you.

Natural Alternatives to Prozac and Other Pharmaceuticals

In many respects, antidepressants have revolutionized the treatment of depression. By rebalancing the brain's neurotransmitters, they impact mood at the biochemical level and allow the tormented sufferer to achieve emotional equilibrium. However, not everyone responds to these drugs favorably. For some people, the side effects are too harsh, while others fail to experience the desired relief.

Fortunately, nutritionally oriented doctors and herbalists have researched a number of natural therapeutic substances, such as herbs, vitamins, and amino acids, that may alleviate depression. What follows is a brief summary of the most commonly used alternative modalities. While I did not use these remedies during my depressive episode, I have since used St. John's Wort and fish oil and have heard positive anecdotal reports from other patients. Although scientific studies of St. John's Wort have been done in Germany, many of the other remedies have not been subjected to the same rigorous double-blind studies that are used with pharmaceutical drugs. This is largely because no one has put up the millions of dollars that would be needed to research the safety and effectiveness of these compounds.

Because even "natural" substances can produce strong reactions in sensitive individuals, anyone taking these remedies should do so under the supervision of a nutritionally oriented physician (psychiatrist, family doctor, chiropractor, or naturopath). As with antidepressants, it is important to try one natural remedy at a time until you discover what works. Moreover, you should not switch from a prescription antidepressant to any of these supplements without first consulting your health care provider.

St. John's Wort

St. John's Wort *(Hypericum perforatum)* is the star attraction in the field of natural alternatives to Prozac. The yellow flowering tops of St. John's Wort have been consumed for centuries in tea or olive oil extract for a variety of nervous conditions. In 1994, physicians in Germany prescribed sixty-six million daily doses of St. John's Wort, making it the country's medication of choice for the treatment of mild to moderate depression.

Patients who respond to St. John's Wort show an improvement in mood and ability to carry out their daily routine. Symptoms such as sadness, hopelessness, feelings of worthlessness, exhaustion, and poor sleep also decrease. In one study, St. John's Wort was as effective as the prescription antidepressant Imipramine for treating mild to moderate depression (it is less effective for major depression). Moreover, St. John's Wort is relatively free of side effects when compared to pharmaceutical antidepressants (common side effects are gastrointestinal symptoms, allergy, fatigue, and increased sensitivity to light).

The standard dosage of St. John's Wort prescribed by the European doctors is a 0.3 percent extract of the active ingredient, hypericin, taken in 300 milligram capsules, three times a day. A person using St. John's Wort should be monitored for four to six weeks before evaluating its effectiveness. In addition, St. John's Wort should not be taken along with the traditional antidepressants because of potential unwanted drug interactions. If you are already taking Prozac or another antidepressant and would like to try St. John's Wort, consult with a psychiatrist or other medical practitioner and wean yourself from the pharmaceutical before you start the St. John's Wort.

5-Hydroxy-Tryptophan

L-tryptophan is an amino acid that serves as a metabolic precursor to the neurotransmitter serotonin (the one that is affected by SSRI drugs such as Prozac, Zoloft, and the like). L-tryptophan was quite popular in treating depression and insomnia during the 1980s. However, in 1990 the substance was deemed responsible for a number of deaths and was pulled from the market in the United States. Although the deaths were later attributed to a contaminated non-pharmaceutical-grade product made by one particular manufacturer, L-tryptophan is currently available only by prescription in the United States. (Ironically, just four days after L-tryptophan was banned, the March 26, 1990, issue of *Newsweek* announced "Prozac: A Breakthrough Drug for Depression.")

However, a product similar to L-tryptophan, 5-hydroxy-tryptophan, is currently available over the counter. A metabolite of tryptophan (it forms from the breakdown of tryptophan in the body), 5-HTP is a precursor to serotonin that may work even better than tryptophan. In a head-to-head study conducted by German and Swiss researchers in 1991, 5-HTP and the antidepressant Luvox were shown to be equally effective in treating depression over a six-week period. Since then, 5-HTP has been used by many people to lower their current dosages of antidepressants or to replace them completely. Such adjustments should be made under the care of your psychiatrist or physician.

S-Adenosylmethionine (SAMe or SAM-e)

Along with 5-HTP, S-Adenosylmethionine (SAMe) is one of today's most popular natural antidepressants. SAMe is a metabolite of the amino acid methionine. All of the major neurotransmitters that are thought to be deficient in people suffering from depression—serotonin, norepinephrine, and dopamine—need sufficient quantities of SAMe for their synthesis. Although they also need SAMe for their breakdown, it appears that therapeutic doses of SAMe boost levels of serotonin as well as norepinephrine and dopamine.

One of the advantages of SAMe is that its side effects are extremely well tolerated (in controlled trials, people reported more side effects with a placebo). "It appears that S-Adenosylmethionine is a rapid and effective treatment for major depression and has few side effects," wrote Kim Bell and her associates at the University of California.

Studies show that depressions marked by lethargy, apathy, guilt, and suicidal impulses may be the most responsive to SAMe. According to Richard Brown of Columbia University, patients report a dramatic increase in energy levels after taking SAMe. Brown also recommends SAMe for people suffering from SAD (seasonal affective disorder), postpartum depression, menopausal mood swings, sleep disturbances, and PMS. As with 5-HTP, if you are on a conventional antidepressant, consult with your prescriber if you are thinking of taking SAMe.*

Kava Extract

Kava (Piper methysticum) is a member of the pepper family, which is native to the South Pacific. Its tuberous rootstock is used to make a beverage (also called kava) that is believed to make people happy and sociable. Hence, it has been used for hundreds of years in native ceremonies and celebrations. In recent years, many people in Western cultures have prepared and ingested the beverage, reporting similar tranquilizing and uplifting effects.

Like St. John's Wort, kava extracts are gaining popularity in European countries for treating depression and anxiety. The active ingredients in kava are the kavalactones, although several other components seem to be involved as well. In a number of double-blind studies, individuals taking kava extract containing 70 percent kavalactones showed improvement in symptoms of anxiety as measured by several standardized psychological tests, including the Hamilton Anxiety Scale. In addition, unlike the benzodiazepines—such as Xanax and Ativan—that are prescribed for anxiety, kava extract neither impairs mental functioning nor promotes sedation.

Another problem with benzodiazepines is that the body gradually adapts to their presence, so it takes more of the drug over time to produce the same effect. This condition, known as *tolerance,* does not seem to occur with kavalactones.

Finally, although no significant side effects have been reported from taking kava at the normal levels, some case reports suggest that

---

* Syd Baumel, *Dealing with Depression Naturally* (Los Angeles: Keats Publishing, 2000), 116–118.

kava may interfere with dopamine and worsen Parkinson's disease. Until this issue is resolved, kava should not be used by patients who have this illness.* In addition, kava should not be combined with other tranquilizers such as alcohol, since there may be unwanted chemical reactions.

Treating Underlying Metabolic and Endocrine Disorders

Untreated endocrine problems of all sorts are recognized as having the potential to cause mood difficulties. The most common of these is depression caused by hypothyroidism (an underactive thyroid), which can be successfully treated using thyroid medication. Other medical conditions that may exacerbate or even cause depressive symptoms are chronic fatigue syndrome, candidasis (a fungal over-growth), reactive hypoglycemia, hormonal imbalances, vitamin and mineral deficiencies, and amino acid deficiencies. The diagnosis and treatment of such conditions should always be done by a qualified health care professional.

Vitamin and Mineral Supplementation

Many clinicians believe that supplementing your food intake with certain vitamins, minerals, and amino acids may also help to balance your brain chemistry.

Vitamins B6 and B3

The entire vitamin B complex is known to maintain and promote normal mental functioning. Deficiencies of any or all of these vitamins can produce significant symptoms relating to depression, e.g., anxiety, irritability, lethargy, and fatigue. Although the research remains inconsistent, several studies indicate that vitamin B6 supplementation helps

---

* Michael Murray, *Natural Alternatives to Prozac*, (New York: William Morrow and Co., 1996) 140–150.

alleviate depression associated with premenstrual syndrome. Since oral contraceptives can deplete the body of vitamin B6, women taking birth control pills also need to supplement their diets with B6. In addition, niacinamide, a form of vitamin B3, has shown some success in alleviating both depression and anxiety.

Folic Acid

A large percentage of depressed people have low levels of the B vitamin folic acid. Anyone suffering from chronic depression should be evaluated by a nutritionally oriented doctor for a possible folic acid deficiency. Folic acid is usually taken with vitamin B12 and is best supervised by a physician. Large doses of folic acid may contribute to mania. Thus, anyone with a bipolar disorder should be evaluated by a qualified health care provider before trying this supplement.*

Omega-3 Fatty Acids and Fish Oil

In a study published in 1999, Andrew Stoll, M.D., of Harvard University found that fish oil proved so therapeutic for patients with bipolar disorder he ended the study early to put everyone on the fish oil regimen. Stoll found that 90 percent of the subjects given high doses of fish oil experienced a significant reduction of their symptoms of depression.

The therapeutic aspect of fish oil consists of omega-3 essential fatty acids. Omega-3 fatty acids are integral components of the brain's cellular membranes, including the crucial synapses where chemical messages are transmitted from cell to cell. Although other types of fatty acids (such as those from meat) are available, the brain prefers to use the long-chain polyunsaturated essential fatty acids (EFAs) to build its neuronal membranes. Stoll and his colleagues believe that when the EFAs are incorporated into the neuronal membranes, the neurons become more electrochemically stable and less

---

* E. Reynolds et al, "Folic Deficiency in Depressive Illness," *British Journal of Psychiatry,* 117: 287–92.

likely to "fly off the handle." This effect both stabilizes people who suffer from bipolar disorder and prevents depression.

Stoll and other researchers believe that the increasing rates of depression in Western cultures correspond to a loss of omega-3 fatty acids from the Western diet, due to modern farming and food processing. And in countries such as Japan, where per capita intake of fish is 150 pounds (compared to 25 to 70 pounds in the U.S. and Canada), the rate of major depression is thirty times lower.

To supplement your diet with omega-3 fatty acids, eat lots of deep-sea cold-water fish such as salmon and sardines. Michael Norden of the University of Washington speculates that omega-3s, which organisms produce more abundantly to adapt to cold weather, might be therapeutic for winter depression. This idea gains credence from the fact that the traditional Inuit people did not get depressed and suicidal during winters of total darkness. Their diet was filled with omega-3s from northern fish and marine animals.

In addition to eating lots of fish, you can take daily doses of fish oil from cod liver oil (my first choice) or from the many EFA fish oil supplements that are now on the market. For those who are strictly vegetarian, linseed oil and flax seed oil are also rich in EFAs. Make sure that you purchase unrefined oils that have been mechanically or expeller pressed from organically grown seeds.*

GABA (Gamma Amino Butryic Acid)

GABA is usually classified as an amino acid, although it actually serves as a neurotransmitter (there are more GABA sites in the brain than for other neurotransmitters, such as dopamine or serotonin). GABA basically acts as an inhibitory transmitter, keeping the brain and body from going into overdrive. GABA supplements seem to be quite effective for anxiety disorders as well as insomnia (especially the type of insomnia where racing thoughts keep you from falling asleep). Hence, those suffering from depression exacerbated by anxiety might want to consider taking this supplement.

---

* Syd Baumel, *Dealing With Depression Naturally* (Los Angeles: Keats Publishing, 2000), 104–110.

Other Amino Acids

Amino acids are chains of proteins that are the building blocks of the physical body. Some nutritionally orientated physicians believe that taking amino acids can help your body to restock the brain's supply of vital neurotransmitters such as serotonin and norepinephrine.

L-tyrosine

L-tyrosine is an amino acid that serves as a precursor to the neuro-transmitters norepinephrine and dopamine, which have been shown to be deficient in many depressives. Adding supplements of this amino acid may help the body to form more of these neurotransmitters during difficult times. Tyrosine may also be helpful in cases where clinical or subclinical thyroid disease is present.

L-phenylalynine and DL-phenylalynine

Phenylalynine is a precursor to tyrosine, and so exhibits many of the same effects. In addition, phenylalynine supplements can help your body produce a substance called phenylethylamine, which is also present in chocolate and marijuana and which the body creates in greater amounts when the individual is in love. Phenylethylamine is supposedly present to a greater degree in the DL form of phenylalynine than in the L form; however, the DL form may be more likely to increase blood pressure. (DL is a mixture of the essential amino acid L-phenylalynine and its essential mirror image, D-phenylalynine.)

Phosphatidylserine (PS)

PS is one of a class of substances known as phospholipids. The permeability of brain-cell membranes depends on adequate amounts of these substances. Some studies have shown PS to be an effective antidepressant in the elderly. PS may work by suppressing the production of cortisol, a naturally occurring steroid hormone whose levels are elevated in depressed people.

Dehydroepiandrosterone (DHEA)

DHEA is a naturally occurring androgen produced by the adrenal glands. It is found abundantly in plasma and brain tissue and is the precursor of many hormones produced by the adrenals. DHEA seems to alleviate some of the effects of aging, such as fatigue and muscle weakness. Levels of DHEA may be lower in depressed patients, such that supplementation with DHEA may reduce symptoms.* However, since DHEA is a hormone, you should not take it without having your doctor check your blood level of the hormone. Also, check with your physician before adding it to your diet if you are on an anti-depressant, a thyroid medication, insulin, or estrogen.

Alternative Medical Therapies

In addition to the herbs, vitamins, minerals, and amino acids listed above, a number of alternative medical therapies are available to treat depression. These include:

- acupuncture
- aromatherapy
- Bach flower remedies (and other flower essences)
- herbal remedies
- chiropractic
- homeopathy
- reiki healing
- therapeutic gemstones

Although these modalities lie outside of mainstream medicine, I have seen them alleviate depression in certain individuals, especially those people who are sensitive to subtle energies and for whom traditional medicine has not worked.

If you are interested in trying one or more of these alternative approaches, consult first with the health provider who is treating you for depression. Because of their noninvasive nature, you may be able to employ these therapies at the same time that you are receiving standard treatment (medication and/or psychotherapy).

---

* Owen Wolkowitz, Victor I. Reus, et al, "Double Blind Treatment of Major Depression With Dehydroepiandrosterone," *American Journal of Psychiatry* 156 (1999): 646–649.

This Week's Goals and Assignments

Here are your assignments for the upcoming week:

1. Fill out the Assessing My Medication inventory below. If you have any questions or concerns about your current medication regimen, make it a goal to talk with your current prescriber.

2. Fill out your weekly goal sheet.

Ongoing Self-Care Activities

- Read your vision statement.
- Chart your moods in the Daily Mood Diary.
- Meet with your recovery partner.
- Do some form of exercise or movement (three times or more a week).
- Drink at least sixty-four ounces of water, sipping throughout the day.

Assessing My Medication

1. What is my previous history with psychiatric medication?

2. What psychiatric medications, both conventional and alternative, am I currently taking? If I am not currently taking medication, what is the reason? Am I open to trying medication?

3. What kinds of results am I getting from my current medications?

4. What aspects of taking my medication do I like? What would I like to see change?

5. What is my attitude about taking medication? Do I feel any shame, embarrassment, or ambivalence? Would I be willing to discuss these feelings with my counselor or prescriber? (If so, make this your weekly goal.)

My Goal Sheet for Week 4

This week's starting date:_____ My recovery partner:_____

Date and time we will connect: _____

Goal or goals: _____

_____

Benefits of attaining this goal:_____

_____

Action plan:_____

_____

Ongoing goals (check off the ones as you accomplish them)
_____ Read my vision statement daily (upon awakening or before bed)
_____ Chart my moods in the Daily Mood Diary
_____ Participate in some form of exercise or movement
_____ This was my average mood on the daily mood scale (–5 to +5)

How was my mood this week?

Record your moods below for each day of the week. (–5 to +5)

Day	Mood	Comments
Mon		
Tue		
Wed		
Thu		
Fri		
Sat		
Sun		

Cognitive Restructuring: Making Your Mind Your Friend

The mind is its own place, and in itself
Can make a heav'n of hell, or a hell of heav'n.

—JOHN MILTON

FIFTH WEEK OVERVIEW

In this week, you will learn how to change your mood by changing the way you think about yourself and the world.

In the previous two weeks, we learned how changing our physiology through physical self-care and antidepressants can lead to a better mood. Just as changing our body's physiology can change the way we feel, so too can our thoughts affect our mood. Every thought that you and I think produces a chemical reaction in the brain, which in turn corresponds to a feeling. As one brain scientist explained it, every thought has a neurochemical equivalent! (See diagram below.)

thought ⟶ chemical reaction ⟶ feeling

To illustrate this principle, let us imagine the following situation. It is the middle of January and, for the fifteenth straight day, it's raining in

Portland. Let's call this "an event." In response to this event, person #1 complains, "These gray days are driving me nuts. Why did I ever leave California?" Meanwhile, person #2 exclaims, "Hooray for the rain! Now there will be snow in the mountains so I can go skiing this weekend."

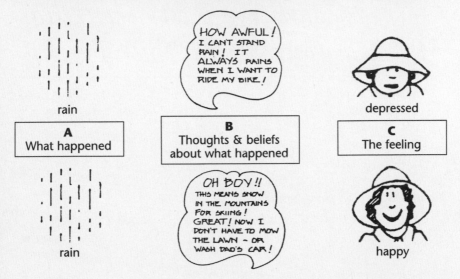

Notice that the same circumstance produced two entirely different feelings. Although we are taught to believe that events *cause* us to have certain feelings, it is not so. Rather, it is our *interpretation of the event* or how we think about it that elicits our feelings.

Looking at the illustration above, what would happen if the depressed person changed his or her thoughts about the rain? Wouldn't that person's feelings change, too? This principle is critical in managing depression, since people who are prone to depression tend to look at the world in a way that produces feelings of melancholy.

Take a moment and complete the following sentences on a separate piece of paper or in your Better Mood Journal:

I am . . .
Most people . . .
The world is . . .
When I think about my future, I see . . .

---

* Illustration reprinted with the permission of Timberline Press, Inc.

Do not stop after completing each sentence once. Complete the phrases over and over, and don't stop until you have run out of conclusions.

If the general tenor of your conclusions seemed bleak or gloomy, you are suffering from what psychiatrist Aaron Beck calls "the cognitive triad for depression." It consists of:

1. A negative view of yourself.

2. A negative interpretation of the world.

3. Negative expectations for the future. Comedian Lily Tomlin echoed this mindset when she said, "Things will get worse before they get worse."

Such a tendency to "see through a glass darkly" is usually caused by two things.

1. **A person's brain biochemistry and temperament.** In chapter 9, we learned that some infants come into this world with a temperament and personality that is especially fearful, pessimistic, and withdrawn. Childhood trauma can also adversely impact the brain chemistry and nervous system.

2. **Our habits of negative thinking,** most of which we learned through our upbringing and conditioning. (For example, a parent who worries a lot will inadvertently teach his or her child to worry, too.) Fortunately, psychologists have developed a process called "cognitive restructuring," which allows you to *identify* and *release* the negative thinking that feeds and accentuates depression.

    At the center of cognitive restructuring are "cognitive distortions"—automatic negative thought patterns that people have about themselves, others, and the world. These thinking errors distort reality, thereby contributing to feelings of loneliness, alienation, stress, anger, helplessness, distrust, and fear. Synonyms for cognitive distortions are:
    • "Stinking thinking" (from Alcoholics Anonymous)
    • Irrational beliefs (from Rational Emotive Therapy)
    • ANTS—automatic negative thoughts
    • "junk thoughts"—like junk food—unhealthy thoughts

The process of cognitive restructuring involves becoming aware of our negative thoughts, challenging their assumptions, and then replacing them, as demonstrated in the following three-step process.

The Ten Thinking Errors
Known As Cognitive Distortions

Painful feelings are often the result of distorted, negative thinking. Here are some common cognitive distortions.

1. All-or-nothing thinking. You see things in black-and-white categories, e.g., "If I don't do something perfectly, I'm a failure."

2. Overgeneralization. You see a single negative event as a never-ending pattern of defeat by using words such as "never" or "always." In response to finding some bird droppings on his car, a depressed salesperson exclaims, "Just my luck! Birds are *always* crapping on my car."

3. Mental filter. You pick out a single negative detail and dwell on it exclusively.

4. Disqualifying the positive. You reject anything positive that happens, insisting that it doesn't count.

5. Magnification or minimization.You exaggerate the importance of some things (such as your faults) and minimize others (such as your desirable qualities).

6. Jumping to conclusions. You make a negative interpretation, even though there are no definite facts to support the conclusion.
   a) Mind reading. You conclude that someone else is reacting negatively to you without checking it out.
   b) Fortune-telling. You are convinced that things will turn out badly, i.e., "I lost my job so I'm going to lose my house." This is also called "catastrophizing" or "awfulizing."

7. Emotional reasoning. You assume that negative emotions reflect the way things really are, i.e., "It feels like this depression will never end, therefore it must be so." Or, "I'm scared of flying, therefore it must be unsafe."

8. "Should" statements. You use these on yourself and produce guilt. Directing these statements toward others can make you angry and resentful. Similar to "musts, "ought-tos," and "have-tos."

9. Labeling and mislabeling. This is an extreme form of overgeneralization. Instead of saying, "I made a mistake," you say, "I'm a loser." Mislabeling can be directed at others as well, e.g., "He's a jerk." This leads to dehumanization.

10. Personalization and blame. You hold yourself personally responsible for an event that isn't under your control, e.g., "my son got a bad report card so I must be a bad parent." Blame holds the other person responsible—"My marriage is bad because my spouse is a jerk."

1. Become aware that your mind is engaging in negative thinking. Identify the self-defeating negative thought or self-statement. Then say out loud, "CANCEL! CANCEL!"
2. Identify the specific distortion. Use the table on the adjacent page to locate the cognitive distortion behind each thought.
3. Replace each distortion with a more rational or realistic thought, and note how you feel.

For example, let's say that Henry is contemplating his upcoming job interview. As he waits for the interviewer, Henry thinks to himself, "I'll probably blow it. My mind will go blank, and I won't be able to think of anything to say." These thoughts send a signal to Henry's brain that initiates chemical reactions, which in turn create feelings of fear and anxiety.

Fortunately, Henry has been practicing cognitive restructuring. Suddenly, he becomes aware of his negative self-talk and repeats to himself, "CANCEL! CANCEL!" Henry then identifies the cognitive distortion of "fortune-telling/catastrophizing" (see item 6b from the cognitive distortions list). He replaces the distortion with a more realistic assessment of the situation, e.g., "I have prepared extremely well for this interview. If I stay focused on what I know, I'll be fine."

Cognitive restructuring is based on an ancient metaphysical principle known as "thought substitution," described here by Emmet Fox:

> One of the great mental laws is the Law of Substitution. This means that the only way to get rid of a certain thought is to substitute another one for it. You cannot dismiss a thought directly. You can do so only by substituting another one for it. If I say to you, "Do not think of the Statue of Liberty," of course, you immediately think of it. But if you become interested in something else, you forget all about the Statue of Liberty—and this is a case of substitution.

Working with Core Beliefs

One discovers that destiny can be directed, that one does not have to remain in bondage to the first wax imprint made in childhood. One need not be branded by the first pattern. Once the deforming mirror is smashed, there is a possibility of wholeness; there is a possibility of joy.
—ANAIS NÏN

In practicing cognitive restructuring, we need to change not only our present negative thinking but also the dysfunctional assumptions and *core beliefs* that underlie that thinking (see Disempowering Core Beliefs). Many of these negative beliefs were formed in early childhood when parents, teachers, relatives, our religious upbringing, society, and television all gave us a model of *who we were* and *how the world worked*. Because young children have not developed the faculty of discrimination, this programming went directly into our brains unedited.

The Cognitive Model of Depression shows how programming can contaminate our thinking. A young child who experiences criticism from her parents comes to believe, "I'm unlovable" and "If I don't achieve, I am worthless." Years later, this person is involved in a relationship breakup that activates these core beliefs and elicits cognitive distortions such as "Nobody loves me" (overgeneralization), "I can't live without him" (all-or-nothing thinking), and "I'll never find anybody like that" (fortune-telling). The repetition of this thinking elicits the symptoms of depression.

Disempowering Core Beliefs

The following are some of the common negative core beliefs that contribute to the negative thinking associated with depression and anxiety. Note which ones you identify with. For each belief, you may want to ask yourself "Where did this belief come from?" and "What more empowering belief can I put in its place?"

About Yourself

- I don't deserve love.
- I must earn love.
- I'm not lovable.
- I'm incompetent.
- I'm not important.
- I'm not creative.
- I must please others.
- I don't fit in.
- I'm not capable.
- My opinions don't count.
- I'm a bad person.
- I can't do it.
- I'm dumb.
- I'm not as smart as others.
- I'm clumsy.
- I'm ugly.
- I fail no matter how hard I try.
- I don't deserve to succeed.
- I don't deserve pleasure.
- It's not okay to feel good.
- I can't have what I want.
- I don't deserve happiness.
- I'm a loser.
- I can't be myself.
- It's not okay to show my feelings.

About the World

- The world is unsafe.
- The world is unhappy.
- Money doesn't grow on trees.
- Nice guys finish last.
- Life's a bitch and then you die.
- Life is only about suffering.
- The world is against me.

About Relationships

- I can't find love.
- I'll never find the right person.
- Men/women can't be trusted.
- If I love I'll be hurt.
- I can't risk being in a relationship.
- I can't make it without you.
- My partner can't make it without me.
- Marriage is a trap.
- I must control my partner.
- Relationships can't last.
- Divorce is a sin.
- The one I love will abandon me.
- I'm not meant to have a relationship.
- People I depend on will let me down.

Cognitive Model of Depression

Early Experience
Criticism and rejection from parents

↓

Formation of Dysfunctional Assumptions and Beliefs
I'm incompetent. I'm unlovable.
If I don't achieve highly, I'm worthless.
Unless I'm loved, I can't be happy.

↓

Critical Incident(s)
(Perception of) rejection by partner.

↓

Activation of Assumptions and Beliefs

↓

Negative Automatic Thoughts
Nobody loves me. I can't do anything right.
I'm nothing. I can't live without him or her.
I can't bear it. I shall never find anyone else like that.

↓ ↑ ↓ ↑ ↓

Symptoms of Depression

↓

Behavioral
- Lowered activity levels
- Slowness
- Withdrawal from
  positive activities
- Impaired coping with
  practical problems

Affective
- Sadness
- Guilt
- Shame
- Anxiety
- Anger

Motivational
- Apathy
- Inertia
- Overwhelmed by
  ordinary tasks
- Loss of self-reliance

Cognitive
- Indecisiveness
- Poor concentration
  and memory

Physical
- Sleep disturbance
- Loss of appetite
- Loss of sexual desire
- Rumination

Although we had no control over our early programming, as adults we have both the power and the responsibility to change unwanted patterns. The first step in releasing our core beliefs is to become aware of them, to make what is unconscious conscious. You can begin this process by reading over the Disempowering Core Beliefs listings and noting which ones you identify with.

If your limiting core beliefs arose from early trauma or abuse, it may be necessary to grieve the loss in therapy and do other related healing. Ultimately, you can use affirmations (which we will be covering in Week 7) to help program your mind with new and more empowering beliefs.

This Week's Goals and Assignments

Here are your assignments for the upcoming week:

1. Fill out the Assessing My Habits of Thinking inventory.

2. Over the next week, record any upsetting events or feelings in your Daily Mood Log. Note how your negative thoughts about events produce distressing feelings.

3. Take at least one of these *events* or *feelings* and use the "Cognitive Restructuring Worksheet" on page 219 to identify and release the negative thinking that led to the upsetting mood. Share this process with your recovery partner during your weekly check-in. Here is a summary of how to use the worksheet.

   Step 1: Describe the upsetting situation or event (it can also be an upsetting thought).
   Step 2: Record your negative feelings.
   Step 3: Use the three-column technique to change your thinking.
   • In column 1, list your ANTS, your automatic negative thoughts.
   • In column 2, identify the distortion behind each negative thought.
   • In column 3, write a rebuttal in the form of a more realistic or rational thought.

This bit of mental alchemy can significantly reduce your symptoms of anxiety and depression. Depending on the intensity of those symptoms, you may wish to practice cognitive restructuring several times a day or several times an hour to keep yourself from drifting into negative thinking.

Assessing My Habits of Thinking

Please take a few moments to answer the following questions as a way of assessing the quality of your thinking habits. You can write in the space provided or in your Better Mood Journal.

1. Do I notice when I engage in thinking errors known as cognitive distortions? Which do I employ most often? Please refer to The Ten Thinking Errors Known as Cognitive Distortions.

2. When I become aware of my automatic negative thoughts, how quickly do I replace them with more realistic, rational ones?

3. Much of our negative thinking grows out of core beliefs about ourselves and the world that we learned in early childhood. Examples of negative core beliefs include, "I am unlovable," "Life is about struggle," "I am incompetent," "My worth is based on what I accomplish," and "Big boys don't cry."

What core beliefs or attitudes do I have that contribute to my negative thinking? Refer to Disempowering Core Beliefs on page 213 to see some examples.

Ongoing Self-Care Activities

- Read your vision statement.
- Chart your moods in the Daily Mood Diary.
- Meet with your recovery partner.
- Formulate a goal for your weekly goal sheet.
- Exercise (three or more times a week).
- Drink at least sixty-four ounces of water, sipping throughout the day.

ABC Daily Mood Log

Use this ABC Daily Mood Log to keep track of the events and circumstances in your life that trigger negative thoughts that lead to painful feelings. I have provided some examples to get you started.

Date	A Actual event	B My negative thoughts and beliefs	C Emotional consequences
April 4	Boss seems annoyed	What have I done? If I keep making him mad, I will get fired.	Anxious, worried
April 5	Friend didn't want to go to the movies	He must be mad at me	Sad, feel rejected

Cognitive Restructuring Worksheet Example

Step 1: Describe the situation or event: Henry is contemplating his upcoming job interview.

Step 2: Record your negative feelings (sad, angry, afraid, helpless, etc.): Henry feels anxious, fearful, and worried. He is also a bit agitated.

Step 3: Use the three-column technique to change your thinking.

A **Automatic Negative Thoughts (ANTS)**	B **Cognitive Distortion**	C **Rebuttal: Substitute Realistic Thoughts**
"I'll probably blow it. My mind will go blank, and I won't be able to think of anything to say."	Fortune-telling	"I have prepared well. Just breathe during the interview and all will be okay."
"He's probably just giving me the interview because he knows my father."	Mind reading	"I really don't know what the boss is thinking."
"I don't really have that much to offer. He probably has other applicants who are more qualified than I am."	Discounting the positive and jumping to conclusions	"I have a lot of qualifications for the job. Otherwise, I wouldn't have gotten the interview."
"I'll probably make a fool of myself."	Labeling and fortune-telling	"In the past, I have done well at interviews."
"If I blow it, it would be a disaster."	Magnification and catastrophizing	"This is not the only job out there. Not getting the job could be a learning experience."

Cognitive Restructuring Worksheet*

Step 1: Describe the situation or event.

Step 2: Record your negative feelings (sad, angry, afraid, helpless, etc.)

Step Three: Use the three-column technique to change your thinking.

A Automatic Negative Thoughts (ANTS)	B Cognitive Distortion	C Rebuttal: Substitute Realistic Thoughts

* Adapted from David Burn's *Feeling Good Handbook,* (New York: Viking Penguin, 1999).

My Goal Sheet for Week 5

This week's starting date: _____ My recovery partner: _____

Date and time we will connect: _____

Goal or goals: _____

_____

Benefits of attaining this goal: _____

_____

Action plan: _____

_____

Ongoing goals (check off the ones as you accomplish them)
_____ Read my vision statement daily (upon awakening or before bed)
_____ Chart my moods in the Daily Mood Diary
_____ Participate in some form of exercise or movement
_____ Monitor my self-talk with the Cognitive Restructuring Worksheet
_____ This was my average mood on the daily mood scale (–5 to +5)

How was my mood this week?

Record your moods below for each day of the week. (–5 to +5)

Day	Mood	Comments
Mon		
Tue		
Wed		
Thu		
Fri		
Sat		
Sun		

Learning to Think Like an Optimist

Most people are about as happy as they make up their minds to be.

—ABRAHAM LINCOLN

SIXTH WEEK OVERVIEW

In this week, you will learn techniques that will help you to think more positively.

Last week, in the lesson on cognitive restructuring, we learned that how we interpret or think about the events in our lives creates our feelings—not the events themselves. Now we are ready to take this process one step further and learn how to consciously cultivate an optimistic attitude. Training your mind to see life's glass as "half full" rather than "half empty" (as the pessimist does) can have a profound impact on your mental health.

Whether you are a pessimist or an optimist can have a significant impact on the state of your mental and physical health. Hundreds of studies show that pessimists give up more easily and become depressed more often. Optimists, on the other hand, do much better in school, in work, and on the playing field. Their health is generally good, and they age with fewer physical complaints than the rest of us. When optimists run for office, they are more likely to win than pessimists.

Like myself, if you suffer from depression and anxiety, your temperament and brain chemistry probably predispose you to think pessimistically. Nonetheless, researchers have demonstrated that a pessimistic mindset can be *modified* or significantly *altered* through learning new mental habits. In this week's lesson, we will learn a new set of cognitive skills that can help any pessimistic person to think more like an optimist. As a born pessimist who has practiced these techniques for years, I can assure you that they work.

The Key to Optimism: Shifting Your Mental Focus

In our lesson last week on cognitive therapy, we learned that there are always two aspects to any event or situation in our lives:

- The situation itself
- Our interpretation of the situation

Psychiatrist and concentration camp survivor Victor Frankl called this ability to choose our attitude in any given circumstance "the last of the human freedoms."

The reason we have this freedom is that situations are never totally black or white (see the yin yang symbol on the opposite page). Life is a mixture of light and dark, positive and negative. Or, as they say in the martial arts, every situation has both an inherent advantage and an inherent disadvantage. If this is true, then why not choose to focus on what is advantageous? This is precisely what the person with an optimistic mindset is able to do. Let's explore some tools that make this possible.

Optimist's Tool #1: An Attitude of Gratitude

Count your blessings, not your crosses,
Count your gains, not your losses.
Count your joys instead of your woes,
Count your friends instead of your foes.
Covet your health, not your wealth.
—PROVERB

What if you began each day by asking the following questions? "What are the positive aspects of my life right now? What can I be grateful for? What is working to support me in my health and healing?" If you thought long enough you would probably uncover a blessing or two, "The sun is shining; I have a roof over my head; I have loving friendships; I am not in physical pain; I can see and hear; I have enough to eat; I feel love for my child." Focusing on *what is working* in your life instead of what is not actually changes brain chemistry and allows you to counteract the negative thinking that is the hallmark of depression. There may be times, however, that you are extremely depressed and can't see *anything* positive in your life. If so, try not to get down on yourself. Your imbalanced brain is distorting your perception of reality. See if you can find others around you who can reflect back to you what is working even if you can't perceive it yourself.

The yin yang symbol is an ancient Chinese image that portrays the universe as an interplay of opposites—light and dark, night and day, positive and negative, and so on. Note that within the dark side of the circle lies a small circle of light. Hence, even that which we consider painful contains the seed of something redemptive.

Expressing gratitude does not mean denying pain or uncomfortable feelings. It doesn't mean pretending something is wonderful when it clearly is not. But when we focus *exclusively* on those dark and painful places, we close ourselves to the gifts that the universe brings.

As you take time each day to count your blessings and give thanks, you will learn to see the good wherever you look. This is how the great Zen master Banzan achieved enlightenment. One day, while walking in the marketplace, he overheard a conversation between a butcher and his customer.

"Give me the best piece of meat you have," said the customer.

"Every piece of meat I have is the best," the butcher replied. "There is no piece of meat here that is not the best."

Upon hearing this, Banzan became enlightened—he realized that every moment in life, like every piece of meat, contained something to be grateful for.*

Optimist's Tool #2: Reframing

Everything can be taken from a man but one thing—the ability to choose one's attitude in any given set of circumstances.
—VICTOR FRANKL

While most of us find it easy to be grateful when life is going well, what about during the bad times? Finding the good can be accomplished even during challenging situations by practicing reframing—the art of taking a difficult situation and putting a new frame around it so you focus on the inherent advantage. Actor Christopher Reeve practiced reframing his life. The actor who played Superman is bravely trying to accomplish the superhuman feat of learning to walk after being paralyzed by a spinal chord injury. During his treadmill therapy, Reeve unexpectedly broke his left leg. He had developed osteoporosis from a lack of calcium, and the strain of the exercise caused his femur to snap. Although the injury was discouraging, Reeve was quick to reframe the situation. "If I hadn't known to up

---

* Eckhart Tolle, *The Power of Now* (Novato, California: New World Library, 2001), 161.

What Is Your Explanatory Style?

According to Martin Seligman, author of the groundbreaking book *Learned Optimism,* optimists and pessimists have two very different methods of explaining misfortune. Seligman has found that:

- Pessimists see difficult times as *permanent* and *enduring,* while optimists know that "This, too, shall pass."
- Optimists see their troubles as specific to the situation; pessimists *generalize their misfortune* to see it as occurring everywhere. For example, the optimist who had a bad math teacher might say, "Mr. Jones is unfair," while the pessimist would say, "All math teachers are unfair."
- Pessimists see misfortune as their fault, while the optimist is more likely to blame the circumstances. For example, the pessimist who was hitless in a baseball game might say, "It's my fault we lost," while the optimist would conclude, "That pitcher was just too good." (Ironically, when good events occur, the explanatory styles of optimist and pessimist reverse. The optimist sees the good situation as enduring and brought on by his or her own good works; the pessimist sees a positive circumstance as temporary and caused by external factors.)

While normally it is a sign of mental health to assume responsibility for what happens to us and not to blame the other fellow or fate, depressed people often take too much responsibility for their painful situation. In such cases, assigning cause to outer circumstances can be a healthy thing.

If you identify with the pessimistic explanatory style, you can use the principles of cognitive restructuring from last week, as well as the techniques you learn this week, to interpret your world more like an optimist. Remember, you have the ability to choose your point of view.

my calcium, I would have been in trouble when I tried to walk," he said. My legs would have turned to powder. I'm lucky that this happened now."*

My favorite reframing story concerns the optimistic and pessimistic brothers, Davey and Joey. The parents were tired of seeing Davey always cheerful and Joey always gloomy, so they arranged a unique experiment for their birthdays (the boys were born only a few days apart). For Joey they purchased a Shetland pony; for Davey, a room full of horse manure. They left the boys alone with their new presents and checked back with them an hour later. True to form, Joey was whining away. "The horse isn't the right color, the saddle is too big," he moaned. It seemed that nothing could satisfy him.

Then the parents turned their attention to Davey, expecting him to be in the same melancholic state. Instead, they found him enthusiastically diving into and playing with the manure.

"What's going on?" they inquired. "How can you be happy with such a yucky birthday present?"

"Don't you see?" Davey replied. "With all of this horse poop around, there must be a pony hiding somewhere!"

Optimist's Tool #3:
The Blessing in Disguise Principle

There is no such thing as a problem without a gift for you in its hands.
You seek problems because you need their gifts.
—RICHARD BACH

In searching for his pony, little Davey was affirming his belief in the "blessing in disguise principle," that good things can arise out of difficult (or even tragic) circumstances. For example, American cyclist Lance Armstrong, winner of three consecutive Tour de France bicycle races, credits his success with getting testicular cancer. "Before I faced cancer I was on cruise control," Armstrong recalls. "Cancer taught me to fight and to persevere. Without those lessons, I would not have

---

* Russell Scott Smith, "Man of Steel Resolve," *Us Weekly,* 20 November, 2000: 78.

David's Story:
What Happens When You Can't Be Grateful?

What do you do when you are so down and discouraged about being depressed that you are angry at God and the universe for playing such an awful trick on you? What if none of the medications or treatments are working, and no one has found any decent alternatives? How do you find gratitude when you are in the black hole of despair and there's no relief?

This is how I felt at the depth of my depression. Many people tried to get me to focus on the positive, but such encouragement only made me angry. Although they were well meaning, these folks had no idea how hopeless the situation was. Who were they to tell me to count my blessings when all I could see was that hell surrounded me?

After I recovered and looked back on my ordeal, I could see positive things that I couldn't see at the time. I was not homeless. I had a dedicated therapist, loving friends, and my physical health remained intact. These were all supports that helped get me through. I'm glad that I did hang on. As a survivor, I feel stronger now than before my breakdown.

---

become a champion." Ironically, the cancer gave Armstrong a second gift by taking thirty pounds off his upper body. His lighter weight and the reduction in his wind resistance made him a faster rider.*

Another example of the blessing in disguise principle occurred in the life of Morrie Schwartz, a wise and loving psychology professor at Brandeis University. In his mid-seventies, the healthy Schwartz was stricken with Lou Gehrig's disease, a terminal condition. Learning of Schwartz's illness, Mitch Albom, a former student, tracked his old professor and recorded their final conversations in the bestselling book *Tuesdays with Morrie*. If Schwartz had not contracted this terrible disease, his wisdom and life-changing philosophy would have remained hidden from the world.

---

* From an interview on "Charlie Rose," PBS television, August 3, 2001.

Examples of the blessing in disguise principle abound if we choose to look for them. Take a moment and think of an example from your own life. You will have the opportunity to write about your experience at the end of the chapter.

Optimism: A Habit of Thinking

Learning to think optimistically is as simple as shifting one's perspective. But choosing to look at life differently does not occur overnight. As David's story reminds us, a person who is experiencing an episode of major depression cannot will himself to think positively. In such cases, the brain's extreme biochemical imbalance makes it virtually impossible to hold a positive thought for any length of time. This is where physiological interventions such as medications and alternative therapies can work wonders. It is also essential to have others around you who can keep the faith that you will get better even when you cannot.

Once you are stabilized, however, you can consciously practice optimistic ways of thinking until they become a mental habit. Remember, every thought has a neurochemical equivalent. Research at the State University of New York at Stoneybrook have shown that changing one's thinking has been shown to rebalance the brain's neurotransmitters as effectively as antidepressants. Cultivating an optimistic attitude will reap benefits both in your current mood and in helping to prevent a future depressive downturn.

This Week's Goals and Assignments

1. You are now midway through the 12-week program. Congratulations for having come this far! Look back over the goals for yourself that you wrote during week one (page 151). How close are you to meeting them? Write down any progress you have made as well as any obstacles that you still face.

2. Fill out the Assessing My Optimism Inventory on the next page.

3. Begin a gratitude journal. At the end of each day, write down in a notebook or journal an example of something that you are grateful for. This could be either:

- an ongoing blessing in your life (such as your health, having a roof over your head, a good job, a loving relationship, or a pet, etc.)
- something that happened during the day that you appreciated

Ongoing Self-Care Activities

- Read your vision statement.
- Chart your moods in the Daily Mood Diary.
- Meet with your recovery partner.
- Formulate a goal for your weekly goal sheet.
- Exercise (three or more times a week).
- Drink at least sixty-four ounces of water, sipping throughout the day.
- Use your Cognitive Restructuring Worksheet to identify and replace your negative thinking.

Assessing My Optimism Inventory

Please take a few moments to answer the following questions as a way of assessing the quality of your thinking habits. You can write in the space provided or in your Better Mood Journal.

1. When I face a challenging situation, do I try to find the inherent advantage in the circumstance?

2. Am I in the habit of counting my blessings, i.e., focusing on what is working in my life?

3. Try this reframing exercise: Look back at your life and find an event or circumstance where something painful occurred that afterward led to something good or positive. First write about the event and then about the positive outcome that occurred afterward (e.g., you lost one job only to find a better one).

If you couldn't think of anything to say right now, let it be okay. I believe, however, that if you search your heart, you can find an example of the blessing in disguise principle, even if it is something very small.

My Goal Sheet for Week 6

This week's starting date: _____   My recovery partner:_____

Date and time we will connect:_____

Goal or goals: _____

_____

Benefits of attaining this goal: _____

_____

Action plan:_____

_____

Ongoing goals (check off the ones as you accomplish them)
_____ Read my vision statement daily (upon awakening or before bed)
_____ Chart my moods in the Daily Mood Diary
_____ Participate in some form of exercise or movement
_____ Monitor my self-talk with the Cognitive Restructuring Worksheet
_____ This was my average mood on the daily mood scale (–5 to +5)

How was my mood this week?

Record your moods below for each day of the week. (–5 to +5)

Day	Mood	Comments
Mon		
Tue		
Wed		
Thu		
Fri		
Sat		
Sun		

The Road to Self-Esteem

I am the greatest. I said that even before I knew I was. Don't tell me I can't do something. Don't tell me it's impossible. Don't tell me I'm not the greatest. I'm the double greatest.

—MUHAMMAD ALI

SEVENTH WEEK OVERVIEW

In this week, you will learn specific techniques for developing positive self-worth and self-esteem.

Over the past two weeks, we have explored the second pillar of the better mood program—mental and emotional self-care. Specifically, we have learned that our mind has the ability to choose what it will focus on—and that *what* it focuses on affects how we feel and whether we view the world optimistically or pessimistically. Now it is time to turn the power of our thoughts inward—to examine how we value and esteem ourselves. Do we focus primarily on our strengths and gifts or on our faults and shortcomings? Do we emphasize our successes or our failures? These kinds of evaluations add up to our sense of self-esteem—whether we feel good about ourselves, or feel inadequate.

My experience in running healing from depression support groups shows that positive self-esteem is a powerful antidote to depression. When we truly value ourselves and feel that we are worthwhile, we are

231

much more likely to engage in the self-nurturing strategies that will help us get well and stay well. A person with healthy self-esteem says, "Because I am of value, I deserve to feel better. I am committed to doing whatever it takes to bring about my healing."

Unfortunately, people who become depressed find that their self-esteem plummets like a stock market in free fall. As author and recovering depressive William Styron wrote, "I felt like an absolute, loathsome completely worthless object who hadn't done anything and whose life trajectory had gone up and then was plunged down to absolute zero." Styron's friend, TV journalist Mike Wallace, added about his own depression, "I felt lower than a snake's belly. I thought the world would be better off without me."

Fortunately, depression is cyclic. When people emerge from an episode, they often feel good enough to start repairing and strengthening their self-esteem. In this week, we will learn a number of powerful tools to bring this about.

Self-Esteem Booster #1: Speaking to Yourself in a Loving Manner

What we say to ourselves and how we say it has a powerful impact on how we feel. Each of us participates in a silent inner conversation known as *self-talk*. This self-talk consists of two inner voices that engage in an ongoing dialogue. The first of these voices, known as the *"Yes" voice,* represents the part of the psyche that is loving and affirming. The Yes voice is a source of peacefulness and strength. It taps into our natural curiosity, wonder, vitality, spontaneity, creativity, and joy.

The opposing voice is called the *"No" voice.* This is the part of the psyche that engages in negative, fearful self-talk. It is the voice of doubt, worry, anxiety, limitation, shame, and self-hate.

Here are some examples of what these two voices say.

Yes Voice	No Voice
I can.	I can't.
I am okay.	I'm no good.
I can handle it.	I can't do it.

I am special.	I'm a loser.
I will get through this hard time.	I will never be happy again.
I am afraid, but I will act anyway.	I can't act because I am too afraid.
I can make a difference.	I am powerless.
I am smart.	I'm a dumbbell.
I am good looking.	I am ugly.

Clearly, the more our self-talk arises out of the Yes voice, the healthier our self-esteem will be. A simple way to reinforce the Yes voice is through the use of affirmations. An affirmation is a positive thought or idea that you consciously focus on in order to produce a desired result. The result may be a specific *goal* or *outcome* (doing well in school, making new friends, improving one's health) or an improved *attitude* or *state of mind* (experiencing self-love, overcoming fear). You can create an affirmation for virtually any need, goal, or challenge in your life.

Characteristics of Self-Esteem

Individuals with high self-esteem exhibit the following characteristics. They:

- feel they are important, that they matter
- are responsible—to themselves and to others
- have a strong sense of self; they act independently and are not easily influenced by others
- acknowledge their abilities and talents and are proud of what they do
- believe in and have faith in themselves; they are able to risk and to face challenges
- express many types of emotions and feelings
- have a high tolerance for frustration
- exhibit emotional self-control
- feel connected to others, have good communication skills, and know how to make friends
- care about their personal appearance and take care of their bodies

Affirmations for Self-Esteem

I like myself unconditionally.

I value myself.

I am a valuable person who deserves to be whole and well.

I treat myself as I would my own best friend.

I honor and celebrate my own uniqueness.

I am one of a kind.

I deserve to be happy.

I am capable, competent, and worthy.

I treat myself to the very best.

I am a good person.

I love myself just the way I am.

I accept myself as I am.

I am me, and I am enough.

I feel good about me.

I like my essence.

I take responsibility for my well-being.

I take good care of myself.

I respect who I am.

I am confident and self-assured.

I am a work in progress, growing and evolving.

I am the master of my fate. I am the captain of my soul.

Because they say Yes! to a person's inner being, affirmations are ideally suited for building self-esteem. My favorite self-esteem affirmation, *I am me, and I am enough,* beautifully conveys the sense of being okay at the core level. A sample of other uplifting self-esteem affirmations appears on the opposite page.

Creating Your Own Affirmation

Affirmations work best when they arise from within. Here is a process that I have used with great success in my groups.

Close your eyes. Go back in time and picture *three* different moments in your life when you felt proud or good about yourself. Perhaps you were engaging in a positive action, or someone gave you a compliment that pointed out one of your strengths. In each of these instances, think of an adjective that you could use to describe yourself in that moment.

Next, take one of those adjectives and complete these sentences to yourself:

- I am _____.
- (State your name), you are _____.

For example, if I saw myself as courageous, my affirmations would be: *I am courageous,* and *Douglas, you are courageous.*

Now, open your eyes and use each of the three adjectives to complete the self-statements below.

- I am _____ (State your name), you are _____
- I am _____ (State your name), you are _____
- I am _____ (State your name), you are _____

As you read your affirmations aloud, ask yourself, "How does it feel to say something positive *about* myself and *to* myself? Does it bring up any feelings of resistance and unworthiness?" (Techniques for responding to negative voices from our subconscious are covered in my books *Words That Heal* and *Listening to Your Inner Voice.*)

I also recommend that you give your affirmation to a friend and ask him or her to repeat it back to you in the second tense—i.e., my partner Joan, would say to me, "Douglas, you are courageous." Again, ask yourself, "What feelings come up when I hear this positive self-statement from another person?"

If you want to further increase the effectiveness of your affirmation, repeat it while *looking in the mirror.* (This will really test your ability to receive compliments.) If you can bear with the discomfort and embarrassment of hearing something wonderful about yourself, this exercise will really boost your self-esteem.

Henry Ford once said, "If you think you can, you can. If you think you can't, you can't. Either way, you are right." Through the power of our words, we have the ability to shape our inner and outer reality. When we learn to speak to ourselves in a loving and kind way, we will both feel better and attract positive experiences in the outer world.

Self-Esteem Booster #2: Taming the Inner Critic

When people first start to use affirmations, they often experience a disconcerting phenomenon. Each time they say their affirmation, a second voice jumps in to oppose the affirmation. In my book *Words That Heal,* I give the example of a client who used Muhammad Ali's famous affirmation "I am the greatest" to build his self-esteem. Here is how his inner self-talk played out.

Affirmation	What Comes Up
I am the greatest.	I'm afraid you're not.
I am the greatest.	In fact, you're a real loser.
I am the greatest.	You can't do anything right!

Another name for this disparaging No voice is the *inner critic.* The inner critic is the negative inner voice that constantly judges, criticizes, and attacks us. Here are some of the inner critic's favorite tactics. The inner critic:

- *blames you* for things that go wrong.
- *compares you to others*—to their achievements and abilities—and finds you wanting. Unfortunately, measuring ourselves by external markers and standards is rampant in our culture. Growing up, we are conditioned to base our self-worth on our looks, how well we do in school, our popularity, or our skill in sports. Later on, it's how much money we make, the model of our car, the size of our home, or the status of our job.
- *sets impossible standards of perfection* and hounds you for the smallest mistake.
- *keeps an album of your failures,* but never once reminds you of your strengths and abilities.
- has a script telling you how you ought to live; the inner critic *"shoulds"* all over you.
- *calls you names*—stupid, incompetent, weak, selfish, defective, ugly—and makes you believe that they are all true.
- loves to focus on *what you didn't do right* instead of what you did right. The inner critic produces SHAME: Should Have Already Mastered Everything.
- employs the cognitive distortion of *overgeneralization* by using the words *always* and *never*—i.e., "You *always* mess up," or "You *always* screw up a relationship," or "You *never* do anything on time."*

The inner critic resembles what John Bradshaw calls "the shaming voices in our head," which reinforce our sense of unworthiness and failure. In the perennial TV show *Charlie Brown's Christmas Special,* Charlie Brown repeatedly asks, "Why is it that everything I touch gets ruined?" Millions of people around the country repeat this shaming self-talk each and every day.

Strategies for Responding to the Inner Critic

The inner critic is usually some internalized critical parent or other authority who judged, criticized, or put us down when we were children. Now that the voice has become incorporated into our own internal self-talk, it is up to us to disarm him or her. Eleanor Roosevelt said,

---

* Patrick Fanning and Matthew McKay, *Self-Esteem* (Oakland: New Harbinger Publications, 1994), 34.

"Nobody can make you feel inferior without your permission." At some point, we gave the inner critic the power to make us feel inferior; now is the time to take our power back. The process for accomplishing this is the same as for cognitive restructuring: becoming aware of the inner critic, disputing the validity of what the critic is saying, and replacing the critic's voice with a realistic, positive self-statement. Here are the steps.

Step #1: Become aware of the inner critic's negative voice. The first step in any change process is awareness. Start to notice when you put yourself down. It helps when you give the inner critic a name, e.g., "the bully," "the critic," "the judge," "Mr./Ms. Perfect," "Martha" (a parent's name), "Mr./Ms. Kick-Ass, Hard-Ass." This helps to differentiate between you and the critic.

Step #2: Halt what the critic is saying. After becoming aware of the critic's voice, you then short-circuit the negative self-talk and stop it in its tracks. The following howitzer mantras are selected words and phrases that are designed to talk back to the inner critic:

- Stop that!
- Shut up!
- Get lost!
- Lies, lies, and more lies.
- I beg to disagree, Mother.
- I beg to disagree, Father.
- I beg to disagree (fill in the name).
- What you are saying is absolute nonsense.
- CANCEL! CANCEL!

Step 3: Use affirmations to replace the critic's negative self-talk with a more realistic and compassionate view of yourself. Here are some examples:

Inner Critic's Self-Talk	Replacement Affirmation
You're not good enough.	I'm okay.
I hate myself.	I like myself.
What a jerk!	I'm a nice person.
You're stupid.	I'm smart.
You're ugly.	I'm attractive.

You're fat.	I like my body.
You're a butthead.	I'm hip.
You're a loser.	I'm a winner.
You're worthless.	I'm awesome.
You can't do anything right.	There are many things I can do well.
No one cares about what I have to say.	I have important things to share.
You're not good enough.	I am fine the way I am.
You could have done better.	I did the best I could.
You don't measure up.	I am me and I am enough.
You'll never be a success.	By my standards, I already am a success.

Ultimately, the best way to inoculate yourself against the inner critic is to practice self-acceptance. The inner critic's power comes from your belief that you are not okay the way you are. Once you start to have compassion for yourself and practice self-forgiveness, the inner critic's power over you will diminish. This brings us to our next topic.

Self-Esteem Booster #3: Letting Go of Blame through Self-Forgiveness

To err is human, to forgive divine.
—ALFRED, LORD TENNYSON

One of the inner critic's favorite activities is to blame you for things that went wrong in the past. The critic has no trouble pointing out past blunders (which we all make) and then holding you accountable. For example, I have clients who are still upset with themselves for:

- dropping out of school
- going off their medication and having a relapse
- getting into drugs and alcohol
- passing up a golden business opportunity
- having an unhappy marriage
- inadvertently hurting themselves or another person

Some of these incidents occurred thirty to forty years ago. Nonetheless, people continue to mentally beat themselves up and hold themselves in contempt. Such self-blame and guilt further debilitates their already damaged self-esteem.

Healing from depression means that we release this self-blame and learn to forgive ourselves. We have compassion for ourselves by seeing that we were doing the best we could with the awareness we had at the time. The following process will help bring this realization home.

Self-Forgiveness Exercise

Think of a past incident for which you have not forgiven yourself. It could be something recent or something that occurred long ago. Try to pick an experience that is only mildly to moderately distressing; it is better to deal with the heavy stuff when you have had more practice with this process.

Now ask yourself, "If I could go back in time and *bring my current knowledge and awareness with me,* how would I have handled the situation? Would I have acted differently?"

Answering these questions will help you to see that you probably *did not* have your current wisdom and knowledge available to you in the past. You made the best choice you could with the limited awareness you possessed.

When we can accept that we truly were doing our best, a huge burden is lifted from our shoulders and psyche. We literally feel lighter as feelings of guilt and heaviness that accompany our depression are slowly released. This process is not an easy one, nor does it occur overnight. If you wish to explore the possibility of practicing self-forgiveness (or forgiving another person), I suggest that you work with a trained counselor or spiritual advisor. There are also excellent books and resources on forgiveness that are widely available in bookstores and libraries.

Self-Esteem Booster #4:
Overcoming the Stigma of Depression

Despite the fact that modern medicine recognizes that depression, like heart disease, is an *organic* condition whose seat resides in a disturbed brain, a societal view still persists that depression is the result of a weak will or a character deficit. Too often, a person suffering from anxiety or depression internalizes this stigma and suffers from what family therapist John Bradshaw calls "toxic shame"—the belief that one is flawed and defective *at the core*. While guilt says "I *made* a mistake." Shame says "I *am* a mistake." As one client recently confessed, "I feel like I'm damaged goods."

Here are two powerful strategies that you can use to dissolve this debilitating shame so you don't have to feel bad about feeling bad.

Healing strategy #1: Make a distinction between who you are and your condition. If you feel ashamed about having a diagnosis of depression, it is important to separate yourself from your condition. The label "depression" does not define who you are but *how you are suffering*. Think of yourself as a *normal person* responding to an *abnormal condition*. Your spiritual essence transcends depression and cannot be touched by it or by any illness. As my friend Mary Morrissey has said:

> There is something about you that isn't touched by your circumstances. There's something about you that no matter whatever happened to you, it can't really harm you unless you agree to that harm. You have a kind of power, an essence to you, that's beyond anything that can happen to you. Who you are is an invisible, spiritual dweller, evolving, and that soul continues to evolve even after the doorway we call death.

Here is a delightful story that speaks directly to this truth.

The $20 Bill Story

A well-known speaker started off his seminar by holding up a $20 bill. He asked the two hundred people in the room, "Who would like this $20 bill?" Hands started going up. He said, "I'm going to give this $20 bill to one of you, but first, let me do this." He proceeded to crumple up the dollar bill. He then asked, "Who still wants it?" The hands went up in the air. "Well," he replied, "what if I do this?" He then dropped the bill to the ground and started to grind it into the floor with his shoe. He picked it up, now all crumpled and dirty. "Now who wants it?" Still, the hands went up into the air.

"My friends," the speaker said, "you have all learned a very valuable lesson. No matter what I did to the money, you still wanted it because it did not decrease in value. It was still worth $20. Many times in life, we are dropped, crumpled, and ground into the dirt by the decisions we make and the circumstances that come our way. We feel as though we are worthless. But no matter what has happened or what will happen, you will never lose your value.

"You are special. Don't ever forget it."

This story makes it clear that even if we suffer from depression, there is a basic core of wholeness and goodness that is our true essence. Affirming this inner essence can help us maintain our self-esteem, as our bodies and emotions struggle to return to wellness.

Healing strategy #2: Reframe your battle against depression as a heroic struggle. When I work with people who have spent their lives battling psychiatric illnesses, I do not see wimps. I see strong and courageous individuals who have the Herculean task of bearing and transforming intense pain. Like St. George who slayed the dragon, their task is to conquer their inner demons. I am reminded of what Christopher Reeve said about this type of heroism shortly after he became paralyzed:

> When the first Superman movie came out, I was frequently asked, "What is a hero?" My answer was that a hero is someone who commits a courageous action without considering the consequences—a soldier who crawls out of a foxhole to drag an injured buddy to safety. I also meant people who are slightly larger than life: Houdini and Lindbergh, John Wayne, J.F.K., and Joe Dimaggio. Now, my answer is completely different. I think of a hero as an ordinary individual who finds the strength to persevere and endure in spite of overwhelming obstacles.*

---

* Christopher Reeve, *Still Me* (New York: Random House, 1998), jacket text.

Diana's Story: Breaking the Silence

I am fifty-three years old, and for the past thirty-four years I have had schizo-affective disorder. I am also bipolar. I have been married for thirty years, am the mother of five children, and have three lovely grandchildren.

Twenty years ago, when my children were ten, eight, five, and one, I was hospitalized for a suicide attempt. I was taken to a psychiatric hospital in the middle of the night and did not see my children again for seven weeks. My husband and mother cared for the children, but no one ever explained the nature of my illness to them. They were just told, "Mommy needs a rest. She is sick." Everything was hushed up, such was the stigma with regard to mental illness. I was hospitalized three more times after that, but the silence continued.

Finally, after thirty-four years of therapy, my counselor suggested that we have a family meeting to talk openly about my psychiatric condition. By this time, my children were thirty, twenty-eight, twenty-five, twenty-one, and eighteen. Although we planned to meet for an hour, the session lasted two and a half hours. For the first time, my children got to learn the truth. All of those questions that had been on their minds finally got asked and answered. Throughout the meeting there were many tears and hugs. The meeting was such a success that *all* of the participants wanted to meet with my therapist again in two to three weeks.

Afterward, my children told me that this meeting was long overdue. Now that they are becoming educated about my condition, they no longer have to wonder what is wrong with me or be afraid of what they don't understand.

I do believe that the terrible stigma of mental illness is gradually decreasing. Although the meeting was initially stressful for me, it was very beneficial for my children. Since the meeting, my children take the initiative and ask me how I am feeling, and they aren't making as many demands on me. But most of all, I don't have to hide my illness anymore!

In this sense, every one of us who has ever struggled with crippling depression or anxiety is a hero—and there certainly is no shame in that.

Just as recovering from depression is a lifelong journey, so too is overcoming its stigma. The key, I believe, lies in self-love and self-acceptance. This is where support groups are immensely helpful. The healing of shame begins when we come out of hiding and let others witness our affliction. Their acceptance of us allows us to accept ourselves. Ultimately, we can love and embrace *all* of ourself including those parts that we had considered unacceptable.

This Week's Goals and Assignments

Here are your assignments for the coming week:

1. Fill out the Assessing My Self-Esteem inventory on page 247.

2. Choose one of the affirmations that you created in the affirmation exercise and repeat it to yourself throughout the week. Try saying it while looking in the mirror.

Ongoing Self-Care Activities

- Chart your moods in the Daily Mood Diary.
- Meet with your recovery partner.
- Formulate a goal for your weekly goal sheet.
- Exercise (three or more times a week).
- Drink at least sixty-four ounces of water, sipping throughout the day.
- Use your Cognitive Restructuring Worksheet to identify and replace your negative thinking.
- Write down any blessings in your gratitude journal. If you can't find anything to be grateful for, let it be okay. The most important thing is to be honest with what you are feeling right now.

My Goal Sheet for Week 7

This week's starting date: _____ My recovery partner: _____

Date and time we will connect: _____

Goal or goals: _____

_____

Benefits of attaining this goal: _____

_____

Action plan: _____

_____

Ongoing goals (check off the ones as you accomplish them)

_____ Read my vision statement daily (upon awakening or before bed)

_____ Chart my moods in the Daily Mood Diary

_____ Participate in some form of exercise or movement

_____ Monitor my self-talk with the Cognitive Restructuring Worksheet

_____ This was my average mood on the daily mood scale (–5 to +5)

How was my mood this week?

Record your moods below for each day of the week. (–5 to +5)

Day	Mood	Comments
Mon		
Tue		
Wed		
Thu		
Fri		
Sat		
Sun		

No Less Than Greatness

Nelson Mandela spoke the following lines from Marianne Williamson's book
A Return to Love in his 1994 Inaugural address as he assumed the presi-
dency of South Africa. They are a wonderful affirmation of the self-love
that leads to positive self-esteem.

Our deepest fear is not that we are inadequate.
Our deepest fear is that we are powerful beyond measure.
It is our Light, not our Darkness, that most frightens us.
We ask ourselves, who am I to be brilliant, gorgeous,
    talented, fabulous?

Actually, who are you NOT to be?

You are a child of God. Your playing small does not serve the world.
There is nothing enlightened about shrinking so that other people
    won't feel insecure around you.
We were born to make manifest the glory of God that is within us.
It is not just in some of us; it is in everyone.
As we let our own Light shine, we unconsciously give people
    permission to do the same.
As we are liberated from our fear, our presence automatically
    liberates others.

Assessing My Self-Esteem

The following questions are designed to help you assess your self-esteem. You can answer in the spaces provided or in your Better Mood Journal.

1. What is the nature of my self-talk? Is it mostly encouraging and affirming or fearful and negative? Do I see the glass as half-empty or half-full?

2. What tools do I use (such as affirmations) to consciously bring positive beliefs and attitudes into my life so I may think more optimistically?

3. Do I spend as much time praising myself as I do criticizing myself? What strategies have I developed to respond to my inner critic?

4. Have I ever felt shame or negative feelings about myself for having been depressed or anxious? How have I responded to these feelings?

(continued on next page)

5. Are there any areas in my life where I have not forgiven myself for mistakes I have made in the past? Am I open to seeing that perhaps I did the best I could at the time with the awareness that I had?

6. What are the most important lessons I have learned from my depression and/or anxiety? Have I received any gifts or valuable teachings from my experience?

Expanding Your Social Support

No man is an island, entire of itself;
every man is a piece of the continent, a part of the main.

—JOHN DONNE

EIGHTH WEEK OVERVIEW

In this week, you will learn ways to strengthen your connections with other people, thereby creating a solid foundation of social support.

In weeks three through seven, you learned how caring for your physical body, releasing cognitive distortions, cultivating optimism, and building self-esteem through positive self-talk can help improve your mood. Now it is time to focus on the importance of connection and intimacy. In my personal experience of surviving a depressive episode, social support was an essential ingredient in my healing. Having relationships not only helped to alleviate my depression, but has also played a huge part in preventing its recurrence.

Social scientists have documented that social support provides a major buffer against stress, protects against mental decline, bolsters the immune system, and contributes to longevity. Our culture values independence and individualism. But when solitude is not balanced by connectedness, the ensuing isolation can lead to mental and physical illness. Conversely, when people experience meaningful connections

249

with friends, work, a hobby, a pet, or anything beyond themselves, healing can result.

A dramatic example of this principle is the Rosetto study which was recounted in Dean Ornish's groundbreaking book *Love and Survival.* Rosetto is an Italian American town in eastern Pennsylvania that, at the turn of the century, had a far lower mortality rate from heart disease when compared to adjacent towns, even though the risk factors for heart disease were the same (smoking, high-fat diet, alcohol consumption, and so on). One major difference was that the people from Rosetto had a high degree of social homogeneity, close family ties, and cohesive family relationships. When, in the 1970s, the third generation fell prey to the influences of the surrounding culture and the townspeople became fragmented and isolated, the incidence of death from heart disease rose to the same level as in neighboring towns.

Many other studies found in *Love and Survival,* unequivocally demonstrate that love and intimacy promote mental and physical health. I have identified six types of connection that I believe are extremely helpful to healing from depression:

- family and close friends
- mental health professionals
- mentors and allies
- group support
- community service
- relationships with animals

Let's explore these support systems in detail.

Family and close friends. This is often the first line of defense against emotional or physical illness. During my depressive episode, I was fortunate to have my partner, Joan, as my caretaker. In addition, I had three or four close friends who took shifts to help care for me.

In researching this section, I read numerous first-person accounts of people who survived life-threatening depressive episodes. Each of these survivors—such as writer William Styron, TV reporter

Mike Wallace, newspaper reporter Tracy Thompson, and psychologists Kay Jamison and Martha Manning—had the loyal and steady support of family (spouses, family, and children) and friends. (Books written by these authors are listed in the bibliography.) As novelist and recovering depressive Andrew Solomon wrote:

> Recovery depends enormously on support. The depressives I've met who have done the best were cushioned with love. Nothing taught me more about the love of my father and my friends than my own depression.

There are also times, though fewer, where relationships on the job can provide significant support.

Mental health professionals. Not everyone is fortunate enough to have a loving spouse, parent, or close group of friends. However, there are a great many qualified and compassionate health care professionals who offer care and treatment for depression. These include psychologists, psychiatrists, psychiatric nurse practitioners, clinical social workers, marriage and family therapists, pastoral counselors, clergy, and drug and alcohol counselors.

By now, the eighth week of the program, you should be connected with a counselor, therapist, and/or prescriber. If this is not the case and you would like to form such a relationship, please refer to the information contained in Week 2.

Mentors and allies. Allies and mentors include support people such as a rabbi, minister, priest, 12-step sponsor, teacher, coach, or any trusted person in whom you can confide. Such individuals can listen to and validate your feelings and help with problem-solving even though you may not have a professional relationship with them.

Group support. A sense of belonging to a community makes us feel part of a larger whole, which in turn promotes a sense of well-being. Examples of group support include:

- a sports team
- a book club
- a church group
- a women's or men's group
- group psychotherapy
- a 12-step group such as AA, NA (Narcotics Anonymous), ACOA (Adult Children of Alcoholics), EA (Emotions Anonymous), and OA (Overeaters Anonymous)
- any self-help group that focuses on an issue you are dealing with, where you can gain and give help and encouragement. Examples include a diabetes support group, Weight Watchers, a job search group, or a depression support group
- a Master Mind group (I will discuss Master Mind groups in the chapter on spiritual support)

I have always been a huge believer in the power of community as it is expressed in groups. In his classic work, *The Principles and Practice of Group Psychotherapy,* Irvin Yalom identifies eleven "therapeutic factors" that are universally present in the group experience. These include:

- the installation of hope
- the imparting of information
- universality (the realization that I am not alone, that other people share my suffering)
- group cohesiveness
- altruism (having the opportunity to give to other members)

The value of altruism is depicted by the Hassidic story about a rabbi who had a conversation with the Lord about Heaven and Hell. "I will show you Hell," said the Lord, and led the rabbi into a room containing a group of famished, desperate people sitting around a large, circular table. In the center of the table rested an enormous pot of stew, more than enough for everyone. The smell of the stew was delicious and made the rabbi's mouth water. Yet, no one ate. Each diner at the table held a very long-handled spoon—long enough to reach the pot and scoop up a spoonful of stew, but too long to get the food into one's mouth. The rabbi saw that their suffering was indeed terrible and bowed his head in compassion.

The Power of Social Support:
Lessons Learned from Geese

Geese, like human beings, are social animals. Recent scientific discoveries about why geese fly in a V formation reveal five important lessons about our interdependence and our need for each other.

Fact #1: As each bird flaps its wings, it creates an uplift for the bird following behind. By flowing in a big V formation, the whole flock adds at least 71 percent greater flying range than if each bird flew on its own.

Our Lesson: By sharing a common direction and sense of community with others, you get where you are going more quickly and easily because you are traveling on the thrust of one another.

Fact #2: Whenever a goose falls out of formation, it suddenly feels the drag of resistance of flying alone, so it quickly gets back into formation and takes advantage of the lifting power of the bird immediately in front.

Our Lesson: There is strength, power, and safety in numbers when we travel in the same direction with others who share a common goal.

Fact #3: When the lead goose gets tired, it rotates back into formation, and another goose flies at the point position.

Our Lesson: It pays to take turns doing the hard jobs and sharing the leadership. This means that sometimes you will be the pillar for others; at other times they will rely on your strength.

Fact #4: The geese in formation honk from behind to encourage those up front to keep up their speed.

Our Lesson: We all need to give and receive active support and appreciation.

Fact #5: When a goose gets sick or wounded, two geese drop out of formation and follow it down to help and protect it. They stay with the goose until the crisis resolves. Then, they launch out on their own with another formation, or they catch up with the original flock.

Our Lesson: Like the geese, we need to stand by each other in times of need as well as when we are strong.

"Now I will show you Heaven," said the Lord, and they entered another room, identical to the first—the same large, round table, the same enormous pot of stew, the same long-handled spoons. Yet, there was gaiety in the air, and everyone appeared well nourished, plump, and exuberant. The rabbi could not understand and looked to the Lord. "It is simple," said the Lord. "You see, the people in this room have learned to feed each other."

Ever since hearing this story, I continue to picture the diners in heaven using their overly long spoons to feed each other across the table. Herein lies the beauty of group support—that in extending ourselves in compassion to help others, we become fed and nourished.

Check with your local hospitals, mental health centers, or the National Alliance for the Mentally Ill (800-950-NAMI) to see whether any depression or anxiety support groups exist in your area. Or you may participate in one of the groups listed at the beginning of this section.

Another option is to ask a counselor or a person recovering from depression who is trained in group facilitation to start a depression or anxiety support group for you. For the past year, I have been facilitating such groups and can attest to how much more quickly people heal when they come together in community. Please refer to Appendix B to learn the specific steps to form a support group.

> Life's most persistent and urgent question is,
> "What are you doing for others?"
> —MARTIN LUTHER KING, JR.

Community service. Serving others—by volunteering in the community or by helping someone in need—is a marvelous way to experience interconnectedness and the therapeutic factor of altruism. A fundamental symptom of depression (and unhappiness in general) is self-absorption. Service allows us to transcend our suffering by shifting our focus away from ourselves. As author Tracy Thompson writes of her own recovery in her memoir *The Beast*, "Help others. Be of service. Only in this way will you find your way out of the prison of self." In this vein, an article in *Psychology Today* reports that volunteer work

The Prayer of Saint Francis of Assisi

This is one of my favorite prayers and is a perfect expression of the principle of selfless service, a way of giving that comes back to us tenfold.

Lord, make me an instrument of Your peace.
Where there is hatred, let me sow love.
Where there is injury, pardon.
Where there is doubt, faith.
Where there is despair, hope.
Where there is darkness, light.
Where there is sadness, joy.
O, Divine Master, grant that I
may not so much seek
To be consoled as to console.
To be understood as to understand.
To be loved as to love.
For it is in giving that we receive.
It is in pardoning that we are pardoned.
And it is in dying that we are born to eternal life.

leads to a phenomenon called "helper's high"—a physiological change in the body that produces physical and emotional well-being, as well as relief from stress-related disorders.*

The amount of service that you perform does not have to be large. If you are feeling limited in your capacity to give, start with some form of service that requires a low level of commitment—such as nurturing a pet or a plant. Extending yourself even a little bit will be good for the recipient and good for you.

Mary Todd Lincoln, wife of President Lincoln, serves as an intriguing example of the therapeutic value of altruism. She and her husband

---

* Alan Luk, "Helper's High," *Psychology Today*, October 1988, Volume 22, 310: 39, 42.

suffered clinical depression throughout their lives due to the early death of a parent—Abe his mother, and Mary her father. (The death of a parent before the age of eleven is a major predictor of depression in later years.) In the midst of the Civil War, Mary experienced a second depressive breakdown, triggered by the loss of her favorite son and the absence of her husband, who was preoccupied with wartime activities. Shortly after her boy's death, Mary began to volunteer as a nurse's aide in Civil War hospitals. Although the drop of a book at home would have set off a panic attack, to the amazement of her friends, Mary was able to stay calm amidst the sounds and shrieks of the tormented patients. By taking the focus off herself through serving others, she was able to transcend her fears.

Relationships with animals. In addition to the support of human beings, I want to mention the support of animals, especially pets. The unconditional love that we give to and receive from our animal friends can be as healing as human love. (This is why pets are increasingly brought to hospital wards and nursing homes.) A loving relationship with a cherished pet provides a level of bonding and intimacy that can strengthen your psychological immune system and help keep depression at bay.

I know about this connection firsthand. In the depths of my depressive episode, I adopted a stray cat named Gabriel from the Humane Society. A month later, Gabriel was hit by a car. The operation to repair his fractured jaw was prohibitively expensive (I was unable to work because of my illness), and I considered the option of having him put to sleep.

Then a medical intuitive who specialized in working with animals told me that Gabriel was not ready to make his transition as he had "much more to do in this lifetime." She encouraged me to proceed with the operation, saying that Gabriel was a mirror for me, and that as he regained his strength and vitality, so would I. Over the next six months, this is precisely what occurred.

To illustrate the healing power of animals, I share the following letter I received from one of my workshop students.

The most precious things in life aren't things

Dear Douglas,

Kansas City is now cold and wet—pretty typical for this time of year. I just wanted to let you know that my depression has been in remission since September 9. That is a record of almost three years. Remember my crazy dog? Well, he has grown and matured enough since you last saw him and had enough training to make him a Service Dog. He goes almost everywhere with me. My doctor gives a lot of credit for my newfound health to the dog. He thinks the dog was sent by God with a purpose in my life.

Warmly,
Jenny

Expanding Your Support Network

Given the importance of social support to mental and physical health, it is important to ask ourselves, "How can I expand my circle of support? How can I meet new people and make new friends?" Having multiple sources of support is especially important for anyone suffering from depression. Given the severity of the disorder, the depressed individual can easily wear out a friend or family member. As I learned through my own episode, it takes a whole village to see someone through a dark night of the soul.

Here are a few ways that you can create more support in your life:

- Take a class in something that interests you. This is a tried and tested way to meet like-minded folks.

- Participate in a community activity, such as hiking, dancing, recycling cleanups, or fund-raising activities such as Race for the Cure.
- If you live alone, find a roommate.
- If you are single, join a singles' group.
- Do volunteer work.
- Participate in activities at your church, synagogue, or spiritual community.
- Join a support group.

Once you meet people, the best way to build supportive relationships is to spend quality time in *mutually enjoyable* activities—long walks, a meal, a movie or concert, and so on. As you share common interests with people of a like mind, you will feel closer and more connected to them. At some point, you may wish to determine whether a new friend is the type of person who can be of support to you. Ask yourself, "Is this person comfortable with intense feelings? Can he or she listen without judging or jumping in to fix the problem?"

If this is someone who you feel safe with and want to be a member of your mental health support team, you can do the following:

- Ask whether they are willing to be a supporter. Tell them what you need from the relationship.
- Say that you are willing to be their supporter so it is clear that the relationship is a two-way street.
- Assure them that you have other people in your support network so they will not have to be available for your support at all times.

Blocks to Asking for Support

While people who suffer from depression and anxiety need more support than the average person, they often have the hardest time asking for it. Reasons may include:

- natural shyness
- not feeling deserving (Why would anyone want to support a wretch like me?)
- fear of being rejected or ridiculed
- hopelessness—it won't matter anyway
- shame—feeling embarrassed about asking for help

Sherry's Story: Early Morning Telephone Angels

In the latter part of December, just days before Christmas, I had just ended a ten-year relationship with a man that I still have great feelings for. In addition, I became victim of an airborne mold that contaminated my rented apartment and made me extremely ill. The trauma of ending the relationship, losing my home, and the blow to my health, sent me into a severe depression. I soon became very suicidal, as I could see no way out of what was happening to me. I had discovered that my worst time was usually first thing in the morning, but that frequently if I talked to someone—even over the phone—I could get myself into a better frame of mind. I thought to myself, "Wouldn't it be great if I had a program in place where someone would call me every morning?"

I shared my request with a minister at my church, and we put out the word for volunteers. I quickly was presented with seven people, for the seven days of the week. One person had promised to call me every Monday, another every Tuesday, and so on. On the many days that I awoke with that horrible feeling in my head, I could always count on someone calling me at about 9:00 A.M. to check on me. They were there to listen, and to encourage me to get dressed. Sometimes we would say a prayer; at other times my telephone angel would give me a simple affirmation to say throughout the day. On the days I woke up feeling pretty well, I could talk to my caller about the good feelings I had and about how to make them last the rest of the day.

It is now two months later, and my healing is definitely happening. The people of my church can see the great improvement. I am coming alive again. I am learning to focus again, to start my world over again. I have an apartment of my own again and am slowly finding that many of the personal possessions, which I had been told I had lost have been cleaned and are being returned to me. What a blessing it is to know that I *can* reach out to people for help and that people really do care about me and will support me in any way they can.

I am truly grateful.

Feelings of unworthiness and the fear of rejection often lie at the root of many depressed people's social phobia. Both of these can be overcome through counseling, and in some cases medication. Try saying the affirmation, *"I am a lovable person and who is worthy of support, attention, respect, and love."* If your immediate response is, "No, I'm not!" you may want to explore the source of that belief. You'll probably find that it is rooted in the early childhood experience of not feeling unconditionally loved. This universal wound can be healed by creating new imprints, either with your therapist or another loving presence. Ultimately, you can learn to reparent yourself and give yourself the unconditional love and attention that you deserve.

Arnold Patent, an old teacher of mine, was found of saying, "The universe is a 'mutual support system'." If we look at the interconnectedness among the communities on our planet and the symbiosis between plants and animals, we understand that we are not meant to go through life alone—or to struggle with depression alone. Before my illness, I was a believer in the healing power of love and community. As I continue my recovery, I have come to believe that a potential gift of depression is its ability motivate us to reach out to others for connection, love, and support.

This Week's Goals and Assignments

Here is your assignment for the coming week:

1. Fill out the Assessing My Social Support inventory and the Creating Goals for Social Support sheet that follow. Choose a goal from this sheet as a goal for the week.

Ongoing Self-Care Activities

- Read your vision statement.
- Chart your moods in the Daily Mood Diary.
- Meet with your recovery partner.
- Formulate a goal for your weekly goal sheet.
- Exercise (three or more times a week).
- Drink at least sixty-four ounces of water, sipping throughout the day.
- Use your Cognitive Restructuring Worksheet to identify and replace your negative thinking.
- Locate an affirmation that has meaning for you and repeat it daily.
- Continue filling out your gratitude journal to the best of your ability.

Assessing My Social Support

Please take a few moments to answer the following questions as a way of assessing the quality of social support in your life. You can write in the space provided or use a blank piece of paper.

1. What makes a person supportive for me?

2. What are the main sources of social support in my life? (Choose from family, friends, work relationships, group support, and an ally or mentor.) How often do I meet with these people?

3. How satisfying are my personal relationships? Can I be my true self with the people with whom I associate? Are there people in whom I can confide?

4. Do I feel loved, valued, and appreciated by others? Do I have opportunities to express my love and caring to others?

5. Do I feel part of a community? Am I involved in a regular support group, such as a 12-step group or a Master Mind group?

6. Do I do volunteer work or belong to a social organization?

7. How is my social life?

8. What are some things that I can do to attract new support into my life?

9. Do I have any blocks to my asking for and receiving support? If so, how might I deal with them?

Creating Goals for Social Support

Using the answers from your Assessing My Social Support inventory, write down the social support you now have and the support that you would like to incorporate into your life.

Social support I now have:
1.
2.
3.

Social support I would like to make part of my life:
1.
2.
3.

Take one of these and make it a goal for the week.

My Goal Sheet for Week 8

This week's starting date: _____ My recovery partner:_____

Date and time we will connect: _____

Goal or goals: _____

_____

Benefits of attaining this goal: _____

_____

Action plan: _____

_____

Ongoing goals (check off the ones as you accomplish them)

_____ Read my vision statement daily (upon awakening or before bed)

_____ Chart my moods in the Daily Mood Diary

_____ Participate in some form of exercise or movement

_____ Monitor my self-talk with the Cognitive Restructuring Worksheet

_____ This was my average mood on the daily mood scale (–5 to +5)

How was my mood this week?

Record your moods below for each day of the week. (–5 to +5)

Day	Mood	Comments
Mon		
Tue		
Wed		
Thu		
Fri		
Sat		
Sun		

The Healing Power of Spirit

At the hospital I was separated from alcohol for the last time. There I humbly offered myself to God as I understood Him, to do with me as He would. I placed myself unreservedly under his care and protection. I have not had a drink since.

—BILL W., founder of Alcoholics Anonymous

NINTH WEEK OVERVIEW

In this week, you will learn how feeling spiritually connected to a benevolent universe can alleviate symptoms of anxiety and depression.

In weeks one through eight, we have focused on the physical, mental, and social supports that can help a person to heal from depression and anxiety. Now we are ready to address the next level of healing—the spiritual dimension. Spiritual resources such as faith, hope, and courage are every bit as important to the person recovering from depression as are the more tangible tools of medicine and psychology.

Mental health researchers have defined a phenomenon known as "religious coping"*—a reliance on a spiritual belief or activity to help manage emotional stress or physical discomfort. In other words, people with a defined spiritual philosophy or worldview seem to cope better

---

* Kenneth Parament, *Religion and Prevention in Mental Health* (New York: Haworth Press, 1992).

265

with life's crises and challenges. (An example of religious coping occurred when my friend's ninety-four-year-old mother used her religious faith and support from her church community to make a remarkable recovery from breast cancer surgery.) A 1999 Duke University study of four thousand adults found that attendance at a house of worship was related to lower rates of anxiety and depression. It was this type of spiritual coping that led me to my ultimate healing. Various aspects of spirituality can be used to promote emotional serenity.

Throughout this chapter, I will be using the term "God" to describe a higher power or creative intelligence that infuses the universe. If the traditional concept of God seems alien to you, you may wish to think of such ideas as the vastness of the human spirit, an intelligent order in nature, the life force, creative inspiration, or qualities such as goodness, truth, love, beauty, peace, justice, and so on. The words we use are less important than the universal reality they describe.

Prayer

Ask and ye shall receive. Seek and ye shall find.
Knock and the door shall be opened. For everyone who asks receives,
and he who seeks finds, and to him who knocks, it shall be opened.
—MATT. 7:1–3

As far as I know, there are no scientific studies that document the efficacy of prayer in the healing of depression or other forms of mental illness. There do exist, however, documented cases about the success of prayer in physical healing, as shown in Larry Dossey's book, *Healing Words.*

If prayer can alter physical matter, and the brain is made of material substance, then it seems reasonable that prayer can impact the brain chemistry that creates depression. (I have my own experience to testify to this truth.) Thus, I would encourage anyone with a depressive illness to combine prayer with the traditional treatment modalities.

There are many different types of prayer. The success of prayer does not depend on your religious persuasion. (As AA is fond of saying, "There are no atheists in the foxholes.") If the word "prayer" seems too religious, think of it as a way of connecting with your higher power. Here is a beautiful poem, sent by a visitor to my Web site, which beautifully describes God's loving response to a prayer for healing.

Judith's Story: Calling Me

The darkness engulfed my soul;
My screams of pain deafened me,
Falling further away from reality.
Quieting the din of the storm,
You reached for me gently,
Within Your warmth I began to see.
Your love broke through,
And You patiently awaited,
Until at last the darkness faded.

[rmc 1981 revised 2000]

To my Lord that came for me,
Deep within the darkness,
To suffer not eternally.

Ideally, prayer should be connected with action. As one spiritual teacher put it, "You don't pray and then hang out in bed with your sneakers on. *Pray* as if everything depended on God, but *act* as if everything depended on you."

There is no right way to pray. The sincerity of your request and your intention to heal is more important than the structure you use. If you bring a pure heart to your inner altar and remain open to the presence of grace, who knows what miracles may occur?

As I learned in my own healing, group energy increases prayer's potency and effectiveness. If you wish to have people pray for you, it is most effective to have them do so as a cohesive unit. If you can't get your support people to meet as a single group, you can still ask people in different locations to pray for you (preferably at a specific time of day).

In addition, you may place your name on a prayer list where it will be prayed over for thirty days or more. The following prayer ministries are also listed in Appendix C with descriptions of their services, Web sites, and mailing addresses.

Silent Unity
    816-929-2000
    800-669-7729
    E-mail: unity@unityworldhq.org

World Ministry of Prayer
    213-385-0209
    800-421-9600
    E-mail: inquiry@wmop.org

Inspiration for Better Living and 24-Hour Ear-to-Ear Prayer Ministry
    773-568-1717
    800-447-6343

Living Enrichment Center Ministry of Prayer
    503-582-4218
    E-mail: prayer@lecworld.org

Christ Church Unity Prayer Ministry
    619-282-7609

Meditation

Peace is not the absence of the storm,
but serenity within the storm.
—ALCOHOLICS ANONYMOUS

The eleventh step of the 12-step program states that we "seek through prayer and meditation to improve our contact with our Higher Power." While prayer is our way of talking to God, meditation is how we listen to the response. There are many meditation techniques from a variety of spiritual traditions that are designed to take you to a place of stillness and receptivity. Perhaps the simplest one is described in Herbert Benson's classic work, *The Relaxation Response,* in which you breathe in to the words "I am" and breath out to the word "relaxed." Since many people in the modern world are overly mentally active, a walking meditation (consciously focusing on each step) is an excellent way to calm your mind while burning off nervous energy. Other meditative focuses include reading a scripture or other source of inspiration, listening to relaxing music, or taking a walk outdoors.

When you meditate, your goal is not to *do* anything, but rather to *be* with yourself and with spirit in a relaxed and receptive way. There are a number of benefits to this contemplative state:

- **Becoming quiet in meditation can help stop unwanted and counterproductive thoughts** that contribute to depression and anxiety. When your mind is not at peace, it is like a candle that flickers in wind; Buddhists call this the "monkey mind" (picture a monkey wildly jumping from branch to branch.) Or imagine your untamed mind to be like a racing train. Meditation can be compared to stopping the train, getting off, and sitting by a still lake.

    When practicing meditation, your goal is not to control your thoughts, but rather to observe them from a detached, calm space known as the *witness*, i.e., the place from which you witness your thoughts. Whenever you notice your mind wandering, you gently bring it back to your point of focus (e.g., your breathing) and continue to be still.

- **Spending time in meditation can allow you to pay attention to yourself in a healthy way.** Think of your meditation as a time-out period when you can ask yourself, "How do I feel in this moment? Is there anything special that I need right now?" These personal check-ins can alert you if you are emotionally or physically off-center and help you to get back on track.

- **Centering yourself opens you to spiritual guidance through listening to the still small voice within.** (That still small voice is both our inner wisdom and communication from a higher power.) People who suffer from depression have difficulty making decisions. While your personality may feel stuck in indecision, there is a wiser part of you that knows what is for your highest good. When you relax and open yourself to a higher wisdom, you can receive insight and answers to important questions without effort or struggle.

- **Stilling the mind makes it possible to connect with the part of yourself that is beyond your depression.** No matter how severe your psychiatric symptoms may be, there is a part of you that is not touched by those circumstances. This spiritual essence is called by many names—the Christ self, the Buddha self, the Divine self, and so on. Once you touch this place, even for a few seconds, you have a new way of understanding who you really are. Instead of saying, "I am a depressed and anxious person," you can affirm, "I am a spiritual being who is experiencing the pain of depression." Making the distinction between *the real you* (that is, whole and complete) and your *outer circumstances* helps to diminish the sense of shame that so often accompanies depression.

Ideally, you should make it a goal to meditate at approximately the same time each day. Try to find a quiet, comfortable environment where you can spend five to twenty minutes without being disturbed. Most spiritual teachers recommend meditating first thing in the morning, although your schedule may dictate that afternoons or evenings are best.

Keeping the Faith in the Midst of Pain

*In the depth of winter, I finally learned that
within me there lay an invincible summer.*
—ALBERT CAMUS

Physicist Albert Einstein, named by *Time* magazine as the "Person of the 20th Century," was also a great philosopher and mystic. According to a famous story, Einstein's last words as he lay on his deathbed were, "There is only one fundamental question to ask: *Is the universe friendly?*"

How you answer Einstein's question may have a significant impact on how you face and cope with depression. Do you believe, as the *I Ching,* the Chinese book of changes, says, that "Everything serves to further," or as Paul the Apostle writes, "All things work together for good to them that love God"?* Or do you identify with the melancholic Hamlet, who proclaimed that life is "a tale told by an idiot, full of sound and fury, signifying nothing"?

---

* Rom. 8:28

When we choose to hold the view that the universe is benevolent and supportive, we are far more likely to adopt the optimistic way of thinking that we described in Week 6. Moreover, believing in a benevolent universe also gives you the faith that in times of trouble, invisible means of support will become available. One of my spiritual mentors, Mary Morrissey, is fond of saying that God is greater than any *condition* or *circumstance* in your life. Mary often advises, "Instead of telling God how big your problems are, tell your problems how big your God is."

My faith in this principle was severely challenged during my recent depressive episode when my sick brain made it impossible for me to see my way out of the darkness. I was convinced that God had abandoned me to a horrible fate from which there was no escape. Many who are in the throes of a major depression also report experiencing this inconsolable desolation.

To bolster my faltering faith, I followed the advice of a friend and collected many "messages of hope" taken from the Book of Psalms; from my own book, *I Am With You Always;* and from other inspirational sources. Reading these words on a daily basis helped give my soul the strength to manage the pain until it shifted. I present a sample of these life-affirming words in Promises of Deliverance on the following pages in the hope that they may offer similar reassurance to others that there really is a light at the end of the tunnel.

Spiritual Community

All spiritual traditions emphasize joining with others as a way to gain assistance in strengthening one's spiritual life. One of the Buddha's main teachings was to "seek the *sangha,*" a community of like-minded believers. Similarly, one of the greatest spiritual movements of the twentieth century—Alcoholics Anonymous—has made community fellowship the foundation of its healing work.

A special kind of spiritual community that has made a huge difference in my life is the Master Mind group. Napoleon Hill first coined the term "Master Mind" in his classic book, *Think and Grow Rich*. Hill discovered that successful businesspeople did not succeed

Promises of Deliverance

God is our refuge and strength, a very present help in trouble.
Therefore will we not fear, though the earth be removed,
and the mountains be carried to the midst of the sea.
—PSALM 46:1–2

The Lord is my light and my salvation; whom shall I fear?
The Lord is the strength of my life; of whom shall I be afraid?
—PSALM 27:1–2

Though I walk through the shadow of the valley of death, I will fear no evil;
for thou art with me; thy rod and thy staff they comfort me.
—PSALM 23

The will of God will never take you where the grace of God will not
protect you. Don't give up five minutes before the miracle.
—ALCOHOLICS ANONYMOUS

In the depth of winter, I finally learned that within me
there lay an invincible summer.
—ALBERT CAMUS

The Lord is near to them that are brokenhearted, and He saves those that
are humble in spirit. Many are the afflictions of the righteous, but the Lord
delivers him out of them all.
—PSALM 34:19–20

I will turn their mourning into joy, and will comfort them,
and will make them rejoice from their sorrow.
—JER. 31:13

Remember, no human condition is ever permanent; then you will not
be overjoyed in good fortune nor too sorrowful in misfortune.
—SOCRATES

For I reckon that the sufferings of this present time are not worthy
to be compared to the glory which shall be revealed in us.
—ROM. 8:18

Our greatest glory is not in never falling,
but in rising every time we fall.
—BUDDHA

Though he fall he shall not be utterly cast down,
for the Lord upholds him with His hand.
—PSALM 37:24

Although the world is full of suffering,
it is also full of the overcoming of it.
—HELEN KELLER

Enlightenment begins on the other side of despair.
—SARTRE

But they that wait upon the Lord shall renew their faith:
they shall mount up with wings as eagles.
They shall run and not be weary, and they shall walk and not faint.
—ISA. 40:31

Sometimes I get discouraged and feel my work's in vain;
But then the Holy Spirit revives my soul again.
—MARTIN LUTHER KING, JR.

The Light of God surrounds me.
The Love of God enfolds me.
The Power of God protects me.
The Presence of God watches over me.
Wherever I am, God is.
—THE PRAYER OF PROTECTION

Let nothing disturb thee, nothing affright thee.
All things are passing, God never changes.
Patient endurance attaineth to all things.
Who God possesses, in nothing is wanting.
Alone God suffices.
—ST. THERESA OF AVILA

on their own, but depended on a "brain trust"—a group of people whom they consulted before making important decisions. Hill called this process of cooperation "the principle of the Master Mind." He writes:

> The human mind is a form of energy. When two or more minds cooperate in harmony, they form a great "bank" of energy plus a third, invisible force, which can be likened to a Master Mind. The Master Mind is yours to use as you desire. It is the master way to use organized and directed knowledge as a road to life-long power.

Years later, Unity minister Jack Boland integrated Hill's idea with the recovery model and equated the term Master Mind with one's higher power. (Boland was a recovering alcoholic who brilliantly synthesized the principles of the 12 steps and New Thought spirituality.)

Today, Master Mind meetings perform the same function as the brain trusts of Hill's time. A Master Mind group consists of two or more persons (two to six is ideal, eight is maximum), who meet regularly in an atmosphere of trust and harmony to provide each person with support and encouragement for the attainment of their goals. Master Mind partners believe for each other what each cannot believe alone.

In a Master Mind meeting, each member is encouraged to surrender to the Master Mind (i.e., turn over to one's higher power) any problem areas, challenges, needs for healing, and heartfelt goals. When such requests are fully and honestly made, spirit provides answers and solutions in the most amazing way.

During the past four years of my recovery, I have met regularly with my current Master Mind team, which grew out of my original Living Enrichment Center prayer group. Each week I share my goals for my health, relationships, finances, vocation, spiritual growth, and so on. The social and spiritual support I have received from this process has played an instrumental role in the writing of this book and in the formation of my depression support groups. (To learn more about the Master Mind process, write Master Mind Publishing, P.O. Box 1830, Warren, Michigan 48090-1830, or call 800-256-1984.)

Like a 12-step group or any support group, a Master Mind group is really about creating a field of love through which divine love can flow and heal. This kind of loving energy serves as a healing balm for the symptoms of anxiety and depression. Whether it is a Master Mind group or your church or temple, joining together with others in spiritual community will greatly enhance your mental and emotional well-being.

Using the Twelve Steps of AA to Heal from Depression

Religion is for people who are afraid of going to hell.
Spirituality is for people who have already been there.
—ALCOHOLICS ANONYMOUS

Although I have never suffered from a drug or alcohol addiction, during my episode of depression I often turned to the principles of the recovery movement and the Twelve Steps of AA as a source of healing and spiritual inspiration. This was no accident, for I now see a direct correlation between recovery from alcoholism and other addictions and recovery from mental illness.

To begin with, a substantial number of people with mental illness also suffer from drug and/or alcohol abuse. While 13.5 percent of the general population suffer from alcoholism, 22.3 percent suffer from both alcoholism and psychiatric disorders. (And 6.1 percent suffer from drug abuse, while 14.7 percent suffer from both drug abuse and mental illness.)* One reason for this relationship is that dopamine, a chemical that drives the brain's reward systems, is implicated in both addictions and depression. As Kathleen DesMaisons explains in her book *Potatoes Not Prozac*, the same diet that was developed to prevent relapse into alcoholism also works to heal depression. In fact, the parallels between the two conditions are so great that some see them as underlying aspects of the same disorder.

---

* Lisa Dixon and Jane De Veau, "Dual Diagnosis: The Double Challenge," *NAMI Advocate*, Volume 20, Number 5 (April/May 1999): 16.

The Twelve Steps

(slightly amended from AA)

1. We admitted we were powerless over our addiction (and depression)—and that our lives had become unmanageable.

2. We came to believe that a Power greater than ourselves could restore us to sanity.

3. We made a decision to turn our will and our lives over to the care of this Higher Power, as we understood Him, Her, or It.

4. We made a searching and fearless moral inventory of ourselves.

5. We admitted to our Higher Power, to ourselves, and to another human being the exact nature of our wrongs.

6. We were entirely ready to have our Higher Power remove all these defects of character.

In addition to their physical similarities, addiction and depression have a number of psychological and spiritual parallels. In both disorders, the sufferer is dealing with a force that is outside his or her control. As step 1 of the twelve steps states, "We admitted we were powerless over addiction—and that our lives had become unmanageable." In a similar fashion, the severe psychiatric symptoms of clinical depression cannot be healed through willpower alone. One cannot "snap out" of being depressed.

Healing from addiction or depression is not a one-time event. The person who has stopped drinking does not refer to himself as a recovered alcoholic or an ex-alcoholic, but a *recovering* alcoholic. Similarly, staying free from depression is an ongoing process. This understanding leads both the alcoholic and the depressive to live life one day

7. We humbly asked our Higher Power to remove our shortcomings.

8. We made a list of all persons we had harmed, and became willing to make amends to them all.

9. We made direct amends to such people wherever possible, except when to do so would injure them or others.

10. We continued to take personal inventory, and when we were wrong, promptly admitted it.

11. We sought through prayer and meditation to improve our conscious contact with our Higher Power as we understood Him, Her, or It, praying only for knowledge of our Higher Power's will for us and the power to carry that out.

12. Having had a spiritual awakening as a result of these steps, we tried to carry this message to others and to practice these principles in all of our affairs.

at a time, doing what is necessary to stay sober and emotionally stable twenty-four hours at a time. To accomplish this end, AA's relapse prevention strategies are wonderfully suited for helping the previously depressed person take care of himself or herself (see Week 12).

Another key to recovery from addiction is the Serenity Prayer: "God, grant me the serenity to accept the things I cannot change, the courage to change the things I can, and the wisdom to know the difference." Likewise, the depressive must learn to accept those things that are outside his or her personal control—such as genetics and temperament—and then change the things that he or she can control—attitudes, behaviors, diet, exercise, willingness to seek help, and so on.

Also, people who suffer from depression report that many of the aphorisms from the recovery movement contain practical wisdom that help them stay serene, productive, and at peace, one day at a time. Here are a few favorites:

- one day at a time
- easy does it
- utilize, don't analyze
- act as if
- first be willing, then get busy
- don't give up five minutes before the miracle

Because of this close connection between recovery from depression and recovery from drugs or alcohol, many depressives receive support from attending 12-step meetings such as Al-Anon, Emotions Anonymous, and Adult Children of Alcoholics.

Finding Purpose and Meaning

Social scientists have long observed that rates of depression decrease during wartime and rise during peacetime. This is because during war, people have a clear sense of focus and mission, i.e., achieving military victory. This phenomenon demonstrates the importance of having purpose and meaning in our lives. During his concentration camp experience, psychiatrist Victor Frankl discovered that if a prisoner had a purpose for living after the war, he would be more likely to survive.

After the war, Frankl realized that the need for meaning was not just applicable to prisoners of war; it was a universal human need. In his role as a psychiatrist, Frankl discovered that many types of mental illness—including depression—improved when a person found a worthwhile purpose upon which to base his or her life. Conversely, he saw many people succumb to depression when they felt they had nothing to live for.

An example of someone who has found great purpose and meaning in her life is wildlife advocate Jane Goodall. Ms. Goodall first became recognized for her work with chimpanzees at the Gombe Preserve in Africa where she demonstrated that chimps had the ability to make and use tools, a province thought to be exclusive to humans. Since then she has founded Roots and Shoots, an environmental and humanitarian movement for young people, with branches in fifty-seven countries. Asked why she didn't return to the peaceful reserve of Gombe to continue her scientific studies, Goodall replied:

> I feel the need to make people see what we are doing to the environment. At this point, the more people I reach, the more I accomplish. I miss Gombe and my wonderful years in the forest, but if I were to go back to that, I wouldn't feel I was doing what I should be doing.

Here is a woman who clearly has a purpose in her life. Her sense of mission no doubt has allowed her to maintain an exhausting travel schedule in which she is booked four years in advance and never stays in one place more than three weeks at a time.

This Week's Goals and Assignments

This is your assignment for the coming week:

1. Fill out the Assessing My Connection to Spirit inventory and the Creating Goals for Spiritual Connection sheet that follow. Choose a goal from this sheet as a goal for the week.

Ongoing Self-Care Activities

- Read your vision statement.
- Chart your moods in the Daily Mood Diary.
- Meet with your recovery partner.
- Formulate a goal for your weekly goal sheet.
- Exercise (three or more times a week).
- Drink at least sixty-four ounces of water, sipping throughout the day.
- Use your Cognitive Restructuring Worksheet to identify and replace your negative thinking.
- Work with your daily affirmation.
- Continue filling out your gratitude journal to the best of your ability.

Assessing My Connection to Spirit

Please take a few moments to answer the following questions to assess the quality of spiritual connection in your life. You can write in the space provided or use a blank piece of paper.

1. What are the main sources of spiritual support in my life? Do I belong to a spiritual community?

2. What would I consider my main types of spiritual practice? What activities do I engage in, such as prayer and meditation, that help me to feel connected with spirit or to something larger than myself?

3. How do my spiritual beliefs or practices help me to deal with the day-to-day challenges in my life?

4. Does my life have a sense of meaning and purpose? What gives my life its meaning? Do I feel that I am serving a greater purpose?

5. What is my world view? Do I see the universe as basically benevolent and supportive? How was the concept of God presented to me as a child—as a God of love or a God of punishment? Have I changed my views as I have grown older?

6. When painful things happen, do I think that I am being punished for something I did in the past? Or do I have a different explanation? How do I explain my suffering?

Creating Goals for Spiritual Connection

Using the answers from your "Assessing My Connection to Spirit" inventory, write down the spiritual support you now have and the support that you would like to incorporate into your life.

Spiritual support I now have:

1.
2.
3.

Spiritual support I would like to make part of my life:

1.
2.
3.

Take one of these and make it a goal for the week.

My Goal Sheet for Week 9

This week's starting date: _____ My recovery partner: _____

Date and time we will connect: _____

Goal or goals: _____

_____

Benefits of attaining this goal: _____

_____

Action plan: _____

_____

Ongoing goals (check off the ones as you accomplish them)

_____ Read my vision statement daily (upon awakening or before bed)

_____ Chart my moods in the Daily Mood Diary

_____ Participate in some form of exercise or movement

_____ Monitor my self-talk with the Cognitive Restructuring Worksheet

_____ This was my average mood on the daily mood scale (–5 to +5)

How was my mood this week?

Record your moods below for each day of the week. (–5 to +5)

Day	Mood	Comments
Mon		
Tue		
Wed		
Thu		
Fri		
Sat		
Sun		

Creating a Healthy Lifestyle

Those who do not find some time every day for health must one day sacrifice a lot of time for illness.

—FATHER SEBASTIAN KNEIPP

TENTH WEEK OVERVIEW

In this week, you will learn specific lifestyle habits that will elevate your mood when they become part of your daily routine.

In the previous nine weeks of our better mood recovery program, I have shared various self-care strategies that are designed to rewire the brain and help you to heal from anxiety and depression. These strategies have focused on the physical, mental and emotional, social, and spiritual dimensions of life.

This week we are going to look at other self-care activities that do not fit under any of these four categories. I have organized them under the theme of "lifestyle habits" because they represent specific *behaviors* that you can incorporate into your daily life to enhance your mood.

Lifestyle Habit #1:
Create Structure and Routine

Having the right amount of structure and routine in your daily life is essential to good mental health. Optimal amounts of structure decrease anxiety and help stabilize emotions. Without adequate structure and a regular routine, people prone to depression can become excessively involuted and self-absorbed. This is why I awaken, exercise, eat, see students, write, and socialize at approximately the same time each day. Having a stable routine gives me something to look forward to. Having something predictable to focus on each day calms my anxiety as effectively as any tranquilizer—and without the side effects.

The importance of structure in alleviating anxiety took on critical importance during my last depressive episode. Weekends were my most challenging times because of the lack of structure. During the week, I was able to attend a full-time day treatment program, where I could focus my agitated energies. There was no such built-in structure on the weekends, and so I did my best to improvise. Making appointments with friends to go hiking was my best strategy. And on Sunday mornings I attended worship services at the Living Enrichment Center, not because of a spiritual hunger, but because I needed someplace to go. It was this decision that ultimately attracted the support group that saved my life.

Lifestyle Habit #2:
Connect with the Natural World

Scientific evidence reveals that any contact with nature, even a view of trees from a window, can improve coping ability and mental functioning in people who are ill or under stress. Whether it's watching a moonrise over a mountain peak, a sunset over the ocean, or simply taking a leisurely walk in your city park, spending time in nature can elicit a healing connection to Mother Earth.

Hiking outdoors (in the woods, on the beach, and so on) is particularly beneficial because it combines the advantage of aerobic exercise with the feelings of awe and reverence that accompany being in the natural world. As John Muir, the founder of the American conservation movement, said over one hundred years ago:

> Climb the mountains. Get their glad tidings. Let the winds and the storms blow their energy into you, and watch your cares drop off like autumn leaves.

Lifestyle Habit #3: Be Exposed to Natural Light

Part of connecting to nature means getting plenty of exposure to natural light. Many spiritual paths teach that God and light are one and the same. For those people who are light sensitive, inadequate exposure to light can create depressive syndromes such as seasonal affective disorder (SAD). If you live in a dark climate and suffer from SAD, use full-spectrum lights or halogen lamps to enhance your exposure to light. In addition, spend as much time outdoors as you can. Research shows that early morning light is the most beneficial. If you find yourself working indoors, try to have your desk situated by a window. (Please refer to Appendix A to learn more about SAD.)

Lifestyle Habit #4: Find Employment and Right Livelihood

When asked for his definition of mental health, Sigmund Freud replied, "The ability to work and to love." Employment is therapeutic for a variety of reasons: it draws us outside of ourselves, it brings us into contact with other people, and it gives us a sense of identity and independence. (Volunteer work provides many of the same benefits.) As one middle-aged woman recently testified at a mental health conference, "The most important factor in my recovery was being able to return to work!" Conversely, I have seen depression brought on by a person's lack of employment or being involved in work that does not express a genuine passion.

Work issues are prominent in the depression support groups that I run. Prior to joining the groups, many of my clients had been forced to leave their jobs or careers because of their depression and anxiety. As they have healed, their desire and ability to work has reemerged. Returning to work has constituted a huge turning point in their recovery.

A more challenging group of clients are those folks whose high-stress (and sometimes abusive) jobs are "driving them crazy," i.e., exacerbating the symptoms of anxiety and depression. To leave the job, however, would mean replacing job stress with financial stress. (One option to replace lost income is to apply for Social Security disability. See chapter 12, "*Financially Surviving a Depressive Episode.*")

The ideal way to resolve such a dilemma is through the practice of "right livelihood," which originated as an aspect of the Buddha's Noble Eightfold Path to enlightenment. (The other seven elements of the Eightfold Path are right view, right thinking, right speech, right action, right diligence, right mindfulness, and right concentration.) To practice right livelihood means finding a way to earn a living such that what you do is beneficial to humans, animals, plants, and the earth—or at least minimally harmful. Right livelihood is about expressing your natural talents and gifts in a way that brings you joy, blesses the world, and produces a livable income. It is an expression of your deepest self that:

- produces something of personal value to others
- gives you a fair return, providing for your needs but not your greed
- gives you a sense of being a valued part of your community
- provides intrinsic satisfaction
- gives expression to the values you live by

Many practitioners of right livelihood agree on three basic guiding principles.

1. I do this work because I love doing it; I feel full when I am doing it.

2. I find my *primary* reward in serving people and creating something meaningful, beautiful, or useful. (Depending on the profession, you may still earn a high income, but making money is not the primary motivation.)

3. My relationship to my fellow human beings and the planet is based on sharing and cooperating, rather than competing.

Marie's Story:
Overcoming Depression Through Right Employment

At age fifty-one, I had become very isolated as I searched for satisfying employment. Although I had received a formal education in art and had worked within women's social-change arenas for years, I was struggling to find a fit as I wandered through lengthy periods of unemployment, debt, and dissolution.

In the absence of work, my sense of self-worth became easily confused. I began to doubt myself, to wonder about my reason for doing things, and to blame myself for the failure to do things right. My feelings of alienation grew, and the need for distraction and avoidance mounted. Comfort from overwhelming anxiety became my daily goal. Food, drink, and sleep became my best friends. I became disconnected from all of the healthy structures of my life.

Finally, I decided to break my self-imposed isolation and admit that I was deeply depressed and needed help. I joined Douglas's support group, where I was able to regain a larger perspective as I listened to other people who were struggling through their own dread and darkness. I was challenged to identify my own defeating patterns, and to create a positive vision and work at affirming my life every day. It felt good to ask for help and to receive it. I reached out to employment service support and found nonjudgmental people who validated my efforts and provided networking ideas for my job search.

After I succeeded in finding a meaningful job and work with people with whom I could identify, I was able to relax deep within myself. I could lower my shoulders and let air deep into the bottom of my stomach. My feelings of alienation lessened. My creative energy began to flow again. I began to regain my confidence and belief in my true nature. I got back in touch with my wealth of life experience and skills, which I share in my new job. I was able to see and feel the life surrounding me, and to feel grateful to be alive. I find myself saying "Thank you, thank you, thank you," many times a day.

Clearly, the passion and joy that we experience when we find our right livelihood are wonderful antidotes to depression as well as a blessing for the entire planet. (Two excellent resources on finding fulfilling work are *Wishcraft,* by Barbara Sher, and *Your Heart's Desire: Instructions for Creating the Life You Really Want,* by Sonia Choquette.)

Lifestyle Habit #5: Find Time to Relax

While work is therapeutic, too much work and not enough play can put you out of balance. In recent years, Americans have become more and more time deprived. We live in a type-A culture where people become, in the words of John Bradshaw, "human doings" and not "human beings." (Remember when Sundays were a day of rest?) As an antidote to such overactivity, see whether you can schedule in periods of time to relax and just be.

Relaxation comes in many forms:

- going to a movie
- reading a book
- talking with friends
- listening to or playing music
- going fishing
- writing letters
- taking a leisurely walk
- soaking in a warm bath
- taking naps
- playing sports
- cooking or baking

Find your own special activity and structure it into your day.

While it can be tempting to use alcohol to relax (or to use caffeine to focus), you run the risk of developing a new problem—chemical dependency. If you feel stressed, there are a variety of tools—such as deep breathing, exercise, massage, hydrotherapy, listening to relaxing music, positive self-talk, or prescribed medication—that can help you to relax (see also the stress-reduction techniques listed in Week 11).

Ideas for Pleasurable Activities

The following are some ideas for activities that can help you to bring more joy and pleasure into your life. While reading over the list below, ask yourself, "What things are pleasurable, used to be pleasurable, or might be pleasurable?" Then, write down four choices in the space provided. I could:

- go for a walk
- watch the sunrise or sunset
- tell a funny joke
- receive a massage
- sit in a hot tub
- see a special play
- drive to the beach
- pet an animal
- talk to a friend
- create with clay
- make a collage
- go sailing or canoeing
- go star gazing
- jump on a trampoline
- watch the clouds
- enjoy a good cup of tea
- go on a camping trip
- do a gentle stretch
- attend a concert
- write in my journal
- rent a good video
- do aerobics or go dancing
- think of something I am grateful for
- share a hug with a loved one
- watch a funny movie
- listen to relaxing music
- take a warm bath
- play a musical instrument
- spend time in the garden
- swim, float, or wade in the water
- treat myself to a nutritious meal
- attend a favorite sports event
- make a bouquet of flowers
- draw or paint a picture
- go on a favorite hike
- play golf or tennis
- ride a bike
- read a special novel or magazine
- visit a museum or art gallery
- practice deep breathing
- spend time with a friend
- enjoy the beauty of nature
- take a vacation
- repeat a favorite affirmation
- do yoga
- think of an enjoyable memory
- buy myself a special gift

Four Activities That Could Bring Me Joy

1.
2.
3.
4.

Lifestyle Habit #6:
Find Ways to Experience Pleasure

Related to the idea of relaxing is that of experiencing joy or pleasure. Since the absence of pleasure is one of the key symptoms of depression, incorporating pleasure into your life will be curative. Take a look at the list of Ideas for Pleasurable Activities on the previous page. As you read over the list, see whether you can locate activities that are enjoyable, used to be enjoyable, or might be enjoyable—e.g., eating a good meal, working in the garden, nurturing a pet, or spending time with friends. Write down the activities that you would enjoy in the space provided or in your Better Mood Journal. You can also ask yourself the following questions:

- "Is this activity something I would prefer to do by myself or with other people?"
- "Is it something I can start enjoying now, or do I need to plan for it?"
- "Will I have the opportunity to laugh?"
- "What are this activity's benefits? How likely is it to lift me out of my normal worrisome state?"

You can use the week-at-a-glance planner provided at the end of this section to schedule enjoyable activities into your weekly routine. Even finding just one pleasurable activity a week can be an important first step in feeling better.

Another way to experience pleasure is to create a library of positive memories. Make a list of the happiest moments of your life. Then go back in time and relive them, using your five senses to re-create, in exquisite detail, those joyful experiences. Because the brain cannot differentiate between a real or imagined experience, its neurochemicals will take on the same mood-enhancing configuration as they did when the original events occurred. In the future, when you are feeling low or need some inspiration, you can reexperience those pleasant memories.

Lifestyle Habit #7: Get into the Flow

When I was in graduate school, I asked one of my psychology professors how she helped her clients heal from depression.

"That's easy," Carolyn replied. "The cure for depression is involvement."

Reflecting on my professor's comment, I realized that the ending of my previous depressive episodes had always corresponded to committing myself to a new creative idea or passion. I also realized that when I was truly involved in an all-consuming project or focus, I did not experience the symptoms of depression and anxiety.

Recently this truth has been corroborated by psychologist Mihalyi Csikszentmihalyi at the University of Chicago. Mike, as his friends call him, has written a groundbreaking book called *Flow: The Psychology of Optimal Living*. According to Mihalyi, activities that produce flow are a remedy for "psychic entropy"—the mind's tendency to become random and chaotic when not focused on a purposeful goal-directed activity.

Here are Mihalyi's eight conditions of flow:

1. *You have a clearly defined goal with clear steps on how to reach it.*

2. *You receive clear and immediate feedback about how you are doing.* For example, in tennis, each time you hit the ball, you quickly discover how good a shot it was. Knowing how well you are doing keeps you focused on the activity.

3. *The challenge of the activity matches your skills.* For example, in tennis, you would select an opponent with matching skills to avoid being overwhelmed by the other person's superior ability or being bored because you are so much better.

4. *You feel totally focused on what you are doing.* Your focus becomes a single beam of concentrated attention.

5. *You live in the present moment.* Worries or concerns about the past or future do not intrude on your consciousness. Neither do the concerns or frustration of daily life.

6. *You lose yourself in the activity,* no longer aware of yourself as a separate entity. Self-forgetfulness leads to a sense of self-transcendence.

Even though you forget yourself in the moment, you can look
back at yourself afterward and feel good about what you have
accomplished.

7. *You feel a sense of control and mastery over your experience.*

8. *Your experience of time is transformed.* Hours may feel like minutes, or
a few seconds can seem to take fifteen to twenty minutes. An example of the latter is a dancer doing a pirouette where so much is packed
into the moment that time becomes expanded rather than condensed.

Flow is the experience of true enjoyment. In flow, you take on new
challenges and learn new skills, always moving forward toward higher
levels of complexity and mastery (e.g., the chess player who plays at
greater levels of skill as he improves his game).

Look to your own life. Have you ever experienced a time when you
were so focused and motivated that you felt alert, energized, and free of
self-consciousness? Were you dancing, gardening, working on a car,
playing an instrument, hiking, experiencing a runner's high, playing
your favorite sport, making a painting or sculpture, singing in a choir,
teaching a child, or helping another? See if you can identify any prior
flow experiences, and then bring them into your daily or weekly routine.

Of course, in the midst of a severe depressive episode, getting into
the flow may be next to impossible. The best time to use flow as an
antidote for depression and anxiety is when you are in remission. Then,
you can use it as preventative medicine, a way of strengthening your
psychological immune system so dips in mood become less likely.

Lifestyle Habit #8:
Tune into the Healing Power of Music

Aside from soothing the savage beast, music can be a balm for those
suffering from depression and anxiety. Many spiritual traditions use
sound vibrations to calm the emotions, still the mind, and restore
hope and inspiration. (Think of the soothing, reverential tones of
Gregorian chants.) Music can be very relaxing, especially when it follows a rhythm of sixty to seventy beats per second. Or, a rousing
symphony can be just what you need to feel renewed and energized.

In my recovery program, I make use of music in two ways. In the morning, I play inspiring music (such as Johnny Nash's "I Can See Clearly Now") to motivate me as I ride my stationary bike for a half hour. In the evening, I play classical music or a relaxation tape to help me wind down at the end of the day.

Ask yourself, "What kind of music makes me feel better?" Make a catalog of your favorite musical tunes, noting which ones are relaxing and which can be used for inspiration. You may want to make a tape or CD that you can play as a daily mood enhancer. (An example of a wonderful song that provides hope and encouragement is Billy Joel's "You're Only Human," also known as "Second Wind.")

Lifestyle Habit #9: Take Time to Laugh

The proverb "Laughter is good medicine" is more than just a saying. Ever since Norman Cousins published his memoir, *Anatomy of An Illness,* in which he describes how he healed himself of a fatal illness through Vitamin C and laughter, the medical world has come to recognize the therapeutic value of humor. William Fry, Jr., who has done research on the physiology of humor for the past forty-five years, lends support to Cousins's notion that laughter is like "internal jogging." Laughter enhances respiration and circulation, oxygenates the blood, decreases stress hormones in the brain, and prevents hardening of the attitudes.

There are numerous accounts in the medical literature of people healed through humor. In one instance, an elderly man was admitted to a hospital suffering from severe depression, having not eaten or spoken for several days. Shortly afterward, a clown entered his room, and within thirty minutes, the patient was laughing, eating, and talking.* In recent times, the most well-known practitioner of humor and medicine is Patch Adams, M.D., who adopts the role of a clown to bring joy and healing to the patients of his Gesundheit Institute in rural West Virginia (www.patchadams.org).

---

* Raymond Moody, *Laugh After Laugh* (Jacksonville: Headwaters Press, 1978), 21.

There are numerous ways that you can build laughter into your daily environment—having a humorous poster in your home or at the office, reading your favorite comic strip, telling jokes with your friends, receiving jokes over the Internet, or renting films with your favorite comedians. Consider, "S/He who laughs, lasts." It is almost impossible to feel depressed or anxious in the middle of a good belly laugh.

Lifestyle Habit #10: Bring Beauty into Your Life

The ancient Greeks knew of the healing power of beauty. Beauty brings balance and harmony to the soul. Many things can bring beauty into your environment: beautiful works of art (which can be reproductions and therefore inexpensive); nature calendars; gorgeous fabrics, rugs, and tapestries; and your favorite colors. According to Dr. Andrew Weil,

---

Take Time for Twelve Things
by Paul Bragg

1. Take time to Work; it is the price of success.
2. Take time to Think; it is the source of power.
3. Take time to Play; it is the secret of youth.
4. Take time to Read; it is the foundation of knowledge.
5. Take time to Worship; it is the highway of reverence and washes the dust of earth from our eyes.
6. Take time to help and enjoy Friends; it is the source of happiness.
7. Take time to Love; it is the sacrament of life.
8. Take time to Dream; it hitches the soul to the stars.
9. Take time to Laugh; it is the singing that helps with life's loads.
10. Take time for Beauty; it is everywhere in nature.
11. Take time for Health; it is the true wealth and treasure of life.
12. Take time to Plan; it is the secret of having the time for the first eleven things.

---

bringing flowers into your home is a wonderful way to delight the senses and raise your spirits. Working in the garden, strolling in a park, or hiking in the forest are ways to experience the beauty of nature.

Lifestyle Habit #11: Practice Time Management

Creating a healthy lifestyle means bringing mood-enhancing habits and activities into your daily life. The key to making this happen is learning to manage your time. Taking the time to plan is the secret to creating a lifestyle that truly nurtures and supports you (see Paul Bragg's poem, "Take Time for Twelve Things").

I first read about time management in Alan Lakein's classic book *How to Get Control of Your Time and Your Life*. According to Lakein, successful time management begins with considering your values and making a list of what is truly important in your life. After listing those things that are most important to you, Lakein suggests that you prioritize your goals by assigning an A to those items that have high value, a B to those items that have medium value, and a C to those items that have the lowest value. Finally, Lakein suggests that you make a daily to-do list, blocking out periods of time each day to work on those high-priority A goals.

Lakein's effective ABC priority system is based on the famous 80/20 rule, discovered by Italian economist Vlifredo Pareto, who noted that if all items are arranged in order of value, then 80 percent of the value would come from 20 percent of the items. (I learned this in the sales industry when I discovered that 80 percent of my income came from 20 percent of my customers.)

The 80/20 rule explains why 80 percent of our tasks in life are C's (low-value goals), and that, although A's takes more work than C's, they provide far more value in the long run. For example, let's say that you make regular exercise one of your high-priority goals. Although you may prefer to clean out your desk than work out at the gym, your A goal of physical exercise will pay the greater dividends in helping you to heal from depression. That is why exercise should always be a part of your daily routine.

This Week's Goals and Assignments

These are your assignments for the coming work:

1. Fill out the Assessing My Lifestyle Habits inventory and the Creating Goals for Lifestyle Habits sheet that follow.

2. Make several photocopies of the 24-Hour Healthy Self-Care Activity Schedule on page 301 (or create your own). Then, after answering the questions in the Assessing My Lifestyle Habits inventory, write down those self-care activities that have become part of your daily routine since starting the better mood recovery program. Include everything that you have been doing over the past ten weeks, including daily exercise, reading your vision statement, seeing your counselor, attending a support group, filling out your Daily Mood Diary, and your spiritual practice. Also include the pleasurable activities you listed earlier in this section.

An example of my own Healthy Self-Care Activities schedule is provided on page 300 to give you a model of how you can make your healthy lifestyle habits an integral part of your recovery plan.

Ongoing Self-Care Activities

- Read your vision statement.
- Chart your moods in the Daily Mood Diary.
- Meet with your recovery partner.
- Formulate a goal for your weekly goal sheet.
- Exercise (three or more times a week).
- Drink at least sixty-four ounces of water, sipping throughout the day.
- Use your Cognitive Restructuring Worksheet to identify and replace your negative thinking.
- Continue filling out your gratitude journal to the best of your ability. Work with your daily affirmation.

Assessing My Lifestyle Habits

Please take a few moments to answer the following questions to assess the quality of your lifestyle habits. You can write in the space provided or use your Better Mood Journal.

1. How much structure and routine do I have daily? Too much, too little, or just the right amount?

2. Do I find time each week to connect with the natural world?

3. Am I taking any health risks? What is my daily intake of alcohol, tobacco, or other potentially harmful substances? If these habits exist, how am I trying to change them?

4. Do I take time to relax and just be? Do I take time for personal reflection? How do I renew myself?

(continued on next page)

5. What truly nurtures me? What brings me joy? What activities are fun or pleasurable? Am I finding time for them in my life?

6. Do I have any creative outlets? If so, what are they?

7. What kind of music makes me feel better? Which music most relaxes me? Which music most energizes and inspires me?

8. Are there any colors that I am attracted to? What colors do I like to wear or have in my environment?

9. What makes me laugh? How often do I laugh? Am I around people who share my sense of humor?

10. Have I discovered my gift(s) to the world? Am I using them? Do I have the opportunity to express them in my work?

11. What would I do if I knew I couldn't fail?

Creating Goals for Lifestyle Habits

Using the answers from your Assessing My Lifestyle Habits inventory and the topics discussed in this section, write down your current lifestyle habits and the habits that you would like to incorporate into your life.

Positive lifestyle habits that I am already practicing:
1.
2.
3.

Positive lifestyle habits that I would like to make part of my life:
1.
2.
3.

Douglas' Healthy Self-Care Activities

Week of July 19

	M	T	W	T	F	S	S
5:00 A.M.							
6:00							
7:00							
8:00							
9:00	Meditate	Meditate	Meditate	Meditate	Meditate	Meditate	Meditate
10:00	Ride bicycle	Ride bicycle	Ride bicycle	Ride bicycle	Ride bicycle	Ride bicycle	Ride bicycle
11:00							Church
12:00 P.M.							
1:00		Therapy				Hike	↓
2:00							
3:00							
4:00				Support group		↓	
5:00				↓			
6:00	Swim		Swim		Swim		
7:00							
8:00							
9:00					Movie with friend		
10:00	Read	Read	Read	Read	Read	Read	Read
11:00		Hot tub		Sauna			
12:00 A.M.	Sleep	Sleep	Sleep	Sleep	Sleep	Sleep	Sleep
1:00							
2:00							
3:00							
4:00							

My 24-Hour Healthy Self-Care Activity Schedule

Week of

	M	T	W	T	F	S	S
5:00 A.M.							
6:00							
7:00							
8:00							
9:00							
10:00							
11:00							
12:00 P.M.							
1:00							
2:00							
3:00							
4:00							
5:00							
6:00							
7:00							
8:00							
9:00							
10:00							
11:00							
12:00 A.M.							
1:00							
2:00							
3:00							
4:00							

My Goal Sheet for Week 10

This week's starting date: _____   My recovery partner: _____

Date and time we will connect: _____

Goal or goals: _____

_____

Benefits of attaining this goal: _____

_____

Action plan: _____

_____

Ongoing goals (check off the ones as you accomplish them)

_____ Read my vision statement daily (upon awakening or before bed)

_____ Chart my moods in the Daily Mood Diary

_____ Participate in some form of exercise or movement

_____ Monitor my self-talk with the Cognitive Restructuring Worksheet

_____ My average mood this week on the Daily Mood Scale (–5 to +5)

How was my mood this week?

Record your moods below for each day of the week. (–5 to +5)

Day	Mood	Comments
Mon		
Tue		
Wed		
Thu		
Fri		
Sat		
Sun		

Stress Reduction and Pain Management

The goal of stress reduction is to respond to stress instead of reacting.
—TERESA KEANE, R.N.

ELEVENTH WEEK OVERVIEW

In this week, you will learn a simple and effective mind and body approach to relieving stress and coping with the pain of depression.

Over the past ten weeks, you have learned a five-part, better mood program consisting of physical self-care, mental and emotional self-care, social support, and lifestyle habits. In the next two weeks, we will be focusing on the process of "relapse prevention"—maintaining a better mood. A key component of keeping your mood even and consistent is learning how to deal with stress in your life. Depression and anxiety do not occur in a vacuum. Although one may be genetically and temperamentally predisposed to depression, it normally takes a triggering stressor such as a personal loss, financial setback, or illness to elicit severe symptoms. Although we all experience these kinds of stresses, those of us who are predisposed to depression and anxiety are more vulnerable than the norm to the debilitating effects of stress. This is why stress-reduction skills are a critical piece to your recovery program.

303

The Fight-or-Flight Response

A good way to understand the effects of stress on your body is to look at the fight-or-flight response. Let's suppose you are taking a leisurely hike on a wilderness trail, and a bear jumps out of the woods. Once you spot the bear, your body turns on an automatic survival mechanism known as the fight-or-flight response. The brain's hypothalamus and pituitary glands secrete hormones that tell the adrenal gland to release adrenaline. Within seconds, the following changes occur in your body:

- your breathing increases
- your heart rate and blood pressure skyrocket
- you become mentally alert
- your blood flows away from the digestive organs to the skeletal muscles, causing digestion to shut down
- your muscles become tense as you prepare to fight or flee
- your sex drive decreases
- your immune system shuts down

When the fight-or-flight response is activated, your body halts its long-term projects (digestion, tissue repair, immune functioning, and so on) and focuses on getting you out of danger. Once you make it to safety and perceive that the threat has passed, your systems return to normal.

In modern civilization, we don't have to worry about fending off bears or other predators; instead we experience *chronic psychological* and *social stressors,* such as conflicts at work or home, a child on drugs, an ongoing physical ailment, or worries about money. Even though these stressors are not lifethreatening—and in some cases may be only imagined (such as when we worry about the future)— the brain still releases the powerful hormones that activate the fight-or-flight response. Over time, this unremitting stress wears down the body and causes stress-related illnesses.

Depression and anxiety are two such stress-related illnesses. In his book *Why Zebras Don't Get Ulcers,* neuroscientist Robert Sapolsky states that 50 percent of people with clinical depression have abnormally elevated glucocorticoids levels, while people who suffer from anxiety disorders have too-high levels of adrenaline. (Glucocorticoids are steroids, like the anabolic steroids banned in the Olympics, that work with adrenaline to activate the fight-or-flight mechanism). Perhaps this is why 80 percent of people with depression also suffer anxiety; in both cases, the adrenal glands are oversecreting hormones that keep the body and mind on continuous red alert.

Noticing the First Signs of Stress

We can think of stress as lying on a continuum. At the low end of the continuum is healthy stress, such as the nervousness you might feel before preparing a dinner party or going on a rafting trip. As the stress increases, you cross a midpoint and experience unhealthy stress. (Many of the symptoms of stress are identical to those of anxiety and depression.) Here are some symptoms of stress.

1. **Mental symptoms**
   - anxious thoughts
   - poor concentration
   - problems with memory

2. **Emotional symptoms**
   - mood swings
   - feelings of irritability and restlessness
   - depression
   - fear and anxiety
   - anger

3. **Behavioral symptoms**
   - avoidance of responsibilities
   - negative changes in eating, smoking, or drinking
   - withdrawal from friends and difficulties getting along with people
   - sleep problems

4. **Physiological problems**
   - stiff, aching tense muscles
   - tension headaches or grinding of teeth
   - stomachache, nausea, or vomiting
   - exhaustion, shakiness, or nervousness
   - increased heart rate, blood pressure, or respiration

Having read this list, ask yourself the following questions (you will have the opportunity to record your answers in the stress inventory at the end of this section):

- "What is the target symptom that lets me know that I've crossed the line into unhealthy stress? What is the first indication that I am slipping?"
- "What are the external stressors that most often trigger my stress response?" (Examples may include hot weather, traffic, difficult people, managed care, or financial obligations.) "Are there ways that I can avoid these triggers?"

To further help you evaluate the presence of stressful events in your life, you can also refer to the Holmes Rahe Social Readjustment Scale on the opposite page. This scale was developed by two psychiatrists who interviewed hundreds of people of varying ages and backgrounds and asked them to rank their relative amount of readjustment to meet a series of life events. Note that each stressful readjustment is assigned a numerical value from 1 to 100. According to Holmes and Rahe, the higher your score, the greater your risk of developing stress-related symptoms or illnesses. For example, those people who have accumulated a total of 300 or more points over the past year have an 80 percent chance of getting sick in the near future; those with a score between 200 and 300 have a 50 percent chance of becoming ill. Evaluate your own score to determine how you are being impacted by environmental changes in your life.

The Relaxation Response

Fortunately, the debilitating conditions of chronic stress can be changed. There is a counterbalancing mechanism in the brain known as the *relaxation response,* which produces the *opposite* effects of the fight-or-flight response. When your relaxation response is activated, your:

- breathing decreases
- heart rate and blood pressure decrease
- mind slows down

The Holmes Rahe Social Readjustment Scale

Life Event	Value
Death of a spouse	100
Divorce	73
Marital separation	65
Jail term	63
Death of a close family member	63
Personal injury or illness	53
Marriage	50
Fired from work	47
Marital reconciliation	45
Retirement	45
Change in family member's health	44
Pregnancy	40
Sex difficulties	39
Addition to family	39
Business readjustment	39
Change in financial status	38
Death of a close friend	37
Change to a different line of work	36
Change in number of marital arguments	36
Mortgage or loan for large purchase	31
Foreclosure of mortgage or loan	30
Change in work responsibilities	29
Son or daughter leaving home	29
Trouble with in-laws	29
Outstanding personal achievement	28
Spouse begins or stops work	26
Starting or finishing school	26
Change in living conditions	25
Revision of personal habits	24
Trouble with boss	23
Change in work hours or conditions	20
Change in residence	20
Change in schools	20
Change in recreational habits	19
Change in church activities	19
Change in social activities	18
Mortgage or loan for a lesser purchase	17
Change in sleeping habits	16
Change in number of family gatherings	15
Change in eating habits	15
Vacation	13
Christmas season	12
Minor violation of the law	10

- blood flows back toward the digestive organs
- muscles relax
- immune system returns to normal
- metabolism decreases

Thus, the key to undoing the chronic stress that can lead to depression and anxiety is to:

- notice when you have crossed the line into unhealthy stress
- elicit the relaxation response, which will counteract the effects of the stress and return the body to a more balanced state

The relaxation response has two primary components:

- focusing your attention
- passively disregarding your thoughts; you assume the position of "witness" and passively notice your thoughts without trying to change or control them

Guidelines for Practicing the Relaxation Response

With regular practice, you will be able to elicit this relaxation response at will. Here is how Herbert Benson, the doctor who first coined the term "relaxation response," teaches the process to his patients:*

When: The best time to practice the relaxation response is when you are undisturbed. Doing it in the morning can set your mood for the day. Try to avoid practicing within two hours of a meal, as digestion seems to interfere with elicitation of the relaxation response.

Where: Find a quiet place where outside noise is minimal. Pick a spot that feels safe and protected.

Position: Sit or lie down in any position that feels comfortable. If you sit in a chair, select one that has good back support.

Length of practice: Try to set aside ten to twenty minutes once or twice a day. It is important to practice regularly so the relaxation response becomes as automatic as the stress response.

---

* Herbert Benson, *The Relaxation Response* (New York: HarperCollins, 2000), 12–13.

Instructions for focusing your mind:

- Sit quietly in a comfortable position and close your eyes.
- Relax your muscles, beginning at the soles of your feet and slowly work up to your face.
- Breathe in and out through your nose, becoming aware of the rhythm of your breathing. On the out breath, say the word "one" silently to yourself. For example, breathe in, breathe out, think "one"; breathe in, breathe out, think "one." Breathe easily and naturally.
- Continue for ten to twenty minutes. You may open your eyes to check the time, but do not use an alarm. When you are finished, sit quietly for several minutes, first with your eyes closed and then with your eyes opened. Do not stand up for a few minutes.
- During the relaxation process, maintain a passive attitude and permit relaxation to occur at its own pace. When you notice your mind beginning to wander, gently refocus your attention on the word "one" (or any other word that you choose as your focus word). Remain a neutral witness, and watch your mind involved in thoughts.
- Practice this for five weeks. Over time, the relaxation response should come easily and naturally. The more you practice, the more quickly you will enter a state of serenity and peace.

While practicing the relaxation response, your goal is to move your awareness into your right brain so you can observe how your left brain is perceiving events. If you are not perceiving a situation correctly, your fight-or-flight mechanism may be activated when you don't need it. For example, being late on a mortgage payment is a true concern, but it is not a life-threatening emergency. However, if you worry about the mortgage all day long, you will elicit the fight-or-flight response and create unnecessary stress-related symptoms. (The cognitive restructuring techniques you learned during Weeks 5 and 6 are also well suited for countering the stressful effects of worry.)

Other Relaxation Techniques

In their book *The Relaxation and Stress Reduction Workbook*, Martha Davis, R. Eshelman, and Matthew McKay provide an in-depth explanation of the following relaxation techniques and how to use them in your life:

- **Progressive muscle relaxation.** This is a deep, muscle-relaxation process that is based on the premise that the body responds to anxiety with muscle tension. Thus, when the muscles become relaxed, stress and anxiety fade away.
- **Meditation.** There are many types of meditation practices, all of which seem to work equally well.
- **Autogenic training.** This is a series of techniques, first developed in Germany, that induces relaxation through thinking about warmth and heaviness in the extremities.
- **Self-massage.**
- **Visual imagery.**
- **Hypnosis.**
- **Yoga.**

Stress and Other People

Although other people are our main source of support in healing from depression, they can also be a source of stress. According to researchers, those people with problems at work or with interpersonal conflicts at home are three to five times as likely to get a cold as those without such problems. Life abounds with conflicts with our spouse, children, coworkers, or boss—not to mention all of the ethnic hatreds and wars on the planet. "Hell is—other people?" noted the philosopher Sartre.

At the height of the Cold War, when the United States and the Soviet Union were spending trillions on armaments, one commentator noted, "That's a lot of money to spend on a relationship problem." While our own squabbles may not compare to a superpower struggle, they can produce significant personal stress.

Learning to communicate clearly and compassionately is a skill that can be learned. There is a lot of good information out there, both in book and in seminar form. (Two good books are *How to Talk So Kids Will Listen and Listen So Kids Will Talk* by Adele Faber and Elaine Mazlish and Marshall Rosenberg's *Nonviolent Communication: A Language of Compassion*.)

If conflicts with a spouse, child, other family member, boss or co-worker, or anyone else are disturbing your serenity and you can't work them out on your own, locate a professional mediator or family therapist. The dividends you reap in your mental and physical health will be well worth it.

Managing the Pain of Depression and Anxiety

One of the biggest challenges of depression and anxiety is dealing with chronic, unrelenting mental and emotional pain. This pain can vary from mild pain (–1 on our Daily Mood Scale) to the immense agony of a –5. A good way to visualize this challenge is shown in the image of a scale as depicted below.

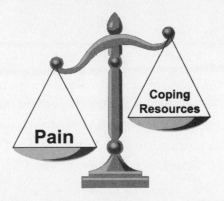

On one side of the scale is pain; on the other side are coping resources. When your emotional pain exceeds your resources for coping with the pain, the pain becomes unbearable (this, and the belief that there is no hope for change, can lead to suicidal thinking). To get the scales back in balance, you can do one of two things: discover ways to reduce the pain or increase your coping resources. Here are some tools and strategies that can accomplish both objectives.

Monitor the level of your pain. Rate your day-to-day pain using the –5 to +5 Daily Mood Scale and enter the numbers in the Daily Mood Diary in Week 2.

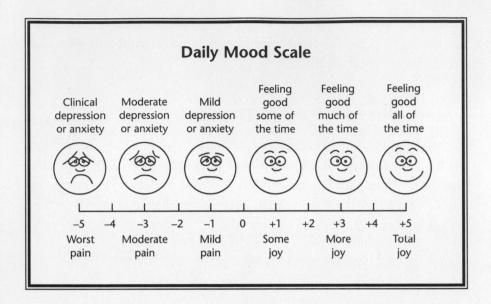

Daily Mood Scale

You can also expand your diary to include pain scores during the morning, afternoon, and evening. Over time, you may be able to see patterns. For example, many people find that their depression or anxiety is worse in the morning and improves as the day goes on. This was true for me, and nights were the only time I felt any relief.

Change your physiology. There are many ways you can alter the state of your physical body:

- *Use progressive muscle relaxation*—tense and relax each muscle group, starting with your feet, calves, and upper legs, and working your way up to your shoulders, neck, and head and then down your arms.
- *Exercise hard*—do one hundred jumping jacks or run in place, swim until you drop, hit a punching bag, and so on.
- *Sit in a warm bath or hot tub.* One of my personal favorites.
- *Drink hot milk.* The calcium seems to relax some people.
- *Massage* your neck and scalp, calves and feet, or have someone else give you a massage.
- *Alternate hot and cold water.* Get in a hot or warm shower and then gradually make the temperature as cold as you can stand it; then make it as hot as you can stand it; then go back to cold. Repeat this as many times as you wish, ending with cold water.

- *Breathe deeply.* This especially helps with decreasing anxiety.
- *Change your facial expression*—try a half smile. Tense and relax your facial muscles.
- *Increase your overall physical activity* if you can. Exercise may be the last thing you want to do when you are severely depressed, but its benefits are more than worth the effort. Exercise makes muscles feel better, improves sleep, eases the symptoms of anxiety and depression, builds fitness, helps manage weight, boosts self-esteem, and can increase your sense of empowerment.

Monitor your self-talk. While you may not be able to control the level of pain that you feel, you can control what you think and say about it. For example, in chapter 5 of my personal narrative I relate how I called up my friend Teresa and screamed, *"This pain is unbearable!"* Teresa instructed me to change my statement to, "The pain is *barely bearable.*" When I took her advice and shifted the wording, I felt less distraught. I had given myself a new message—that although this was really hard, I could handle it.

Use distraction techniques to refocus your attention away from the pain. You can distract yourself and take a break from the pain using a variety of methods:

- *Do some activities.* Busy yourself with a hobby, go to a movie, take a walk, visit a museum, clean the kitchen, work in the garden.
- *Turn your mind to other thoughts.* Count to ten, think of something pleasurable from the past, solve a puzzle, work on a jigsaw puzzle, read a good novel (if you can concentrate), watch a TV show or a video.
- *Use intense sensations.* Hold ice in your hand, squeeze a rubber ball very hard, listen to loud music, yell out loud.
- *Contribute to others.* Help someone else in need, do volunteer work. If you can muster the energy to reach out, you will be lifted out of your own cares as you focus on the welfare of others.

Soothe yourself with the five senses. Enhance your well being with:

- *Vision.* Purchase a beautiful flower and look at it. Gaze at the stars and moon at night. Watch a beautiful sunset or sunrise. View a pretty photograph or a favorite picture of someone you love.

- *Hearing.* Listen to melodious and soothing or inspiring and passionate music. Listen to the sounds of nature or tapes of these
sounds—birds singing, leaves falling, ocean waves crashing, wind
rustling through trees. Sing your favorite song.
- *Smell.* Surround yourself with your favorite scents or fragrances—
perfumes, essential oils, or aromatherapy. Buy some fresh-cut roses
or other fragrant flowers and deeply inhale their scents. Take a
walk in the woods, smell some freshly mowed grass, or immerse
yourself in the aromas of your favorite bakery.
- *Taste.* Have a favorite meal. Make yourself a soothing drink such
as herbal tea or hot chocolate (avoid alcohol; also avoid caffeine
if you are anxious). Taste samples of flavors in an ice cream store.
Treat yourself to a meal you've always wanted, or make your
favorite meal. Eat slowly, savoring each delicious bite.
- *Touch.* Take a bubble bath or sit in a hot tub. Pet your cat or
dog (or a friend's) or pet one at the animal shelter. Have someone
rub your feet with rich body lotion. Get a therapeutic massage.
Give and receive hugs. Walk barefoot in the grass. Hug a tree.
Sit in a comfortable chair. Let the warm breezes of a summer's
night caress your skin.

Soothe yourself using mental imagery. Picture a scene in nature
where you feel relaxed and nurtured. Some examples are:

- lying on a warm, tropical beach
- hiking through a verdant green forest
- sitting on a hill or mountain peak that overlooks a gorgeous valley
- walking through a meadow with colorful wildflowers
- swimming in the ocean or a clear lake

Or you can visualize a sanctuary such as a church, temple, or a special
place from childhood where you felt nurtured and safe.*

Call on your spiritual reserves. Open your heart in prayer to God
or your higher power. Ask for the strength to bear the pain in this

---

* Many of the distraction and soothing strategies from the above points were adapted
from the *Skills Training Manual for Treating Borderline Personality Disorder*, by Marsha
Linehan, (New York, The Guilford Press, 1993.)

moment until it repatterns (see my dark night of the soul prayer at the end of chapter 4).

Find or create some purpose, meaning, or value in the pain. Ask that your suffering be redemptive (i.e., some good may arise out of your pain).

Set up support systems. The pain of depression is made worse by isolation and loneliness; on the other hand, love and intimacy, connection and community produce pain-killing endorphins in the brain. Maximizing your social support will help you on the road to recovery. Having support also means that you are receiving proper medical treatment for your condition by seeing a counselor and/or a prescriber for medication.

Practice mindfulness. Focus your attention on what you are doing right now. Put your entire attention on the physical sensations that accompany ordinary tasks (e.g., doing the dishes, walking, doing the laundry, or weeding the garden). If you start to feel the sensation of pain, let it wash over you like a wave. Breathe into the pain instead of fighting it.

Live one day at a time. Remember the saying "Yard by yard, life is hard. Inch by inch, it's a cinch." Break your pain down into manageable parts. Practice getting through each day. If a day seems too much, try to make it through each hour; if an hour seems too long, set your sights on getting through each minute or second.

Practice acceptance. There is a psychological truth that states "Whatever you resist persists" (i.e., resistance to pain creates more pain). Instead of fighting your pain or telling yourself that you shouldn't be feeling this way, try to accept where you are right now. Practicing acceptance does not mean being passive. Do whatever it takes to improve your situation, while recognizing that this is your life for the moment, and you are going to make the best of it.

Using these strategies will not make all of your pain go away overnight. But it should tip the scales in favor of your coping resources so that you can bear the pain until it repatterns. Of course, if you are severely depressed or anxious, it may seem too hard to practice these strategies. If this is the case, ask your recovery partner or other support person to give you the encouragement and help you need to work with these tools. In the meantime, remember Robert Schuller's maxim: Tough times never last, but tough people (i.e., those who don't give up) do.

This Week's Goals and Assignments

This is your assignment for the coming week:

1. Fill out the My Stress Management inventory. Make it a goal of the week to practice the relaxation response for two or more days. Keep your Better Mood Journal by your side and write down any thoughts or feelings that come up. Share them with your recovery partner or your mental health professional.

Ongoing Self-Care Activities

- Read your vision statement.
- Chart your moods in the Daily Mood Diary.
- Meet with your recovery partner.
- Formulate a goal for your weekly goal sheet.
- Exercise (three or more times a week).
- Drink at least sixty-four ounces of water, sipping throughout the day.
- Use your Cognitive Restructuring Worksheet to identify and replace your negative thinking.
- Continue filling out your gratitude journal to the best of your ability.
- Refer to your 24-Hour Healthy Self-Care Activity Schedule as a way to structure your day with healthy lifestyle activities.

My Stress Management

1. What is the target symptom that lets me know that I've crossed the line into unhealthy stress? What is the first indication that I am slipping?

2. What are the external stressors that most often trigger my stress response? (Examples may include hot weather, traffic, difficult people, managed care, or financial obligations.) Are there ways to avoid these triggers?

3. What is the quality of my interpersonal relationships? How am I handling any interpersonal conflicts that may be arising?

4. How am I handling the pain of depression and/or anxiety? What coping resources am I using? Does my pain exceed my coping resources? If so, what am I doing to get the scales back in balance?

My Goal Sheet for Week 11

This week's starting date:_____   My recovery partner:_____

Date and time we will connect: _____

Goal or goals: _____

_____

Benefits of attaining this goal:_____

_____

Action plan:_____

_____

Ongoing goals (check off the ones as you accomplish them)
_____ Read my vision statement daily (upon awakening or before bed)
_____ Chart my moods in the Daily Mood Diary
_____ Participate in some form of exercise or movement
_____ Monitor my self-talk with the Cognitive Restructuring Worksheet
_____ This was my average mood on the daily mood scale (–5 to +5)

How was my mood this week?

Record your moods below for each day of the week. (–5 to +5)

Day	Mood	Comments
Mon		
Tue		
Wed		
Thu		
Fri		
Sat		
Sun		

Relapse Prevention

Depression is recurring and cyclic. What we have is treatments, not cures. You're never really free of it; you are always living in the shadow of it. You always have to be prepared for a recurrence and be ready to stave it off.
— ANDREW SOLOMON, *The Noonday Demon*

TWELFTH WEEK OVERVIEW

In this week, you will learn the basics of relapse prevention, learning how to identify and respond to outer and inner stressors so you can maintain emotional stability.

L ast week we began the process of relapse prevention by examining how to deal with life's stressors by calming the nervous system through practicing the relaxation response. Now, you are ready to take the next step and create a comprehensive and personalized relapse-prevention program that will show you specific steps to take if you find yourself slipping back into anxiety and depression. Relapse prevention is a critical part of the better mood recovery program because surviving an episode is not like having the measles—one does not develop an immunity to the disease. Although the symptoms of depression can be controlled, the underlying predisposition does not go away. While it is true that some individuals experience just one major depressive episode in a lifetime, half of those who have been severely depressed are at risk to become depressed again.

What can you do to decrease the likelihood of having another depressive episode? The first step is to realize that recovering from depression is not a one-time event, but an ongoing process. While utilizing the tools of the better mood recovery program can help our brains and nervous systems to stay well, there are times when powerful external stressors or internal biochemical anomalies will disrupt the brain's delicate balance. In such instances, we need a plan for identifying and responding to symptoms before they get out of hand and lead to another breakdown. This process of nipping depression in the bud is known as "relapse prevention."

Relapse prevention can be compared to fighting off a cold. When you first feel yourself coming down with a cold or flu, the proper response is to drink tea, take vitamin C, and rest. If, however, you ignore early warning signs and continue with your busy life, the cold might enter your lungs and turn into bronchitis. If you continue to ignore your body's cry for help, the infection may penetrate deeper into the lungs and become pneumonia. If the case is serious enough, you'll have to be hospitalized.

In a similar manner, depression can easily sneak up on you if you are not paying attention. Fortunately, having a depressive breakdown does not occur overnight. Clinical depression is a *gradual* process of falling out of recovery, ultimately leading to the inability to function. By regularly monitoring the state of your body, mind, and spirit, you can identify relapse symptoms early on and take action to prevent a return to major depression. In addition, you may want to ask a good friend or family member to monitor your moods, since an objective person may be able to spot the return of symptoms before you can.

Identifying Relapse Triggers

Last week we learned the principles of stress management—how to activate the relaxation response in order to free the body from the damaging fight-or-flight response. Relapse prevention takes stress reduction one step further by identifying those particular stressors (which I will call *triggers*) that can initiate the symptoms of anxiety and depression. Triggers can manifest as thoughts, events, or situations. An example of a trigger for a compulsive overeater would be a slice of chocolate cake; for an alcoholic, it would be finding himself or herself in a bar and being offered a free drink; for a compulsive gambler, it would be playing a game of video poker.

Each of us has our own unique set of triggers. Some of these triggers can be linked to traumatic events from our past. Examples of such triggers include:

- a man who was verbally abused as a child becomes despondent when he is criticized by his spouse.
- a teenage boy whose mother died when he was nine experiences sadness and depression each year around the anniversary of her death.
- a woman who was sexually abused as a girl turns to food each evening to fill her emptiness and to comfort herself. Nighttime is when the abuse occurred.

Other triggers include financial setbacks, health challenges, loss, role transitions, social isolation, and career changes. Of these, the most powerful trigger seems to be loss. Relationship break-ups, divorce, the death of a parent, the death of a grandparent, and even the loss of a pet have the potential to send us spiraling downward into depression. Humans are intensely social animals, and our desire for connectedness is both our greatest strength and our greatest vulnerability.

Another way to understand triggers is to use the acronym HALT, which stands for hungry, angry, lonely, and tired. (This term comes from Alcoholics Anonymous.) Whenever a person is hungry, angry, lonely, or tired, he or she is more likely to reach for booze or drugs. For people who suffer from a mood disorder, being overly hungry, angry, lonely, or tired can make us more vulnerable to experiencing symptoms of anxiety or depression.

Finally, remember that *stress of any kind* is a potential trigger for relapse. Thus, it is important to regularly practice the relaxation response that you learned last week.

Avoiding Triggers

An excellent relapse-prevention strategy is to stay away from circumstances that have the potential to serve as triggers. Here are some situations that my clients try to avoid:

- violent movies
- extreme heat (e.g., being in a car on a hot day)
- eating sugar when feeling blue
- taking on too many projects
- being around argumentative people
- losing sleep

You will have the opportunity to list your personal triggers when you fill out your personalized relapse-prevention plan at the end of this section.

Recognizing and Responding to Triggers

Once you know what your triggers are, your job is to be on the lookout for the return of the symptoms of anxiety and depression when a trigger is activated. These symptoms occur in three stages:

1. early warning signs

2. the beginning of a crisis (the onset of moderate symptoms)

3. a full-blown crisis (the onset of severe symptoms that can lead to a breakdown)

Stage 1: Early warning signs. Early warning signs are those subtle changes of thinking, feeling, and behaving that indicate a worsening of your condition. While they are usually associated with a triggering event, they may also come out of the blue. Often they go unnoticed because they are subtle or because you are not paying attention.

Here is one example. A few weeks ago, my nephew, who is in recovery from a bipolar disorder, looked more tired than usual.

"You look a bit beat," I observed.

"Well, to tell you the truth, my sleep cycles have been a bit off," Jesse replied.

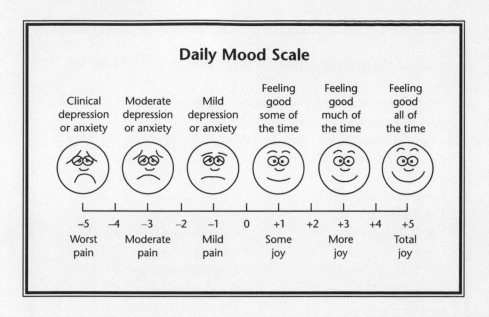

I became suspicious and, upon further questioning, I learned that Jesse wasn't getting to sleep until three in the morning. Since sleep disruption is often a prelude to a manic episode, I told Jesse that his sleep irregularities should be dealt with as soon as possible. (This story will be continued later in the section.)

You can refer to the Early Warning Signs of Depression and Anxiety sidebar on page 324 to help you create your own list of symptoms that signal a mood disorder onset. Compare this to the daily moods you are tracking on your Daily Mood Scale. As long as your ratings remain between a –2 and +2, you are experiencing normal fluctuations in mood. If, however, they creep up to a –3 or –4, and remain there for more than a week, you are in mild danger of relapse. (If you have bipolar disorder, ratings of 4 and above could be warning signs of an oncoming mania.) If these scores occur, you can implement the following coping strategies (if a clear external stressor such as a divorce or other major loss is evoking this pain, you may not be suffering from clinical depression, but should still take these steps):

- Check to see that your daily exercise regimen has not lapsed. If it has, get back on your schedule.
- Check to see that your diet and sleep cycles are normal.

Early Warning Signs of Depression and Anxiety

The following are some of the common symptoms associated with the onset of depressive and anxiety disorders. Create a list of your own warning signs, and keep it by your Daily Mood Diary so you will note the return of any symptoms. Warning signs include:

- lack of motivation
- insomnia
- low energy level
- poor appetite
- low self-esteem
- social withdrawal
- bleak feelings
- getting upset easily
- difficulty concentrating
- slow movement
- chronic aches and pains
- feeling of emptiness
- excessive crying
- hopelessness
- feeling fragile
- lack of interest in self-care
- excessive worry
- catastrophizing
- restlessness
- obsessive thoughts
- stomachaches
- shortness of breath
- excessive fears

- chronic sadness
- sleeping too much
- excess fatigue
- eating too much
- feeling worthless
- feeling hopeless
- feeling dead inside
- apathy
- inability to make decisions
- agitation
- excessive guilt
- irritability
- addictive behavior
- suicidal feelings
- feeling overwhelmed
- nervousness
- rumination
- irritability
- being keyed up
- shallow breathing
- feelings of panic
- dizziness
- feeling out of control

- Make an appointment with your therapist. Discuss any significant stressors you may be experiencing, such as domestic conflicts, problems at work, health challenges, or financial worries.
- Do something nurturing for yourself (e.g.,take the day off, spend time in nature, get a loving massage, or hang out with a good friend).

Stage 2: The beginning of a crisis—things are breaking down. Despite your best efforts, your symptoms may progress to a point where they begin to interfere with your normal functioning. In such a case, your symptoms would register a –4 or worse on the Daily Mood Scale for at least a week. Rather than toughing it out, now is the time to reach out for support. Here are some good ways to take care of yourself:

- Call your psychiatrist or prescriber to evaluate and possibly adjust your medication.
- Call your therapist or counselor for an emergency session.
- Call your support team to let them know you are in crisis.
- Take three days off from your responsibilities.
- Have a friend come over and stay with you until your symptoms diminish.
- If you are open to prayer, call one of the telephone prayer ministries listed in Appendix C and ask to be placed on their prayer list.
- Do something nurturing for your physical body, such as going on a long walk, practicing yoga, or taking a bath or a Jacuzzi.
- Monitor your thoughts. If you are beginning to catastrophize, tell yourself that, with the right support, you can make it through this period.

An example of successfully handling a Stage 2 crisis can be seen in Jesse's story, which I began earlier. About a week after telling me about his sleep irregularities, he phoned me and said that he was unable to concentrate enough to complete two relatively easy college term papers. He also dropped an introductory astronomy course because he had not been able to concentrate enough to study for an upcoming test. The night before, he had admitted himself to the emergency room, complaining of fatigue and dehydration.

I remembered that just eighteen months ago, Jesse had phoned complaining of similar symptoms while attending college away from home. With no family member nearby to lend support, he stopped eating and became nearly catatonic.

Fortunately, Jesse agreed with my suggestion to attend a local day treatment program—a structured, full-time regimen of group and individual psychotherapy. (See chapter 3 of my personal narrative for a more detailed description of a day treatment program.) Within a few days of attending day treatment, Jesse's eating, drinking, and sleeping patterns became normalized. Within two weeks, he was able to attend the program part-time. A month later he was discharged. With the permission of some of his college instructors, he was able to make up his coursework over the summer. (Jesse's story supports the idea that it is helpful to have a buddy or someone in your life who can recognize and evaluate potential warning signs before they get out of hand.)

Stage 3: A full-blown crisis—the symptoms become extreme. Stage 3 takes place when the symptoms of Stage 2 have not been successfully resolved and you are beginning an episode of clinical depression or panic disorder. The numbers on your Daily Mood Scale are likely to be close to –5.

Ideally, you should take the same actions that were outlined in Stage 2, i.e., enlisting your support team to help you deal with your crisis. However, your symptoms may have become so disabling that others need to take responsibility for your care and make decisions for you. (This is what occurred during my last episode when my partner and friends decided that I needed to be hospitalized.)

Take a moment and consider one or more people whom you would trust to act on your behalf if you became disabled by severe psychiatric symptoms. In the next few days, ask them whether they would like to become your supporters and advocates in the event of a relapse. Good candidates include a primary care mental health professional, a family member, or a good friend. (You will have the opportunity to write their names and numbers in your personalized relapse-prevention plan at the end of this section.)

In addition, you might ask one of these people to monitor your moods and behaviors on a regular basis when you are well. Since we don't always see ourselves with 20/20 vision, an objective observer may be more adept at noticing the early warning signs of relapse and reporting those changes to you.

Avoiding the Hole in the Sidewalk

The following story, *The Hole in the Sidewalk* by Portia Nelson, is a wonderful metaphor for relapse prevention. Think of the hole as some stressor or habit pattern (e.g., not getting enough rest) that increases the likelihood that you will slip back into anxiety or depression. Recovery is a function of learning to make new and healthier choices that will decrease the likelihood that you will fall into the pit.

The Hole in the Sidewalk
    Chapter 1: I walk down the street. There is a deep hole in the sidewalk. I don't see it. I fall in. I feel lost and hopeless. It isn't my fault. It takes forever to find my way out.
    Chapter 2: I walk down the same street. There is a deep hole in the sidewalk. I pretend I don't see it. I fall in again. I can't believe I'm in the same place again, but it isn't my fault. It takes a long time to get out.
    Chapter 3: I walk down the same street. There is a deep hole in the sidewalk. I see it. I know it is still there. I still fall in it. It's a habit. My eyes are open. I know where I am. It's my fault. I get out immediately.
    Chapter 4: I walk down the same street, see a deep hole in the sidewalk, and walk around it.
    Chapter 5: I walk down another street.

This Week's Goals and Assignments

These are your assignments for the coming week:

1. Fill out the My Personalized Relapse-Prevention Plan. Take as much time as you need. You may want to answer the questions on a separate piece of paper. I strongly advise that you keep a copy for yourself and then give a copy to each of the people whom you list as your supporters in question #3. Also, show it to your recovery partner.

   Think of this document as a valuable piece of insurance. Ideally, it will serve as a road map that will prevent you from becoming ill and will show you how to take actions that will restore your stability and wellness.

2. In addition, if you have been previously hospitalized, you may want to create a Relapse Prevention Document, in which you authorize certain people to act on your behalf if your symptoms disable you.

   In such a document you would list the following:
   • your early warning signs of depression
   • signs that the symptoms are worsening
   • the names and phone numbers of your support team and health care professionals
   • the actions you authorize others to take
   • the facilities where you would willing to be admitted
   • the name of your attorney (if you have one)

You would then *sign* and *date* this document, and give it to all the members of your support team.

Ongoing Self-Care Activities

• Read your vision statement.
• Chart your moods in the Daily Mood Diary.
• Meet with your recovery partner.
• Formulate a goal for your weekly goal sheet.
• Exercise (three or more times a week) and drink adequate water.
• Use your Cognitive Restructuring Worksheet and gratitude journal to the best of your ability.
• Practice the relaxation response for ten to twenty minutes a day.

My Personalized Relapse-Prevention Plan

Answering the questions that follow will help you to identify the thoughts and behaviors that are your personal warning signs of relapse. They will also help you to specify actions that you can take once you become aware of those warning signs.

1. What are the warnings that indicate that I am becoming depressed or anxious? (You may want to review what led up to any previous depressive episodes in order to answer this question.)

2. When I notice these warning signs, what actions might I take that will even out my mood? (Refer to the list of early warnings signs you made earlier in this section.)

3. Whom can I call or talk with to get support? Whom will I share my relapse warning signs with? Please list (if you can) three or more people below:

        NAME   PHONE NUMBER

a.

b.

c.

(continued on next page)

4. Sometimes others spot relapse warnings signs in me before I do. How would I respond if others expressed concern that I am in danger of relapse?

5. What are my personal "triggers"—those thoughts, events, or situations that can initiate symptoms of depression or anxiety?

6. What steps can I take to reduce the chance of being depressed or anxious in those situations?

7. Is it possible to avoid such triggers altogether? How might I do so?

8. What are some of my old ways of thinking (cognitive distortions) that I have seen produce feelings of depression or anxiety?

9. What are some new thoughts or beliefs that I can use to challenge those old ways of thinking?

10. Are there any changes I could make in my daily activities that would reduce the risk of relapse?

11. What areas of my life am I still working on in my ongoing recovery work?

My Goal Sheet for Week 12

This week's starting date: _____ My recovery partner: _____

Date and time we will connect: _____

Goal or goals: _____

_____

Benefits of attaining this goal: _____

_____

Action plan: _____

_____

Ongoing goals (check off the ones as you accomplish them)

_____ Read my vision statement daily (upon awakening or before bed)

_____ Chart my moods in the Daily Mood Diary

_____ Participate in some form of exercise or movement

_____ Monitor my self-talk with the Cognitive Restructuring Worksheet

_____ This was my average mood on the daily mood scale (–5 to +5)

How was my mood this week?

Record your moods below for each day of the week. (–5 to +5)

Day	Mood	Comments
Mon		
Tue		
Wed		
Thu		
Fri		
Sat		
Sun		

Living in Recovery

God, grant me the serenity to accept the things I cannot change, the courage to change the things I can, and the wisdom to know the difference.

—SERENITY PRAYER

THIRTEENTH WEEK OVERVIEW

In this week, you will explore how to build on the foundation you have created by making the better mood recovery program a way of life.

Congratulations! You have just completed the first twelve weeks of the better mood recovery program. I hope that the program has lived up to its name and that you are closer to recovery than you were twelve weeks ago—or whenever you began. (Remember, you can take as long as you need to complete the program.) To summarize what we have covered:

- In Week 1, you learned the importance of setting the intention to heal and forming a clear vision statement of health and wellness.
- In Week 2, you learned that reaching out for support is essential to recovery from depression.
- In Week 3, you learned that good mental health begins with caring for the physical body and its needs.
- In Week 4, you learned about the role of antidepressant medications in healing from depression.

- In Week 5, you learned how to use the principles of cognitive therapy to identify and release cognitive distortions and disempowering beliefs.
- In Week 6, you learned how to use the tools of gratitude and reframing to cultivate an optimistic attitude.
- In Week 7, you learned how to build and enhance your self-esteem.
- In Week 8, you learned how to expand the social support in your life.
- In Week 9, you learned how spiritual beliefs and practices can help you cope with and, in many cases, improve the symptoms of depression and anxiety.
- In Week 10, you learned how specific lifestyle habits that have been shown to enhance mood become part of a daily routine.
- In Week 11, you learned how to elicit the relaxation response as a way to alleviate physical and emotional stress.
- In Week 12, you learned how to develop a personalized relapse-prevention plan that gives you specific steps to take if you find yourself slipping back into anxiety and depression.

As a result of learning about these tools and strategies, you are hopefully practicing some of the following self-care activities:

- reading your vision statement of health and wellness on a regular basis
- charting your moods on the Daily Mood Diary
- meeting with your recovery partner and/or mental health professional
- engaging in some type of exercise or movement three or more times a week
- drinking adequate amounts of water
- using your Cognitive Restructuring Worksheet to release negative thoughts and beliefs
- writing in your gratitude journal to record what is positive in your life
- practicing the relaxation response daily or finding some other way to relax your mind and body
- finding times during the week to participate in pleasurable activities
- participating in some kind of spiritual activity that is in alignment with your core values and beliefs

Healing from Depression and Anxiety:
My Personalized Better Mood Recovery Program

The goal: To experience a better mood, free from depression and anxiety.

In the space below, write down those self-care activities that are now a part of your daily life. As you learn the better mood recovery program, you will be adding new tools and activities to the list.

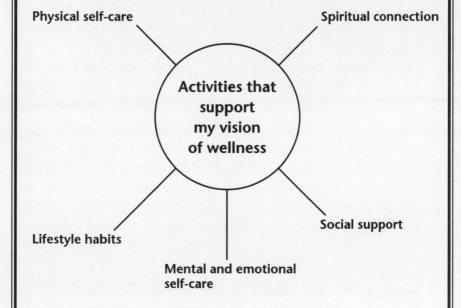

Physical self-care

Spiritual connection

Activities that support my vision of wellness

Lifestyle habits

Social support

Mental and emotional self-care

Assessing Your Progress

The first thing I would like you to do is to assess what progress you have made over the past twelve weeks.

Let's start by looking over the goals for the better mood recovery program that you wrote the first week. Have you met any of these goals? If so, which ones? If you have not yet achieved your goals, are you aware of any progress you have made toward them?

Now look at your vision statement from Week 1. Have any of the goals or desires contained in your vision statement come to pass? Do you feel that your vision of wellness is any more real now than it was when you first started the recovery program? Do you want to revise your vision statement in light of what you have learned?

Look through your ratings in the Daily Mood Diary from the past few weeks. How do the numbers of your general mood compare now to where they were twelve weeks ago? Have you noticed any movement out of the negative numbers into the positive ones?

Take a moment and turn to page 140, where you listed the self-care activities that you were practicing at the beginning of the program. Then, ask yourself, "Which self-care activities have I since added to my life?" Write down in pen *all* of the self-care activities that you are now practicing in your life in the blank template on page 335. You may wish to refer to your 24-Hour Self-Care Activity Schedule, which lists these activities (see Week 10).

When you have completed this process, you will have a clear picture of your Better Mood Recovery Program as it exists *right now*. Has it changed from where you were at the beginning of the program?

I do hope that in answering the above questions you have been able to see *measurable progress* in your situation. If you have not seen such progress (or perhaps feel worse), please consider answering the following questions:

- Have there been any major stressful events in your life over the past twelve weeks?
- Have you been faithfully applying the principles and tools of this program?

- Has your medication decreased in effectiveness? If so, you might want to pursue a medication change or adjustment.
- Have you been working with a counselor and/or a recovery partner over the past twelve weeks?
- Have you been receiving adequate social support?

If any of the above areas have been out of balance, making proper adjustments can get you back on track. Don't give up. Keep trying. Review the twelve-week program and continue using its tools until something clicks.

Taking the Next Steps

Now that you have looked back and assessed your progress, it is time to look ahead and see where you want to go. Here are some suggestions:

- Set your continued intention to heal. As always, your desire to be well and the clarity you have in creating a vision of healing are the driving forces behind your recovery. On a separate piece of paper, write your vision of wellness as it exists right now. Continue to read your vision statement on a daily basis, revising it as you feel called to do so.
- Set new goals. I encourage you to create a new set of mental health goals for the next twelve weeks. The goal sheet that you used at the beginning of this program is reprinted on the following page for your use. Use your vision statement and your desire to reduce your current symptoms as a way of defining new goals.

Another way you can create more goals is to turn to the Personalized Better Mood Recovery Program diagram that you just created. Ask yourself, "Are there any *new* self-care activities that I would like to add to my current program?" If the answer is "Yes," write them down in pencil below the current self-care activities that you listed in ink. You may also transfer them to your new goals sheet.

- **Continue to use your weekly goal sheets** to break your long-term goals into manageable parts.

My New Goals for the Better Mood
Recovery Program

In the space below, list at least three goals that reflect the changes that you would like to see over the next twelve weeks. These goals should reflect changes in the following areas of your life:

- your thinking
- your feelings
- your physical well-being
- your behaviors

One simple way to create a goal is to take a current symptom (e.g., poor sleep) and turn it into its opposite (sound and restful sleep). Thus, the problem of low self-esteem would become the goal of healthy self-esteem, the problem of difficulty making decisions would become the goal of improvement in decision making, and so on.

To locate symptoms you wish to heal, you can refer to the symptoms you listed on question 4 of the Anxiety and Depression Symptoms Inventory in chapter 9. Now, proceed to write your goals.

Goals
1.

2.

3.

List any further goals below.

- Starting with Week 3, Physical Self-Care, go back over the program. Or review the sections in any order that suits you. Whatever your strategy, continue to build upon the foundation of wellness that you have created. The more of these self-care strategies that you apply in your daily life, the better you will feel and the more likely that the demons of depression and anxiety will be kept at bay.

As you may have surmised, there is nothing new or radical in what I have suggested here. The better mood recovery program is a simple integrated approach to living a healthy and balanced life. But simple does not mean easy. Developing and sticking to good habits requires persistence and discipline (ask anyone who has quit smoking). But the dedication is worth it. Having spent too many days in the darkness, I do not wish to return; and I am confident that you don't either.

Remember that, for progress to occur, you will need the support of other people. Continue to meet with your recovery partner as well as with your mental health professional. Stay involved with people, whether it is through your family, friends, church, work, or a volunteer position. Set a goal to join a depression support group such as the one described in Appendix B. If you can't find one, 12-step groups or other support groups are also excellent. (By the time this book is published, I hope to be running small support groups over the Internet. Contact me at dbloch@teleport.com if you are interested.)

Also, remember that progress toward health is not a straight line. Periods of forward movement are sometimes interrupted by unwanted setbacks. Take heart that progress will continue, as shown by Patricia's story on the next page.

Above all, try to be at peace with your condition. Some people have diabetes, others heart disease; you get to deal with depression. By applying the strategies described in this program, and by drawing upon other resources listed in this book, you can take small steps to improve the quality of your life. Remember, life is not always about fairness, but rather about how gracefully we learn the teachings of our unique path. Best wishes on your transformational journey.

Patricia's Story:
"I Am Grateful for the Little Things"

The following story was written by one of my group members who describes the long and arduous period of rebuilding her life after a serious breakdown at the age of twenty-six.

Twelve years ago, I had a job in the center of the New York art world. It was all the things I had ever dreamed it could be: high powered, glamorous, exciting, financially remunerative. I could afford my own apartment in Manhattan, occasional trips to Europe, good books, wonderful food. I spent the summers working in the Hamptons, was strong and fit and loving New York. Then, due to some badly administered prescription drugs, I had a horrible nervous breakdown. The drug reaction created a combination of high anxiety, severe depression, and obsessive-compulsive disorder that had me washing my hands hundreds of times a day. I left New York for Ohio, for what I thought would be a few months, to try to put myself back together again. I never lived in New York again.

It was my psychiatrist in Ohio who gave me the first ray of hope that I could get better. "Your house (psyche) has been razed to the ground," Dr. Swanson said. "We will rebuild it, with a foundation so strong it will never fall down again." It took ten years for the rebuilding to occur, for me to come all the way back, mentally and emotionally. For the first two years, I couldn't even work. Simple chores like mopping the floor, grocery shopping, or doing laundry that I once would have done without a second thought took hours and left me exhausted. I often fell asleep after finishing one of them, although I slept eleven hours every night.

My first job, after two years of gradual healing, was as a bus girl. Whereas once I made many thousands of dollars a year, I now worked for a meal and a few dollars an hour. But that job gave me enough confidence to apply for my next job, as a bookstore clerk. After three more years, I was about

70 percent back. I fell in love, married a wonderful man, and moved to the Pacific Northwest, still working for a bookstore. Then, I took a stint in an art-supply store for two years. Finally, I was able to reenter the art world on a very small scale. Now, I work at the library, paint, show, and teach. My marriage is solid. I'm back to 100 percent of where I was before, emotionally, mentally, and artistically and beginning to push beyond that to deeper levels of healing.

I am so very grateful to have my life back again. When I remember what it was like to be sick, I almost cry with relief and gratitude that I once again have a mind that works and a spirit that can feel joy as well as sadness. I am most grateful for the little things, the simple things—waking up slowly over a cup of coffee; basking in the warmth of the returning sun; lying on the couch and reading the Sunday paper; losing myself in a good book; trading stories and jokes over dinner with a good friend; watching the light glisten on the leaves; listening to bird song, the wind in the trees, or the sound of a slow soaking; feeling at peace; going for a quiet walk in the park; taking a road trip alone to the mountains, absorbing the landscape along the way; feeling both loving and lovable; and most of all, being able to paint again.

I have rebuilt my life, in many ways better than before. I doubt that I shall ever again have the material abundance that I once had. But I have learned that material things can vanish in an instant. I put more value on relationships, spiritual and artistic growth, building community, healing self, and on others than on reacquiring the things I once owned. I am hopeful that I have reached the goal that my psychiatrist set for me when we first met in the hospital—to rebuild my house on a foundation so strong it will never fall down again. I feel like *Estelle peixa*, Portuguese for starfish, an idiom meaning "the creature that regenerates from deep wounds and creates joy."

PART THREE

Crisis Management
and Other Issues

Are You a Survivor?

When people are confronted by extreme trauma, they respond in a number of ways. Some individuals are broken by their experience. Others limp their way through. But a small minority actually emerge in a stronger and better state. These "triumphant survivors" have been able to overcome disastrous childhoods or major setbacks in their lives.

Researchers such as psychologist Al Siebert (author of *The Survivor Personality*) have found that such people are endowed with certain attitudes or emotional resources, such as a sense of humor, flexibility, the ability to be empathetic, the ability to pick the most positive and useful interpretation for any situation, and—perhaps most importantly—the ability to reach out for help. Surgeon Bernie Siegel worked with people suffering from cancer who exhibited these attributes and called them "exceptional patients."

When questioned about their recovery, triumphant survivors state, "The critical issue for me was not what has happened, but *What am I going to do about it?*" After their ordeal has passed, survivors are often inspired to share their story with others. Part of their message is this: "Out of misfortune, some good can emerge."

People who are suffering from depression can apply many of the qualities of the survivor personality.

CHAPTER ELEVEN

Therapeutic Interventions for When Things Are Falling Apart

Don't give up five minutes before the miracle.

—ALCOHOLICS ANONYMOUS

In the preceding pages, I outlined a systematic, step-by-step twelve-week plan for recovering from depression and anxiety. There are times, however, when the disabling affects of these disorders can make it difficult or impossible to start this program—or to complete it.

I know this to be true from personal experience. At the height of my agitated depression, I could not have participated in the exercises in this book. My ongoing anxiety meant that I couldn't sit still long enough to read. I lost my ability to focus and to concentrate. Most important, when I looked into the future, I could not envision recovery.

If you are in a similar situation, where your symptoms are seriously interfering with your ability to function, here are some suggestions:

- Turn to the suggestions and coping strategies for getting out of hell that I outlined in the introduction to the better mood recovery program (pages 133 to 135).
- Read the section on pain management (pages 309 to 314) from Week 11 of the better mood recovery program.

- Read over the coping strategies for Stage 3 (major crisis) from Week 12 on (page 326). Make sure that you are in daily contact with members of your support team (your therapist, prescriber, family or friends, and so on).

To further support you in your quest for healing, I would like to share five additional crisis-intervention strategies for dealing with intense pain:

- hospitalization
- electroconvulsive therapy (ECT—a way of jolting the brain back into balance through an electrical stimulus)
- two milder forms of ECT—rapid transcranial magnetic stimulation (RTMS) and vagus nerve stimulation (VNS)
- suicide prevention

Let's explore these intervention strategies now.

Hospitalization: When Is It Appropriate?

The very idea of going to a psychiatric hospital is anathema to most people. The idea of being "locked up" in a "funny farm" or "loony bin" elicits feelings of shame and stigma. Columnist Art Buchwald recounted how he felt "humiliated" and like "a total failure" when he was hospitalized for his manic depression.

There are times, however, when a person who is severely depressed or anxious should consider committing himself or herself to a psychiatric ward for a period of time. Hospitalization may be a positive option for you when:

- you are suicidal
- you are psychotic (hearing voices, feeling paranoid, or having delusional beliefs)
- you are harming yourself in some way or are afraid you will harm others
- you are unable to perform the tasks of daily living (for yourself and others), such as bathing, feeding, dressing, or getting out of bed
- you cannot handle being left alone

- you feel that you can no longer cope
- you lack the support you need to keep you safe
- your medication requires monitoring or changing

If you need to go to the hospital, remember that it is a temporary situation designed to keep you safe. Try to let go of any feelings of shame or failure. You are still a worthy person regardless of your external circumstances.

Unfortunately, hospital stays are shorter than they might ideally be. When William Styron experienced his depressive breakdown in 1985, he convalesced for six weeks, a respite that he credits with saving his life. Today, in the age of managed care, such multiweek stays are unheard of, unless you have the money to pay for a private hospital that specializes in long-term residential care. While I am not advocating returning to a time when chronically mentally ill people were warehoused in large institutions, it is clear that the pendulum has swung too far in the opposite direction.

Electroconvulsive Therapy: The Method of Last Resort

Electroconvulsive therapy (ECT), also known as electric shock therapy, is by far the most controversial modality in the treatment of depression. Much of the public's concerns about ECT arises from the gruesome way in which the treatment has been portrayed by the popular media. Many people still cringe when they recall the memory of Jack Nicholson being punished with ECT treatments in the film *One Flew Over the Cuckoo's Nest*. The idea of having electrical currents forced through one's brain inspires fear and terror while conjuring images of Frankenstein, mad scientists, and electrocution. Can such a seemingly barbaric practice be effective in treating severe depression? In the following pages, we will explore the pros and cons of ECT.*

---

* "Electroconvulsive Therapy, NIH Consensus Statement," The National Institute of Health's Consensus Development Conference Statement, 1–23.

What Is ECT?

Electroconvulsive therapy is a treatment for severe mental illness in which the brain is stimulated with a strong electrical current that induces a seizure, similar to those of epilepsy. In a manner that is not understood, this seizure rearranges the brain's neurochemistry, resulting in an elevation of mood.

ECT was first introduced in the United States in the 1940s and 1950s. During that time, the treatment was often administered to the most severely disturbed patients residing in large mental institutions. As often occurs with new therapies, ECT was used for a variety of disorders, frequently in high doses and for long periods. Many of these efforts proved ineffective, and some even harmful. Moreover, ECT was used as a means of managing unruly patients for whom other treatments were not then available. This contributed to the perception of ECT as an abusive instrument of behavioral control for chronically ill patients. With the introduction of effective drugs for the treatment of mental illness, the use of ECT declined. Recently, however, as safer and less traumatic ways of administering ECT have evolved, the treatment has made a comeback.

How Effective Is ECT in Treating Mental Disorders?

The efficacy of ECT has been established most convincingly in the treatment of delusional and severe endogenous depressions (the latter is what I experienced), which make up a clinically important minority of depressive disorders. Some studies find ECT to be as effective as antidepressants, while others find ECT to be superior to medication. The literature also indicates that ECT, when compared with antidepressants, has a more rapid onset of action.

A nurse at one hospital reported, "I have seen severely depressed people who were unable to dress or feed themselves; I had to change their diapers because they were so regressed and withdrawn. By the end of their ECT treatments they were smiling and eating and drinking on their own. It's as if they were brought back from the dead."*

---

* *Harvard Mental Health Newsletter,* June 1997.

Although ECT can jolt people out of severe depression and mania, recovery is not necessarily permanent. Relapse rates in the year following ECT are likely to be high unless maintenance anti-depressant medications are subsequently prescribed. In other instances, maintenance doses of ECT are given two to six times a year to prevent relapse. ECT is also useful in certain types of schizophrenia, although antipsychotic drugs remain the first line of treatment.

How Is ECT Administered?

During an ECT treatment, the patient is given a number of medications and muscle relaxants, and stimulus electrodes are placed on the head, either on one or both temporal lobes (for unilateral or bilateral ECT, respectively). After the muscle relaxant has taken effect, the brain is stimulated with an electrical pulse lasting from a quarter of a second to two seconds. The pulse induces a seizure that usually lasts from thirty seconds to two minutes, during which time the patient is closely monitored. After the treatment, the patient is brought to a recovery room where he or she remains until awake.

The number of ECT treatments in a course of therapy varies between six and twelve. Treatments are given three times a week, for two to four weeks. Following ECT, most depressed patients are continued on antidepressant medication or lithium to reduce the risk of relapse. Sometimes physicians give maintenance doses of ECT to their patients on an outpatient basis.

What Are the Risks and Adverse Effects of ECT?

ECT is clearly less dangerous than it once was. Over the years, safer methods of administration have been developed, including the use of short-acting anesthetics, muscle relaxants, and adequate oxygenation, all of which have reduced the risks of physical injury and mortality. Yet, even under optimal administration conditions, the ECT seizure produces two main reactions—transient post-treatment confusion and spotty but persistent memory loss.

Immediately after awakening from the treatment, the patient experiences confusion, temporary memory loss, and headache. Some people compare their experience to having a bad hangover. The time it takes to recover clear consciousness varies from several minutes to several hours, the exact length depending on the type of ECT administered (stimulating both hemispheres produces more confusion than unilateral ECT), as well as individual differences in the patients' response patterns.

ECT's second side effect is memory loss that persists after the termination of a normal course of treatment. This amnesia seems to surround events that occurred around the time of the treatment, either several weeks before or after. For example, the patient may not remember who took him to the hospital or what gifts he gave a month before the treatment. The ability to learn and retain new information does not seem to be adversely affected, although learning difficulties may exist during the first few weeks after the treatment.

Because there is also a wide difference in individual perception of the memory deficit, the subjective loss can be extremely distressing to some and of little concern to others. For example, many patients who complain about autobiographical memory loss say that being free of depression is well worth whatever memory disruption they experience. Others insist, though, that they have suffered a terrible disruption to their memory and to their lives. Although the second group is in the minority, accounts of their suffering must be taken seriously. Such accounts indicate that ECT carries definite risk and that it should be used only if the depression or manic depression is severely debilitating or life threatening.

Conclusion

ECT remains controversial despite its potential benefits. This controversy is perpetuated by the following factors: the nature of the treatment itself, its history of abuse, unfavorable media presentations, compelling testimony of former patients, special attention by the legal system, uneven distribution of ECT use among practitioners and facilities, and significant side effects. Nonetheless, ECT has been shown to be effective for a narrow range of severe psychiatric disorders— delusional and severe endogenous depression, manic episodes, and certain schizophrenic syndromes.

Much additional research is needed into the basic mechanisms by which ECT exerts its therapeutic effects. Studies are also needed to better identify groups for whom the treatment is particularly beneficial (or toxic) and to refine techniques that will maximize the treatment's effectiveness and reduce side effects. Rigorous double blind studies must be implemented to:

- determine whether and when ECT is effective
- carefully document side effects
- identify potential patients at risk

In this manner, ECT can be administered in the right way, at the right time, for the right patients.

Rapid Transcranial Magnetic Stimulation: Healing the Brain Magnetically

While ECT can be an effective means of treating serious depression, its invasive nature has long been a source of controversy. Now, there is a promising alternative that works on the same principle as ECT, but may be less traumatic. An experimental procedure known as rapid transcranial magnetic stimulation (RTMS) uses a powerful magnet to deliver an electric jolt to the brain in the same manner as ECT, but without electrical stimulation to unnecessary parts of the brain. Scientists believe that the technique works like a heart defibrillator. The electric voltage that passes through the brain causes its neurons to fire at once, and somehow this action seems to reset the rate at which the brain releases its various neurotransmitters.

In clinical trials, some people who have failed to improve by using medication and other therapies have responded to RTMS treatments within six days, and the majority are significantly better after two weeks of twenty-minute daily treatments. Because of its newness, no one knows whether these benefits will last longer than six months, but preliminary indications are promising. Like ECT, RTMS will most likely be used to jump-start the brain so other forms of medical care can then be used to maintain the patient's well-being over the long haul.

Magnetic therapy has been a viable medical therapy for thousands of years. Having a gentler form of ECT available is exciting news for people who suffer from long-term treatment-resistant depression.*

Vagus Nerve Stimulation

A second alternative to ECT that uses the same principles but in a milder fashion is called vagus nerve stimulation (VNS). Like ECT, VNS attempts to rearrange the brain's chemical soup through electrical stimulation. The key to its success is the vagus nerve (in Greek, vagus means "wanderer"), which, like a winding river, meanders for about twenty-two inches through an adult's upper body. The vagus functions as the brain's information superhighway, carrying signals to and from the brain from the vital organs below. When you feel your heart racing, the information is being transmitted to your brain through your vagus nerve.

Here's how VNS works. Doctors implant a device much like a heart pacemaker into the patient's chest and run a wire to the vagus nerve in the patient's neck. The vagus nerve carries signals from the battery-powered device into the brain (a thirty-second impulse is sent every three minutes). According to doctors, more than 80 percent of the electrical signals applied to the vagus nerve reach the brain and activate areas that regulate moods.

The battery-operated device, about the size of a stopwatch, lasts for five to ten years. Doctors can adjust the signals sent to the brain by using a computer and a wand with a magnet. Patients can also turn the device on and off with the magnet, which is important since the device can change their voice when it sends out a signal, although the change is hard to detect during normal conversation.

The vagus nerve stimulator is still in its experimental phase, although initial findings are extremely promising. A number of success stories have been published in the press, and the VNS device is now being marketed in Europe and Canada. A preliminary study is

---

* Joannie M. Schrof and Stacey Schultz, "Melancholy Nation: Depression Is on the Rise, Despite Prozac, But New Drugs Could Offer Help," *U.S. News and World Report*, 8 March, 1999, Volume 126, Number 9: 63.

underway in the United States, and the results are due to be published in the spring of 2002. You can learn about this study and the VNS device by visiting www.cyberonics.com.

How to Cope with Suicidal Feelings— in Yourself and Others

The ultimate tragedy of mood disorders is suicide. Suicide is a double disaster. Not only does it prematurely end a life, it wreaks havoc on the lives of those left behind. Devastated survivors can be traumatized by feelings of grief, guilt, anger, resentment, and confusion. "There was no time to say good-bye," and "Perhaps I could have done more," are examples of comments that are made by shell-shocked friends and relatives. A good friend of mine told me that her heart "shut down" for *thirty years* after her older brother committed suicide when she was nineteen. Moreover, the stigma surrounding suicide makes it very difficult for family members to talk about what has happened.

Suicide has been defined as a permanent solution to a temporary problem. For the person caught in the black hole of depression, however, there is nothing temporary about the hell he or she is experiencing. The resulting sense of hopelessness is the *major trigger* for suicidal thoughts, feelings, and attempts. This hopelessness includes:

- no hope for the future
- no hope that things will ever change
- no hope that you will ever be well or stable
- no hope that you will be able to meet your goals in life (or even have goals)
- no hope that the pain will ever stop
- no hope that you can do anything to change it

When your psyche is assailed by this level of despair, suicide feels like the only way out. If you are feeling suicidal, here are some thoughts that can help you to counter the suicidal urge:

- Remember that you are under the influence of a "drug" called depression that is distorting your view of reality. As a result, your feelings of hopelessness do not accurately reflect your true potential for recovery.

- Depression, like everything else in the physical world, is cyclic. In most cases, it comes and goes; it has a beginning and an end. A useful affirmation to repeat is, "Nothing stays the same forever. This, too, shall pass."

- An *overwhelming majority* of people who have suffered from suicidal feelings have fully recovered. The *odds* that you will get better are *in your favor.*

- If you have family and/or friends in your life, realize that they will be devastated by losing you. Their suffering will only add to the existing suffering in the world.

- Use the techniques described in the daily survival plan in this book, in the better mood recovery program, to increase your coping resources and to keep yourself safe.

- Remember that feelings and actions are two different things. Just because you feel like killing yourself, it doesn't mean you have to act on it this minute. This is one time when procrastination is a good idea.

- Do not remain alone when you are feeling suicidal. If you are feeling overwhelmed, ask for help. Set up a suicide support system with people who can spot your mood swings even before you do and will take action to keep you safe. Make a pact that you will contact them when you are feeling suicidal. If you don't have friends who can do this, try to locate a depression support group at a hospital or clinic.

- Use your local crisis hotline as a resource. Their job is to support you through your struggle, one day at a time. If you don't have a local hotline, call 888-SUICIDE (888-784-2433).

- Regulate anything in your environment that may be used to harm you. Flush old medications down the toilet, keeping only small quantities of those you take regularly. Dispose of all firearms you have or give them to a support person for safekeeping.

Remember, people do get through this, even when they feel as bad as you do right now. Here is a passage from Kathy Cronkite's *At the Edge of Darkness* that was very helpful in restoring my hope:

Part of the anxiety and dread of depression is that "storm in the brain" that blocks out all possibility of sunlight. In the depths of despair that by definition murders faith, courage may have to suffice. Keep slogging. Even if you don't believe it at the moment, remind yourself of the existence of good. Reassure yourself: "Once I enjoyed 'X,' I will again." The *disease* may have turned off the spigot of love, but it will come back.

Coping With Suicidal Pain

The diagram below, which we used in our section on pain management (Week 11), also offers a model for understanding suicidal pain. On one side of the scale is pain, on the other are your coping resources. Suicidal thoughts flood your mind when your emotional pain exceeds your resources for coping with the pain. To get the scales back in balance, you can do one of two things: discover a way to reduce the pain or find a way to increase your coping resources. The tools throughout the book are designed to do both.

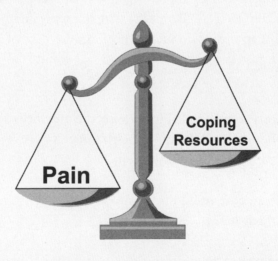

When Someone You Know Is Suicidal

Many people have mistaken ideas about the suicidal feelings that result from major depression. Depressed people who say they are suicidal are often not taken seriously by their friends and family. (For example, the day before a fourteen-year-old boy went on a shooting spree in a Georgia school, he told his friend that he wanted to kill himself. "You're crazy," came the reply.) What follows are some dos and don'ts on what to say to a suicidal individual.*

DO ask people with suicidal symptoms whether they are considering killing themselves. Contrary to popular opinion, it will not reinforce the idea. "In fact, it can prevent suicide," says Dr. Joseph Richman, professor of psychiatry at the Albert Einstein College of Medicine in New York. Since the suicidal person feels isolated and alienated, the fact that someone is concerned can have a healing effect.

DON'T act shocked or disapproving if the answer to the question "Are you suicidal?" is "Yes." Don't say that suicide is dumb or that the person should snap out of it. Suicidal feelings are part of being clinically depressed, just as a high white blood cell count is a symptom of an infection.

DON'T lecture a suicidal individual about the morality or immorality of suicide or about responsibility to their family. A person in a state of despair needs support, not an argument.

DO remove from easy reach any guns or razors, scissors, drugs, or other means of self-harm.

DO assure the person that although it may not feel like it, suicidal feelings are temporary.

---

* Taken from Caryl Stein, "Why Depression Is a Silent Killer," *Parade Magazine,* 28 September, 1997: 4–5.

DO ask the person whether he or she has a specific plan. If the answer is yes, ask him or her to describe it in detail. If the description seems convincing, urge the person to call their mental health professional right away. If he or she is not seeing a therapist or psychiatrist, offer a ride to an emergency room for evaluation or call the local crisis line or 888-SUICIDE (888-784-2433.) If the person is drunk or high, the risk of self-harm is greatly increased.

DO make a "no suicide" contract. This means that the person agrees (in words or in writing) that if he or she feels on the verge of hurting himself or herself, he or she will not do anything until first calling you or another support person. You, in turn, promise that you will be available to help in any way you can. It is best if the suicidal person has prepared a list of people (three or more is ideal) that he or she can contact in the midst of a crisis.

DON'T promise to keep the suicidal feelings a secret. Such a decision can block much-needed support and put the person at greater risk. If a person needs help from a medical professional or a crisis-intervention center, make sure that he or she gets it, even if you have to go along.

DO pay particular attention to the period after a depressive episode, when the person is beginning to feel better and has more energy. Ironically, this may be a time when he or she is more vulnerable to suicide.

DO assure the person that depression is a treatable illness and that help is available. If the individual is too depressed to find support, do what you can to help him or her find support systems, psychotherapy, medical treatment, and support groups.

DO call a suicide hotline or crisis hotline if you have any questions about how to deal with a person you think may be suicidal. Help is available for you, the caregiver.

Facts about Suicide

Statistics
- More than thirty-two thousand people in the U.S. kill themselves every year.
- Suicide is the eighth leading cause of death in the U.S.
- Each day, eighty-five people commit suicide and about two thousand attempt it.
- A person commits suicide about every fifteen minutes in the U.S., but it is estimated that an attempt is made once a minute.
- Sixty percent of all people who commit suicide kill themselves with firearms.
- There are four male suicides for every female suicide. However, at least twice as many females as males attempt suicide.
- Seventy-five percent of all suicides are committed by white males.

Youth
- Suicide is the second leading cause of death among college students.
- Suicide is the third leading cause of death among all those fifteen to thirty-four years old.
- Suicide is the fourth leading cause of death among all those ten to fourteen years old.
- The suicide rate for young men (fifteen to twenty-four) has tripled since 1950, while for young women (fifteen to twenty-four) it has more than doubled.
- The suicide rate for children (ten to fourteen) has more than doubled over the last fifteen years.

Facts about Suicide

Depression

- More than 60 percent of all people who commit suicide suffer from major depression. If one includes alcoholics who are depressed, this figure rises to over 75 percent.
- About 15 percent of the population will suffer from clinical depression at some point in their lives. Thirty percent of all clinically depressed patients attempt suicide; half of them succeed.

Alcohol and Suicide

- Ninety-six percent of alcoholics who commit suicide continue their substance abuse up to the end of their lives.
- Alcoholism is a factor in about 30 percent of all completed suicides.
- Eighteen percent of alcoholics die by suicide; 87 percent of these deaths are males.

Firearms and Suicide

- Death by firearms is the fastest growing method of suicide.
- Firearms are now used in more suicides than homicides.
- States with stricter gun control laws have lower rates of suicide.

Figures are based on 1995 United States statistics.
Source: American Foundation for Suicide Prevention.

There are a number of telephone hotlines and Internet sites that can provide immediate support and relief for anyone who is struggling with feelings of suicide, including the following:

- American Suicide Survival Line 888-SUICIDE (888-784-2433). This nationwide suicide telephone hotline provides free twenty-four-hour crisis counseling for people who are suicidal or who are suffering the pain of depression.
- The Samaritans Suicide Hotline, 212-673-3000, jo@samaritans.org. They will respond to your E-mail within twenty-four hours.
- Covenant House Nineline, 800-999-9999, www.covenanthouse.org. This hotline provides crisis intervention, support, and referrals for youth and adults in crisis, including those who are feeling depressed and suicidal.
- If you are thinking about suicide, read this first: www.metanoia.org/suicide/. This is an excellent Web site that I visited when I was suicidal. I credit it with being one of the factors that prevented me from taking my life.
- Suicide Awareness Voices of Education, www.save.org/index.html. This is the Web site for SA\VE whose mission is to educate others about suicide and to speak for suicide survivors. I frequented this Internet site when I was suicidal and found it to be extremely helpful.

These phone numbers and Internet addresses are repeated in Appendix C, along with other resources. In addition, on July 28, 1999, the Surgeon General of the United States officially recognized suicide as a national health crisis and issued "The Surgeon General's Call to Action to Prevent Suicide." To learn more about this important campaign to raise awareness about the causes and prevention fo suicide, call the Office of the Surgeon General at 301-443-4000 (or visit the Web site at www.surgeongeneral.gov).

CHAPTER TWELVE

Where Has All the Insurance Gone? Financially Surviving a Depressive Episode

Increasing, the mentally ill have nowhere to go. That's their problem and ours.
—MICHAEL WINERIP, *New York Times*

Experiencing a depressive episode in our society is not cheap. Hospital rooms run $800 a day, psychiatrists charge from $150 to $180 an hour, and antidepressants may cost as much as $2.80 a pill. During my depressive episode, I was fortunate to be covered by the group insurance plan from my previous job, which paid for a majority of my hospitalization and outpatient costs. Most people are not so lucky. As a rule, insurance plans are structured so the money allotted for mental health treatment is far less than the funds given for physical health benefits. This means that many people who suffer from depression run out of insurance before they run out of illness.

This lack of parity is most discriminatory for the self-employed. For example, as a self-employed writer, I purchase my insurance from the Providence Health Plan, one of the premier managed care companies in the Pacific Northwest. If I were in a car accident, had a heart attack, or developed an acute infection, my insurance would pay for 80 percent of my hospitalization costs. But if I suffered a relapse into depression and needed to be hospitalized, the Providence Health Plan would pay *absolutely nothing* for my treatment! Moreover, I cannot sign up for better mental health coverage. As incredible as it seems, mental health inpatient benefits for the self-employed are *unavailable* in the state of Oregon.

Day treatment coverage is not much of an improvement. Under current law, the state of Oregon mandates a maximum of $1,000 worth of benefits (which pays for only one week of outpatient care) every twenty-four months. When I attended the day treatment program at the Pacific Counseling Center, it took nine months before I got well. Fortunately, I was covered by my employer's group health plan. But what if I were to have a relapse now? Where would I go? What of other self-employed people who are currently in the hell of depression? How many of them are literally dying because they cannot get the care they deserve? While there have been reports in the media of people dying from physical illnesses that were neglected by the managed care system, no one has reported on suicides due to untreated mental illness. I can assure you that it happens, since untreated depression is the leading cause of suicide.

These discriminatory policies reflect a long-held societal stigma against mental illness. This stigma is reflected in the fact that for every $100 of cost created by mental disorders, thirty cents are spent on research (compare that to $1.63 for cancer research). We will know that attitudes have changed when we see depression awareness booths (just like today's blood-pressure stations) set up in airports and other public facilities, where individuals can receive free screenings to determine whether they suffer from clinical depression or a related mood disorder.

Fortunately, a shift in attitudes is slowly taking place. In the first White House Conference on Mental Health (June 7, 1999), President Clinton stated, "As a nation founded on the principles of equality, it is high time that our health plans treat all Americans equally." He then announced that the federal government, the largest self-insured institution in the country, would amend its insurance coverage so mental health services are *on a par* with physical health treatments. Under the new policy, private health plans covering federal employees and their families *could not* set limits on the number of outpatient visits or days spent in a hospital for treatment of "recognized mental health disorders" such as schizophrenia, bipolar or manic-depressive disorder, and major or clinical depression. Moreover, the policy would bar making copayments higher for mental health disorders than those for the treatment of physical illnesses. The administration hopes that this policy will be a model for the rest of the health care industry. (To learn more about the government's support of mental health reform, visit the White House Web site at www.mentalhealth.gov.)

In this vein, I plan to join with the National Alliance for the Mentally Ill (NAMI) in lobbying the Oregon legislature to pass a law mandating that insurance companies in this state provide equal coverage for mental illness. If you have similar concerns about your state's insurance coverage for mental health, I encourage you to get involved. It is time to put benefits for mental and physical health on an equal playing field, thereby guaranteeing that those who suffer from the terrible malady of mental illness can receive the same compassionate care that is offered to other patients with "physical" problems.

Replacing Lost Income

A second economic challenge that many people suffering from depression face is replacing lost income, especially when the illness is so disabling that the person can no longer work. For those individuals who do not have insurance and/or independent resources, financial support is available, thanks to Social Security benefits provided by the federal government.

A person who can document that he or she is suffering from a disabling mental illness is eligible for SSD (Social Security disability income) and, if his or her income is low enough, for SSI (supplemental security income). After benefits have begun, he or she can then receive Medicare, which pays for inpatient psychiatric care and some outpatient services.

Although the monthly income from SSD and SSI is extremely modest, recipients do seem to get by. During my stay at day treatment, I saw many people who were able to stay and get well because they were supported by disability income and their therapy was paid by Medicare. To learn more about obtaining assistance, you can call the Social Security Administration at 800-772-1013. In addition, a number of attorneys and social workers specialize in helping people with disabilities to apply for Social Security benefits. Ask a local mental health center for a referral or consult the Yellow Pages. Locate the section advertising attorneys, and then look for lawyers who are listed under the subheading, "Social Security."

CHAPTER THIRTEEN

Managing the Anxiety That Often Accompanies Depression

If you're facing terror everyday, it's going to bring Hannibal to his knees.

—JIM BALLENGER

O ver 60 percent of major depressions are accompanied by vary-ing levels of anxious feelings and behavior. (During my illness, my extreme anxiety interfered with my recovery and increased the risk of suicide.) These symptoms may be diagnosed as generalized anxiety disorder, panic disorder, obsessive-compulsive disorder, or post-traumatic stress disorder (PTSD). Here are some techniques that are commonly used to treat mild to severe anxiety.

Medications. The medications most often used to treat anxiety are a class of drugs known as benzodiazepines (also called minor tranquil-izers). These include Xanax, Ativan, and Klonopin. The main prob-lem with these substances is their potential for tolerance, physical dependence, and the likely recurrence of panic and anxiety symp-toms when the medication is stopped. Hence, they are best used for treating short-term anxiety and panic. Because anxiety is so often associated with depressive disorders, it is essential to treat the under-lying depression along with the anxiety disorder. When the depression is healed, symptoms of anxiety often diminish.

Exercise and relaxation techniques. Because anxiety clearly has a physical component (especially when it manifests as a panic attack), techniques for relaxing the body are an important part of your treat-ment plan. These include abdominal breathing, progressive muscle relaxation (relaxing the body's muscle groups), and the relaxation response that we learned in Week 11. You can learn these practices from any mental health professional who teaches relaxation or stress reduction. Regular exercise also has a direct impact on several physi-ological conditions that underlie anxiety. Exercise reduces skeletal muscle tension, metabolizes excess adrenaline and thyroxin in the bloodstream (chemicals that keep one in a state of arousal), and dis-charges pent-up frustration and anger.

Cognitive-behavioral therapy. Cognitive-behavioral therapy is a psychotherapy that helps you to alter anxious self-talk and mistaken beliefs that give your body anxiety-producing messages. For example, saying to yourself, "What if I have an anxiety attack when I'm driving home?" will make it more likely that an attack will ensue. Overcoming negative self-talk involves creating *positive counterstatements*, such as "I can feel anxious and still drive," or "I can handle it." What often underlies our negative self-talk is a set of negative beliefs about our-selves and the world. Examples of such mistaken beliefs are "I am powerless," "Life is dangerous," and "It's not okay to show my feel-ings." Replacing these beliefs with empowering truths can help to heal the roots of anxiety (see How the Same Event Can Result in Different Feelings in Week 5).

Monitoring diet and nutrition. Stimulants such as caffeine and nicotine can aggravate anxiety and leave you more prone to anxiety and panic attacks. Other dietary factors such as sugar, certain food additives, and food sensitivities can make some people feel anxious. Seeing a nutritionally oriented physician or therapist may help you to identify and eliminate possible offending substances from your diet. He or she can also help you to research supplements and herbs (e.g., GABA, Kava, B vitamins, and chamomile and valerian teas) that are known to calm the nervous system.

If you are suffering from a serious anxiety disorder, you may want to locate a clinic in your area that *specializes* in the treatment of anxiety. Your local hospital or mental health clinic can give you a referral. In addition, you may wish to call 800-64-PANIC to receive helpful material from the National Institute of Mental Health. Books and Internet sites on anxiety disorders can be found in Appendix C and in the Recommended Reading section.

CHAPTER FOURTEEN

When Someone You Love Is Depressed

Whatever you give of yourself to somebody else is never lost, no matter what happens to that person.

—FRED ROGERS (aka Mr. Rogers)

The pain of seeing a loved one in the depths of clinical depression is almost as torturous as being depressed oneself. If you are the partner, parent, child, or friend of someone who is undergoing a depressive episode, your understanding of the illness and how you relate to the patient can either support or deter his or her ability to get well. Here are some important ways in which you can help the healing process.

Help the person to recognize that there is a problem. If a friend or family member's activity and outlook on life starts to descend and stays down not just a few days, but for weeks, depression may be the cause. Support is especially crucial, since many people fail to realize that they are depressed. Begin by encouraging your friend to share his or her feelings with you and by showing him or her the Daily Rating Scale for Anxiety and Depression on page 41. Contrary to myth, talking about depression makes things better, not worse. Once it becomes clear that something is amiss, you can suggest that your friend seek professional help. (This is critical since only one-third of people with mood disorders ever receive treatment.)

You can be of further support by accompanying your friend to his or her initial doctor's or therapist's appointment and subsequently monitoring his or her medication. In addition, explain that seeking help for depression does not imply a lack of emotional strength or moral character. On the contrary, it takes both courage and wisdom to know when one is in need of assistance.

Educate yourself about the illness. Whether it is depression, manic depression, anxiety, or something else, learn about symptoms of the illness and how to tell when they are improving. Your feedback to the psychiatrist or therapist about how your friend is faring will help him or her to assess whether a particular treatment is working.

Provide emotional support. Remember, what a person suffering from depression needs most is compassion and understanding. Exhortations to "snap out of it" or "pull yourself up by your own bootstraps" are counterproductive. The best communication is simply to ask, "How can I be of support?" or "How can I help?"

Provide physical support. Often this means participating with your friend in low-stress activities—taking walks, watching movies, going out to eat—that will provide an uplifting focus. In other instances, you can ease the depressed person's burden by helping with their daily routines—running errands, doing shopping, taking the kids out for pizza, cooking, vacuuming the carpet, and so on.

Monitor possible suicidal gestures or threats. Statements such as "I wish I were dead," "The world would be better off without me," or "I want out" must be taken seriously. The belief that people who talk about suicide are only doing it for the attention is just plain wrong. If the person you care about is suicidal, make sure that his or her primary care doctor is informed. Use the suggestions in Week 5, such as the Daily Mood Log and the Cognitive Restructuring

Worksheet, to keep the patient safe. Don't be afraid to talk with the person about his or her suicidal feelings. Meanwhile, hold on to the possibility that your loved one will get better, even if he or she does not believe it.

Don't try to talk the depressed person out of his or her feelings. Listen, even if they are irrational. Suppose the depressive says, "My life is a failure," "Life is not worth living," or "All is hopeless." Telling the person he or she is wrong or arguing will only add to his or her demoralized state. Instead, you might want to say, "I'm sorry that you are feeling so bad. What might we do right now to help you feel better?"

Maintain a healthy detachment. You may become frustrated when your well-meaning advice and emotional reassurance are met with resistance. Do not take your loved one's pessimism personally—it is a symptom of the illness. When the light you shine is sucked into the black hole of depression, you may become angry or disgusted. Direct your frustration at the *illness,* not at the person. People who suffer from depression complain that their families' resentment over their condition often leads to neglect or outright hostility.

Consider praying for your friend's healing. If prayer is something you believe in, turn his or her welfare over to the care of a higher power. In addition, you may wish to place his or her name on a prayer list (see Appendix C for a listing of prayer ministries). Prayer goes directly to a person's unconscious where it will not meet the negative thinking so commonly found in depression. To respect the person's confidentiality, it is best to pray privately. Moreover, if you put a loved one's name on a prayer list, use his or her first name only.

Establish communication with other people in the person's support network. By talking to other caregivers—family members, friends, physicians, therapists, social workers, and clergy—you will obtain additional information and perspective about the depressed person. If possible, arrange for all of the caregivers to meet together in one room for a brainstorming support session. In this way, you will be working as part of a team, not in isolation.

Take good care of yourself and your needs. It is easy to get immersed in your friend's care and lose your own sense of self. You may experience "contagious depression," i.e., taking on the other person's depressive symptoms. Here are some ideas on how to inoculate yourself so you can stay centered enough to truly help:

- Find a safe place to process your feelings. In the role of caregiver, you may feel powerless, helpless, worried, and scared (when you hear talk of suicide), or resentful and frustrated (at your inability to heal the pain). Discharge your frustrations with a trained therapist or a friend; you will be less likely to dump your negative mood (anger, fear, or sadness) on the person who is suffering. Remember, it is okay to have negative thoughts as long as you don't act on them.
- Maintain your routine as much as possible. Although you may need to adjust your work schedule or other routines to accommodate helping a depressed person, keep your life as regular as possible. Don't become so involved in caregiving that you lose touch with your friends and your social support.
- Learn to set limits, especially when you are feeling overwhelmed by the depressed person's pain and tales of woe. To avoid burning out or experiencing hostility toward the depressed person, encourage him or her to seek professional help. Your role is that of a friend or family member, not a therapist or a medical doctor.
- Take breaks. When you start to feel emotionally or physically drained, ask other friends and support people to relieve you. Then do things to nurture yourself.
- Continue to pursue activities that bring you pleasure. Having fun will replenish you so you can keep on giving.
- Give yourself credit for all that you are doing, and realize that you cannot do everything. No matter how much you love another person, you cannot take responsibility for his or her life. Try to distinguish between what you can control (your own responses) and what you cannot (the course of the illness). To this end, you may wish to meditate on AA's version of the "Serenity Prayer." (God,

grant me the serenity to accept the things I cannot change, the courage to change the things I can, and the wisdom to know the difference.)

• Attend support group meetings for families who are dealing with mental illness. The local chapters of the following organizations can provide you with times and locations of such groups: the National Alliance for the Mentally Ill, 800-950-NAMI; the National Depressive and Manic Depressive Association, 800-82-NDMDA; and the Depression and Related Affective Disorder Association, 410-955-4647.

Best Things to Say to Someone Who Is Depressed

It is not easy to know what to say when a person you care about is clinically depressed. Here are some words that will show your support, while acknowledging the person's right to feel his or her feelings:

• "I love you!"
• "I care."
• "You're not alone in this."
• "I'm not going to leave or abandon you."
• "Do you want a hug?"
• "When all this is over, I'll still be here and so will you."
• "Would you like to hold my hand and talk about it?"
• "I can't fully understand what you are feeling, but I can offer my compassion."
• "I'm sorry you're in so much pain."
• "I have empathy for what you are going through."
• "I am not going to leave you. I am going to take care of myself so you don't need to worry that your pain might hurt me."
• "I can't imagine what it's like for you. I just can't imagine how hard it must be."
• "You are important to me."
• "If you need a friend, I am here."

Encourage the person you are caring for to reach out for support. Fortunately, it is possible to take advantage of the strength in numbers principle to bring together a group of committed loving people for the sole purpose of creating a field of loving support that will catalyze the depressed person's healing.

How to Form a Support or Prayer Group for Someone Who Is Depressed

If you know a friend or loved one who is going through an episode of anxiety or depression and you wish to enlist the healing power of a support or prayer group, here are some simple guidelines that will get you started:

- Find at least three people other than yourself (preferably four to six) who would like to participate in such a group.
- Ask your friend who is depressed whether he or she would like to be present during the group meetings. If the person is not able to attend because of the severity of his or her symptoms, let him or her know what you are doing and ask for his or her permission to begin the group.
- Set a regular meeting time—weekly is ideal, although every other week will also work. Meetings can last for sixty to ninety minutes.
- Ask your friend to write a vision statement of wellness, using the instructions in Week 1. If he or she is unable to do so, you can employ the affirmation found in Jesse's story on page 376, or you can create one of your own.
- Pick a facilitator to chair each meeting (the facilitator can remain the same or vary from meeting to meeting).
- Begin the group with an opening affirmation, prayer, or meditation. Once the group has been convened, ask the person needing support to read his or her vision statement to the group. (If the person is not present, one of the other members can read the vision statement.) During this time, each group member imagines the vision becoming manifest. Members can also affirm this reality out loud by saying, "I see your vision coming to pass," or "I see you as whole and well."

    The goal of the meeting is to align the *group* mind with the individual's intention to heal. This, in turn, will bring forth the

Master Mind—a benevolent spiritual energy (see Week 9 for an explanation of the Master Mind concept). When the person's intention to heal, the group's intention, and the Master Mind are all aligned, a loving force is released that has the power to move mountains.

- If the person being supported is present, ask him or her to check in and let the group know how he or she is faring in his recovery. (If the depressed person cannot attend the meeting, the group members can spend the remaining time brainstorming ways to be of support to the patient, as well as giving each other support in their roles of friend and caretaker.) During this sharing, it is the role of each group member to listen attentively. The process works best if people do not interrupt or give advice at this time. After your friend's sharing time is up, the facilitator will ask the person whether he or she would like some feedback from the group. If the person requests feedback, group members can spend some time sharing their perceptions of how the person is doing and offer advice or suggestions.

- Finally, ask whether your friend would like to make a request for *specific support* for the coming week. The request should focus on some aspect of the person's wellness program. The group then affirms the person silently or by using an affirmation such as, *"I see you attaining your goal and hold for you a vision of your success."*

In between meetings, each of the group members should set aside a few minutes *every day* to read the person's vision statement and see him or her as whole and well. The process works best if the entire group (including the individual receiving the support) repeats the visualization at the same time of day. Moreover, if the depressed person is having difficulty reading his or her vision statement, some of the group members can volunteer to call the individual at a specified time of day and stay on the phone while he or she reads the vision out loud. Receiving these daily phone calls from my support team made a huge difference in my recovery.

Over a period of months, this type of daily and weekly focused group support can make a significant impact on your friend's healing. While I cannot provide any guarantee that healing will automatically happen, my experience with this process, both as a patient and as a supporter, has been universally positive.

Examples of Healing

The idea of creating a depression support group first emerged at the peak of my illness when the ministers at the Living Enrichment Center and my friends and family joined together to see if they could collectively do what none could do alone—bring about my healing.

Fortunately, I knew about the first recovery principle—setting the intention to heal. During our initial meeting, I wrote out a simple vision statement of what wellness would look and feel like for me. The group members then agreed to read that vision statement every day at 9 A.M. while picturing me as whole and well. Over the next six months, my symptoms of anxiety and depression went into a complete remission.

About eighteen months later, I had the opportunity to use these principles again on somebody else's behalf. My nephew Jesse had recently been hospitalized for a depressive breakdown that he experienced while attending his first year at college away from home. His symptoms were fairly severe; he wasn't eating, drinking, or speaking. At that point, I asked his father, stepmother, and friends of the family to join with me in forming a prayer support group that would hold a vision of Jesse's recovery. Everyone agreed, and for the next three months we met for ninety minutes every other Sunday evening. During the sessions, we shared our perceptions of how Jesse was doing and how we could support him. At the close of each meeting, we repeated the following affirmation:

> Jesse, I know that you are experiencing a safe passage through
> this dark night of your soul. You notice, accept, and receive all
> the gentle and powerful nurturing from those watching over
> you on your journey. You are returning to us in radiant health
> and bearing glorious treasures.

We also agreed to say this affirmation every day at exactly 8:30 P.M. (Thank God for digital watches with alarms!) Sometimes my alarm would go off in the middle of dinner with a friend. I explained that I had set aside a few minutes to say a prayer for a relative who was ill. Invariably, my friend would join me in saying the affirmation.

Three months later, Jesse was well enough to appear at our Sunday evening sessions. At the meetings, he gave us an update on how he was feeling and formulated some simple goals for the coming two weeks. Meanwhile, his six supporters continued to repeat his affirmation at 8:30 P.M. every day.

In mid-August, Jesse was discharged from the hospital and moved into a group home. Our group had been meeting for six months, the exact length of time that the Living Enrichment group had taken to see me through my condition.

A third manifestation of group support occurred when my publishing assistant discovered that a good friend was experiencing crippling panic attacks. Over a four-month period, my assistant, her husband, and two friends met with their friend, Chris, on a weekly basis. His anxiety decreased and eventually he became well enough to return to work. A year later he got married.

Although the examples of healing that I have shared in this book are not scientific studies, they have convinced me that focused group prayer support can make a difference in a person's recovery. Because I want to see group support adopted by the mental health profession as a low-cost adjunct to the traditional treatment of depression, I would appreciate receiving feedback from any readers who organize a prayer support group for a friend or loved one. My contact information is located on the author information page at the back of the book.

Unfortunately, there are times that, despite one's best efforts, a loved one's healing does not occur. In extreme cases, the depressed person may end his or her life. (This happened to my therapist, Anne, to whom I dedicated this book.) If suicide does occur, the caregiver may need to deal with guilt and self-blame as well as grief through counseling or by joining a survivors of suicide group. Visit the SA\VE Web site (www.save.org/indcx.html) to find out more about such support groups.

Afterword

Wherever a person's deepest wounds exists, that is where his greatest gift to the community lies.

—ROBERT BLY

In contrast to the blackness of my mood, it was a sunny spring day in May of 1997. Using more willpower than faith, I dragged myself to the usual LEC Sunday morning service. Afterward, I found myself in the office of associate minister Michael Moran, a colleague at whose church I had spoken five years before.

"It is the cruelest of ironies," I lamented, "that as students of New Thought spirituality, we understand that thought is creative, that 'whatever the mind can conceive and believe, it can achieve.' But now I suffer from a disease that renders this God-given faculty inoperative! How can I heal myself with principles that you and Mary teach, when my mind, the instrument of my creative imagination, is itself diseased?"

"Do you remember Martin Luther King's words," Michael said, "that for those who are on the spiritual path, suffering can be redemptive?"

"Yes," I replied, "but I can't imagine what good can result from this seemingly insurmountable affliction."

Michael swiveled his chair to the right and gazed out the window. Outside, a robin had just alighted upon a budding lilac tree. Putting his head in his hands, Michael pondered my words for what seemed an interminable length of time, until at last he turned toward me and spoke.

"You are going through this ordeal so one day you can write about it."

"Are you dreaming?" I replied. "I haven't been able to write a word in five years."

"I know it sounds far-fetched, but that's what the Spirit told me."

Two years later, by the grace of God, Michael's uncanny prophecy has come true. Before she died, my therapist and mentor Anne Zimmerman made a similar request—that my next book should emerge from the depths of my inner torment.

And so it appears that I have been called, though not willingly, to share my ordeal as part of the wounded healer tradition. I pray that what I have portrayed—the account of my own struggle with depression, as well as the recovery program I have developed—has been of support to you or a loved one. I hope that this book has shone a light into the darkness that may have engulfed you. Most important, I wish that your suffering, like mine, can be redemptive—that out of the pain of your struggle, some unexpected good may emerge.

May the blessings be.

The Many Faces of Depression

*My creative powers have been reduced to a restless indolence. I cannot
be idle, yet I cannot seem to do anything either. I have no imagination,
no more feeling for nature, and reading has become repugnant to me.
When we are robbed of ourselves, we are robbed of everything!*

—GOETHE

Getting proper help for depression begins with a proper diagnosis.
This is easier said than done, since depression, like the mythological Hydra, is a many-headed beast. There are many types of
depressive disorders, each of which contains a multitude of symptom
patterns and representations.

What follows is a broad overview of the most common depressive
disorders as listed in the *Diagnostic and Statistical Manual of Mental
Disorders (DSM-IV)*. For those who have not studied psychology or
psychiatry, I hope this synopsis provides you with an understanding
of the brain imbalances that may affect you or your loved ones.

Major Depression
(Also Known As Clinical Depression)

This is the mood disorder from which I suffered. As I described in
chapter one of my narrative, clinical depression is not a passing blue
mood or sign of personal weakness. It is a whole body illness that

drastically impacts one's physiology, biochemistry, mood, thoughts, and behavior. It affects the way you eat and sleep, the way you think and feel about yourself, others, and the world.

Depression has both biochemical and environmental roots. As we saw in the better mood recovery program, clinical depression can be treated on a variety of levels, with antidepressant medication and cognitive therapy being the main treatments offered by the medical profession.

Some of the common symptoms of major depression are a sad or persistent blue mood, lack of energy, inability to concentrate, the inability to experience pleasure, loss of appetite, disruption of sleep cycles, physical agitation, feelings of guilt and worthlessness, hopelessness, despair, and suicidal thoughts and/or suicide attempts.

Because depression is invisible, i.e., it does not disfigure the outer body, many people do not take it seriously and think that the sufferer should be able to simply snap out of it. The actual patient may also agree with this assessment and fault himself or herself for having a weak will or a defect in character. Both of these views are incorrect, as depression is clearly a medical condition that emerges from highly afflicted brain chemistry.

Please refer to chapter 9 for additional information about the causes and symptoms of major depression.

Manic Depression
(Also Known as Bipolar Disorder)

Terror drove me from place to place. My breath failed me as I pictured my brain paralyzed. Ah, Clara, no one knows the suffering, the sickness, the despair of this illness, except those so crushed.
—Composer ROBERT SCHUMANN, speaking of his manic depression

Although manic-depressive illness (which affects two to three million people) is less common than major depression, it maintains a high profile because of the many creative artists who have suffered from it. Examples include Edgar Allan Poe, Tennessee Williams, Ezra Pound, Virginia Woolf, Vincent Van Gogh, Alfred Tennyson, Cole

Porter, and Robert Schumann. In recent times, celebrities such as Abbie Hoffman, columnist Art Buchwald, actress Patty Duke, actress Margot Kidder, and CNN's Ted Turner have been similarly afflicted. Manic depression has two distinct sides: the *depressive* state and the *manic* state. Mania is a seemingly heavenly state of mind in which all the world is beautiful and everything seems possible. Here are some of the most common characteristics of mania:

- optimism
- euphoria
- little need for sleep
- little need for food
- irritability
- inflated self-concept
- grandiose schemes
- unrealistic thinking
- poor judgment
- loss of inhibition
- delusional thinking
- outbursts of anger
- increased sexual activity
- impulsivity
- spending large amounts of money
- socially inappropriate behavior
- heightened sense of awareness
- flight of ideas
- racing thoughts
- pressured speech
- tremendous energy
- enhanced creativity
- hyperactivity
- feeling that nothing can go wrong
- alcohol and drug abuse

As Kay Redfield Jamison, a psychologist who is diagnosed with manic depression, writes in her memoir *An Unquiet Mind:*

> When you're high it's tremendous. The ideas and feelings are fast and frequent like shooting stars and you follow them until you find better and brighter ones. Shyness goes. The right words and gestures are suddenly there, the power to captivate others is a felt certainty. Feelings of ease, intensity, power, well-being, financial omnipotence, and euphoria pervade one's marrow.

Upon hearing this description of mania, people often respond, "If this is a disease, where do I sign up for it?" The problem with mania, however, is that due to the impulsivity and poor judgment that it brings, an episode can wreak havoc on family, friends, the community, and the law. Moreover, when the high inevitably wears off, the individual comes crashing down into a state of total darkness and despair. As Jamison describes:

A floridly psychotic mania was followed, inevitably, by a long and lacerating black, suicidal depression. Everything—every thought, word and movement—was an effort. Everything that once was sparkling now was flat. I seemed to myself to be dull, boring, inadequate, thick brained, unlit, unresponsive, chill skinned, bloodless, and sparrow drab. I doubted, completely, my ability to do anything well. It seemed as though my mind had slowed down and burned out to the point of being totally useless.

A well-known myth that perfectly describes the manic depressive's fall from grace is that of Icarus. Icarus, son of the Greek inventor Daedalus (who built the labyrinth), was given wings of wax by his father. Enamored of his new-found ability to fly to great heights, Icarus ignored his father's warning and in a moment of ecstasy flew too close to the sun. The heat of the sun melted the wax that held his wings together, and Icarus crashed into the sea.

The alternation of mania and depression illuminates a second aspect of manic depression—its cyclic nature. Periods of creativity, productivity, and high energy alternate with times of fatigue and apparent indifference. Mania leads to depression, which leads to mania, which becomes depression, and so on. This extreme flip-flop of mood from peaks to valleys and back is extremely dangerous, as shown by the fact that 20 to 25 percent of untreated manic depressives (including many of the artists listed earlier) commit suicide.

Fortunately, manic depression is highly treatable following the discovery of lithium, a simple salt that in 1949 was accidentally found to have a mood-stabilizing effect on bipolar individuals. The downside of lithium treatment is that therapeutic levels of lithium are dangerously close to toxic levels. Lithium poisoning affects the brain and can cause coma and death. Thus, in the initial stages of treatment, lithium concentration in the blood must be frequently monitored. After the lithium blood level stabilizes, levels can be checked every six months.

The side effects of lithium can include hand tremors, excessive thirst, excessive urination, weakness, fatigue, memory problems, diarrhea, and possible interference with kidney function. Lithium is often ineffective in treating bipolar patients who are rapid cyclers—those who experience four or more manic-depressive cycles per year. For these and other patients who fail to stabilize on lithium, the drugs Depakote and Tegretol (originally anti-seizure medications) are also available. For some doctors, Depakote is now the drug of choice, rather than lithium, because its long-term side effects are considered safer.

In addition to taking medication, bipolar individuals can employ a number of preventive strategies to decrease the likelihood of having a full-blown manic attack, such as:

- Recognizing the early warning signs of mania—e.g., insomnia, surges of energy, making lots of plans, grandiose thinking, speeded-up thinking, overcommitment, excessive euphoria, or spending too much money. Let friends and family know of these symptoms so they can also become alerted to the start of a manic episode.
- Creating a stable lifestyle in which you keep regular sleep hours. Studies show that intervals between manic episodes are considerably longer in those people who live in stable environments. In addition, eat a diet that is high in complex carbohydrates and protein, avoiding foods, such as simple sugars, that can cause ups and downs. Alcohol and caffeine should also be avoided.
- Using planning and scheduling to stay focused and grounded. Make a list of things to do and stick to it.
- Trying to engage in a daily meditative activity that focuses and calms the mind. If you are too restless for sitting meditation, go for a leisurely walk, taking long, deep breaths along the way.
- Refraining from taking on too many projects or becoming overstimulated. If you feel an excess of energy starting to overtake you, channel it into productive physical activities such as doing the dishes, mopping the floor, cleaning out the basement, or weeding a garden.
- Meeting with psychotherapist and support groups, which can help you to explore the emotional aspects of your illness, as well as provide support during times of stress.
- Calling your doctor or therapist if you feel things are getting out of hand. This is especially true if you start losing sleep, as sleep deprivation is one of the major contributors to mania.
- Asking a good friend or family member to track your activity level. Sometimes a manic episode can sneak up on you, and an objective person may be able to spot it before it gets out of hand.

Books, organizations, and support groups for manic depression are listed in the Resources for Wellness section in Appendix C.

Dysthymia

"Good morning, Eeyore," said Pooh.
"Good morning, Pooh Bear," said Eeyore gloomily.
"If it is a good morning," he said, "which I doubt," said he.
—A. A. MILNE, *The House at Pooh Corner*

In addition to major depression, there exists another type of depressive illness—dysthymia—that is far less severe, though crippling in its own way. Dysthymia consists of long-term chronic symptoms that do not disable, but keep you from feeling really good or from functioning at full steam. Physically, it is akin to having a chronic low-grade infection—you never develop a full-blown illness, yet you always feel a little run down.

Although dysthymia implies having an inborn tendency to experience a depressed mood, it may also be caused by childhood trauma, adjustment problems during adolescence, difficult life transitions, the trauma of personal losses, unresolved life problems, and chronic stress. Any combination of these factors can lead to an enduring case of the blues.

Some of the most prominent symptoms of dysthymia are:

- depressed mood for most of the day, for more days than not, for at least two years
- difficulties sleeping
- difficulty in experiencing pleasure
- a hopeless or pessimistic outlook
- low energy or fatigue
- low self-esteem
- difficulty concentrating or making decisions
- persistent physical symptoms (such as headaches, digestive disorders, or chronic pain) that do not respond to treatment

A dysthymic disorder is characterized not by episodes of illness, but by the steady presence of symptoms (see the following diagram). Because dysthymia does not incapacitate like major depression, as a rule, dysthymic people do well in psychotherapy (medication can also be used). During stressful times, a person with dysthymia may be catapulted into a major depressive episode, called "double depression."

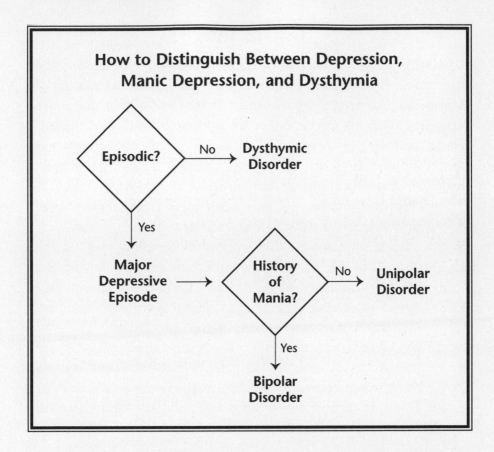

How to Distinguish Between Depression, Manic Depression, and Dysthymia

Dysthymic disorder is a common ailment, affecting about 3 to 5 percent of the general population. Unfortunately, because dysthymia is not as severe as clinical depression, the condition is often undiagnosed or dismissed as a case of psychosomatic illness. ("Your symptoms are all in your head," is the all-too-common response from doctors.) Perhaps the most famous dysthymic is Eeyore, the despondent and downcast donkey in A. A. Milne's *Winnie the Pooh*. If you identify with Eeyore (or feel down in the dumps most of the time), it is important that you consult a qualified mental health professional who can make a correct diagnosis. In addition, you can use the wellness strategies described in the better mood recovery program to improve your mood.

A dysthymic temperament does have positive traits. Dysthymic individuals can be serious, profound, deep, prudent, dependable, industrious, patient, and responsible.

Cyclothymia

Cyclothymia is a milder form of manic depression, characterized by hypomania (a mild form of mania) alternating with mild bouts of depression. The symptoms are similar to those of bipolar illness but less severe. Many cyclothymic disorder patients have difficulty succeeding in their work or social lives since their unpredictable moods and irritability create a great deal of stress, making it difficult to maintain stable personal or professional relationships.

Cyclothymic persons may have a history of multiple geographic moves and alcohol or substance abuse. Nevertheless, when their creative energy is focused toward a worthwhile goal, they may become high achievers in art, business, government, or other endeavors. (The cycles of cyclothymia are far shorter than in manic depression.) The ability to work long hours with a minimum of sleep when they are hypomanic often leads to periods of great productivity.

If you identify with the diagnosis of cyclothymia, you may use the wellness strategies described for manic depression, as well as those in the better mood recovery program, to elevate and stabilize your mood. If your highs and lows begin to intensify, seek treatment with a psychiatrist or mental health professional.

Postpartum Depression

In the period that follows giving birth to a child, many women experience some type of emotional disturbance or mental dysfunction. A large percentage of the time, these baby blues are characterized by grief, tearfulness, irritability, and clinging dependence. These feelings, which may last several days, have been ascribed to the woman's rapid change in hormonal levels, the stress of childbirth, and her awareness of the increased responsibility that motherhood brings.

In some cases, however, the baby blues take on a life of their own, lasting weeks, months, and even years. When this occurs, the woman suffers from *postpartum depression*—a syndrome very much like a major depressive disorder. This depression may also be accompanied by anxiety and panic. In extreme cases, symptoms may include psychotic features and delusions, especially concerning the newborn infant. There may be suicidal ideation and obsessive thoughts of violence to the child.

It is estimated that approximately four hundred thousand women in the United States experience postpartum depression, usually six to eight weeks after giving birth. Postpartum depression is a treatable illness that responds to the following modalities:

- recognizing and accepting the disorder
- breaking negative thought patterns
- creating support systems
- reducing stressors in one's life
- exercise and proper diet
- medication (antidepressants and antianxiety drugs)
- psychotherapy

A good introduction to this often-undiagnosed disorder is contained in the book *This Isn't What I Expected* by Karen Kleiman, M.S.W., and Valerie Raskin, M.D. You might also visit the Web site of the organization Depression After Delivery at www.behavenet.com/dadinc.

Seasonal Affective Disorder (SAD)

There's a certain Slant of light,
Winter Afternoons—
That oppresses, like the Heft
Of Cathedral Tunes—
Heavenly Hurt, it gives us.
—EMILY DICKINSON

Patients with seasonal affective disorder tend to experience depressive symptoms during a particular time of the year, most commonly fall or winter. They often become depressed in October or November and remit in April or May. The symptoms of SAD, also known as "winter depression," are listed below:

- altered sleep patterns, with an overall increase in the amount of sleep
- difficulty in getting out of bed in the morning and getting going
- increased lethargy and fatigue
- apathy, sadness, and/or irritability
- increased appetite, carbohydrate craving, and weight gain
- decreased physical activity

Researchers believe that seasonal affective disorder is caused by winter's reduction in daylight hours, which desynchronizes the body clock and disturbs the circadian rhythms. Winter depression is usually treated by morning exposure to bright artificial light (see Appendix C for addresses of light box companies). With appropriately timed light exposure, the body's circadian rhythms can become resynchronized and the symptoms of SAD resolve.

In addition, it is important for the person with SAD to get as much natural light as possible. Here are some suggestions:

- Lighten up your home. Use white wallpaper and light-colored carpet instead of dark paneling and dark carpet.
- Live in dwellings with large windows.
- Allow light to shine through doors and windows when temperatures are moderate. Trim hedges around windows to let more light in.
- Exercise outdoors.
- Set up reading or work spaces near a window.
- Ask to sit near a window in restaurants, classrooms, or at your workplace.
- Arrange a winter vacation in a warm, sunny climate if possible.
- Put off large undertakings until summer.

Although the most common form of recurrent seasonal depressions in northern countries is the winter SAD, researchers at the National Institute of Mental Health have uncovered a type of summer depression that occurs during June, July, and August. Summer SAD tends to occur more in the southern states such as Florida, as well as in Japan and China. Summer depressives frequently ascribe their symptoms to the severe heat of summer, although in some instances the depressions are triggered by intense light.

For further information or support about SAD, contact your doctor or visit the Web site of the Society for Light Treatment and Biological Rhythms at www.websciences.org/sltbr. Norman Rosenthal's seminal book *Winter Blues* is also a good resource.

Situational Depression

Unlike clinical depression, which is rooted in a biochemical imbalance in the brain and nervous system, situational depression (formerly known as exogenous or reactive depression) is often the result of an identifiable stressful life situation, such as:

- the death of a spouse, parent, or child
- a divorce
- the loss of a job
- a financial or health setback
- a change of residence
- an accident or being the victim of violence
- chronic sexual dysfunction

In circumstances such as these, it would be unusual not to be sad or depressed. Symptoms of situational depression may include insomnia, anxiety, mood swings, and a host of somatic (body-centered) complaints.

Although less debilitating over the long term than clinical depression, situational depression can be extremely painful—as evidenced by the person whose loneliness brought on by a recent divorce becomes intensified over the Christmas holidays. Thus it is very important to reach out and seek help. Here are some steps you can take:

- Seek help that is appropriate to the type of challenge you are facing. For example, if you have experienced a personal loss, enter into bereavement counseling and/or join a bereavement support group. If your challenge is monetary or work-related, locate a financial or vocational counselor. If you are experiencing postpartum depression, medical treatment is most likely indicated.

- Use some of the strategies listed in my survival plan in chapter 3 of the narrative, as well those described in the better mood recovery program. Providing for your physical, emotional, and spiritual needs will help you to remain balanced during this challenging period. If you feel that you need to take medication as a temporary support, consult your physician or therapist.
- Tell yourself, "This, too, shall pass." Fortunately, your depression is likely to lift when circumstances change back to normal. Realize, however, that you may need to be patient with the process. It may take years to fully grieve a divorce or other major loss.

Existential Depression

A specific kind of situational depression is known as existential depression, brought on by a *crisis of meaning* or *purpose* in one's life. Any significant transition, especially a change of roles in family or work, can trigger this crisis. A well-known account of existential depression occurred in the life of the famous Russian novelist Leo Tolstoy. In mid-life, while enjoying health, wealth, and great literary fame, Tolstoy fell into a deep despair as he asked himself, "Is this all there is?" Out of his quest for something more, Tolstoy underwent a religious conversion and formulated a philosophy of nonviolence, renunciation of wealth, self-improvement through physical work, and nonparticipation in institutions that created social injustice. Tolstoy's ideas had a profound influence on many social reformers, including Mahatma Gandhi and Martin Luther King, Jr.

The importance of dealing with existential issues should not be underestimated. A number of clinicians have reported that depression (as well as chronic fatigue syndrome) has a strong connection with a person's lack of success in finding his passion—i.e., not being involved in work or other activities that feed the core self. After all, Sigmund Freud defined mental health as "the ability to work and to love." If either of these two essential needs is missing, even a person with normal brain chemistry is going to feel out of kilter.

Mood Disorders Due to a Medical Condition

Clinical depression commonly co-occurs with general medical illnesses, though it frequently goes undetected and untreated. While the rate of major depression in the community is estimated to be between 2 and 4 percent, among primary care patients it is between 5 and 10 percent. For inpatients, the rate increases to between 10 and 14 percent.

Treating the co-occurring depressive symptoms can improve the outcome of the medical illness, while reducing the patient's emotional and physical pain and disability. Here are some medical conditions that have been implicated as triggering depressive symptoms:

- endocrine conditions such as hypothyroidism
- neurological disorders such as brain tumors
- encephalitis
- epilepsy
- cerebrovascular diseases that cause structural damage to the brain
- viral and bacterial infections
- inflammatory conditions such as rheumatoid arthritis and lupus
- vitamin deficiencies (especially vitamin B_{12}, vitamin C, folic acid, and niacin)
- heart disease
- stroke
- diabetes
- kidney disease
- multiple sclerosis
- cancer

Anyone who suffers from one of these disorders should treat the underlying illness medically and pursue psychotherapy or counseling if depression accompanies the physical illness.

Medication-Induced Depression

Many people do not realize that a number of common prescription drugs have side effects that can induce depression. Thirty years ago, my mother went into a long-term depression as a result of a reaction to the drug Resperine, a high–blood pressure medication. Similarly, my own depression was accelerated by my reaction to large doses of antibiotics given for a leg infection. Prescription drugs with depressive side effects include:

- cardiac drugs and hypertensives
- sedatives
- steroids
- stimulants
- antibiotics
- antifungal drugs
- analgesics

It may be worthwhile to consult the *Physician's Desk Reference (PDR)* or books such as *Worst Pills, Best Pills* (by M. Sidney Wolfe, Larry Sasich, and Rose Ellen Hope) to learn whether depression is a potential side effect of a medication you are taking. In addition, taking recreational drugs or being exposed to toxic chemicals in the environment may have an adverse effect on mood.

Usually, stopping the intake of the offending substance will eliminate the symptoms (as happened in my mother's episode). If depressive symptoms caused by the substance linger, psychological treatment may be necessary.

Substance-Induced Mood Disorder

If you're depressed, you're more likely to use alcohol and other drugs to medicate your feelings. And if you use alcohol and other drugs, you are more likely to develop depression. Thus, alcohol and drug abuse can be both the cause *and* the result of clinical depression.

When you are both depressed and dependent on alcohol or drugs, you are given a dual diagnosis. A dual diagnosis simply means that you suffer from *both* a psychiatric disorder (it may a bipolar disorder or depression) *and* chemical dependency. Having a dual diagnosis complicates the healing process, since it means that you have to overcome two major illnesses in order to get well. Fortunately, many outpatient and residential treatment centers specialize in treating individuals with dual diagnoses. These centers are usually covered by insurance and are able to offer long-term treatment. Check with your local hospital or mental health clinic to learn who offers dual diagnosis treatment in your area.

How to Start a Healing from Depression Support Group in Your Area

In addition to its nightmarish qualities, depression is a lonely experience. Those possessed by melancholy feel cut off from God, removed from themselves, and misunderstood by others. Even family and friends often fail to appreciate the disability and despair of the clinically depressed person. In this context, experiencing the support of others who know and understand your pain can be a lifeline to healing.

During my life-threatening depressive illness, I bemoaned the fact there were no institutional structures (such as a healing from depression support group) designed to help someone with my kind of emotional pain. (As I explained in my personal narrative, there were plenty of chemical dependency treatment programs, but nothing for someone suffering "just from depression.")

After my recovery, I decided to fill this void through creating a course on healing from depression and anxiety. The purpose of this course was to impart practical tools and coping strategies in a caring and supportive environment that would allow members to reduce their symptoms of anxiety and depression. After putting out the word, I expected three or four people to attend the course; instead, thirty showed up. Over the next twelve weeks, I witnessed how the combination of healing information and group support could transform people's moods and lives. I have written this chapter so others with group facilitation experience can duplicate these healing circles in their own communities.

Strengths and Limitations of a Support Group

It is amazingly empowering to have the support of a strong,
motivated, and inspirational group of people.
—SUSAN JEFFERS, *Fear the Fear and Do It Anyway*

A healing from depression support group can serve different purposes.
A depression support group can:

- be a place where you are heard and listened to
- provide a safe place to share emotions
- validate your pain
- be a place to connect with people who *understand* what you are going through because they are there, or have been there
- help you to realize that you are not alone
- be a place to share experiences—what worked and what didn't
- show by example how to bring about wellness

A depression support group cannot:

- provide professional therapy or counseling
- take the pain away
- stop or solve problems—legal problems, interpersonal problems, illness, and so on

Although these groups are therapeutic, they are not a *substitute* for psychotherapy. Many people who suffer from depression experienced trauma in early childhood—such as loss, abandonment, neglect, or abuse. If, during the course of the group, a person goes into crisis or becomes overwhelmed by emotions arising from their unconscious, it is essential to have someone to turn to—a mental health therapist—to process those feelings.

In addition, being in a support group is only one piece of the recovery puzzle. Just as recovering alcoholics go to AA meetings *and* work the program, your involvement in a depression support group should function as part of your *overall better mood recovery program,* as described in the second half of this book. Practicing this program includes:

- composing your vision statement of wellness and reading it each day
- charting your moods on the Daily Mood Scale
- setting and pursuing weekly goals
- being involved in a regular exercise program three or more days a week
- identifying and replacing automatic negative thoughts

The Group's Composition

Your support group can have anywhere from four to ten members, with eight being ideal. The group should include people who have had previous episodes of anxiety or depression and are working on *staying well,* as well as those who are in the middle of an episode and want to *get well.* In this way, the folks who are further along on the path can serve as role models and coaches for their fellow sufferers.

Ground Rules

As in any group experience, there are certain ground rules that will contribute to the success of the experience. Here are the basics:

Confidentiality. Because of the stigma that still exists around depression and "mental illness," it is absolutely essential that group members respect each other's privacy and that whatever is revealed stays in the room. For example, it would be okay to state outside of the meeting that one of the members of the group is bipolar and is taking lithium. But you would not say that Steve Jones is bipolar. Perhaps Steve Jones is an attorney who fears that his clients would lose their trust in him if they learned about his condition. No matter what his profession, Steve's confidentiality must be assured.

Respectful communication. It is the function of the support group to create a safe space where people can feel free to open up and share their deepest feelings. To support this process, communication needs to be respectful, nonviolent, compassionate, and nonjudging. If any disagreement arises, members should use "I" statements as opposed to blaming or putting others down (e.g., "I felt scared when you raised your voice"). Many who suffer from depression and anxiety were raised by critical parents and have internalized that parental criticism. A support group can provide an antidote to internal put-downs by modeling loving and respectful communication.

Avoiding sexual or romantic interactions. Much of the healing in a group arises through the loving, supportive relationships that members develop among themselves. These relationships work best if they remain friendships and do not involve sexual or romantic interactions.

This is a basic ground rule in all group therapy, and there is a good reason for it. The group is a sanctuary in which people feel safe and unconditionally accepted. Romantic involvement brings a different kind of energy—one in which we are appraised and evaluated. In this context, someone invariably ends up feeling rejected or having unfulfilled expectations, which in turn disrupts feelings of safety and trust in the group. To avoid this kind of a morass, it is best to keep the relationships on a friendship level.

Consistent attendance. While traditional 12-step groups are run on a drop-in basis, I have found that group cohesion is best facilitated when the same people show up week to week. Hence, I make it a requirement that members of my support groups attend all of the meetings (unless, of course, things come up such as out-of-town trips or other unforeseen events). I suggest that you begin with a set number of group members and encourage them to come every week. This will create the safety and stability that people need in order to open up and be vulnerable with each other.

When in doubt, communicate. When people come together in a group, it is inevitable that concerns will arise. If at any point in time a member is having difficulty with something in the group process, it is important that that person voice his or her questions or concerns. A cardinal issue for people with depression is feeling powerless. Thus a person might think, "Why bother to speak up since nothing is going to change anyway?"

The other way to respond is to let your needs and wishes be known. In this way, each member can have an impact on the group and shape it more to his or her liking. This sense of empowerment, in itself, is an antidote to depression.

The Meeting's Structure

Set a regular time to meet. Weekly meetings are ideal, although every other week will also work. The length of the meeting can vary. Give yourself at least ninety minutes; two hours is more realistic.

During the meeting, each group member will have the opportunity to share and to receive support from the group. After the facilitator opens the group, the first person begins sharing according to the following format, which parallels the format we used in chapter 14:

1. For the first block of time (usually seven to eight minutes), the person gives an update on his mood (using the –5 to +5 Daily Mood Scale in Week 2) and shares how he or she is faring in his or her recovery—reporting any successes, challenges, insights, and so on. During this sharing, it is the role of each group member to listen attentively. The process works best if people do not interrupt or give advice at this time.

2. After the person's sharing time is up, the facilitator asks whether the person would like some feedback (three to four minutes' worth) from the group. If the person requests feedback, group members can then *validate* the person's experience ("I can hear your frustration"), show *compassion* ("I'm sorry that you hurt"), or offer *reassurance* and *suggestions*.

3. Finally, the facilitator asks whether the person would like to make a request for support for the coming week. Examples include, "I would like support for exercising three times a week," or "I would like support for saying my affirmations on a daily basis," or "I would like support for being more consistent with my daily meditation." The group then affirms the person silently or by using an

affirmation such as, "I see you attaining your goal and hold for you a vision of your success."

Between meetings, each group member holds an image of healing support for each other member. Members can stay in touch with each other by phone, by E-mail, or in person. I find it helpful to pair people up as buddies and ask them to pick a particular time when they will check in with each other.

You may wish to add an educational component to the group experience by choosing a topic for discussion at the beginning of each meeting. Examples include exercise, diet, spirituality, medication, and dealing with family members. (Any topic from the better mood recovery program will do.) In addition, you may wish to bring in outside speakers who can share their areas of expertise.

Here is a lovely meditation that can be used at the close of each meeting:

I put my hand in yours, and together we can do what we could never do alone.

No longer is there a sense of hopelessness; no longer must we depend on our own unsteady willpower.

We are all together now, reaching out our hands for power and strength greater than our own, and as we join hands we find love and understanding beyond our wildest dreams.

Who Should Facilitate the Group?

Since Alcoholics Anonymous began in 1935, AA and the other anonymous groups have been run by lay people in recovery and not by professional drug and alcohol counselors or other mental health professionals. Can this model be replicated by people who suffer from depression and anxiety? I have come to believe that in most cases, one or two people in the group need to assume a leadership position and keep their eyes on the prize, i.e., keep the group focused on the vision of healing and recovery. The group facilitator can be:

- a mental health professional.
- a layperson who is in recovery and has a background in working with groups. (Although I have an MA in counseling, I consider myself to fall in this category. I cofacilitate groups with my partner, Joan, and work under the direction of a clinical supervisor.)

From week to week, the group facilitator will:

- hold the consciousness of healing for the group
- keep the group on track and follow the structure
- respond to any member's symptoms of distress during the meeting
- pair up group members to serve as buddies between sessions
- pick the topic of discussion, if there is an educational component to the group

Professional leadership, of course, introduces the factor of cost. If the group is run through a hospital, it will usually be free or low cost. If you find someone to run the group privately, fees will be a bit higher ($25 to $40 a session), but still far below the cost of individual therapy.

Since people who have long-term depression may be limited in their ability to work (or may be on disability), I have tried to be flexible in my approach to fees. If an individual has a strong intention to heal and has good outside mental health support (through a counselor and/or medical prescriber), I will offer a partial scholarship or let the person make payments over a longer period of time.

If you are a counselor or therapist who wishes to start a depression support group in your community, I highly encourage you to do so. There is a real need for this kind of group. If I can be of any help, please feel free to call or E-mail me (see About the Author at the back of the book for my contact information).

Changes in Membership

Groups are organic living organisms that, like all living systems, go through cycles of death and rebirth. Hence, there will come a time when either a group member wishes to leave, or someone new wishes to join. Similarly, there may come a time in your recovery program when you (or another member) will decide to take a break. (How does one know when it is time to leave? M. Scott Peck says that the time to begin therapy is when you feel stuck, and the time to end is when you can become your own therapist.) A person wanting to leave should pick a time to do closure and to say good-bye to the group. (Because depression is a recurrent disorder, a group member may wish to continue attending the support group on a weekly basis, even when he or she is feeling well.)

If someone expresses interest in joining the group, the facilitator should consider the following questions:

- Do we have room for a new member (I recommend keeping membership under ten)?
- Is this the right time to have a new person join the group? Are we as a group ready?

If the answer to these two questions is "yes," the facilitator should set up an intake meeting with the prospective member. In addition to taking a case history, it is important to ask the applicant why he or she wants to attend the group and what he or she hopes to get out of it. If the individual seems like a good fit, the facilitator can invite the person to attend a group meeting to test the waters.

In the years since I began facilitating healing from depression support groups, the greatest complaint I have heard from my clients is their inability to find others outside the group who truly understand their condition. In this context, they greatly appreciate the contact and support they receive from their fellow group members. As one client commented, "Joining this depression support group has made my recovery possible." It is my hope that the millions of people who suffer from depression and anxiety can follow suit and join together in a healing community, thereby accomplishing together what they cannot do alone.

Resources for Wellnesss

Give a man a fish and you feed him for a day.
Teach a man how to fish and you feed him for a lifetime.

—Japanese proverb

Clinical depression is a serious, complex, and often deadly illness. Fortunately, many excellent books, organizations, and Web sites now exist that can lead the sufferer and his or her family out of the darkness. Following is a compilation of resources that I have found to be particularly helpful in my recovery. I recommend these materials in the hopes that you, too, may receive healing and inspiration from them.

Healing On-line: Internet Sites for Depression and Other Mood Disorders

I am a lover of books. As a writer of twenty-one years, books are my favorite means of learning about the world. But when I became depressed and my ability to concentrate was limited, I discovered another pathway to knowledge—the Internet. In the late evening, when the black cloud lifted enough to give me a few moments of respite, I would turn on my computer and surf the Net to gain valuable tips from my fellow sufferers.

The Internet is one of the best sources of information about depression and mental disorders (if not *the* best) that is available to the

general public. Hundreds of sites (as well as support groups) offer compassionate, commonsense, and clinically up-to-date help and support.

The following sites will start you on your journey toward healing. I have personally visited each of these locations and testify to
their excellence. Many of them have links to other sites, which have
links to more sites, and so on. The resources are endless.

Please note, though, that Internet sites are constantly being
updated and revised. These URL addresses are current as of November 2001.

If you discover that any of them have changed, please E-mail me
(see About the Author for my contact information), and I will make
the appropriate corrections for the next edition of this book.

Mental Health Net
www.mentalhelp.net/

This award-winning site lists over seven thousand resources in the
mental health field. It offers straightforward information on an easy-to-
navigate site. The information is targeted toward both the lay public and
professionals. A Reading Room offers access to books, articles, advice
columns, opinion polls, roundtables, and an index of discussion forums.

Mental Health Net Suicide Prevention Links
www.mentalhelp.net/guide/suicidal.html

This Web site offers an extensive collection of links provided by
Mental Health Net. It is incredibly comprehensive and gives you the
opportunity to be on a suicide support mailing list.

Internet Mental Health
www.mentalhealth.com

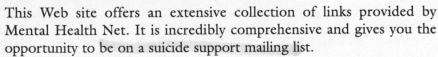

This site functions as a World Wide Web mental health page. The site's
goal is to improve understanding, diagnosis, and treatment of mental illness throughout the world. One of its special features is descriptions,
treatments, and research findings for the fifty-two most common mental
disorders. It also lists the sixty-seven most common psychiatric drugs,
including: indications, contraindications, warnings, precautions, adverse
effects, dosage, and research findings. This site also has a links page that
will connect you with over a hundred other mental health Web sites that
offer free mental health information.

Dr. Ivan's Depression Central

www.psycom.net/depression.central.html

This site is one of the Internet's clearinghouses for information on all types of depressive disorders and on the most effective treatments for individuals suffering from major depression, manic depression (bipolar disorder), cyclothymia, dysthymia, and other mood disorders. It contains an amazing amount of information, more than I have seen in any single book volume.

Mental Health Infosource

www.mhsource.com

This site has several excellent features, including the invitation to submit questions to an expert clinician on any aspect of mental health. It also has an excellent on-line directory of mental health resources available on the Internet.

Psych Central: Dr. John Grohol's Mental Health Page

www.psychcentral.com

Started in 1995, this site is a personalized one-stop index for psychology and mental health issues, resources, and people on the Internet. This is another comprehensive, compassionate source of information.

Dr. Grohol's Suicide Help Line

www.grohol.com/helpme.htm

Dr. Grohol's suicide help line, a part of his excellent mental health home page.

Alt.Support.Depression FAQ

www.stripe.colorado.edu/~judy/depression/asdfaq.html

Alt.Support.Depression is a newsgroup for people who suffer from all forms of depression, and for others who may want to learn more about these disorders. This Web site contains frequently asked questions (FAQs) about depression, including its causes, symptoms, medication, and treatments—as well as things you can do to help yourself. In addition, it contains information on where to get help and on books to read, a list of famous people who suffer from depression, Internet resources, and instructions for posting anonymously.

The Anxiety Panic Internet Resource (tAPir)

www.algy.com/anxiety/index.html

This is a grassroots project involving thousands of people interested in anxiety disorders such as panic attacks, phobias, shyness, generalized anxiety, obsessive-compulsive behavior, and post-traumatic stress disorder. It is a self-help network, replete with an on-line bookstore, that is dedicated to overcoming and curing anxiety disorders.

Depression.com

www.depression.com

This is another good Web site that contains a wide array of information on depression. The site is supported in part by a grant from Bristol-Meyer-Squibb, so there may be a slight bias toward medication.

Haveaheart's Home

www.geocities.com/HotSprings/3628/index.html

This Web site contains several articles on depression and manic depression, written by someone who has struggled with his own depression and suicidal thoughts.

Suicide Help

www.metanoia.org/suicide/

This is an excellent resource that I read when I was suicidal. The writer compassionately takes you by the hand and describes why and how you should hold on to life, even in the face of overwhelming pain. This site was one of the factors that prevented me from taking my life.

SA\VE (Suicide Awareness Voices of Education)

612-946-7998

E-mail: save@winternet.com

www.save.org/index.html

This is the Web site for SA\VE (Suicide Awareness Voices of Education), whose mission is to educate others about suicide and to speak for suicide survivors. I also visited this Internet site when I was suicidal and found it to be extremely helpful.

www.save.org/question.html

Visit this SA\VE link to get the answers to the most frequently asked questions about suicide prevention.

The Samaritans
www.mentalhelp.net/samaritans/
The Samaritans' United States home page, describes their services in support of suicidal individuals.

Depression After Delivery, Inc.
www.behavenet.com/dadinc
This site provides information and support for women who are experiencing postpartum depression, as well as for health care professionals.

Wing of Madness
www.wingofmadness.com/
Another good Web site that contains a plethora of information on depression and mood disorders.

Pendulum Resource Center for Bipolar Illness
www.pendulum.org/
This is a great site for everything you would want to know about manic depression.

Internet Depression Resource List
www.execpc.com/~corbeau
This site has great links to other pages.

Andrew's Depression Page
www.blarg.net/~charlatn/Depression.html
This is another good resource.

Famous People Who Have Suffered From Depression or Manic Depression
www.frii.com/~parrot/living.html
A list of living celebrities who have publicly stated that they have experienced manic depression or depression in their lives.

Society for Light Treatment and Biological Rhythms
www. websciences.org/sltbr
Visit this site to learn about the current research on light therapy for the treatment of biological rhythm disorders.

The Web of Addictions
www.well.com/user/woa/

This group is dedicated to providing accurate information about alcohol and other drug addictions. It is also a resource for teachers, students, and others who need factual information about abused drugs.

The National Clearinghouse for Alcohol and Drug Information Line
www.health.org/links/reglink.htm

This site provides great links to other Web sites that have information on healing from drug and alcohol abuse.

Finally, here are two Web sites on sleep and sleep disorders.

Sleepnet.com and The Sleep Well
www.sleepnet.com
www.stanford.edu./~dement/

Mental Health Advocacy and Consumer Organizations

Many organizations are dedicated to providing healing information and support to those who suffer from mood disorders and other types of emotional pain. Contact the following agencies for information about depression, sources of treatment, and local community support groups.

Depression Awareness, Recognition, and Treatment Program (D/ART) National Institute of Mental Health
5600 Fishers Lane, Room 10-85
Rockville, MD 20857-8030
800-421-4211
301-443-4513
www.nimh.nih.gov
Write or call for free informational brochures about depression and anxiety disorders.

National Alliance for the Mentally Ill (NAMI)
2107 Wilson Blvd., Suite 300
Colonial Place 3
Arlington, VA 22201
800-950-NAMI
www.nami.org
The nation's voice on mental illness, NAMI is the national umbrella organization for more than a thousand local support and advocacy groups for families and individuals affected by serious mental illnesses. Contact them to learn more about groups in your area, and how to connect with local affiliates.

Depressive and Related Affective Disorder Association (DRADA)
Johns Hopkins Hospital
Meyer 3-181
600 North Wolfe Street
Baltimore, MD 21287
410-955-4647
www.med.jhu.edu/drada
Call to be put in touch with support groups in your area.

National Foundation for Depressive Illness
P.O. Box 2257
New York, NY 10016
800-239-1265
www.depression.org
This organization refers people to physicians who treat depression using biological (i.e., antidepressant) therapies.

National Depressive and Manic Depressive Association (NDMDA)
730 North Franklin, Suite 501
Chicago, IL 60610
800-82-NDMDA
www.ndmda.org
This nonprofit group provides educational information about depressive and manic depressive illness. Call for support groups.

The Dana Alliance for Brain Initiatives
745 Fifth Avenue, Suite 700
New York, NY 10151
212-223-4040
www.dana.org/brainweb
This organization supports cutting-edge research on a number of brain diseases and disorders, including depression.

National Alliance for Research on Schizophrenia and Depression (NARSAD)
60 Cutter Mill Road, Suite 200
Great Neck, NY 11021
516-829-0091
www.narsad.org
This group raises funds for research on mental illness. They also provide informational brochures.

National Mental Health Association (NMHA)
1021 Prince Street
Alexandria, VA 22314
800-969-NMHA
www. nmha.org
Established in 1909 by former psychiatric patient Clifford W. Beers, the NMHA is dedicated to promoting mental health and preventing mental disorders through advocacy, education, research, and service. They have more than 330 affiliates nationwide. Call for literature.

Depression After Delivery, Inc.
P.O. Box 278
Belle Mead, NJ 08502
908-575-9121; 215-295-3994 (professional inquiries)
800-944-4PPD (information request line)
www.behavenet.com/dadinc
This organization offers education, information, and referral for women and families coping with mental health issues associated with childbearing, both during and after pregnancy. Be sure to visit their Web site to learn about postpartum depression and its treatment.

Anxiety Disorders Association of America
11900 Parklawn Drive, Suite 100
Rockville, MD 20852
301-231-9350
www.adaa.org
This nonprofit organization has a number of excellent self-help publications, books, and tapes on healing from anxiety disorders.

Depression Wellness Network
9550 Roosevelt Way NE, #210
Seattle, WA 98115
206-528-9975
206-528-9832 fax
E-mail: dwnetwork@uswest.net
www.depressionwellness.net
Depression Wellness Network is committed to educating, supporting, and connecting those interested in the holistic care of depression. It offers educational material, support groups, workshops and training, and well-being services—such as Reiki clinics and yoga classes—and membership benefits.

National Self-Help Clearinghouse
365 Fifth Avenue, Suite 3300
New York, NY 10016
212-817-1822
www.selfhelpweb.org
www.cmhc.com/selfhelp
This Web site puts you in direct contact with self-help groups. This organization refers people to local self-help clearinghouses, who then refer you to local self-help groups.

National Mental Health Consumer Self-Help Clearinghouse
1211 Chestnut Street, Suite 1207
Philadelphia, PA 19107
215-751-1820
800-553-4539
www.mhselfhelp.org
This organization disseminates information to mental health consumers on how to start one's own mental health self-help group and how to locate self-help groups in your local area.

Enviro-Med
1600 SE 141st Avenue
Vancouver, WA 98683
800-222-3296
E-mail: info@bio-light.com
www.bio-light.com
This group offers light systems for the treatment of biological rhythm
disorders—e.g., seasonal affective disorder and sleep disturbances due to
jet lag and changes in work schedules.

SunBox Company
19217 Orbit Drive
Gaithersburg, MD 20879
800-548-3968
E-mail: sunbox@aol.com
www. sunboxco.com
This company offers bright light therapy units for the treatment of biological rhythm disorders, as well as dawn simulators that will create the
experience of sunrise indoors.

For information about light therapy contact:

NIMH Seasonal Studies Program
Building 10, Room 4S-239
9000 Rockville Pike
Bethesda, MD 20892
800-421-4211

The Northwest Neurodevelopmental Training Center
P.O. Box 406
Woodburn, OR 97071
503-981-0635
E-mail: nntc@open.org
www.open.org/nntc
This center investigates brain injuries or developmental dysfunctions in
the nervous system as possible causes of mental and emotional disorders.

Suicide Prevention Organizations

The following groups are dedicated to providing information about suicide prevention and support for those who are suicidal.

American Association of Suicidology
4201 Connecticut Avenue NW, Suite 408
Washington, DC 20008
202-237-2280
202-237-2282 fax
www.suicidology.org
This group offers books, pamphlets, journals, and workshops on suicide prevention.

American Foundation for Suicide Prevention
120 Wall Street, 22nd Floor
New York, NY 10005
888-333-AFSP
212-363-6237 fax
www.afsp.org
This foundation funds research, education, and treatment programs aimed at preventing suicide.

SA\VE (Suicide Awareness Voices of Education)
7317 Cahill Rd., Suite 207
Minneapolis, MN 55439
952-946-7998
www.save.org/index.html
This organization's mission is to educate others about suicide and to speak for suicide survivors. I visited their Internet site when I was suicidal and found it to be extremely helpful.

American Suicide Survival Line
888-SUICIDE, 888-784-2433 (toll free)
The nationwide toll-free suicide hotline provides free twenty-four-hour crisis counseling for people who are suicidal or who are suffering the pain of depression. Confidentiality is assured. Case management is also offered to connect people with healing resources in their local communities.

The Samaritans Suicide Hotline
617-247-0220; 212-673-3000; 401-272-4044
E-mail: jo@samaritans.org
www.mentalhelp.net/samaritans/ (U.K. Web site)
www.samaritansnyc.org (New York Web site)
The Samaritans is a United Kingdom charity, founded in 1953, which exists to provide confidential emotional support to any person who is suicidal or despairing, and to increase public awareness of issues around suicide and depression. This service is provided twenty-four hours every day by trained volunteers. It is free. You are guaranteed absolute confidentiality and that you will not be judged. Your E-mail will be answered within twenty-four hours. The phone numbers can be called from anywhere in the United States.

Covenant House Nineline
346 W. 17th Street
New York, NY 10011
800-999-9999
www.covenanthouse.org
This hotline provides crisis intervention, support, and referrals for youth in crisis—for runaways, abandoned youth, and those who are depressed or suicidal. Help is also available for adults.

Surgeon General's Call to Action to Prevent Suicide
202-690-7694
202-690-6960 fax
www.surgeongeneral.gov
In June 1999, the Surgeon General of the United States defined suicide as a "major public health problem." Consequently, the surgeon general's office has developed a national strategy for suicide prevention. For a free copy of the report, visit the Web site or call.

National Institute of Mental Health (NIMH)
Suicide Research Consortium
www.nimh.nih.gov/research/suicide.htm
This branch of the National Institute of Mental Health coordinates program development in suicide research across the country and disseminates science-based information on suicidology to the public, media, and policymakers.

12-Step Recovery Groups

Contact these groups for meeting locations in your area.

Alcoholics Anonymous World Service Office
475 Riverside Drive
New York, NY 10115
212-870-3400
www.aa.org

Narcotics Anonymous World Service Office
P.O. Box 9999
Van Nuys, CA 91409
818-773-9999
www.na.org

Cocaine Anonymous World Service Office
P.O. Box 2000
Los Angeles, CA 90049
310-559-5883
310-559-2554 fax
E-mail: cawso@ca.org
www.ca.org

Al-Anon and Alateen Family Group Headquarters
1600 Corporate Landing Way
Virginia Beach, VA 23454
800-344-2666
757-563-1655 fax
www.al-anon.alateen.org
Al-Anon and Alateen are offshoots of AA, and are designed to support
families and friends of alcoholics or those dealing with substance abuse.
Call for meeting locations in your area.

Emotions Anonymous World Service Office
P.O. Box 4245
St. Paul, MN 55104
651-647-9712
651-647-1593 fax
www.mtn.org/EA
Emotions Anonymous is a 12-step fellowship composed of people who come together in weekly meetings for the purpose of working toward recovery from a wide variety of emotional difficulties, including depression and anxiety. Call for meeting locations.

Overeaters Anonymous World Service Office
6075 Zenith Court NE
Rio Rancho, NM 87124
505-891-2664
505-891-4320 fax
E-mail: overeatr@technet.nm.org
www.overeatersanonymous.org

National Clearinghouse for Alcohol and Drug Information (NCADI)
111426-28 Rockville Pike
Rockville, MD 20852
800-729-6686
www.health.org/index.htm
NCADI is the world's largest resource for current information and materials concerning substance abuse.

Associations of Mental Health Professionals

These professional organizations can be contacted for referrals to mental health professionals in your area.

American Psychiatric Association
1400 K Street NW
Washington, DC 20005
202-682-6220
www.psych.org

American Psychological Association
750 First Street NE
Washington, DC 20002
202-336-5800
www.apa.org

National Association of Social Workers
750 First Street NE
Washington, DC 20002
800-638-8799
www.socialworkers.org

American Society of Clinical Hypnosis
33 West Grand Avenue
Chicago, IL 60610
312-645-9810

American Association for Marriage and Family Therapy
1133 Fifteenth Street NW, Suite 300
Washington, DC 20005
202-452-0109
www.aamft.org

American Association of Pastoral Counselors
9504-A Lee Highway
Fairfax, VA 22301
703-385-6967
www.aapc.org

American Mental Health Alliance (AMHA)
877-264-2007 (toll free)
E-mail: AMHA@mental-health-coop.com
www.mental-health-coop.com/index.html
AMHA is a growing grassroots national alliance of over two thousand
mental health practitioners, including psychiatrists, psychologists, licensed
social workers, and other licensed mental-health practitioners. Its goal is
to develop a caring and respectful mental health care delivery system that
provides an alternative to the managed care systems.

Telephone Prayer Ministries

The turning point in my healing from depression came when a group of people started to pray for me. In addition to receiving support from the Living Enrichment Center group, I called a number of telephone prayer ministries and asked them to hold a vision of my wellness.

I believe that such telephone ministries perform a valuable service to all who seek prayer support. Having a prayer partner is not only consoling, but the presence of two or more souls activates an energy field that can attract divine healing and grace. Please feel free to use the following resources as spirit directs you.

Silent Unity
1901 NW Blue Parkway
Unity Village, MO 64065
800-669-7729
816-251-3554 fax
E-mail: unity@unityworldhq.org
The granddaddy of prayer ministries was founded in 1890 by Charles and Myrtle Fillmore as the Society of Silent Help. Initially, all requests for prayer arrived by mail, but soon people turned to the telephone and called in their prayers. Today, telephone lines are open twenty-four hours a day, seven days a week. When you call, you will speak to a live person who will respond to your request with an affirmative prayer treatment. The Silent Unity prayer team will pray over your request for thirty day. In addition, you may ask to be sent a healing affirmation and support literature.

World Ministry of Prayer
3251 West Sixth Street
P.O. Box 75127
Los Angeles, CA 90075-0127
213-385-0209, 800-421-9600
213-388-1926 fax
E-mail: inquiry@wmop.org
www.wmop.org
Run by the Church of Religious Science, this live twenty-four-hour prayer line functions like that of Silent Unity. When you call, a person will pray with you over your request. The prayer team will hold you in the light for the next thirty days and will send you a letter of support, as well as two or three affirmations. This is an excellent prayer ministry.

Inspiration for Better Living and 24-Hour Ear-to-Ear Prayer Ministry

11901 S. Ashland Avenue
Chicago, IL 60643
773-568-1717
800-447-6343

This is another fine twenty-four-hour prayer line. Someone will speak to you in person and send you a prayer response, including an affirmation. You might also request their "Daily Inspiration for Better Living," a series of daily affirmations and meditations for each month.

Christ Church Unity Prayer Ministry

3770 Altadena Avenue
San Diego, CA 92195
619-282-7609

Run by the Christ Church Unity in San Diego, this twenty-four-hour telephone prayer line was designed to serve the church congregants, but receives requests from the entire Southern California area, as well as the rest of the country. I have visited their Prayer Tower, which is filled with a consciousness of light and love. You will receive a written response to your prayer request, which will be prayed over for thirty days.

Living Enrichment Center Ministry of Prayer

29500 SW Grahams Ferry Road
Wilsonville, OR 97070
503-582-4218
503-682-4275 fax
E-mail: prayer@lecworld.org
www.lecworld.org

This is not a telephone ministry per se, but I list it because it is the ministry where I work in the Pacific Northwest. When you call, you will hear a taped inspirational message and will have the opportunity to leave your prayer request on a message line. Although you will not speak to a live person, your prayers will be answered by mail (if you leave your address) and will be prayed over for thirty days. You can also send your requests by E-mail.

Recommended Reading

For those people whose depression and/or anxiety has not impaired their ability to read, I wish to recommend some excellent books and articles on the subject of depression and other mood disorders. I have organized my bibliography around specific themes so you can easily locate the appropriate book to speak to your particular needs. In addition, I have annotated some of the listings, offering my specific reasons for recommending a particular book.

Memoirs of Melancholy

Each of the following works presents a beautiful and compelling account of the author's unique struggle with the hell of depression, and how he or she made it through to the other side.

Callahan, Steven. *Adrift: Seventy-Six Days Lost at Sea*. Boston: Houghton Mifflin, 1986. A book about situational depression brought on by a life and death struggle. The book-on-tape, read by Dick Estelle, is must listening.

Cronkite, Kathy. *On the Edge of Darkness: Conversations About Conquering Depression*. New York: Doubleday, 1994.

Danquah, Meri Nana-Ama. *Willow Weep for Me: A Black Woman's Journey Through Depression*. New York: WW Norton & Co., 1998.

Dravecky, Jan, *A Joy I'd Never Known*. Grand Rapids: Zondervan Publishing House, 1996. An evangelical account of God's role in healing depression.

Duke, Patty, and Gloria Hochman. *A Brilliant Madness: Living with Manic-Depressive Illness*. New York: Bantam Books, 1992.

Filips, Janet. "Father John's Resurrection: A Priest Credits Prozac and
    Prayer for Pulling Him Out of His Depression." *The Oregonian*
    Section B (February 10, 1995): pp. 1–2.

Hampton, Russell. *The Far Side of Despair: A Personal Account of
    Depression.* Chicago: Nelson-Hall, 1975. (Out of print, but available
    in libraries.)

Jamison, Kay Redfield. *An Unquiet Mind.* New York: Alfred A. Knopf,
    1995. The classic memoir about manic-depressive illness.

Kaysen, Susanna. *Girl, Interrupted.* New York: Random House, 1993.
    A compelling account of the author's two-year stay at McLean
    Hospital at a time when psychiatric hospitals still provided long-
    term care.

Manning, Martha. *Undercurrents: A Therapist's Reckoning with Her
    Own Depression.* San Francisco: HarperSanFrancisco, 1994.
    A moving story that describes the author's recovery from major
    depression through ECT.

Plath, Sylvia. *The Bell Jar.* New York: Harper and Row, 1971.

Reeve, Christopher. *Still Me.* New York: Random House, 1998. An
    inspirational account of one man's courageous battle to heal.
    The lessons can apply to healing from depression.

Smith, Jeffrey. *Where the Roots Reach for Water: A Personal and Natural
    History of Melancholia.* New York: North Point Press, 1999. A
    literary and psychological account of depression.

Solomon, Andrew. *The Noonday Demon: An Atlas of Depression.* New
    York: Scribner, 2001. Depression is examined in personal, cultural,
    and scientific terms. A monumental work.

———. "Anatomy of Melancholy." *New Yorker,* Volume 73, Number
    42 (January 12, 1998) 46 (14). An excellent melding of memoir
    and informational reporting.

Styron, William. *Darkness Visible: A Memoir of Madness.* New York:
    Vintage Books, 1990. During my depressive episode, this book
    was my bible. Here was someone who truly understood what my
    hell was like, and described it in exquisite detail.

Thompson, Tracy. *The Beast: A Reckoning with Depression.* New York:
    GP Putnam and Sons, 1995. A *Washington Post* reporter vividly
    portrays her experience with depression and the road to healing.

Thorne, Julia. *You Are Not Alone: Words of Experience and Hope for the
    Journey Through Depression.* New York: HarperPerennial, 1993.
    The author, who suffered from depression, has compiled short
    first-person accounts by fellow sufferers.

Wurtzel, Elizabeth. *Prozac Nation: Young and Depressed in America*. Boston: Houghton-Mifflin Company, 1994. A funny, witty, and poignant tale.

Books and Articles on the Treatment of Depression and Other Mood Disorders

Baumel, Syd. *Dealing With Depression Naturally*. Los Angeles: Keats Publishing, 2000. The best guide to alternatives to conventional antidepressants.

Beck, Aaron. *Cognitive Therapy of Depression*. New York: Guilford Press, 1979.

Berger, Diane, and Lisa Berger. *We Heard the Angels of Madness: A Family Guide to Coping With Manic Depression*. New York: William Morrow, 1992.

Bloomfield, Harold, and Peter McWilliams. *How to Heal from Depression*. Los Angeles: Prelude Press, 1994.

Bourne, Edmund J. *The Anxiety and Phobia Workbook*. Oakland: New Harbinger Publications, 1995. An excellent resource for coping with panic and anxiety.

Callahan, Rachel, and Rea McDonnell. *God Is Close to the Brokenhearted: Good News for Those Who Are Depressed*. Cincinnati, Ohio: St. Anthony Messenger Press, 1996.

Cobain, Bev. *When Nothing Matters Anymore: A Survival Guide for Depressed Teens*. Minneapolis: Free Spirit Press, 1998. Bev Cobain, the cousin of rock star Kurt Cobain, who took his own life in 1994, has created a much-needed resource for young people with depression.

Cohen, David B. *Out of the Blue: Depression and Human Nature*. New York: WW Norton, 1994.

Conroy, David L. *Out of the Nightmare: Recovering from Depression and Suicidal Pain*. New York: New Liberty Press, 1991. Promotes the theory that suicide occurs when pain exceeds one's coping resources.

Copeland, Mary Ellen. *The Depression Workbook: A Guide to Living with Depression and Manic Depression*. Oakland: New Harbinger Publications, 1992. A superb resource.

Cousens, Gabriel. *Depression: Free for Life*. New York: William Morrow and Co., 2000. A comprehensive overview of holistic treatments.

DesMaisons, Kathleen. *Potatoes Not Prozac*. New York: Simon and Schuster, 1998. Controlling depression through diet.

Elkins, Rita. *Depression and Natural Medicine: A Nutritional Approach to Depression and Mood Swings.* Pleasant Grove, Utah: Woodland Publishing, 1995.

Engler, Jack, and Daniel Goleman. *A Consumer's Guide to Psychotherapy.* New York: Simon and Schuster, 1992. A truly comprehensive manual.

Fassler, David, and Lynne S. Dumas. *Help Me, I'm Sad: Recognizing, Treating and Preventing Childhood and Adolescent Depression.* New York: Viking, 1997. A comprehensive and compassionate work for children and their parents.

Garbarino, James. *Lost Boys: Why Our Sons Turn Violent and How We Can Save Them.* New York: Simon and Schuster, 1999.

Garland, Jane. E. *Depression Is the Pits, But I'm Getting Better: A Guide for Adolescents.* Washington, D.C.: Magination Press, 1997. An easy-to-understand guide to teenage depression.

Gilbert, Binford W. *The Pastoral Care of Depression.* Binghampton, NY: Haworth Press, 1998.

Glenmullen, Joseph. *Prozac Backlash.* New York: Simon and Schuster, 2000. A powerful book that documents the downside of prescription antidepressants.

Goleman, Daniel. "The Rising Cost of Modernity: Depression." *New York Times* (December 8, 1992) B5.

Gorman, Jack M. *The Essential Guide to Psychiatric Drugs.* New York: St. Martin's Griffin, 1997.

Hirschfield, Robert. *When the Blues Won't Go Away: New Approaches to Dysthymic Disorder and Other Forms of Low-Grade Chronic Depression.* New York: Macmillan, 1991.

Kindlan, Dan, and Michael Thompson. *Raising Cain: Protecting the Emotional Life of Boys.* New York: Ballantine Books, 1999.

Kleiman, Karen R., and Valerie D. Raskin. *This Isn't What I Expected: Recognizing and Recovering from Depression and Anxiety after Childbirth.* New York: Bantam, 1994.

Klerman, Gerald, and Myrna Weissman. *Interpersonal Psychotherapy of Depression.* Northvale, NJ: Aronson Press, 1994.

Marano, Hara Estroff. "Depression: Beyond Serotonin." *Psychology Today,* Volume 32, Number 2 (March–April 1999): 30.

Meehan, Brian. "Shedding Light, Hope on Dark Side of Teen Years." *The Oregonian* (May 17, 1999): A-1.

Moody, Rick. "Why I Pray." *Esquire* Volume 128, #4 (October 1997): 92 (5). A moving account of one person's healing from depression through the power of prayer.

Murray, Michael. *Natural Alternatives to Prozac*. New York: William Morrow and Company, 1996. A comprehensive and well-researched account of the most common natural remedies for depression.

Nelson, John, and Andrea Nelson, editors. *Sacred Sorrows: Embracing and Transforming Depression*. New York: Tarcher/Putnam, 1996. A fine compilation.

Norden, Michael J. *Beyond Prozac: Brain-Toxic Lifestyles, Natural Antidotes and New Generation Antidepressants*. New York: Regan-Books (HarperCollins), 1995.

O., Jack. *Dealing with Depression in 12-Step Recovery*. Seattle: Glen Abbey Books, 1990.

O'Connor, Richard. *Undoing Depression*. Boston: Little, Brown and Co., 1997.

Owen, Patricia. *I Can See Tomorrow: A Guide to Living with Depression*. Center City, MN: Hazelden, 1995.

Papolos, Demitri and Janice Papolos. *Overcoming Depression*. New York: HarperPerennial, 1992.

Quinn, Brian P. *The Depression Sourcebook*. Chicago: Contemporary Books, 1997.

Quinnett, Paul. *Suicide: The Forever Decision*. New York: Crossroad, 1997. A helpful treatise on suicide prevention.

Real, Terrance. *I Don't Want to Talk About It: Overcoming the Secret Legacy of Male Depression*. New York: Scribner, 1997. An exceptional book that explores the world of men's depression.

Rosen, Laura Epstein, and Xavier Francisco Amador. *When Someone You Love Is Depressed: How to Help Your Loved One without Losing Yourself*. New York: The Free Press (Simon and Schuster), 1996. A well-researched and helpful book on how to support a friend or loved one who is depressed.

Rosenthal, Norman. *Winter Blues*. New York: Guilford Publications, 1998. The classic book on seasonal affective disorder.

Schrof, Joannie M., and Stacey Schultz. "Melancholy Nation: Depression Is on the Rise, Despite Prozac, But New Drugs Could Offer Help." *U.S. News and World Report* Volume 126, #9 (March 8, 1999): 57.

Seligman, Martin. *Helplessness: On Depression, Development and Death*. San Francisco: W.H. Freeman and Company, 1995.

———. *Learned Optimism*. New York: Alfred A. Knopf, 1990. A great book on changing your thinking.

Sheffield, Anne. *How You Can Survive When They're Depressed*. New York: Harmony, 1998. An excellent guide for learning how to cope with a loved one's depression.

Slagle, Patricia, M.D. *The Way Up from Down: A Safe New Program that Relieves Low Moods and Depression with Amino Acids and Vitamin Supplements.* New York: St. Martin's Press, 1987.

Smyth, Angela. *Seasonal Affective Disorder.* San Francisco: Thoesons, 1992.

Solomon, Andrew. *The Noonday Demon.* New York: Scribner, 2001. A monumental work that covers all aspects of depression.

U.S. Public Health Service. *The Surgeon General's Call to Action to Prevent Suicide.* Washington, D.C., 1999.

Valenstein, Elliot S. *Blaming the Brain: The Truth About Drugs and Mental Health.* New York: Free Press, 1998.

Washington, Harriet. "Infection Connection." *Psychology Today* (July/August 1999): 43 (5).

Whybrow, Peter. *A Mood Apart.* New York: Basic Books, 1997. A profound and eloquent introduction to the science of mood.

Wolfe, Sidney M., Larry D. Sasich, Rose-Ellen Hope, and Public Citizens' Health Research Group. *Worst Pills, Best Pills: A Consumer's Guide to Avoiding Drug-Induced Death or Illness.* New York: Pocket Books, 1999.

Yapko, Michael D. *Breaking the Patterns of Depression.* New York: Doubleday, 1997.

Zuess, Jonathan. *The Wisdom of Depression.* New York: Harmony Books 1998.

General Health-Physical and Psychological

Davis, Martha, R. Eschelman, and Matthew McKay. *The Relaxation and Stress Reduction Workbook.* Oakland, CA: New Harbinger Publications (fourth edition), 1995. The classic book on stress management.

Dossey, Larry. *Healing Words: The Power of Prayer and the Practice of Medicine.* San Francisco: HarperSanFrancisco, 1993.

Dreher, Henry. *The Immune Power Personality.* New York: E.P. Dutton, 1995.

Dufty, William. *Sugar Blues.* New York: Warner Books, 1986.

Frankl, Victor E. *Man's Search for Meaning.* New York: Simon and Schuster, 1984. A philosophy of meaning developed in the concentration camps. One of the most important books of the twentieth century.

Hauri, Peter. *No More Sleepless Nights.* New York: John A. Wiley & Sons, 1990.

Hutschnecker, Arnold. *The Will to Live.* New York: Simon and Schuster, 1986.

Kabit-Zinn, Jon. *Full Catastrophe Living: Using the Wisdom of Your Body and Mind to Face Stress, Pain and Illness.* New York: Dell Publishing, 1990.

Kaplan, Harold I., Benjamin J. Saddock, and Jack A. Grebb. *Kaplan and Saddock's Synopsis of Psychiatry,* seventh edition. Baltimore: Williams and Wilkens, 1994.

Ornish, Dean. *Love and Survival: The Scientific Basis for the Healing Power of Intimacy.* New York: HarperCollins, 1987.

Peck, M. Scott. *The Road Less Traveled.* New York: Simon and Schuster, 1979. This popular treatise on psychology and spirituality is my all-time personal favorite.

Pert, Candace. *Molecules of Emotion.* New York: Scribner, 1997

Siebert, Al. *The Survivor Personality.* Portland, OR: Practical Psychology Press, 1993.

Siegel, Bernie. *Love, Medicine, and Miracles: Lessons Learned About Self-Healing From a Surgeon's Experience with Exceptional Patients.* New York: Harper and Row, 1986.

Stearns, Ann Kaiser. *Living Through Personal Crisis.* Chicago: The Thomas More Press, 1984.

Viorst, Judith. *Necessary Losses.* New York: Simon and Schuster, 1986.

Weil, Andrew. *Spontaneous Healing: How to Discover and Enhance Your Body's Natural Ability to Maintain and Heal Itself.* New York: Alfred A. Knopf, 1995.

Zi, Nancy. *The Art of Breathing.* Glendale, CA: ViVi Company, 1997.

Spiritual Inspiration

This is by no means a complete listing of the many inspiring books that are in print. They have, however, been of particular comfort to me over the years, and especially so during my dark night of the soul.

Bach, Marcus. *The Power of Serendipity: The Art of Finding Valuable or Agreeable Things not Sought For.* Marina del Rey, CA: Devorss Publications, 1970.

Eadie, Betty. *Embraced by the Light.* Carson City, NV: Gold Leaf Press, 1994. A stirring account of a near-death experience.

Fahy, Mary. *The Tree That Survived the Winter.* Mahwah, NJ: Paulist Press, 1989.

Fox, Emmet. *The Sermon on the Mount.* San Francisco: HarperSan-Francisco, 1992.

————. *Power through Constructive Thinking.* Cutchogue, NY: Buccaneer Books, 1994.

Freeman, James Dillet. *The Story of Unity*. Unity Village, MO: Unity
Books, 1991.

Kuhlman, Katherine. *I Believe in Miracles*. North Brunswick, NJ:
Bridge-Logos Publishers, 1992.

Paulus, Trina. *Hope for the Flowers*. Mahwah, NJ: Paulist Press, 1972.
An allegory about the meaning of life, told by a caterpillar.

Saint-Exupery, Antoine de. *The Little Prince*. New York: Harcourt,
Brace, Jovanovich, 1971.

Taize Monks. *Songs and Prayers from Taize*. Chicago: GIA Publications,
1991.

Wilber, Ken. *Grace and Grit: Spirituality and Healing in the Life and
Death of Treya Killam Wilber*. Boston: Shambhala Publications,
1991. A masterful and moving account of a courageous woman's
battle with cancer.

Books on Social and Ecological Change

We cannot separate our mental health from the health of the social and
physical environments in which we live. Self-transformation and societal
transformation go hand in hand. The following books point the way
toward a sustainable and just future for ourselves and our children.

Brown, Lester R. *State of the World*. New York: WW Norton & Co. A
yearly Worldwatch Institute report on progress toward a sustainable society.

Callenbach, Ernest. *Ecotopia*. New York: Bantam, 1973.

Capra, Fritjof. *The Web of Life: A New Scientific Understanding of
Living Systems*. New York: Doubleday, 1996.

Eisler, Riane. *The Chalice and the Blade*. Cambridge, MA: Harper and
Row, 1987.

Fox, Matthew. *The Reinvention of Work: A New Vision of Livelihood for
Our Time*. San Francisco: HarperSanFrancisco, 1994.

Gore, Al. *Earth in the Balance: Ecology and the Human Spirit*. Boston:
Houghton-Mifflin, 1994.

Greider, William. *Who Will Tell the People: The Betrayal of American
Democracy*. New York: Simon and Schuster, 1992.

Hartmann, Thom. *The Last Hours of Ancient Sunlight*. New York:
Harmony Books, 1999. A call to planetary transformation.

Hawken, Paul. *The Ecology of Commerce: A Declaration of Sustainability*.
New York: HarperCollins, 1993. Required reading. The first
book to design a comprehensive system that makes conservation
profitable, productive, and possible.

Huxley, Aldous. *Brave New World and Brave New World Revisited.* New York: HarperPerennial Library, 1965. Huxley's brilliant satire about a socially engineered pseudo-utopia is more relevant today than ever.

Korten, David. *The Post-Corporate World: Life After Capitalism.* Hartford, CT: Kumarian Press, 1996. Provides specific alternatives to the present economic system.

Mander, Jerry. *In the Absence of the Sacred: The Failure of Technology and the Survival of the Indian Nations.* San Francisco: Sierra Club Books, 1991. Mander speaks passionately about the plight of indigenous cultures, whose wisdom we need to create a sustainable future for our planet.

New Dimensions Foundation. *Deep Ecology for the 21st Century.* San Francisco, 1999. Thirteen hours of interviews with Dr. David Suzuki, Fritjof Capra, Paul Ehrlich, Arne Naess, George Sessions, Paul Shepherd, Gary Snyder, Ted Roszak, Edward Abbey, Cecelia Lanman, Tim Hermach, John Seed, Julia "Butterfly" Hill, Dave Foreman. To order the whole set or individual tapes, call 800-935-8273.

Peck, M. Scott. *The Different Drum: Community-Making and Peace.* New York: Simon and Schuster, 1987.

Robbins, John. *Diet for a New America.* Tiburon, CA: H.J. Kramer, 1998.

Schaef, Anne Wilson. *When Society Becomes an Addict.* San Francisco: Harper and Row, 1987.

Schor, Juliet B. *The Overworked American: The Unexpected Decline of Leisure.* New York: Basic Books, 1991. Schor advocates a scaling back of consumerism so people can escape the cycle of "work and spend" and reclaim their leisure.

Schumacher, E.F. *Small Is Beautiful: Economics As If People Mattered.* New York: Harper and Row, 1973.

Suzuki, David. *The Sacred Balance: Rediscovering Our Place in Nature.* Amherst, NY: Prometheus Books, 1998. A comprehensive and highly readable book from a leading environmental writer.

Credits

Grateful acknowledgment is made for permission to reprint the following:

431

About the Author

Douglas Bloch is an author, teacher, and counselor who writes and speaks on the topics of psychology, healing, and spirituality. He earned his B.A. in Psychology from New York University and an M.A. in Counseling from the University of Oregon. He is the author of ten books, including the inspirational self-help trilogy *Words That Heal: Affirmations and Meditations for Daily Living; Listening to Your Inner Voice;* and *I Am With You Always,* as well as the parenting book, *Positive Self-Talk for Children.*

Douglas lives in Portland, Oregon, with his partner, Joan, their cat, Gabriel, and two parakeets Sebastian and Sabrina. He is available for *lectures* and *workshops*. You may contact him at:

4226 NE 23rd Avenue Portland, OR 97211
503-284-2848; fax: 503-284-6754
E-mail:dbloch@teleport.com
www.healingfromdepression.com

Services Offered
by Douglas Bloch

1. **"Healing from Depression and Anxiety" Class and Support Group.** This is ideal if you live in or near Portland, Oregon, and wish to join with other people in a support goup setting to apply the tools of the better mood recovery program. Please call or E-mail me to receive an application to register for the course.

2. **"Healing from Depression and Anxiety" Correspondence Course.** This twelve-week course is suited for those people who live outside the Portland area and wish to receive individual coaching on how to apply the better mood recovery program in their life. Contact me for information on how to start the program.

3. If you have any uplifting stories concerning how you or someone you know recovered from depression, anxiety, or any dark night of the soul experience, please write or send me an E-mail. I look forward to hearing from you.

Healing Books and Tapes by Douglas Bloch

Healing From Depression: 12 Weeks to a Better Mood. A comprehensive body, mind, and spirit recovery program on healing from depression.

Words That Heal. Both a self-help primer on affirmations and a source of daily inspiration. Contains fifty-two meditations that provide comfort, upliftment, and support. Endorsed by John Bradshaw and Jerry Jampolsky.

Listening to Your Inner Voice. The sequel to *Words That Heal.* How to discover the truth within you and let it guide your way.

I Am With You Always. A treasury of inspirational quotations, poems, and prayers from history's great spiritual teachers, philosophers, and artists.

Positive Self-Talk for Children. How to use affirmations to build self-esteem in children. A guide for parents, teachers, and counselors.

Order Form

Name _____

Street Address _____

City, State, Zip _____

Healing from Depression   # _____ × $15/copy = _____

Words That Heal   # _____ × $13/copy = _____

Listening to Your Inner Voice   # _____ × $11/copy = _____

I Am With You Always   # _____ × $13/copy = _____

Positive Self-Talk for Children   # _____ × $14/copy = _____

Postage ($3.50 for the first item; $1.00 for each additional) _____

Total Cost (make check payable to Pallas Communications) _____

Please mail the order and payment to:

Douglas Bloch

4226 NE 23rd Avenue

Portland, OR 97211

503-284-2848

Delivery will take 7 to 10 days.

Index

435

I know it's hard, but hang in there.
Take one day at a time.
Don't give up five minutes before the miracle.

If you are on the edge of the abyss, don't jump.
If you are going through hell, don't stop.
As long as you are breathing, there is hope.
As long as day follows night, there is hope.
Nothing stays the same forever.
Set an intention to heal,
reach out for support, and you will find help.

www.healingfromdepression.com